SCALES
AND
STONES

SCALES AND STONES

AD KRASIKOV

DEDICATION

Scales and Stones is dedicated to the misfits, the dreamers, the ones who dance to their own beat; thank you for making the world a colorful, whimsical, joyful place.

Thank you for believing.

ACKNOWLEDGMENTS

The making of Scales and Stones was a long road with many twists and turns, and many versions. Thank you to my husband and children who encouraged me. My children know the characters nearly as well as I do and love them just as much.

Thank you to my friends who stood by me and believed in me. Your faith, loyalty and love kept me anchored in a sea of self-doubt.

Thank you to my friend and hairstylist who let me read the first five chapters out loud while getting highlights. By the middle of the first chapter, the salon had gone quiet, and I had an enraptured audience. When I quit reading, I had the other ladies in the salon asking where they could buy the book. It was a wonderful and humbling experience that made me want to keep writing.

Thank you for reading *Scales and Stones*, may you find a bit of whimsy in your everyday, and may you choose to live joyfully.

CHAPTER 1

Viggo's pencil moves effortlessly over the paper shading the scales of a dragon's brow. Many such images fill his sketchbook, memories of the soul he carries.

He glances at the contract under his pad, the words "Marriage Agreement" stand out in bold print. He sets his pencil on the desk and leans back in the leather office chair. The air conditioner kicks on as he rests his hands behind his head.

An agreement made between two clans to bind their most powerful souls together, never mind the humans who bear them. He finds himself vaguely curious about what the girl looks like; not that it matters, he'll honor the agreement.

Dane enters, wearing a tailored pair of slacks and a silk shirt and tie. He looks the part of a wealthy playboy. Viggo leans forward, resting his arms on the aged wooden desk and arches his eyebrows in question.

"The girl is missing."

Sliding his sketchpad to the side, Viggo picks up the contract and thumbs through it. "We can't let what we have worked generations for fail because a seventeen-year-old ran away."

Viggo sets the document down and paces to a window that overlooks the bay. His reflection greets him in the glass. Tall, athletic with dramatic good looks, he can have any girl he wants, except the one he's supposed to marry.

"You will find the girl."

Viggo's shoulders relax at the sound of IlliaVaa's voice. He greets his twin as she enters and leans against the leather sofa, her tall willowy frame clad in a pale rose dress befitting the summer afternoon. "Then, go with Dane and bring back my bride."

✿ ✿ ✿ ✿ ✿

When you live in a world of science and technology, learning that everything considered fantasy is real is like stepping into a movie, only life has consequences and movies end.

The shop door chimes as a lanky blue-haired teen in a graphic T-shirt and saggy jeans enters. He waves at Cate when she cheerily welcomes him, the fluorescent lights twinkle off his many piercings. Cate scratches at the scales along the back of her neck. Since her sixteenth birthday, they started appearing. Blue-green, iridescent, and reptilian looking. At least body modification is a thing and if anyone asks, she can say her mom did it at her tattoo and piercing parlor.

The door chimes and Cate welcomes a slender well-built man in a light gray suit. He looks to be in his early twenties, accompanied by the most beautiful woman she's ever seen. Tall, with hair darker than a starless night, light blue eyes, and flawless skin. As if Cate did not already feel inadequate, in faded jeans and a ponytail. "Can I help you?"

Before answering, the man tilts his head and looks down his nose at the blue-haired teen. With a furtive glance at Cate, the teen hastily exits. The door bangs closed and the woman steps to the counter. "I'm thinking about a navel piercing."

Cate guides the woman to a jewelry case. As she examines the barbells and captive bead rings, the man sets a legal-sized manilla folder on the counter.

"I'm looking for Emily Reddington." The woman off-handedly announces as she points to a sapphire barbell. "I like that one, but I'm not sure I'm ready for the commitment."

"Emily works tomorrow. Why don't you think about it if you're not ready?" The woman focuses on Cate. Her eyes shift, the pupils elongating. This isn't the first odd thing to happen in the parlor and Cate manages to keep her cool. "Is there anything else I can show you?"

The woman sidles to the front door, locks it, and switches off the open sign. When she looks at Cate again, her eyes are normal. "I'm IlliaVaa and this is Dane. We are legal representatives of the Dragotian family here to serve Emily Reddington with court documents."

"I told you she doesn't work today. Why did you lock the door?"

"Customers would make things messy. Besides, you are Emily's daughter, and the agreement has everything to do with you." Cate's gaze drifts from the envelope to the man.

"I never said I was Emily's daughter."

"You didn't have to."

Dane lunges for Cate. She leaps over the glass counter, putting distance between them. IlliaVaa claps with delight at Cate's agility as Dane stalks the counter's edge. Reaching the front counter, Cate's hands roam under the Formica looking for the revolver Emily keeps there but pulls out her cell phone instead.

IlliaVaa plucks it from her hand. "Now, now. I said it would get messy if anyone would walk-in. Don't worry about your mother. Everything she needs to know is in this folder. Please, come with us."

"I'm not going anywhere." Cate backs against the wall. "What kind of document makes you think you can kidnap me?"

"A marriage agreement."

Cate freezes in shock and Dane grabs her by the arms, taking advantage of her momentary confusion. "A marriage agreement? That's ridiculous."

IlliaVaa warmly smiles. "Would it make you feel any better to know your fiancé feels the same?"

"Then why?"

"Because some things are bigger than us or what we want." IlliaVaa trades places with Dane, her grip less bruising. "Traveling is disorienting the first time."

Dane turns his back to them, muttering. Cate's too numb to struggle. None of this feels real. It's like watching a movie where the heroes magically disappear through a swirling portal. Only, it's real. It isn't swirling and it's a hole. That's the only way to describe it – a hole that shows another place.

IlliaVaa drags her to it, and it's as if the movement activates her brain. Cate plants her feet and puts all her effort into being as heavy as she can be. But it doesn't stop IlliaVaa from tossing her into the hole or following after.

It feels like a bucket of ice water is poured on Cate's head. All her nerves tingle, her skin shivers, and her stomach clenches. She looks behind them – the parlor is gone. The hole is gone.

They are standing at the edge of a dense forest looking on sculpted grounds leading to an expansive stone mansion. Cate's legs give out and she drops to the grass.

"Where are we?!" Cate screams. Tears flood her eyes as she launches from the ground at Dane. He dodges. She turns and catches the sleeve of his jacket. He shrugs out of her hold. "Take me home!"

"You *are* home." He shouts back and follows IlliaVaa across the sculpted grounds toward the mansion.

Cate sits on her knees and buries her face in her hands. Tears fall until there is no more to shed. Her heart aches. She pushes to her feet, her knees damp and muddy with strands of grass clinging to them.

She wipes her face and straightens her back. Taking a deep breath, she turns in a circle and takes stock of her surroundings. There is no one, just a forest behind and an isolated mansion in front.

Cate takes a slow breath, gathers her courage, and walks with heavy steps to the mansion.

IlliaVaa sits on the patio on an outdoor couch sipping from a steaming mug. "I bet a hot bath would feel pretty good right now."

"I don't have any clothes."

"Of course, you do." IlliaVaa brightly smiles and leads Cate inside. It's like walking into a five-star hotel. Immaculate, professionally decorated. All style and little warmth. "Your suite is on the second floor, next to mine." IlliaVaa leads her up a sweeping staircase.

"Can I have my phone?"

"Tomorrow, after you meet my brother."

"Your brother?"

IlliaVaa pushes open a door. "This is your room."

Cate sits on the end of the bed. "Where are we?"

IlliaVaa sits next to her and starts to set her hand on Cate's when Cate pulls away. "I should have anticipated you would know nothing of the agreement, especially given that your mom kidnapped you and hid you for the last fifteen years."

"I don't believe you."

IlliaVaa straightens her shoulders and takes a long slow breath. "When you were two, your parents made a legal agreement with my parents for you to marry my brother. A year later, your mother disappeared with you."

"My mom wouldn't…."

"Maybe she regretted it, and your father wouldn't break the agreement." IlliaVaa stands and looks down at Cate. "Take a hot bath, I'll have dinner brought to your room. Tomorrow, after you meet my brother, you can call your mom."

"Give me a phone and I'll call the police."

IlliaVaa laughs as she crosses to the door. "It wouldn't matter if you did. Your mom is at fault, not us. You'd only be getting her in trouble. By the way, we're still in the U.S., that's as much as I can say about where we are."

❀ ❀ ❀ ❀ ❀

"Well done." Dane bows his head, accepting Viggo's compliment. "Tell me about her."

Dane swirls the whiskey in his shot glass contemplating how to answer. "Young. She may be a seventeen-year-old human, but it's clear her dragon hasn't manifested."

Viggo's pencil stops. "Are you sure you have the right girl?"

"Yes."

Viggo closes his sketchbook and leans back in his chair. "How could such a powerful soul not manifest?"

"Her mother isn't dragon-souled. Perhaps, living among humans, has prolonged her adolescence."

"My father made our dragons manifest before puberty. Perhaps his methods will work on the girl."

"I doubt her father will agree to such methods."

"She's my betrothed."

"Yes, but she isn't your wife – yet."

"Have you told her father we've found her?" Dane shakes his head. "Then, I'll do it after I meet her tomorrow. We have details to attend to and it would be best in person."

Dane swallows the shot of liquor and moves to leave. At the door, he stops. "Maybe it's because her dragon hasn't manifested, but I want to warn you." Viggo's eyes meet his and Dane second guesses how blunt he was about to be. Tempering his words, he says, "Don't expect a version of IlliaVaa."

Viggo laughs. "We're all gawky and awkward in adolescence, a dragon's no different."

❀ ❀ ❀ ❀ ❀

It feels like she's in some crazy dream. One she should wake from anytime. A part of her wants to think everything that's happening isn't real, but another part knows it is. Sometime during the night, someone came in and cleared the dishes – taking away the dinner she didn't eat.

Cate opens the closet and walks inside. One side is lined with drawers, the other with dresses, pants, and shirts. She grabs a robe and slides it on as IlliaVaa appears in the closet.

"Good morning. I wasn't sure of your size, so I bought a lot of different things."

Cate blinks at her, uncomfortable with the intrusion but unwilling to offend someone who could become an ally. "You bought all this?"

IlliaVaa smiles and it's like the sun peeking through clouds. "I hope there's something in here that's your style. I admit, I bought things I like so I can borrow them."

IlliaVaa slides hangers around evaluating outfits. "You're meeting my brother for the first time today." She selects a light gauzy dress and holds it up to Cate. Wrinkling her nose, she puts it back. "You've got a good figure. We should pick something that highlights it."

IlliaVaa switches to the drawers, her fingers swiftly move from piece to piece. "Aha!" She turns and hands Cate a skirt and silk tank top. "Put these on and come back."

Reluctantly, Cate goes into the bathroom and slides into the skirt. It's short. Her mom would never let her out of the house in it. The top goes easily over her head. Feeling very exposed, she returns to the closet. IlliaVaa shoves a long-sleeved lace top at her. Cate slides it on and buttons it up.

IlliaVaa shakes her head and bats Cate's hand away, unbuttoning the top two buttons. She steps back and analyzes her work, as if studying a mannequin. Slowly, she nods in approval. "Wedges, that's what would look best."

With shoes in hand, she leads Cate to the bathroom and pushes her down on a stool. "I don't have a sister and no female friends, so girl-time is long overdue."

"I can do my own hair."

IlliaVaa gives her a stern look and opens drawers, pulling out a curling iron, hair spray, comb, and makeup. An hour later, Cate stares into the mirror. Her long dirty-blonde hair has been curled and teased into a messy bun with wisps framing her face. Her features perfectly highlighted, and her green eyes look larger than usual.

"Now, you can meet my brother. Ready?"

Cate's heart flutters. "When can I talk with my mom?"

IlliaVaa's perfect lips briefly twitch into a frown before her radiant smile returns. "Tonight, at the latest." She lightly runs her thumb down the back of Cate's neck. "It might be best to remove the lace. You really should show off your scales."

IlliaVaa turns around and lifts her own hair. Red scales disappear beneath her collar. Cate stands, filled with a fervent desire to see them more closely. "They're beautiful, like having rubies under your skin."

IlliaVaa drops her hair and turns, her nose inches from Cate's. "Maybe we should unbutton it, at least."

Cate's not sure why she's nervous. She was kidnapped. Why should she care about the impression she makes? She's only bidding time until she can escape. Under IlliaVaa's watchful eyes, she unbuttons the lace shirt.

Viggo leans in the doorway of what was his father's study. Its heavy dark furniture reminds him of the man who furnished it. Few of the memories are fond.

He turns at the sound of IlliaVaa's voice, watching with cool detachment as his sister escorts his future bride. Dane's assessment was accurate. Compared to his sister's dark beauty, the girl is little more than a flash of sunlight.

"Viggo!" IlliaVaa calls brightly, her keen eyes catch sight of him in the dimly lit hall. He steps forward and the girl stops. There's nothing shy or coy about her.

Shapely legs, a slim waist – as his eyes reach hers, they flash like firecrackers. "Welcome." He attempts to show warmth, but there's little there. "I am Viggo, and you are the daughter of Kith Ender and Emily Reddington."

"Cate, my name is Cate." She steps closer to him; within reach should he choose to extend his hand. "Return me to my mom."

He halves the distance between them. "Our parents chose to align our clans through our marriage. It is for neither of us to dispute."

She tilts her head to look up at him. "I will decide who I marry when I marry. This is the twenty-first century, not medieval Europe."

He shrugs. "It is a legal matter."

She turns, intending to storm up the stairs, but her scales glint in the sunlight snagging his gaze. He grabs her shoulder, stopping her. With his free hand, he pulls the lace down. Wide, brilliant, iridescent blue-green scales descend from her hair and disappear beneath the tank top. She dips her shoulder and breaks free of his grip. He raptly watches as she flees up the stairs and out of his sight.

CHAPTER 2

Cate opens each drawer, throwing clothes on the floor, until she finds a pair of jeans and a woman's fitted t-shirt. Yanking the skirt and tank off, she changes. Next, she ditches the wedges for a pair of slip-on sneakers.

Leaving the closet, looking like a twister tore through it, she stops in the bathroom to pull pins from her hair. Shaking it loose with her fingers, she flees the suite. She can hear Viggo and IlliaVaa talking at the bottom of the stairs and goes the other direction in search for another way to the first floor.

The first room is a library, while the last door in the hall is locked. Cate circles back. Their voices still carry up the stairs. Sticking close to the wall, she tries to make herself small as she crosses the top of the open staircase.

The first door leads to a game room, with a pool table, card table, and retro-style video games. The next door is a bedroom, while the remaining two doors are locked. Cate leans against the wall. You'd think a house this big would have two staircases.

She wanders back the way she came and hesitates near the staircase, listening. Only, no one's talking. She glances downstairs. The entryway is empty. Slowly, she descends to the first floor.

Curious, she peeks into the room where Viggo had been standing. It's a large, dark study. It feels ominous, like someone's watching from the desk. She shivers, leaving the study behind, and enters a great room divided by types of furniture into a sitting room, dining room, and kitchen.

IlliaVaa enters the kitchen from the far side of the room. She's distracted as she opens the refrigerator and snags a bottle of water. IlliaVaa looks up from her place at the bar and calls her name. She offers Cate a gentle smile. "You look more natural like this. The untamed mane suits you."

Cate's shoulders droop, as she joins IlliaVaa. "When can I call my mom?"

IlliaVaa pulls a cell phone from her pocket and puts in on the counter. "Now. Viggo's only demand is that your conversation must be on speaker, and I have to be your witness."

"Witness? Seems more like guard."

"Do you want to call your mom or not?"

"Where's *my* phone?"

"Don't worry, Hunter transferred all the numbers to this phone and made sure your photos were saved to the cloud."

Cate gives her a confused look as IlliaVaa presses a contact titled "Emily" and speaker. "Who's Hunter?" The question is quickly forgotten as Emily answers.

"Hello?"

"Mom!"

"Oh, my beautiful girl, where are you? Are you okay?" Tears fill Cate's eyes with the raw emotion in her mom's voice. It's clear she's been crying.

"I'm okay."

"They haven't hurt you, have they?"

"Mom, I'm okay. It's like a five-star hotel."

"Mrs. Reddington," IlliaVaa interrupts, "I speak on behalf of the Dragotian clan. You have been served the legal agreement in which you and Kith Ender agreed to the marriage of your daughter, Cate, to Viggo, son of Vanor. As stated in the agreement, the Dragotian clan is to take possession of Cate in her seventeenth year to be wed on her eighteen birthday. You were in violation of said agreement, and that violation has been rectified."

"Rectified! You're talking about my daughter not a car."

"Kith, Enderen clan leader, is meeting in-person with Viggo, Dragotian clan leader, as we speak to finalize the agreement and put into action the events previously outlined. In that Viggo desires an amicable relationship with his future wife, please expect a daily call from Cate at 5 p.m. MT."

IlliaVaa steps back from the counter and gestures to the phone. Cate blinks trying to absorb the last few minutes of conversation. "Cate? Are you still there, Honey?"

"Yeah, Mom, I'm here."

"I love you, Sweetheart."

"I love you, Mom."

"Stay strong. I'll figure something out, even if I have to find your father and…."

"Time is up. Please expect Cate's call tomorrow. If you do not answer, she will try again the next day." Before Cate can react, IlliaVaa presses End and pockets the phone.

"Really? That's it. That's all I get?"

IlliaVaa chugs half the water bottle before answering. "You talked with her, didn't you? She knows that you're alive. She knows why you vanished. She knows that all of it was preventable if she had only kept the agreement."

"You're blaming this on my mom?"

IlliaVaa leads Cate to the sitting area and plops on a sofa. "I blame our parents for the whole thing, not just your mom. Look, you and Viggo are clan pawns. Do you think my brother wants to marry a girl he's never met? He's handsome, smart, and rich. He can pick any girl but instead he must marry you."

"It's not like I'm an ogre."

IlliaVaa almost spits out a mouthful of water but manages to swallow it before laughing out loud. "You're right. You're far from being an ogre."

A door opens and closes in the direction IlliaVaa entered the kitchen. Cate watches, expecting Viggo or Dane. Instead, a tall dark-haired muscular man wearing a black t-shirt and jeans appears. He grabs a water bottle before heading upstairs.

IlliaVaa clears her throat and Cate turns back to find IlliaVaa intently staring at her. "That's Hunter. He's our older brother."

Cate frowns, her brows draw down. "Wouldn't that make him clan leader?"

IlliaVaa shakes her head, answering instead with a question. "Why do we have scales?"

"Because we are dragon-souled." It had surprised Cate to learn on her sixteenth birthday that her father's family-line is one of a few surviving clans of humans entrusted to carry the souls of dragons.

"Exactly. When a dragon-souled dies, the dragon's soul it carries passes to another in its bloodline. Unfortunately, Hunter is not dragon-souled. He is merely human."

"Merely human? You make being human sound less than being dragon-souled."

The look IlliaVaa gives Cate makes her want to slap her. "Of course, humans are less."

"So, by the mere fact that you are a vessel for a dragon's soul, you are better?"

"Yes. We are stronger, faster, and gifted."

"What do you mean, gifted?"

"I forgot that you haven't been living with dragon-souled. Every dragon grants abilities to the human who carries its soul. Dane, for example, can Travel."

"You mean that hole he created to bring us here?"

"Exactly, though I think he is the only Traveler who can use that method. As your dragon becomes aware of you and you of it, your gift will manifest."

"I feel like I've been sucked into some crazy streaming service and my life is a jumble of fantasy movies and video games."

IlliaVaa stands. "Well, I've had enough of babysitting. The house is yours. In the basement, there's a movie room with all the latest services. Watch whatever you want. Oh, and if you go outside, stay out of the woods." Without another word, she leaves and walks out the door.

Viggo presses his palms into the table, a trick since childhood to control his emotions. Kith Ender sits across from him, a large barbaric man with a mane of wild blonde hair and a goatee more white than yellow. "Colorado? She always did favor the mountains." Biceps thicker than most men's calves flex as Kith sips from an oversized coffee mug.

Dane pushes the marriage agreement closer to him. "As stipulated, we have located your daughter. Per the agreement, she will stay with the Dragotian clan through her seventeenth year."

Kith strokes the edges of his goatee. The muscles in his cheek twitch as he drops his hand. "Did you bring a picture?"

Viggo's eyes meet Kith's. In his desire to fulfill the agreement, he had forgotten that the man across from him is a father who hasn't seen his daughter in more than a decade. "I am sorry. Next time…."

Kith smiles. It isn't the kind of smile between friends or even associates. It is the kind of smile that sends enemies fleeing. "How about you take me to her?"

Dane flips to page five of the agreement. "We will hold an engagement party on the thirtieth day. At that time, I will personally escort you, and anyone you'd like to bring, to the event."

Kith never looks at Dane. His eyes remain fixed on Viggo. "Vanos was convinced you carry Xenothgorot's soul. What proof have you?"

Viggo methodically unbuttons and removes his shirt. Bare-chested, he stands and turns his back to the Enderen clan leader. Ruby red scales run from Viggo's hairline down his spine, vanishing beneath the waistline of his pants. He doesn't bother to put the shirt back on. Turning, he faces Kith. "What more do you need?"

The clan leader smirks. His eyes shift to Dane. "See you in thirty days."

After raiding the refrigerator, Cate snags a water bottle and wanders outside. The giant house and sculpted grounds feel empty. And silent. Where did IlliaVaa go?

Thinking about her makes Cate think about the phone she pocketed. Stepping back into the house, her eyes go to where Hunter went... and he did something with her phone. Tracing his steps, she jogs upstairs.

She checks the game room first. Knocks on all the bedroom doors and ends in the library. Unexpectedly, Hunter sits in a recliner, his feet up, reading a book. Cate strides to the chair. "Excuse me."

He keeps reading. It's as if he didn't even hear her.

"Hey, excuse me."

Again, no response. Gritting her teeth, she waves her hand in between the book and his face. He blinks and looks up with annoyance. Sliding a bookmark in place, he sets the book down and pulls a wireless earbud from his ear. "What?"

Music blares from the bud in his hand. No wonder he didn't hear her. "Where's my phone?"

He gives her a puzzled look as he removes the other earbud. "Your phone?"

"The phone you took the contacts out of and saved the photos from?"

Recognition dawns. "Tossed it."

"You tossed my phone?!"

"Authorities can track the last tower it made signal with, so we tossed it in a bin behind some tattoo shop."

Cate grabs his shoulders and gets nearly nose-to-nose with him. "You went back to my mom's shop?"

Hunter shrugs. She pushes away as a cold sinking feeling fills her stomach. "I'm living a nightmare." She reels on Hunter. "You're an accessory to kidnapping, you know."

He picks his book up and puts his earbuds in. She rips the book from his hands and throws it on the ground. He jumps from his chair, towering over her. "What's wrong with you?" He picks up the book, checking it for damage. "You're dragon-souled. You should be with a clan, not living among humans."

"You're human!"

He removes the earbuds. The muscles in his cheeks twitch. "Exactly." Book in hand, he storms from the library.

❀ ❀ ❀ ❀ ❀

IlliaVaa leans against the window frame, watching a cruise ship sail from the bay. Dane hadn't asked her to come, he'd just appeared and whisked her away.

Viggo lies on the leather sofa, his forearm covering his eyes. He'd always preferred the city over the estate, especially when father was alive. It was a respite for him; perhaps, even now, the estate holds too many memories.

"In thirty days, we host an engagement party. I want you to plan it. Invite all the clan leaders and the heads of the Kraeken houses." He sounds tired. "It's warm enough to hold it outside at the estate. Dane and the Traveler's in our employ can ensure everyone arrives and leaves when they're told."

IlliaVaa faces him, outlined by the sunset. "What's the intention of the party?"

He sits and pushes his hands through his hair. "Other than being a stipulation in the agreement, it will be our first introduction as a couple."

IlliaVaa bites back what she wants to say. It's a skill learned after many lashings. Her gift for seeing Truth isn't always appreciated. Instead, she bows her head. "I will do my best to make it worthy of royalty."

CHAPTER 3

C ate wakes to IlliaVaa staring at her from the end of the bed. "What? Why are you here?"

"We have a party to plan and a dress to buy. So much to do and so little time! I never thought you'd wake-up." Impishly, she yanks the covers off as she descends on the closet. "What did you do?"

Cate groans. Dragging herself out of bed, she stumbles to the doorway and yawns. IlliaVaa crouches among articles of clothing, separating them into piles. "Help me fold them."

Sitting in an empty spot, Cate starts folding as IlliaVaa puts her efforts into hanging what should be on a hanger. "Like it or not, you're one of us now. You *are* marrying my brother."

"No, I'm not."

IlliaVaa pauses with a jacket half on the hanger. "You are. Twenty-first century or not, you aren't human, and you don't get to live by their rules."

"Yes, I do. I was human until a year ago when these scales erupted."

IlliaVaa kneels in front of Cate. "You are a human with the privilege of carrying a dragon's soul. The connection makes you stronger and faster than other humans. It enhances all your senses. It will even bestow you with a gift." IlliaVaa lightly touches Cate's face and finishes hanging the jacket.

Taking Cate by the hand, she gently pulls her to her feet and sits her on the bed. "Maybe knowing more about being dragon-souled will help you accept your marriage."

"Not likely, but you can try."

"Dragons come in all sizes and colors, like humans, and have varying natural abilities. Some are large, some small. Some eat cows, others' birds. They lived as any other creature lived. But there came a time when their habitats conflicted with other species, humans included."

"Other species?"

IlliaVaa's blue eyes rest on Cate as if she were the stupidest person on earth. "We carry dragon souls. What other species could I be talking about?"

"You aren't going to say elves, ogres, goblins, pixies...."

"Yes, I am."

Cate rolls her eyes.

"What's so hard to believe? Some have joined humans while others remain aloof, hidden by using a mix of magic and tech." Cate waves her on. "Anyway, a thousand years ago there was a terrible war between the races. It almost wiped us out. Only, a dragon-mage devised a spell to cast dragon souls into humans."

Cate covers a yawn with the back of her hand. "I'm not marrying your brother."

"Fine. According to the agreement, you must live with the Dragotian clan for a year and get married on your eighteenth birthday. You have between now and then to figure out how not to marry him."

"Really? You'll help me."

"No, by that time you will realize how futile your argument is and how awesome Viggo is. In a year, you'll *want* to marry him."

"Why would I want to marry him? I haven't even had a boyfriend."

IlliaVaa's eyes flicker over Cate. "All the better."

There's a knock on the door before it opens revealing Hunter and a cart of food. Cate blushes, thankful she chose to sleep in shorts and a t-shirt.

"What's for breakfast?" IlliaVaa moves to a table by the window.

"Pancakes, scrambled eggs, bagels with cream cheese or butter, and apple juice." Hunter pushes the cart to the table and leaves without giving Cate a second look. Joining IlliaVaa at the table, Cate scoops eggs onto a plate and sips the juice.

"Why is he bringing us breakfast?"

IlliaVaa pauses in spreading cream cheese on a bagel. "Hunter? He's the only servant Viggo trusts with you at the estate. That'll have to change for the party. We'll need to bring back some of the old staff."

"Wait, your brother acts as a servant?"

"He's the estate caretaker." Setting her knife down, IlliaVaa smiles as she says, "After all, he's only human."

✽ ✽ ✽ ✽ ✽

Five o'clock cannot come fast enough. Right as the hand moves, IlliaVaa presses the call button and puts it on speaker. Emily answers at the first ring. "Cate?"

"Hi Mom."

"Can you tell me where you are?"

"Some estate in the middle of the woods. Are you okay?"

Emily laughs. It sounds forced. "I'm okay, you?"

"Fine. You need to remember to eat and sleep."

"I talked to your father today. He said he paid the Dragotian clan leader a visit."

IlliaVaa smiles and points to the phone.

"You really talked to my dad?"

"I didn't leave him because I stopped loving him. I left him because of the agreement. I hoped you would never carry a dragon's soul and that they would never come for you."

Cate's heart clenches, like it's being gripped in an iron fist. "But I do, and they did."

"I didn't mean it like that."

"Time's up. We'll call again tomorrow." With that, IlliaVaa presses End and pockets the phone. Cate stares at the space where the phone had been. Had her mother really wished that she never carried a dragon's soul?

"Why'd you do that?"

"I have strict orders. Sorry, little sister." IlliaVaa lightly touches Cate's arm. "I'm sure your mom loves you. She just doesn't understand. That's why dragon-souled live with other dragons. Humans just don't get it, even humans born of dragons like my brother."

Wanting to change the subject, Cate points to the list on the counter. "How are you going to buy anything without a computer?"

"Who says I don't have a computer?" IlliaVaa flashes a brilliant smile. "Tomorrow, I'll measure you for the gown I'm designing. What do you think about red and green for the party colors?"

"Sounds like Christmas."

"You're right. What about red and blue?"

"Fourth of July?"

IlliaVaa wrinkles her nose. "No, like periwinkle blue tablecloths and runners with red roses, your dress...."

"I really don't care."

"Well, Viggo does, and he prefers black." She falls silent, momentarily lost in thought. As Cate moves to leave, IlliaVaa stops her. "You may not know this, but the Dragotian and Enderen clans are the most powerful of the dragon clans. This party will be attended by everyone who is anyone – even the Kraeken."

"Who are the Kraeken?"

"During the great dragon war, a group of humans developed an enchantment to imbue them with animal abilities. It was a way for them to defend against dragons. To this day, their descendants carry the enchantment."

"Why do we care?"

"Over the centuries, some of the dragon clans have interbred with them."

"So, there are weird animalistic dragon-souled out there?"

IlliaVaa laughs out loud. "Thankfully, not. It seems a child is born with the enchantment or a dragon's soul, never both. Cate, this party is important. It's the first time our people will meet you."

"And?"

"Do you know what your gift is?"

Cate shrugs.

"Have you learned to hear your dragon?"

She shakes her head.

IlliaVaa's lips compress into a thin line. "If I give you an extra five minutes a day to talk to your mom, would you try learning?"

"Make it ten and you've got a deal."

"Done."

❈ ❈ ❈ ❈ ❈

The first three days after their agreement, Cate sat on the stone patio silencing her mind and listening to the thoughts of her dragon. She never heard any thoughts besides her own and got a good sunburn for her efforts.

The next week, IlliaVaa had her running laps around the estate. Running had never been Cate's favorite exercise, and she found herself finding new ways to curse IlliaVaa with each lap.

The third week, IlliaVaa alternated between locking Cate in her room without food or without electricity. Now, into the fourth week, it seems IlliaVaa's creativity has come to an end.

Hunter unlocks the door and pushes the food cart into Cate's room. "Countdown is on. I've been asked to keep you in your room until the big reveal. IlliaVaa will be by later today for your dress fitting, and of course to call your mom."

"Why do you stay?" Leaning against the window, Cate faces him.

Hunter pauses. It's a question he's asked himself many times over the years. "They are my family."

The last few weeks have made a positive change in Cate's appearance. Hunter expected her to look gaunt and worn-out, but instead she appeared fit and healthy. Her skin is clear, her eyes bright, even her hair shines. That isn't the most attractive part about her though. Since the last time he saw her, an aura of danger now lingers about her.

It's hard to pull his eyes away.

"Would you like a book?"

Cate smiles. "I'd love a couple. It's boring talking to myself day-in and day-out."

"What do you like to read?"

"Fantasy, paranormal, romance. Not really into non-fiction."

Hunter opens the door. "Even in your situation, you want to read romance?"

Cate shrugs, feeling her cheeks heat. "Okay, I don't want to read anything about a girl being kidnapped and falling for the guy. Got it?"

"Got it."

Thirty days went faster than Cate imagined. Sitting on the dressing chair with IlliaVaa pinning her hair, Cate's stomach twists in knots.

"Done." IlliaVaa pats her bare shoulder and leaves to get the dress.

Cate closes her eyes and takes a deep breath. Opening them, IlliaVaa hands her the gown. She steps in and holds it in place over the backless bra, while IlliaVaa zips it up on both sides.

Looking over her should, Cate stares at her back. The blue-green gown was designed to display her scales – all of them. Cate's first inclination is to cover up. IlliaVaa pushes her hands down. "You look beautiful."

"Does the back have to be so low?"

Cate tries to pull the dress up as IlliaVaa holds out shoes. "Kitten heels, no stilettos to aerate the grass."

Sliding the shoes on, Cate's heart races. IlliaVaa stands in the bathroom doorway, staring at her. "Viggo will be here soon. You'll walk down with him and make your entrance." She gives Cate an encouraging smile. "I'll see you at the party..."

The woman in the mirror looks like a more mature version of the girl they kidnapped. "Make-up does wonders."

Her father will be at this party. All she must do is get through it. There's a light knocking on the door. Cate crosses the room and opens it.

Viggo stands in the hall, wearing a black suit with a mission-style collar, his hair feathered back from his face. He steps into the room. "You look beautiful." It's the first time he's seen Cate since the day they were introduced. He smiles and it brightens his whole face. "Turn around."

Cate slowly spins in place. When she looks into his eyes, they shine with a new light. "There is no doubt who you are and why you are at my side." He offers his arm, and she lightly sets her hand on it. She can feel her skin flush.

It's like a dream. Walking down a sweeping staircase with a handsome man at her side, everyone watching with envy. When IlliaVaa had said this was an important day for the dragon clans, Cate had never imagined so many people.

At the foot of the stairs, onlookers bow their heads as Viggo leads her through the great room to the patio. Gowns swish and chairs grate against stone as everyone, seated at tables, stands.

Viggo places his hand on hers as he leads her among the tables to a platform. Carefully, they climb metal stairs to stand in front of everyone. From the other side of the platform, a blonde bear of a man in a black suit joins them, his long blonde hair tied into a low ponytail. He steps to a microphone and holds his hands up for silence. "On behalf of the Enderen and Dragotian clans, we welcome you."

Viggo releases Cate and joins the man at the microphone. "I, Viggo, son of Vanos, uphold the agreement made by my father and Kith Ender to marry, Cate, daughter of Kith, in the coming year on April 30th."

"I, Kith Ender, uphold the agreement to unite our children and our clans." Kith and Viggo clasp forearms, as Kith's eyes shift to Cate.

Then, Viggo's at her side and guiding her from the platform. Her knees are weak. This isn't how it was supposed to happen. Her father was supposed to tell him, to tell them all, to get bent and rescue her.

People mill about, offering congratulations. Introductions, names, faces. Why didn't her father take her away? Viggo's hand slides down her back and it snaps her to the present. Reflexively, she pulls from him, but he clasps her tightly to his side.

His grip is iron, and she can't move. Her heart beats like a caged bird. Across from him is a stately woman in a tailored pant suit, and a good-looking man about the same age as Viggo. "Lady v'Lana and Lord d'Gar, let me introduce my fiancée. This is Cate."

Cate blinks. The woman offers a genuine and sad smile. "I am glad to make your acquaintance. May you find happiness in the wisdom of your fathers."

"Thank you." Cate finds herself muttering as the woman leaves. The man inches closer to her and inhales deeply as if Cate were wearing an intoxicating perfume.

"Lord d'Gar, if you get any closer to my fiancée, I will take offense."

Cate looks up at Viggo, hearing a near growl in his tone. D'Gar smirks. "I merely admire your good-fortune, Lord Viggo. Perhaps, you'll allow me a dance with your bride-to-be."

Viggo draws Cate closer. "I think not, as I am a greedy man."

"My loss." D'Gar bows his head to Cate and withdraws.

Viggo leans down, his mouth close to Cate's ear. "Stay at my side."

"I can do little else with how tightly you're holding me." Viggo loosens his grip but does not let go.

For hours, they mingle. Viggo's hand moving from Cate's waist to her back, to her waist. Every time his fingers brush her skin, it's like receiving an electric shock. Twice, she managed to catch sight of IlliaVaa standing at the edge of the crowd. Once, she saw Hunter refilling champagne.

Viggo leads her to the house as the sun sets. "It's time to end the party. Come with me." He guides her inside, surrounded by bodyguards to protect them from well-wishers. Together, they ascend the stairs, and he leads her into the game room. The door closes. They are alone for the first time.

His hand slides from her waist as he sits in a leather chair. He closes his eyes and takes a long slow breath. "You did well." Cate remains silent, watching him. He opens his eyes; his gaze finds hers. "You surprise me."

She reaches into her hair and pulls a pin loose, then another and another until her hair falls around her shoulders. He studies her as if looking at something he cannot explain.

"What?" She asks.

"Do you still believe we kidnapped you even after your father stood on stage and declared your engagement?"

Cate sits in a chair near him, the leather cold on her back. "I've never met my father. That man could have been anyone. As for an engagement, no one has asked me to marry them, and I have given no answer."

Viggo smiles, caught off guard by her answer. She stands with a flourish, and he grabs her wrist before she can leave. "Let me walk you to your room."

Together, they leave the sanctuary of the game room and cross the top of the open staircase. A cacophony of voices fills the hall as Travelers escort groups of people from the estate.

At her door, Viggo pushes it open and stops. He stands close, his chest nearly touching her back. He leans forward; his lips close to her ear. "I look forward to getting to know you and hearing your answer to my proposal."

When he straightens, Cate steps into the bedroom. He closes the door and locks it behind her. Unzipping the dress, she heads to the bathroom.

For the last month, she thought tonight would mean escape. She thought her long-lost father would carry her away; that he'd be her hero. Instead, he gave her to the man who kidnapped her.

What crazy world is this?

Showering, Cate slips into a pair of shorts and a T-shirt, braids her wet hair, and climbs into bed. She's asleep as soon as her head hits the pillow.

CHAPTER 4

Viggo leans against the heavy desk, his hands clasped before him. "My Traveler waits outside." He watches Kith swirl whiskey in a crystal glass, every bit the imposing clan leader. Much like his father had been in this very room.

Kith sips from the glass. The dim light would make it difficult for a human to make out his subtle gestures, but for a dragon-souled, it makes no difference. "Has Cate's gift developed?"

"No."

"Do you know why your dragons are the most powerful of our clans?" When Viggo doesn't answer, Kith finishes the whiskey and sets the glass on a table. He pushes to his feet. "They share the same gift."

The Enderen clan leader walks to the door and reaches for the handle. Before he opens it, he turns back to Viggo. "It has been fourteen years since I've spent time with my daughter. Though not in the agreement, I would look favorably on opportunities to meet with her."

"IlliaVaa will work with you on scheduling times."

Kith nods as he leaves the study.

Viggo pushes off the desk. Unbuttoning his jacket, he runs his hands through his hair. It's been a long day. Seeing Cate in that dress, her beautiful scales dipping below the fabric, it's difficult to think about anything else. How could he not have thought of her, even once, since their first meeting?

At the party, he'd wanted to show her off and at the same time keep her for himself. His hands curl into fists thinking how that wolf, d'Gar, had leaned in to inhale her scent. The door opens and Dane enters. "All the guests are gone. Will you be staying or returning to the city?"

"Staying."

✾ ✾ ✾ ✾ ✾

Viggo rubs sleep out of his eyes and sits, his neck sore from sleeping on the Game room couch. IlliaVaa hands him a cup of black coffee. He sips, enjoying the bitterness. "What did you see at the party?"

"The usual, though there were flashes around Kith Ender and Lady v'Lana." Viggo sips his coffee patiently waiting for her to remember the visions. "Ender balances on a knife's edge. I think it has to do with his wife but something about it relates to Cate."

"With Cate in our care, we don't have to worry. That reminds me, schedule a day a month for him to visit, chaperoned of course."

"Got it. As for V'Lana, there seems to be tension between the Wolves and Eagles."

"If the Wolves steal the throne from the Eagles, power to them." He finishes the coffee and leaves. At the sound of a door closing, he turns to see Hunter coming out of Cate's room. A spike of searing jealousy heats his vision. IlliaVaa clears her throat.

"Hunter takes her meals to her." With the muscles in his jaw working, Viggo leaves IlliaVaa standing in the hall and retreats to his room to shower.

✾ ✾ ✾ ✾ ✾

Cate sits on the closet floor staring listlessly at the clothes. The party was supposed to be her escape, not her high-society introduction. Absently, she scratches at her scales.

A month of solitude and doing whatever IlliaVaa said, for nothing. No dragon gift to save her, no father to whisk her away. Just a nightly call with Mom. Cate sighs.

Until yesterday, Viggo ignored her. But, at the party, he'd kept her close. Even touching her when he could. She shivers at the thought of his hand brushing her scales. "Who does he think he is?" She picks up a shoe and throws it into the clothes, knocking garments off hangers.

Her bedroom door opens and closes. A minute later, IlliaVaa steps into the closet. "I suggest you get dressed, unless you want Viggo to see you in your pajamas."

Cate glares at her, grabbing shorts and an oversized shirt. IlliaVaa moves to the bed as Cate dresses. "He doesn't usually stay here, too many memories of our father."

"I don't care where he stays. I just want to go home."

IlliaVaa frowns. Laying on the bed, she covers her eyes with her forearm. "I think that home no longer exists for you."

"What?" Cate asks, returning to the bedroom after washing her face and brushing her hair. She sits at the little table and picks at the breakfast cart. "I didn't hear what you said."

At the sound of a swift knock, IlliaVaa moves before Cate can put down her fork. She opens the door and steps past Viggo to stand in the hallway, leaving Viggo framed in the doorway. He clears his throat. "Please join me on the patio." He doesn't wait for a response, just turns and leaves.

IlliaVaa stares as Cate continues eating. "Well?"

Finishing her bagel, Cate slips sandals on her feet and follows IlliaVaa to the patio. Viggo sits where sunlight warms the top of his head sipping from a mug. He seems to be enjoying the silence.

Reluctantly, Care admits he's someone she probably would have admired from afar if she saw him at a coffee shop. Someone she would have immediately thought out of her league. She sits across from him; awkwardly aware how short her shorts are as cold metal meets her skin.

He turns to IlliaVaa. "Dane will arrive any minute to take you into the city."

IlliaVaa graces Viggo with an insincere smile before turning to Cate. "See you later." With the elegance of a cat swishing its tail, she stalks from the patio. Viggo sips from the mug. Cate tugs at her sleeves and glances at the sunlight bathing the grass wishing for its warmth.

"What do you know about dragons and dragon-souled?"

"Just what IlliaVaa told me and what I read in a couple books from your library."

"It is a pity you were not raised with your clan." Cate bristles at his tone. "The Great War ended when a triad of rogue mages cast a spell to house dragon souls in humans. The spell affected every living dragon, even those still in eggs. Initially, it was thought dragons would soon return to their bodies, as if their confinement to humans was only a dream.

After several generations of human lives, we realized the truth of the spell. It isn't temporary. It has no end. You see it was cast by a triad - dragon, human and elf - and a triad is required to end it. Only, there are no more dragons." Viggo sips from the mug letting his words sink in.

"Now, only dragon-souled remain. Each dragon grants its human host with gifts. There are common gifts like enhancing the five senses, improving the human body, and such. Then, there are rare gifts like the ability to Travel, to see the future, to see Truth, even to wield magic."

"What's your gift?"

Viggo's eyes lift from the mug to study Cate's face. "Magic."

Cate's the first to look away. "I didn't think it'd be this chilly out here."

Viggo softly chuckles and finishes his drink. "I just told you I wield magic, and you talk about the weather."

"I have scales. Why should it surprise me that you can do magic?"

Leaving the mug on the table, he offers Cate his hand. "Come with me." She stands and tucks her hands in her sleeves rather than accept his. Viggo leads her from the patio, across the manicured lawn to the forest's edge. Without hesitation, he follows a faint path into the woods.

She pauses. "I was told not to enter the woods."

"When you are with me, you have nothing to fear."

Her heart races. It feels like there are unseen watchers waiting for her to cross a boundary. Before Viggo vanishes from sight, she follows.

The path is overgrown, as if no one has walked it in years. She pushes branches out of the way and steps over wildflowers. Viggo's far enough ahead that if she hesitates at all, she'll lose sight of him.

A twig snaps to her right, beyond massive trees and thick brush. Thoughts of watchers feed her fear and she sprints along the trail into a clearing with a stone workshop at its center. Viggo waits in the doorway. Cate glances back, but there's no one there.

She follows Viggo into the dimly lit dust-coated workshop. He faces her and mutters under his breath. Candles flare to life around them, causing Cate to sharply inhale.

"I told you; I wield magic."

"Seeing it is different than hearing it."

He smirks. His fingers move as if writing in the air. The dust disappears, leaving the workshop looking newly built and furnished. Cate wanders inside, her mouth slightly agape.

"Most dragon-souled meet their dragon and learn of their dragon gifts at puberty. My father was anxious to know which dragons IlliaVaa and I carried, so he pushed us from an early age. It was…."

He takes a long breath and glances at the ceiling. "Painful and cruel."

Cate's not sure what to say. Feeling awkward, she steps toward him searching for some way to comfort this stranger who is to become her husband. "It is nearly as cruel that you have not met your dragon." He closes the distance between them. His voice is soft, the tone mesmerizing. "Close your eyes. Calm your breathing and reach down inside yourself."

Cate closes her eyes. She takes a long slow breath and then another. It feels like she's falling, though her feet are firmly on the ground.

"Imagine your dragon is coiled in a cavern, its eyes closed, in a long-deep slumber."

Cate's eyes pop open. "How can I do that when I don't know what my dragon looks like? Is it a long snakelike dragon without wings? Is it a pterodactyl like dragon with its wings attached to its front legs? Is it a four-legged dragon with its wings on its back and horns on its head?"

"It doesn't matter. Imagine it however you want."

"How can I connect with my dragon when I don't know what it looks like?"

Viggo tamps down his frustration and turns away. He sits at a long worktable. He's never had such an irritating companion. Candlelight flickers over a wall of shelves lined with various containers.

"Whose workshop is this?"

"My father's." He absently answers. He leans back in the chair, looking past Cate into his own thoughts. "I haven't been here since he died."

"I'm sorry."

"Don't be. We had a complicated relationship." He leans forward, placing his arms on the table. "I want to help you but I'm not sure how. The methods my father used to bring out my dragon were... well, anyone would call them abusive." He pulls his shirt over his head and sets it on the table. Cate blushes and stares at the opposite wall.

"When I was five, he used a hot knife to cut and sear the wound." He points to a scar on his side. "When that healed, he threw me from the second story window." He shows a long scar on his abdomen. "He fought with my mother over that one. The next several years were a series of beatings, being locked in a dark room, starvation, and over-abundance." He turns away, red scales glisten along his spine, vanishing below his belt. "I'm not sure how my mom died. One day she was comforting me, the next she was gone."

Cate's heart aches for the pain in his voice, for the slump of his posture. She moves beside him and sets her hand on his shoulder. His skin is hot. He takes a ragged breath and straightens. "I can't do those things to you. I won't do them to you to wake your dragon. There must be another way." He grabs her hand, keeping it in place. With his free hand, he gently guides her to stand in front of him. Cate blushes, her eyes drawn to the light patch of black hair on his chest.

"Please, put your shirt back on."

"We are to be married. You'll see a lot more than this in less than a year."

Cate's whole-body flashes hot, as if blushing from head to toe. "Our parents may have agreed to an arranged marriage, but I didn't. You barely even looked at me the first time we met."

Viggo pulls Cate onto his lap. She struggles but cannot free herself. His body is lean and strong, his muscles tight. His voice is hoarse with a tone Cate's never heard before. "I admit I didn't recognize you until yesterday." Viggo's eyes shift, their pupils elongating. "You are the only mate for me."

His grip loosens and Cate leaps up out of his reach. He stalks towards her. "Once we wake your dragon, we will be the most powerful couple ever to have lived."

Cate frowns, her brows furrow. "Powerful?"

"With that power, we will bring back the age of dragons."

"What are you talking about?"

It's like someone doused Viggo with cold water. He grabs his shirt and slides it on, leaving Cate standing in the middle of the workshop. "You will stay here until you know your dragon. Remember, the woods are not safe without me."

CHAPTER 5

The workshop is one large room. Its walls are lined with shelves, each holding various books and containers, skulls, and stones. The farthest wall has a daybed, and off to the side a door that leads to a bathroom.

Cate sighs. Without IlliaVaa, how will she call her mom? Will Viggo even allow it? If she can't talk to her mom, and if her father has already agreed to this ludicrous marriage, then what option does she have?

She pulls open the door and stares at the woods. They're just trees. Why do they feel so ominous?

Back home, she often hiked in the mountains by herself. The forest there felt – lively. The trees aren't so close and the undergrowth not so dense. You can see if an animal is nearby; well, you at least thought you could. Why are these woods so different?

Cate shivers, she never expected such an opportunity would come so soon. If she had, she would have worn jeans and sneakers, not shorts and sandals. Returning to the workshop, she scours it for a bag and stuffs it with a blanket and cup.

With her heart beating like she's a thief sneaking in to steal the crown jewels, she enters the woods from the backside of the cabin and runs.

Hunter leaves the food cart outside Cate's room and knocks on the library door. When there is no response, he enters. Viggo sits at a table lined with books, many lying open and stacked on top of each other. "Where's Cate?"

Viggo doesn't respond.

Hunter walks to the table and leans on it, his face less than a foot from his brother's. "Where's Cate?"

Viggo's eyes lift from the pages he is studying to lock on Hunter's. "You mean the girl I'm to marry?"

Hunter laughs. "Don't worry, *brother,* I'm just a servant here. Where is she so I can take her dinner to her?"

"Leave it. I'll take it when I am finished."

Hunter picks up several of the titles as Viggo goes back to reading. "Dragon history? Didn't you get enough of this when Dad was alive?"

"More than enough, as did you." Viggo closes the book and focuses on Hunter. "Tell me what you've observed about Cate."

Hunter's mouth purses but it is his only display of discomfort. "She's lively, friendly, a good sense of humor, avid reader, and she doesn't sleep much." When Viggo's brows lift, illustrating his thoughts, Hunter clarifies. "She's often up late. When not locked in her room, I'd find her in here."

"Anything unusual?"

"Not that I've seen but my interactions with her have been limited. I can spend more time with her if you want."

Viggo laughs once.

"IlliaVaa tried things father did to her to wake her dragon, but they didn't work. I don't suppose you're thinking about the same thing."

"Actually, I was but I can't do that to her. Father was kinder to IlliaVaa than to me."

"I never envied, either of you, father's attention. Being fully human, I was not the son he wanted nor the son he was proud of."

Viggo turns his attention back to the books.

"Where is she?"

"Unless I tell you otherwise, forget her. I won't harm my future wife."

Hunter bows and leaves. There's only one place Viggo would hide her that he would evade answering – the workshop.

Though the inhabitants of the woods near the workshop have never been friendly, they've always treated Hunter with indifference, allowing him to wander to his heart's content. But, tonight, something feels different.

The woods are silent.

Hunter races along the overgrown path and pulls open the workshop door. It's empty and there's been no signs of Cate along the estate path. Leaving the workshop, he circles the stone building finding crushed grass leading among the dark trees.

Should he get Viggo or go after her? Either way, Cate could already be dead. Following her trail while there is still light, he races into the trees.

At first, Cate had been gripped by excitement and the possibility of escape. After hours of running, her feet hurt, her legs are scraped, and the excitement is gone.

All she can do is keep moving.

In the distance, a wolf howls. She slows, listening. The hairs on the back of her neck stand on end. *Things* move in the darkness. Tall, some shambling, some not. Some watch her from branches, while others peek from ground cover.

"Leave me alone!" She shouts as she drops the bag, with the blanket and cup, and runs. Deftly, she avoids fallen logs and skirts scrub oak.

Hitting a patch of loose rock, her slick-soled sandals slide across the scree. Screaming, she pitches forward down a slope into a narrow ravine landing on a stretch of ground-hugging juniper.

She whimpers, pushing off the juniper to her feet. Shooting pain lances through her ankle. She leans against the side of the ravine to steady herself. Blood leaks from scrapes along her legs.

Shadowy figures lean over the ravine's edge peering at her. "Go away!" She screams. A beast snarls from above and Cate presses herself against the ravine wall. Her heart pounds so fast it feels like it's trying to escape her ribs. Holding her breath, she waits.

Above her something squeals, a wolf snarls, dirt and stones rain down. Then, silence.

A few seconds later, a wolf the size of a pony leaps into the ravine. Cate hops in the opposite direction, her ankle in searing pain. Her internal voice screams that she never should have left the workshop.

"You're hurt. Let me help you."

The voice is rough, deep, raspy, and definitely male – Cate stops and looks back over her shoulder. "Did you speak?" The wolf chuckles and every hair on Cate's body stands on end. "Are you going to eat me?"

"I prefer wild game to scared little girls. Come, climb on my back. I'll get you out of the ravine and to safety."

"Why?"

"Because, I have no love for those who own these lands."

"What about the things up there?"

"I took care of them. Come, I won't hurt you."

Cate swallows her fear and hobbles toward the wolf. It's like staring at some creature from the ice age – massive and terrifying. It lies on its belly. "Climb on my back and hold tightly to my fur or else you'll fall off when I leap out."

Telling herself that if magic and dragons exist in this modern world of technology and science, so can a talking wolf, she climbs on to its back and grabs two fistfuls of hair. When the wolf stands, she lurches sideways nearly falling. Leaning over, she wraps her arms around its neck. Cate closes her eyes as the wolf's muscles bunch, and it leaps from the ravine into the forest. With jarring speed, it races through the trees.

Hunter squares his shoulders and enters the library. He sets the bag down and stands before Viggo. At moments like this, his brother reminds him of their father. He wants to admonish Viggo, to scold him for leaving Cate unattended. But, instead, he clears his throat and waits to speak.

Several minutes pass before Viggo says, "What?"

"Cate is missing."

Viggo smiles. "If that's all you're here to tell me, then leave."

"She left the workshop. I found this bag more than ten miles away. Another five miles from that, I found Cate's blood and several dead Watchers."

Viggo stops breathing. He pushes to his feet and leans against the table. "Speak plainly."

"The Watchers trailed her to the ravine. I found three of the larger watchers torn to shreds and left in the bushes. Cate's tracks end there."

"Her tracks end?"

Hunter nods. "She fell into the ravine. By her foot placement, I think she hurt either her foot or ankle. There are a few steps where her prints merge with that of an exceptionally large wolf."

Viggo's face turns red, from the neck up. "A wolf? Could it have been a Kraeken?"

"Likely, I've never seen a wolf that big that wasn't."

"Call Dane. I want him here. In the meantime, get what you need and track her."

Cate wakes in a comfortable bed covered with a country quilt. She slides her feet to the floor and immediately winces at the pain in her ankle. The scrapes on her legs have been cleaned and covered and her ankle wrapped.

The door opens and a dashing man, with long blonde hair tied at the nape, enters. "Good morning. How's your ankle?"

He smiles and his eyes sparkle. Cate blinks, her brain not yet functioning. He kneels in front of her and casually lifts her foot. She winces as he checks the injured limb. "That hurts." She snaps, pulling her foot from his hands.

The corner of his mouth twitches into a half-smile. "I've made eggs and toast. You should eat." He helps her to her feet, but before she can hobble towards the door, he scoops her into his arms.

"I can walk." She protests.

He doesn't acknowledge the complaint. Outside the door, he carries her down a flight of stairs to a great room and sets her at the table. He then puts a plate in front of her, and one down for himself, joining her.

He pours her a cup of coffee and sips from his own mug.

"Sorry if this sounds rude but how did I get here, and where are we?" She asks, eating a slice of toast.

"My friend brought you. You're about four hours from that ravine he found you in – the one belonging to the Dragotians."

"You know of the Dragotians?"

His smile is warm, friendly, and it makes her feel at ease. "Everyone here knows the Dragotians. They are a very wealthy family. Old money. Either you wandered on their land by mistake or were running from them."

Cate chokes on her toast. He waits patiently as she sips coffee and coughs to clear it. "Thank you, and your friend, for helping me."

"I'm not a friend of Viggo's, but I am not looking to be his enemy either. Was it a mistake?"

"Do you have a phone?"

"Nope. No signal towers nearby. Cell phones don't work, and I never found it worthwhile to bring a landline all this way into the back country."

She finishes the food on her plate and sips the bitter coffee. "I should be going. Do you have a pair of sweatpants I could borrow?"

He glances at her bandaged legs, his eyes lingering on her ankle. "If you are walking, you aren't going anywhere for at least a week. You didn't break it, but you sprained it good."

"I can't wait a week. I need to leave now."

"Running then. If you wait until nightfall, my friend will take you to a safe place with access to a phone."

"Do you mean the wolf?"

"Afraid?"

"A little."

"Good, you should be afraid of an animal his size but don't worry, he won't hurt you."

"Don't think I'm crazy, but I heard him talk."

"Of course, you did. He's Kraeken."

She'd heard that word before, Kraeken. It was at the engagement party. "So, he's a man that can turn into a wolf?"

"Something like that. Are you done with breakfast?" Cate nods and he scoops her into his arms and carries her upstairs. "There's a small bathroom through that door. If you feel like showering, you can."

"Thank you, for everything."

"I wouldn't thank me yet. If you're running from Viggo, then you have a long flight ahead. I'm afraid his reach is quite long." The man gives her a sad smile before leaving.

When Cate wakes, the sun is setting. She hadn't realized she was so tired. There's a quick knock on the door and the man enters. "My friend is downstairs. He says there's a tracker on your trail. You'll need to leave sooner than we thought."

He picks Cate up and carries her down the stairs and out the door. There waits a massive black wolf. Setting Cate beside the beast the man waits for her to climb on its back and hold on to its fur before wishing them safe and fleet travels.

Hunter studies the cabin. It's clear the wolf came here, but did it bring Cate?

Leaving the camouflage of the trees, Hunter knocks on the door. A few seconds later, a tall man opens it. "Good evening, Hunter."

"May I come inside, Eagis?"

The man steps back and welcomes Hunter into the cabin. One large great room and a single bedroom upstairs. Not a lot of area to search. Hunter studies the details of the room, nothing appears out of place.

"Have you seen a girl wandering around? She's seventeen, pretty, wearing shorts and a sweater."

Eagis shakes his head. "Can't say I have. Not many people, besides you, ever visit."

"My brother's fiancée took a stroll and got lost. We're searching the woods for her."

"His fiancée? Well, then, I'll keep my eyes open."

Hunter shakes Eagis' hand and steps outside. The ground near the cabin is too hard to hold prints. Eagis would know that. It wouldn't make sense for them to head back into Dragotian lands, which means they are heading to Kraeken.

CHAPTER 6

A night of riding a wolf through mountainous forests, running from an unwanted marriage, with an aching ankle seems like a dream or something you'd read in a book. Cate lies against the wolf's back and wraps her arms around its neck.

As dawn lights the sky, the wolf slows and howls. A few moments later, there is an answering howl. It changes course, climbing a nearby cliff and descending a crater into a quaint village with a mansion that looks like a castle at the far end.

It's too early for anyone to be awake, but the wolf moves cautiously avoiding attention. Sticking to the forest, it reaches the mansion. Circling wide, it approaches from the back. Cate releases her tight hold and sits upright in time to see a stunning woman, in her middle years, wearing a red sweater and dark jeans appear from a quaint cottage.

Her straight black hair falls below her waist, her black eyes study them. The wolf stops in front of the woman and lies down to make it easier for Cate to step off his back. Seeing her wrapped ankle, the woman lends Cate a hand and helps her inside.

The cottage is warm and smells of hot apple cider. Cate is seated at a table and her ankle propped up on an opposite chair. A few minutes later, the woman returns with a bag of ice and gently sets it on Cate's swollen joint.

When she at last sits near Cate's foot, she slides a mug of cider to Cate. It feels splendid to wrap her fingers around the ceramic mug and have its warmth seep into her. Looking across the table, Cate's heart nearly stops as she gets a good look at the woman across from her. "Lady v'Lana." Cate whispers.

"I am surprised you remember me. Our conversation was quite brief. It seemed your engagement was agreed upon by both sides. If that's true, why would you run away? Or is this all some misunderstanding?"

Cate shakes her head. "No, my father agreed. I never did. I don't want to marry Viggo. Please, do you have a phone? I need to call my mom."

Lady v'Lana sits back and sips her cider. Almost absently, she says, "I have never seen a woman ride a wolf like a horse. It was quite an image, I do say." She glances at Cate's ankle. "Only your injury excuses it."

There's a swift knock and the cottage door opens. A tall, broad-shouldered man, with long black hair tied back at the nape, enters. He staggers as if hit with something unexpected before recovering and pouring his own mug of cider. He joins them at the table. "This is my son, Baen."

"I thought Lord d'Gar was your son."

Baen's eyes darken, but v'Lana generously smiles. "They are twins. Baen leads the pack, while d'Gar leads the family in politics." She turns to her son. "This girl's very existence on our lands – let alone in my cottage – will cause all sorts of problems. Explain."

His eyes lift to hold hers, their gaze is gentle, almost a caress. "Wolf heard the Dragotian watchers chasing someone. When he arrived, he found them about to catch a girl when she slid on loose rock and fell into a ravine."

"Wolf...?" V'Lana shifts her gaze between Cate and Baen. "I see. Lady Cate, you say your marriage is unwanted. Do you not know that it is to unite the most powerful dragons of any of the dragon clans?"

"I don't care. I wasn't raised with a dragon clan. I didn't even know I was dragon-souled until last year. Then, out of nowhere, these people show up and kidnap me saying I am to marry a guy I've never met. All I want is to get back to my mom."

"Using a mobile phone to call your mom is traceable. If you return to your mom, they will surely find you. Viggo will not stop until he has fulfilled his father's vision, and the reason for your arranged marriage."

A tear of frustration rolls down Cate's cheek.

"You're pushing too hard, Mother."

V'Lana turns on Baen. "How long before Viggo shows up with one of his Travelers? How much time do you really think we have?" She faces Cate. "If your dragon joins with Viggo's, you will have enough raw ability to change which soul – and therefore which body – is dominant. People won't be dragon-souled anymore. You will have dragons with human souls hidden deep inside them."

"You're saying that Viggo wants to use me to change the enchantment?"

"Exactly. There is balance in this world. We Kraeken were created to balance out the might and strength of the dragons; now, we breed with them. Dragon-souled were created to teach dragons about humanity, to give them empathy for two-legged ant-like creatures. Only, the creators didn't think it through. They didn't leave any dragons remaining to cast the counter spell. What choice have you, other than to marry Viggo?"

"What if I were to find a way to break the spell? If I did that, I wouldn't need to marry him anymore, right?"

Lady v'Lana straightens, her eyes narrow. "You'd be willing to give up your dragon?"

"Absolutely, if it means I don't have to get married."

"What do you think will happen if dragon souls are no longer contained within humans?"

"They'll return to their bodies or their eggs."

"If a dragon doesn't have a body, its soul will be free, and it will die." Baen's gaze holds Cate's until his words sink in. "Can you live with that?"

"Am I being selfish? I just want to live *my* life, not my dragon's life. And, if I feel that way, maybe the dragons feel that way too. Maybe they just want to live their own lives, not the lives of the humans they're stuck inside."

Lady v'Lana reaches across the table and sets her hand on Cate's arm. "Then, we will help. Baen, will you assist this young woman on her quest?"

Cate mouths, *my quest.*

"I will."

Patting Cate's arm, Lady v'Lana glides to a bookshelf and retrieves a book. She hands it to Cate. "It is said that the victors write history. This history is from the loser's perspective and may shed light on what you need to break the spell."

Cate flips through it.

"Take it with you. You should find a place to rest, at least for a week, so that her ankle is healed. You'll need to find a place no Kraeken will look, nor no dragon. And tell no one, or Viggo's sister will get it out of someone."

"Understood." Baen stands and hugs v'Lana. He then helps Cate to her feet and lends her an arm as she hobbles to the door. He removes a set of keys off a hook and leads Cate to a garage behind the cottage.

"We'll borrow the most non-descript vehicle, a four-door white sedan." He opens the passenger door and helps her inside, then gets in the driver's seat and starts the car.

He pulls from the cottage and down a small drive, past the mansion into the village. Faces move in and out of houses, shop lights turn on and signs switch to open.

"Are all the people who live here wolves?"

Baen smiles. "Not all. Some are dragon-souled, with limited gifts, but with the strength to withstand giving birth to an enchanted being."

They pull out of the village onto a winding mountain road.

"Where are we going?"

"A place I found a few years ago. No one knows about it but me."

"Couldn't we go to Colorado to see my mom?"

"Sorry, but Viggo will have people watching her. If you want to end your engagement, breaking the spell is the best way; otherwise, he'll take you back by whatever means necessary."

"By whatever means necessary, right." Cate leans the chair back and closes her eyes.

❋ ❋ ❋ ❋ ❋

IlliaVaa blinks and walks from Eagis. "A girl was here. He told you that much already. He doesn't know where she went, only that a beast was helping her."

"A beast?"

"Fine, a wolf."

Viggo turns to Dane. "Open a portal to Lady V'Lana's estate."

❋ ❋ ❋ ❋ ❋

Hunter bows before Lord d'Gar. "By chance, my lord, have you given aid to a lost girl?"

D'Gar good-humoredly slaps Hunter on the back. "If I had, she wouldn't be lost. Come, let us greet Lady v'Lana." He leads Hunter through the expansive mansion, outside to the back garden and to a quaint cottage. He knocks and waits for Lady v'Lana to tell them to enter. Minutes pass before the door opens and d'Gar steps inside.

He inhales deeply, his pupils dilate and his cheeks flush. "What is it, my son?"

"Sorry to bother you, Lady v'Lana. Lord Viggo's fiancée took a walk in the woods near our estate and got lost. We've been searching for her to no avail. By chance, have you offered her aid?" Hunter asks, uncomfortable with d'Gar's current state.

"I have not." As v'Lana speaks, Viggo and IlliaVaa step inside the cottage making the small room feel claustrophobic. "Welcome, Lord Viggo. This is unexpected."

IlliaVaa smiles, her eyes capturing v'Lana's gaze. "Cate was here, not long ago. She has no idea where Cate has gone. The only aid offered was ice for a sprained ankle, and she gave Cate a book."

"Weren't you just saying to Hunter you did not offer aid?"

Lady v'Lana shrugs. "This is my house, on my land. I choose what I do here, not you. You are welcome to stay for cider and conversation or you may leave."

Viggo smiles, it is a cold heartless smile. He turns to Lord d'Gar, "I hear you are one of Ka'Lea's suitors. Perhaps, we should travel to the Eagles' Reaches together. I would appreciate your queen's help in finding my bride and can help you press your suit."

"Thank you, Lord Viggo." D'Gar recovers his senses. "I am flattered."

V'Lana watches as Viggo and IlliaVaa escort d'Gar outside. Hunter remains, as Dane creates a portal, and the others step through. "Do you want some cider?"

"I'd love some."

Cate wakes as Baen parks the car. He drops the keys into her hands as they get out. She locks the car. "Wait here."

They are on a mountain pull off. The granite peaks are sharp, evergreens growing along their vertical slopes. It reminds her of home. A few minutes later a massive black wolf stands outside her door. It takes her a second before she realizes the wolf is Baen. Nervously, she climbs on his back.

She leans forward and wraps her arms around his neck. With a bound, he leaps from boulder to boulder, ascending the mountain without walking anywhere that would leave tracks.

On top of the mountain, he follows the same pattern until they are several peaks from the road. Then, he alights on the ground and runs. Cate loses track of time and distance, as the wolf slows and stops at a cabin. "Use the second key to open the door. Please get me a pair of pants and a shirt from the dresser near the bed and put them outside. I'll be back soon."

Cate watches as he walks around the building. Finding the key, she unlocks the door and steps inside. The cabin is tiny, with a bed, a dresser, a bathroom, and a counter with a camp stove for cooking. She opens the dresser and retrieves a shirt and pair of jeans and sets them outside. Closing the door, she sits on the only chair in the room and waits.

After what seems like a long time, Baen enters and locks the door. He sits on the edge of the bed. "How's your ankle?"

"Sore."

He kneels in front of her and removes her shoe and the wrap. She winces. The whole side of her ankle is bruised. "At least, it's not broken."

He smiles up at her. "As simple as it is, anything here is yours. Raid the dresser, the cabinet, and shower when you want. After tonight, the bed is yours too. I should be a gentleman and offer it to you now, but I haven't slept in a couple of days. I hope you understand."

"Understand? You've been more than generous."

He glances at her shyly as he lies on top of the bed and closes his eyes. He's asleep before Cate opens the dresser to find a change of clothes.

It takes longer to shower than she expected, as she babies her ankle. Dressed in a borrowed shirt and sweat shorts, her damp hair braided, she climbs under the covers beside Baen.

Closing her eyes, she reminds herself to relax. The forest is silent. The only sound in the room is Baen's quiet breathing.

She tells herself it's just like a sleepover. Only, he's not a girl and just looking at him makes her heart skip a beat. Unlike Viggo who looks like someone she'd admire but never have, there's something honest and rugged about Baen. Something that makes him approachable.

Odd to think the one I don't stand a chance with is the one I am forcibly engaged to. She giggles and fidgets until her ankle is comfortable. The mattress envelops her, and she drifts into a deep slumber.

Blearily, Cate opens her eyes. Baen lies right beside her, his nose inches from the top of her head, his chest next to her face and his arm draped over her. Light peeks through the curtains. "Baen?" She calls hoping to wake him. He inhales deeply but doesn't move. "Baen?"

He yawns and opens his eyes. "What are you doing on the bed?" He leaps off the mattress as if scalded, hitting his back against the wall. Cate barely stifles a laugh. "I thought you were staying in the chair. You know, just for last night."

Cate shrugs. "You slept on top of the covers, and I slept under them. I thought it would be okay."

"Was it okay?" he asks, pushing his hair from his face. "I didn't do anything, right?"

She smiles. "You didn't do anything."

"Good, okay." He ducks into the bathroom. Cate throws off the covers and hobbles to the table. She'd hand-washed and hung the wrap for her ankle to dry the previous night. Fetching it, she slowly wraps her ankle.

The shower turns on and Cate smiles. In his rush, Baen had forgotten to get fresh clothes. She grabs a new shirt and shorts and sets them on the bed. Then, she unlocks the door and steps outside.

After a while, Baen joins her on the small wooden porch. "You sure nothing happened?"

"Nothing happened." Staring at the sky, she sighs. "You're the first guy I've ever shared a bed with and you're more anxious than I am." Cate blushes, deliberately not looking at him.

He glances down at his hands. "I am a man, and I am a wolf, doesn't that frighten you?"

She laughs. "Why would it? Just a year ago, I learned I carry a dragon's soul and my scales started appearing. Not to mention, I was kidnapped for an arranged marriage where I first learned about the Kraeken, oh and of course magic."

"You've been through a lot in a short time."

"Now, I'm on a quest to free the dragons so I don't have to marry Viggo." She throws her hands in the air. "I am really surprised no one has put a strait jacket on me and thrown me into a padded cell."

"Are you hungry?"

"A little."

Baen lifts her in his arms and carries her inside, setting her gently on the chair. Her cheeks are hot. "I could have walked."

"What do you like to eat? I have nothing fresh – all boxed or canned goods." He sets various cans of vegetables and fruits on the table, followed by cereal boxes, rice, potato flakes, and other items.

"I'll have the mixed fruit with cherries." He hands Cate the can and a spoon and opens a can of green beans for himself.

"We're going to be together a while. So, what would you like to know about me?"

Cate shrugs. "What do you want me to know?"

"I turn twenty in a couple months. I prefer the woods to people. I think arranged marriages should stay in the past. I like to prowl at night, and sometimes prefer being a wolf to being human. What do you want to tell me about you?"

"I don't know. I'm seventeen. I grew up with my mom. I'm supposed to get married on my eighteenth birthday. Which is crazy because I've never even been on a date." Cate finishes the fruit and tosses the can in the trash. "Unless, you call having coffee on the patio with Viggo a date. After coffee, he took me to his father's workshop. He meant for me to stay there and reflect on my dragon or something."

"What happened to you at the Dragotian estate?"

Cate leans against the table, trying to put her thoughts into words. "For a few weeks, IlliaVaa tried to wake my dragon. Nothing she did worked. I only did what she asked because I really thought my father would take me away on the day of the engagement party. Only, he didn't." Tears well in her eyes. "I haven't seen him since I was three." She wipes her cheeks and continues, "The dress I wore dropped embarrassingly low, to show my scales." Cate laughs, but there isn't anything funny in her tone or posture. Her bottom lip trembles. "When Viggo saw me - no, when he saw my scales, he changed."

"How?"

Cate's gaze shifts to the door. "I know my looks are average. I get it. The first time he met me, the day I found out we were engaged, he acted like I was nobody. Barely even looked at me. At the engagement party, he reacted like he had never seen me, like I was the most exotic and beautiful woman he'd ever met. He wouldn't leave my side, took every chance to touch my scales, and even acted jealous when guys talked to me."

She looks down at the table. "I just want a normal life. I want to go home."

Baen quietly stares at her. When he speaks, his voice is gentle. "Maybe you should give yourself a chance to know yourself as a dragon before you find a way to give it all up."

"Are you saying I should marry Viggo?"

He throws his empty can away and moves to the bed. "I'd never say that. I'm going to take a nap." He lies on top of the covers and closes his eyes. Cate props her ankle on top of the table and leans back in the chair. The cabin is eerily quiet. She wonders what her mother is doing.

She closes her eyes, and it feels as if she is falling. When she lands, she's standing in a dark pit and in the middle is a massive blue-green dragon. Its four legs are tucked under it, its wings folded over its back. Cate steps forward, her hand held out to touch the dragon's scaled snout. Hot air greets her as it exhales. Great eyes, like mirrors taller than Cate, flicker open. The dragon rolls its head to study her.

It inhales her scent and lifts its head. It studies the pit, and Cate, and then the pit again. "Who are you?" It asks, its voice rumbling through Cate's body.

"I am Cate."

The dragon lowers its head and takes another whiff. Its nostrils flare and Cate steps back. "Cateian. Well met, I am Rathleon."

"Rathleon, well met."

"Where are we?"

"I think we're in my sub-conscious."

"A dreary place. I much prefer the sea. Climb on my back and we shall go there." Rathleon extends her wing and Cate tentatively climbs the bone, careful of the delicate skin between sections. "Sit at the base of my neck, you'll be safe there." Settling herself, Cate holds on to the massive bone in front of her. Rathleon pumps her wings, her great body lifts from the ground and they soar through the darkness.

No air rushes through her hair, no wind batters her ears. But clearly, they soar higher and higher until both can see through Cate's eyes. "What is this?"

"It's a cabin."

Rathleon perches on a stone, newly imagined by Cate. "I wanted to go to the sea. Why are we in a cabin?"

"We are in the mountains, far from the sea, and my body hosts your soul. Do you not remember what happened?" Rathleon falls silent, patiently waiting for Cate to continue. With what Viggo told her and the histories she read waiting for the engagement party, Cate tells Rathleon of the dragon war and the enchantment. "Tell me of the present."

Cate shares her current predicament, including her engagement and escape. Rathleon shudders and Cate's body follows suit, nearly knocking her foot from the table. "Tell me about the clans." Cate tells her what she knows, though she admits she doesn't know much.

"Are you serious about freeing the dragons?" When Cate assures her that she is, Rathleon smiles displaying dagger-like teeth each the size of a person. "When you wake, you will know what you need to start. Trust I will provide what you need."

Cate opens her eyes to find Baen staring at her. "Are you okay?"

"Yeah, why?"

"You're glowing."

CHAPTER 7

Baen gently sets her on the bed and pulls the covers up to her, then sits beside her. "Maybe, it was a dream."

"Are you a dream? Is this cottage a dream? Am I lying unconscious in Viggo's workshop? Why can't you believe that I talked with my dragon, and she can help?"

"You're too trusting, that's why. You don't even know me. Yet, you got in my car and even slept beside me."

Cate glares at him. He's not wrong. They are alone in a secluded cabin only God knows where and it's not like werewolves have the best reputation, if you believe movies. "I was right to trust you and I'm right to trust my dragon."

"How have you survived in this world?" Shaking his head, he leaves the cabin.

Viggo curses under his breath while he climbs the tower stairs, mumbling about modern technology and elevators. Reaching the end of the staircase, he enters a large circular room. Ka'Lea stands at floor-to-ceiling windows, her gaze focused on something in the distance. Her white hair, ornately plaited, falls to the back of her knees. The hem of her plain white dress, tailored to display her curves, kisses the cool marble tiles. She turns and ice blue eyes meet his.

"To what do I owe this honor?"

Not much older than himself, she's already a widow, with her position and kingdom at risk. "I want what is mine returned. I have proof the Kraeken are involved."

"You're accusing my people of thievery. We'll see."

Together, they descend the tower stairs. Waiting in the formal audience chamber is General Ka'Leel, Ka'Lea's twin brother, IlliaVaa and Lord d'Gar. The leader of the Wolves drops into a low bow.

"Report." Ka'Leel barks.

"This morning, I smelled the scent of Lord Viggo's fiancée in Lady v'Lana's private cottage and Lady v'Lana's car is missing."

Ka'Lea's perfect mouth twists into a cruel smile. "Are you implying that Lady v'Lana kidnapped the woman?"

"No!" d'Gar waves his hands in front of Ka'Lea. "Only that the girl hid in v'Lana's cottage. She has a very distinctive scent; one I won't soon forget."

Ka'Lea turns to Viggo. "A lingering scent is not evidence of thievery."

"We have a treatise, do we not?"

"Our resources are at your disposal, if you can bring proof."

Turning on his heels, Viggo leads IlliaVaa from the audience chamber. In the hall, Dane waits. "Are you tracking Hunter?"

"Yes, he's left the Wolves' Den and is following a mountain road."

"Open a portal to my penthouse."

Cate wakes. Baen's watching her from the chair. "Why aren't you sleeping?"

"I'm not tired." Baen tosses a book on the bed. "Read this."

Cate sets it on the dresser and climbs back under the covers. "I'm sleeping."

Baen climbs on the bed and lies beside her on top of the blankets. "Lady v'Lana was right when she said the book was written by the losers. The dragons were winning the war. It wasn't until the spell was cast that we had any chance." He rolls on his side. She can feel his eyes on her. "If it wasn't for the spell, the dragons would have wiped us out. Is that something you really want to unleash on the world just to avoid getting married?"

She opens her eyes and faces him. "That was a thousand years ago. We didn't have the technology we have now. Besides, I don't think dragons will want to eat people after having lived as people."

He lies on his back facing the ceiling. "If the dragons could be freed, why haven't they been?"

"Because they believe it impossible."

Baen takes a deep breath and rolls to the edge of the bed. Even in the dark, she can see his muscles tighten as he clenches his fists. "I can't do this."

"Do what?"

His voice is deep and throaty when he answers. "Your scent is... too much." He pushes to his feet and moves back to the chair.

Cate sniffs her shirt. She doesn't stink, so what's his problem? "It was okay last night."

He chuckles, the sound makes Cate's heart skip a beat. "I was exhausted. At most, I could hold you. A dragon-souled's scent is seductive to any Kraeken. Yours...." He swallows and slowly exhales. "I need space." He yanks open the door and slams it behind him.

Baen returns the next day, as if nothing happened, and checks her ankle. "It's looking better."

As he moves to the cupboard for a can of apples in cinnamon sauce, Cate asks, "Have you ever heard of a dragon stone?"

Baen picks up the book he gave Cate and flips through it. He hands it to her, open to a page. "Not until I read this."

As he eats, she reads aloud. "For the spell, the dragon supplied a sorcerer's stone, a massive gem used to channel vast amounts of magic. It became known as the Dragon's Stone. After the spell was cast, it broke into three pieces. The dragon's apprentice took the largest stone, while the humans and elves took the other two."

Cate marks the page with her finger. "To undo the spell, we need this stone. Magic to undo magic. We must find the pieces."

"Find them where? Anyone could have the human's piece and elves don't care what happens to humans, not anymore."

"Do you know where to find elves?

"Yeah, but that doesn't mean they'll know where the stone is."

Cate stands, favoring her ankle. "We should leave immediately."

His eyes move from her ankle to the book in her hand. He grabs a bag and packs a couple pairs of jeans, a few shirts, and some clothes for Cate. Placing the book on top, he buckles it closed and hands it to her. "Give me a few minutes, then come outside."

Viggo's pencil scrapes across paper. The image coming to life through shading and careful control of each line. Drawing is his way of dealing with stress, a coping mechanism learned while enduring many of his father's lessons.

IlliaVaa lounges on the couch, idly flipping the pages of a tech magazine.

The pencil stops.

"Has your dragon ever shared memories with you?" Viggo looks up from the paper.

"Like past life memories or do you mean memories of being a dragon?"

"The latter."

"I don't think my dragon was out of its shell when the spell was cast. Why, has yours?"

He pushes his hair from his face. "Yeah, some were beautiful, like soaring above the clouds. Others horrific, like tearing apart villages."

"And now?"

"I keep seeing a regal dragon with blue-green scales, scales like Cate's. It makes me yearn for her, as if we've been apart for centuries."

"You've only been apart for days but maybe your dragon remembers hers and you are feeling what he feels. It would explain why you reacted the way you did when you saw her at the engagement party."

Viggo leans back. "I have never wanted for women. You know that, yet all of them pale compared to Cate."

IlliaVaa sets down the magazine. She used to be close to Viggo before his dragon manifested. But that was before he was interested in girls, money, and power. This isn't a conversation they've ever had.

"We have to find her, not because of the clans or the enchantment, but because I have to rid myself of this obsession."

"You think marrying her will do that?"

Viggo's mind wanders to the workshop when he removed his shirt and showed Cate his scales, when he had pulled her onto his lap. Her skin was so warm, her body lithe and muscular. He's never wanted a woman more in his life. "I do."

Wolf races from mountain to mountain, rock to rock, through streams and along ridges. The night passes to day and day into night. Near dawn, he slows to a stop by a mountain lake bordered on all sides by forest. Cate climbs off his back, and using the backpack as a pillow, lies down to sleep. Wolf lies beside her, his sides heaving, exhausted.

Near noon, hot from lying in the sun, Cate wakes. Testing her ankle, she stands and stretches. Wolf sleeps soundly at her feet, like a massive dog sunning himself.

Cate hobbles to the water and drinks. In the sunlight, near Baen, the forest feels less threatening. Here by the lake, it almost has the same feel as Viggo's woods – like someone or something watches from the deep shadows among the trees.

She takes a step back and then another. Close to the water's edge, a woman moves into the sunlight. Dressed in blue jeans and a T-shirt, with a flannel wrapped around her waist, and her hair in a ponytail, she looks normal. She waves. "Hello."

Cate wipes sweaty palms on her shorts and waves back.

"In case you didn't know, this is private land."

"Sorry, I'll wake my friend and we'll get going."

The woman glances behind Cate, then places both hands on her hips. "Oh, your friend can pass through anytime. It's only your kind that aren't welcome."

Cate mouths, *your kind.*

The woman smiles as two men emerge from the forest shadows. They look like the woman, casually dressed, and nondescript. "Don't try running. We've added a little something to the water that makes humans drowsy and forgetful."

Cate glances at the lake and back at the woman who is looking at her wrist like she's checking the time. "Four, three, two…."

"Why are you counting?" Before the woman says one, the world pitches backward as Cate's eyes close.

CHAPTER 8

Baen growls.

This is not what he meant when he said he'd take her to the elves. Her scent is unmistakable. It's clear she went to the water, then into the woods and not alone. With the strap of the bag in his mouth, he enters the tree line.

Admittedly, he should have warned her. This isn't a place where you wander or follow strangers. No, it's common sense. Why would he need to warn her?

The shifting breeze carries cloying scents better off buried. Nothing moves nearby. It's just his bad luck to have stopped here on a day they checked their boundaries. If only Cate had stayed with him.

❋ ❋ ❋ ❋ ❋

Cate's head hurts. If she could remove it, that would be great. Her stomach clenches, she lurches forward in dry heaves.

She lies on the cool stone floor and presses her hands to her stomach. Another wave of nausea curls her into a tight ball. Her whole-body hurts, even her bones feel like they are on fire. She closes her eyes.

The door opens and someone walks towards her. "Here." Without another word, they leave. When Cate opens her eyes, a cup of water sits on the ground near her.

❀ ❀ ❀ ❀ ❀

Elar had been tracking a stag when he heard a voice, faint and in pain. He'd abandoned the hunt to track the call. Now, standing at the edge of Aelvus, he grimaces. He'd rather deal with humans than step foot in this backwater place.

The voice calls out – louder and more urgent. He drops the cloaking spell. A young girl, maybe fifty, gasps and nearly drops a basket. Elar ignores her, used to such reactions. Following the soulful cry leads him to a shed beneath an ancient pine. A group of elves argue outside the door.

"Are you sure you used the right mixture?'

"It hasn't changed in hundreds of years."

"Then, why isn't she amnesiac?"

"Does it matter? Let's dump her on the highway."

Elar clears his throat. It takes a few minutes before the elves elbow each other into silence. The oldest, a female in jeans and a T-shirt, steps forward. "You are not of Aelvus."

Stating the obvious. A horrible habit of the undisciplined. Elar walks toward the shed and the elves move aside. He pulls open the door and lets his eyes adjust to the dim light. A figure lies curled on the stone.

"We found the human and are dealing with it." It's the annoying female again.

Elar silently enters the shed. The voice cries out – screaming in pain. He glances at the others, no one else appears to have heard it. He kneels next to the figure and lightly brushes her hair from her face. Her eyes flutter open, like perfect pieces of crystal refracting a brilliant rainbow of light, they give him a glimpse of a radiant soul.

Her eyes close and he nearly staggers back on his heels. Chastising himself for the emotional display, he slides his arms underneath the woman and picks her up. Her head falls against his shoulder, her forehead leans against his neck.

"What are you doing?"

Elar walks from the shed into sunlight. Outside, a bevy of elders awaits him. They bow their heads, many crowned with long silver or white hair. The woman who challenged him drops to her knees with the others who had been arguing.

"Elders, we are dealing with the human, as per our law. He has no right to intervene."

If the woman in jeans doesn't hold her tongue, Elar might cut it out. Her saving grace is that his hands are currently occupied. The eldest steps forward and the woman falls silent. "Welcome to Aelvus, Lord Elar. If we have offended the Valley of Mist, please enlighten us."

Elar turns his hard gaze to the elder. "The Valley has received no offense. The queen has written a doctrine concerning the ethical treatment of humans. I will have copies sent for your enlightenment."

The elder's eyes linger on the woman in Elar's arms.

"We merely cause humans to experience amnesia and set them loose near one of their own roads. How is that unethical?" Argues a man on his knees.

Elar doesn't need to glance down to know the pain experienced by the woman in his arms. "Then, why is she dying?"

"Dying?" The eldest lifts his hand and sets it on the woman's forehead. Muttering words of magic, a blue light appears at his fingertips.

The woman's pain, the voice that whimpers in his head, challenges Elar's patience. The eldest takes his hand away. "We await enlightenment." The elder has learned of their mistake.

No other words are necessary. Elar steps through the crowd and leaves Aelvus the way he came, wrapping himself and the woman in a cloaking spell.

Baen wishes he could cover his nose in mud. The scent of decaying flesh overwhelms Cate's scent, drawing him from her trail. Animals and birds, in various states of decay, rot within miles of the lake.

The elves must have done something to the water, and it doesn't only affect humans. He backtracks to the meadow. He'll have to start again.

He sniffs wildflowers to rid his nostrils of the smell of rot, then returns to where Cate entered the forest. Her scent is still there, though growing faint. The first time through, he'd gone north. This time, he heads west.

A faint trail leads among the brush and undergrowth, between ancient trees and seedlings. Baen pauses his paw in the air. Mixed with Cate's scent had been the scent of elves. Now, there's only elves. He lifts his nose; forest scents mingle with the smells of civilization.

He stows the bag beneath the low branches of a pine and pushes through the foliage. He'd wandered through elven settlements before, most in the trees and hidden from passing eyes. This one is on the ground, with beautifully simplistic architecture and minimalistic styling.

Gathered at the base of an ancient tree appears to be a council of elders and a bunch of youth on their knees. Even focused as they are, a wolf his size attracts attention. The eldest among the council turns from the tree and casually approaches him.

Baen can feel the elder attempting to probe his thoughts. Within reach of Baen's teeth, the elder stops. "You are not a mere wolf."

"Where is the girl?"

The elder's eyes widen momentarily before he regains composure. For an elf, it's like he jumped two feet in the air. "Kraeken, we let you be. Kindly maintain peace and leave our forest."

"Give me the girl and peace will be maintained."

"There are none but elves in Aelvus."

Baen lifts his nose, his nostrils flare. "What have you done with her?"

"We let her leave."

A deep-throated growl escapes from Baen as his lips curl over his teeth. "Where?"

"The Valley of Mist."

Hunter peers into the window of the small cabin. There's trash in the bin and the bed's unmade. Someone was staying here until recently. Using his utility knife, he works at the window latch until it gives.

Squeezing through, he pushes the window closed and secures it. Opening the dresser, he finds only men's clothes. The small kitchen holds a few canned goods and several boxes of food.

It's not like Cate had much when she fled, but Hunter expected to find something to prove she'd been here. It's too bad IlliaVaa can't read objects like she can people.

He sits at the table and stares at the bed. Not much to do here. If Cate's really with a Kraeken…. The look on Viggo's face the day after the engagement party, when Viggo stood in the hallway and stared at him coming out of Cate's room. He'd been serving her since they brought her to the estate; yet, on that day, something changed. Hunter's fingers curl into a fist.

She's his brother's fiancée. How could Viggo not trust him?

A portal forms between the table and the bed. Viggo and Dane step through. With a quick glance, Viggo assesses the room. His fingers run along the unmade bed until they rest on the pillow. Picking it up, he presses it to his face and deeply inhales.

In one pull, he tears it in half. The veins on his neck stand out, his skin is red. His eyes are no longer human, slit pupils stare through fluff in the air. "She was here. Her scent is still strong. Find her and bring me the wolf. I will kill him myself and use his pelt for a robe."

With his orders, Hunter unlocks the door and steps outside already scanning for tracks.

Cate doesn't know when she fell asleep, only that she did, and in sleep everything hurt a little bit less. Her dreams had been full of running, of weird forests with giant anime like stags, of flying through clouds and diving toward the ground, of voices arguing in an almost familiar language.

Her gag reflex kicks in, and her eyes fly open. A lean man, with long white hair, thrusts a wooden bowl at her. Cate grabs it and retches, her stomach purging acid that burns her throat. As dry heaves subside, he takes the bowl and hands her a cup of water.

She sips, glad to rinse her mouth. On wobbly legs, she sits up on a couch. "Thank you." Glancing around, she's no longer on a dirt floor but in a comely apartment.

"I am Rimalon. I am what humans call a doctor, among many other things. Your body is ridding itself of poison. I gave you something to assist it, but it will take time and you will be weak."

Cate sips more water. Her abdominal muscles are sore from vomiting and her throat feels raw. Rimalon takes her hand, his fingers deftly feeling her pulse. "Rest. You need sleep, food, and time. I will monitor your progress." Releasing her hand, he reaches for her eyes. Cate pulls back before he can touch her. "If I may, I would like to look at your pupils."

She sits straighter and lets him hold her eyelids open as he studies one eye and then the other. It's awkward having him so close, his clear eyes focused intently on hers. At this distance, she can see fine lines on his nearly ageless face.

Rimalon straightens as a door opens and closes. He pats Cate's shoulder and whispers for her to finish the water. Obediently, she drinks the remainder from the cup tasting crushed mint at the bottom. As she sets the cup down, the most beautiful man she's ever seen walks towards her. Tall, with long mahogany-colored hair held back at the temple by small braids, wearing forest green pants, a light-colored tunic, and knee-high boots.

Rimalon intercepts him, their heads bent close and their voices low. Cate tries to eavesdrop with her dragon-enhanced hearing but still their words are too soft. Straightening, Rimalon addresses Cate. "This is Elar. He is the one who found you and brought you to me. I have given him instructions for your care and will check-in tomorrow." With a soft smile for Cate, Rimalon departs.

Elar silently watches the healer leave before his gaze shifts to her. Her heart skips a beat, even feeling miserable. She pushes to her feet and takes a step towards the door. "Thank you for everything, but I really…." Her legs give out.

Elar catches her before she hits the ground, sweeping her from her feet and into his arms. Her head rests against his shoulder and her arms naturally wrap around his neck. He smells of pine and wildflowers. Too tired to be embarrassed, Cate closes her eyes. He carries her upstairs and gently sets her on top of a soft mattress. Then, he places a thick blanket over her.

The aftertaste of mint is strong, and she asks for another glass of water. A few minutes later, Elar puts one in her hand. The water helps clear her head, even if her limbs are weak. "Thank you for saving me." Her eyes go to his ears, and their upswept lobes and pointed tips.

Taking the empty cup, he retreats. "Sleep, Rimalon says it is what you need now."

It's as if his words are a spell. Her eyes close and her body falls into the gentle rhythm of sleep. Her mind is less scattered, her soul retreating into her sub-conscience seeking her dragon.

She finds it perched on the rock at the edge of her mind. Cate sits beside it. "This body is in pain. You should care for it well. You are not merely human."

"Elves poisoned a lake I drank from."

The dragon turns its long neck, its massive eyes on Cate. "Every race has its good and bad. For a moment, I thought…." The dragon shakes its head. "I never imagined it would be a thousand years."

"I never imagined I'd be engaged to a rich dragon-souled heir, helped by a werewolf, or rescued by an elf. All of this is like a dream, even you."

The dragon chuckles producing a soft sulfurous smoke. "I am a dream."

"You are more than that."

The dragon spreads her wings, flexes them, and tucks them back into place. "I sense them moving but cannot feel the wind. I see through your eyes. I hear through your ears. I yearn to feel the inferno in my chest unleashed and fire along my lips."

"Once I find the pieces of the Stone…."

Her dragon is silent for a long time. "Every child must learn to crawl before they walk. Some never walk but run. Perhaps you will run, Cateian."

CHAPTER 9

Kith completes the bench press and racks the bar. He's worked his chest muscles to the point of fatigue. Sitting, he wipes his face with a towel. Built like a fabled barbarian he doesn't look like a typical middle-aged businessman.

Picking up his water bottle, he chugs it as he leaves the gym and heads to his room to shower. Halfway there, he stops. In the living room, holding their wedding picture in her hand is Emily.

Time hasn't changed her. She sets down the picture and faces him. Her chin's tilted, her nose high. "Where's Cate?"

Her words sting. Seeing her like this, all he wants is to pull her into his arms and kiss her, but she doesn't even ask how he's been, just where their daughter is. It's like her voice restarts his heart. He steps into the living room and sits.

Emily sits beside him, her eyes taking stock. "How have you been?"

There it is. He finishes the water in his bottle and wipes his mouth with the back of his hand. "Cate's with her fiancée, as per the marriage agreement. I keep busy. You?"

"I hate this, Kith. I never wanted it. You know that. Cate's arranged marriage is the only reason I left."

He leans forward, his elbows on his knees. "I told you when you married me that we had no choice in this. You knew what you were getting into, even if you're not dragon-souled."

"I knew but I didn't believe it."

His mouth twists bitterly and he pushes to his feet. "I am not doing this. Stay if you want, leave if you want. I'm taking a shower." The words have the effect he wanted; he can see how they've cut her. Without another word, he leaves her sitting alone on the couch and retreats to his room.

He turns the shower on as hot as he can stand, removes his clothes and steps under the water. It has been fourteen years. He leans against the tiles, letting the water wash away the sweat and fatigue. Fourteen years and her only focus is Cate.

Like her, he'd known what he was getting into when he married Emily. He'd known which soul would pass to their child.

He'd known how Emily would respond, what she'd do. He never blamed her. Not really. His dreams showed him what would come, all he had to do was last through the pain.

Turning off the water, he steps from the shower and wraps a towel around his waist. Opening the door to his room, he stops. Emily stands in the middle staring at his drawings. Pencil sketches of his wife and daughter over the years, all images from his dreams.

He leans against the doorframe. "The agreement set Cate on her destined path. I haven't seen whether she'll marry Viggo or even if she'll remake dragon-kind. I only know that the dragon she carries must be put with the dragon Viggo carries for any future where humankind survives to be possible."

Emily faces him, tear streaks line her cheeks. "She's just a kid."

Kith crosses the space between them and pulls Emily against him. "I couldn't have let her go if you hadn't taken her." His wife looks up into his face. "I miss you both. Even now, I want to take her back and tell them all to go to hell."

Emily wraps her arms around him. "Why can't we?"

"The fate of the world is in our daughter's hands, that's why." He rests his chin on top of her head. "No parent wants to send their child to war, not knowing if they will come back. That's what this is. It's war and it will be waged by Viggo and Cate. I don't know how yet, but when I do know I will give our daughter all the help she will ever need."

Emily tilts her head to stare up into his face. "I've never loved anyone but you."

He looks at the pictures on the wall. "I know."

Elar sets a bowl of oatmeal on the table next to the bed. He'd spent the night watching the girl sleep. Her face peaceful, her breathing deep and even. "Good morning." His voice draws her soul toward him, he can feel her waking. It's an odd feeling being connected to another person like this. She stretches and sits, covering a yawn with her hand. Picking up the oatmeal, she takes a tentative bite.

"This is good. What's in it?"

"Honey and spices." He patiently waits as she eats. When she's finished, he takes the dishes and asks, "What is your name?"

"Cate."

As he walks downstairs, he can feel her eyes on him. When the shower turns on, he returns to his room and leaves clean clothes for her on the bed then slips downstairs in time to open the door for Rimalon.

"I envy you this cottage outside the Valley. How is the girl?"

"She slept through the night and ate well this morning."

"Good. Did you learn anything?"

"Nothing."

"Well, maybe after today's examination, we'll understand better." Rimalon climbs the stairs, with Elar close behind.

Cate sits in the middle of the bed, her wet hair loose, wearing the tunic and leggings. Rimalon sets his bag down and asks Cate for her hand. She holds it out letting him feel her pulse. Next, he holds open her eyes to stare into her pupils.

"I would like to listen to your heart and lungs, would that be okay?" Cate nods and turns her back to him. "I'm going to lift your tunic." Cate holds down the front as Rimalon lifts the back. "Your scales are quite beautiful." Rimalon presses an instrument to Cate's back.

Elar agrees. He's never seen a dragon, but if he had he imagines it would be as beautiful as the girl on the bed.

Rimalon lowers the tunic. "Everything sounds good. How are you feeling?"

"Sore and tired."

"You recovered faster than I thought possible. The more you sleep, the better."

Cate glances from Rimalon to Elar. "It's not that I'm ungrateful, but I have a friend back in the clearing. He's probably trying to find me. I can't just stay here and sleep."

Elar sits forward on the chair as an unfamiliar feeling stirs in his chest.

"I'm traveling with a wolf. He's big with thick black fur."

Rimalon laughs. "You're traveling with a wolf? Not the companion I expected."

"I know it sounds crazy, but not anymore crazy than…."

"Elves?" Rimalon finishes. "It's our own fault. We withdrew from the world and have become the stuff of fairy tales."

"And movies."

"If we find your companion, will you stay and rest?" Elar asks.

Cate turns her gaze at him. She had been avoiding looking at him. He's everything she ever imagined an elf to be. Which makes her think of the fantasies she'd concocted over the years, her cheeks heat. "Sure, if you find him."

Elar's eyes meet hers, as if silently sealing a deal, before he disappears downstairs. Rimalon moves to the chair. "What brought you to the elven border?"

Cate climbs under the covers. Part of her wonders how much she should say, while another part thinks sharing secrets with someone you'll never see again, might be a good thing. "It's a long story."

"If you fall asleep, I'll stay until you wake to finish."

Rimalon reminds Cate of a friendly teacher. "Do elves have arranged marriages?"

He shakes his head. "We live too long to be married to someone we don't love, though it used to happen among the highest-ranking families. Is it still a practice among humans?"

Cate shrugs, deciding to change what she was going to say. "Do you know about the enchantment that put dragon souls into humans?"

"I do."

"Did you know it can't be broken because there aren't dragons anymore?" Cate's eyelids are getting heavy. "What happens to dragons if they can't be free of humans?" This last sentence is slurred as sleep takes her. Rimalon collects his things and goes downstairs to wait for Elar.

It's nearly dark before Elar returns, his face could be carved from stone.

"Dare I ask?" If Elar were a mage, his eyes would be wreaking havoc. "Then, let me distract you. Humans who host the soul of a dragon gain scales around puberty. It's one of the few physical signs of their dragon. Most will have scales on their neck, some run down to their shoulder blades. Only one other that I am aware of has scales that run all the way down their back."

The image of Cate's blue-green scales fills Elar's mind. "Could there be more than two?"

Rimalon folds his hands on his lap. "During the dragon war, the most powerful dragons rose up to lead them. A male and a female." Of all his students, Elar was always the sharpest. "As the girl was falling asleep, she mentioned an arranged marriage, the dragon war and asked what happens when dragons cannot be free of humans?"

Elar's eyes shift to the stairs.

"We've monitored the soul of the male dragon since the enchantment was cast. The female has never appeared, until now." Rimalon leans back on the couch. His keen eyes evaluate every detail of Elar's demeanor. "Why did you agree to find the wolf?"

"Cate needs rest."

"Why the concern?"

Elar has been asking himself that since leaving Aelvus. "I saw her soul."

Rimalon frowns.

Elar's eyes flash with an unreadable emotion. "And he is not a wolf. He is a Kraeken shapeshifter. He's been tracking Cate since she disappeared. He's in the Valley now resting in comfort after causing a scene in the Council."

Now, Rimalon understands Elar's agitated state. He had wanted to keep the girl's existence a secret, but if the Kraeken went to the Council that is now impossible.

The world shifts from her high school hallway lined with lockers to her bedroom in mom's condo above the coffee shop, as is the way of dreams.

It feels so good to be home.

Everything looks like she left it when she went to work: clothes on the floor, jewelry spread over the top of her dresser, and makeup on her desk. Her door opens. She looks up expecting Mom; instead, it's a black-haired guy in jeans and a T-shirt that strains against the muscles of his chest. He looks familiar.

"Where have you been?"

Cate starts to answer, but she can't remember. He closes the distance and pulls her to him, holding her loosely in his arms. He looks down into her eyes. Cate's heart races at his tender expression. "It's time to come home."

"I am home."

He smiles and it softens the severe angles of his face. He leads her from the bedroom into the hall. Only, it isn't the hall they step into but the massive, manicured gardens of the Dragotian estate. Cate turns around, but the apartment is gone.

Now, she knows why he looks familiar. Cold panic floods her limbs. She pulls from his grip and flees into the forest. Her frantic footfalls carry her to the hidden workshop. She races inside and slams the door.

When she turns around, Viggo sits shirtless at the table. He walks to her and leans against the door, boxing her in. Panic and desire war inside her. He leans closer and she can feel the heat of his skin. "It's only a dream." He whispers leaning down to cover her mouth with his.

It feels nothing like a dream. She lifts her hands to push him away and touches the soft hair on his chest. His kiss heats, the pressure from his lips insistent. It's only a dream, she reminds herself, giving in to the kiss. His pulls away, his breathing ragged. "Come back to me."

Cate's heart feels like a caged beast trying to break free. Her lips throb. Looking at him, she can't imagine why she left. Gently, he cups her head with his hands. "We are meant to be."

"Why? Who am I to you? An obligation? A means to an end?"

"I won't lie. First, that's all you were. Not anymore, not after our engagement." He leans in to kiss her, and she stops him. He gives her a rakish grin.

"I never agreed to marry you."

His eyes are hooded, shadows play along his features. "You will."

Cate wakes in a cold sweat. Images of Viggo haunt her as she retreats to the bathroom and a cold shower. When she returns, a new set of clean clothes rests on the bed. Dressed in a green tunic and leggings, she walks downstairs.

Whatever they gave her for the poison seems to also have worked wonders on her ankle. Soundless on bare feet, she emerges into a great room. On one side is a galley style kitchen, on the other built-in bookshelves. Elar sits on the couch, reading. He glances up from the book. "Are you well?"

"I think so. Did you find my friend?"

Elar sets the book on the arm of the couch. He crosses his ankle over his knee and turns his full gaze on Cate. "We didn't need to. It seems he found you. He's a guest in the Valley. I will take you there tomorrow."

"Why not now?"

"You still need rest."

"No, I don't."

"You answered, I think so. That means you are unsure."

Cate crosses her arms over her chest. "Okay, I meant I feel great."

"If Rimalon agrees, I will take you to the Valley."

"Where is he?"

Elar's lips twitch, the corners almost lifting into a smile. "He will return at sunset."

Cate plops onto the couch, a cushion between her and the elf. "Why can't we just go? I'm kinda in a hurry."

Elar openly studies Cate. The way his eyes flow over her is like an artist studying a sculpture. "While we wait, tell me about yourself."

She grimaces. She's getting tired of her own tale. "Not much to tell. I grew up in Colorado and graduated high school early. I work at my mom's shop.... What else do you want to know?"

"Why were you in the forest, near Aelvus? Why are you traveling with a Kraeken shapeshifter?"

Her hands idly pick at the couch cushion. "I ran away."

Elar doesn't react.

The silence makes Cate feel like she needs to explain. "Not from my parents, well not from my mom." It's difficult to look at such a beautiful man while confessing what a mess you are. "From an arranged marriage." Cate's eyes lift from the cushion, trying to read his expression.

"And the Kraeken?"

"He saved me from crazy watcher things and helped me flee the guy I'm supposed to marry."

"If you fled him, why are you still traveling together?"

It's hard to read his body language. He isn't leaning toward her or away. He isn't fidgeting. He's just sitting on the couch talking to her. Should she tell him about the dragon stones or should she not?

His expression softens. "If it is personal…."

"No!" She waves her hands in front of her face. "It's not that. It's just, well, we're on a quest." Elar laughs, surprising them both. It's such a human sound that Cate smiles. "Really, we are."

"I believe you and I have never heard anyone use that turn of phrase. I have read about it, but never heard anyone actually use it."

"Don't elves do that sort of thing? Go on quests?"

He wipes tears from his eyes. "Not really, no." Taking a deep breath, he closes his eyes. It looks to Cate like he's trying to gain control of himself. After a few seconds of measured breathing, he opens his eyes and refocuses on her. "What is your quest?"

Cate chews on her lower lip, trying to decide whether to answer. "Are you done laughing?" His smile lights his eyes. Cate cannot help but smile back. "To find the Dragon Stones."

His smile fades. "I have heard of the Dragon Stones. They are fragments of a powerful artifact."

"Exactly! One was given to the elves."

"Why do you want to find the stones?" Before Elar seemed detached, now he seems aloof, almost cold. He leaves her sitting on the couch to answer a knock at the door and returns with Rimalon in his wake.

Cate glances at Elar as Rimalon examines her. When's he done, Rimalon sits on a chair across from her. "The poison has left your body. How do you feel?"

"Fine."

"Good, that's good." Rimalon's keen eyes shift to Elar. "What has disturbed you?"

Elar opens his mouth to answer and instead sits right next to Cate, close enough that his leg is touching hers. Cate starts to scoot over, but Elar places his hand on her arm.

His touch is light, but it feels like energy pulses through his fingers and through the fabric of the tunic right into her nerves. Under his touch, she settles. "Cate and the Kraeken are on a quest to find the Dragon Stones."

Rimalon coughs. If he had been drinking something, Cate would have said he choked. "Why?"

Baen's words echo in Cate's mind, repeating over and over that she trusts too easily. With her stomach in knots, she decides to tell them. "To free dragon souls."

"You will need a triad of mages for that."

"I have to find the stones before I worry about finding mages."

Rimalon directs his attention to Elar. "I nearly forgot. You are requested by the Council. I will stay with Cate. Perhaps, you can bring her friend when you return."

Elar's leg presses against hers as he stands. His mouth is pressed into a thin line. With a nod to them both, he strides from the cottage with determined steps. Cate sets her hand on the warm cushion where Elar had been sitting a moment before.

Rimalon is the first to break the silence. "Who are you?"

"Cate."

The elf's eyes narrow. *"Nochtann nidhogg."*

A blinding needle of pain sears through the top of Cate's head. She grabs her temples. "Ahh, that hurts! What are you doing?" She squeezes her eyes shut. Rimalon repeats the words, and it feels like hot spikes are driven through her eyes. "Stop!"

She drops to her knees in front of the couch.

"Nochtann fior fine nidhogg."

Cate shrieks, each word Rimalon says tears at her. "Enough!" Roars a voice, not her own. It's deep and resonate yet coming from her own chest. The pain ends. Cate drops her hands and blinks several times to clear her vision.

"Ce tusa nidhogg."

Cate's lips curl over her teeth. "Who are you, elf, to demand I reveal myself?"

Rimalon stands and bows deeply. "I am Rimalon, eldest of the mages of the Valley of Mist. Welcome, Mistress of Dragons."

"You know me?"

"A guess, Mistress. You worked with my sire."

The dragon smiles. "You are Ruthvark's son?"

"You are Rathleon. The only dragon willing to sacrifice to save us all."

The dragon controlling Cate's body looks down at her small hands. "A thousand years. It was never meant to last this long."

"The girl seeks the stones."

"I will help her unite them."

"There has been a thousand years of peace among the non-human races. Freeing the dragons will only bring chaos and war."

"You do not know that."

Rimalon sits beside Cate. "Is this the first time you have woken since the spell was cast?"

"It is."

"Then, you do not know humans. You do not know what the dragons have experienced."

Rage explodes inside Cate – red hot, like a volcano. "*Tuero incendiere.*" Fire erupts along Cate's lips. "Beware Rimalon." The mage's eyes widen in surprise. This close, he can feel the heat from the small flames.

The cottage door opens as Cate stands. "Do not presume." Fire spreads from Cate's mouth, along her shoulders, down to her fingers.

"Cate!" She turns at the sound of Baen's voice. He grabs a blanket and tosses it over her, patting her arms to put out the flames. Only, they don't fade. They burn through the fabric. Elar pushes past him, grabs Cate and runs up the stairs to the bathroom.

Pulling aside the shower curtain, he thrusts her inside and turns on the water. It douses the blanket but does not put out the flames that dance along her skin and burn through the tunic. Her eyes meet his, dragon eyes, with long slit pupils. "*Fin`e incendiere.*" The voice is not Cate's.

The fire fades, her eyes return to normal. Elar turns off the water as Baen fills the doorway with his blocky form. "Are you okay?"

Cate stares at the holes in the tunic, her skin showing through. She pushes up what's left of the sleeves. Her skin is perfect, not a single burn on any of it. "What's wrong with me?"

Rimalon moves Baen and then Elar aside. "Nothing. Elar will get you fresh clothes and then you should sleep. The effects of the magic will hit hard. It always does the first time."

CHAPTER 10

Viggo wakes in sweat-soaked sheets. As the pre-eminent mage, he's pulled other dragons into his lucid dreams but never been pulled into another's. Until now. It takes patience, power and practice. Yet, Cate did it without even knowing it.

He smirks at the memory of their kiss. He'd told her it was only a dream and she'd believed him. Everything that happens in the Dreamscape of a dragon mage is real.

He throws off the covers and heads to the shower. Turning the water on as hot as his human body can handle, he stands under the flow.

As he washes, his mind lingers on the dream and the feeling of Cate on his lap, the warmth of her lips. He turns off the shower and shakes water from his hair. Toweling dry, he selects a tailored black suit with a royal blue shirt and black tie.

By the time he meets Dane in the office, he looks every bit the high-powered executive. Dane hands him a mug of black coffee. "The dragon lords are using your wedding as an excuse to gather the clans."

That's good. He'll need all the dragons in one place and his wedding is the perfect venue. "Perfect, make sure all clan leaders accept the invitation. And extend it to all of their generals as well. Any news from Hunter?"

"None. Why do you trust that human?"

"He's my brother, besides, we all have our uses. Take me to the estate." Viggo finishes his coffee and steps through the portal. He goes straight to the workshop. All who have carried Xenothgorot's soul journaled their lives. He'd never found the journals interesting. But, perhaps, in them is what he needs to know about the dragon's soul Cate carries.

Hunter examines the grass near the lake. The way it lies, a large animal bedded down here. He expects there to be many animal tracks near the water, but there are few. Only the same wandering wolf, from the water into the tree line.

He sticks his fingertip in the water and lifts it to his lips. There's a slightly bitter aftertaste. He's run across this before, where elves slipped something into the water to confuse anyone dumb enough to drink from it.

Thinking about how naïve Cate is, Hunter imagines her bending down to drink. If she did, she would have been carried away. Hunter straightens and faces the woods. Standing on the edge of the lake, right in the tree line is a tall slender girl in blue jeans. She hadn't made any noise, and the wind is blowing the wrong direction for him to smell her. Instead, he'd had the feeling of being watched.

"You are trespassing." There's a slight accent to her words.

"My apologies. I am looking for someone that traveled through here."

He can feel her studying him, deciding what her course of action will be. "Few travel this way but there was a girl."

Hunter suppresses a smile. Elves are naturally reserved and tend not to display outward emotions. "Sandy blonde hair, about this tall?" Hunter lifts his hands to his chest. The girl nods. "Where is she?"

"She was taken to the Valley. To find her, you will have to deeply trespass on our land. Forget her." She steps into the shadows and disappears.

Hunter pulls his phone from his pocket. No signal. He'll have to hike back the way he came, until he can get at least a bar. His hunt has stalled. It's time to call Dane.

V'Lana stands at one of the many floor to ceiling windows, her mind on Baen and where he might be. The glass reflects Ka'Lea's image, from the other side of the room. V'Lana had expected the summons. Yet, standing here waiting for the girl to speak, gnaws at her patience.

She reminds herself, that though young, Ka'Lea is cunning and fierce. In the reflection, Ka'Lea looks pale, her beauty all fragile ice. An illusion. The Eagles have long been marked by their white hair and sharp features.

She shifts so the reflection no longer catches her eyes. D'Gar waits in the audience hall with Ka'Leel. The boys have been friends since they were toddlers. V'Lana lets the memories of their play soften her mood. She'd often visit Ka'Mber when the kids were little. A beautiful girl, inside and out.

"What is your opinion of the Dragotian's fiancée?"

"She looked like a startled doe through most of the party." V'Lana turns from the window to face the Kraeken queen. "I doubt you called me here to gossip."

"Careful with your tone." Ka'Lea's voice is as cool as her looks. "Viggo's appearance was surprising. You should have at least sent word that you assisted her."

"I did not think tea and an ice pack warranted royal notification. As for my stolen car, I have people on it."

"Not sending her back to him with a nice little bow around her neck threatens our treatise."

V'Lana's mind devises and discards reason after reason. "I admit, his portfolio is impressive and as a man, he is quite striking. Perhaps, I was thinking of you. Young and recently widowed."

Ka'Lea smirks. "His scent is heady, that doesn't mean I would consider marrying him. It pleases me that you think of my happiness."

"As my regent, how can I not?"

Ka'Lea approaches and v'Lana's hackles rise or would if she were in wolf form. "I have always been fond of Baen and d'Gar. If I cannot marry for love, I at least want to marry a friend."

"Give yourself time, Ka'Lea. Grieve for L'Syle."

"Marrying L'Syle was my father's decision. Tell Ka'Leel everything you know about the girl. Leave out no small detail." With a clear dismissal, V'Lana bows and departs.

❀ ❀ ❀ ❀ ❀

Cate lies on top of the bed, her eyes wide. She can hear Baen arguing with the elves, though his is the only raised voice.

She lifts her hands, staring at them again. Studying them for any signs of the fire. There are none. It is like it never happened. Tears leak from her eyes, and she wipes them away. She shifts to the edge of the bed and sits, her elbows on her knees and her head in her hands.

It is like when her scales first showed up and her mom told her about her dad and the dragons. It felt like she was making up a story, so Cate did not feel like a freak. And, at first, she had not believed her. It took seeing people in Mom's shop who were not fully human. Even then, Cate could argue it was all body modification.

Only, it was not. Their willingness to talk helped her through her own transformation. At least, she thought it had. She never expected to breathe fire. *Breathe fire!* Is that her gift? Being a fire starter?!

She pushes her hair from her face. Pacing from one side of the floor to the other, she runs her hands along her arms, feeling the fabric beneath her fingers.

It has been a year since her scales erupted. Only a year and now, she can breathe fire. *Crap! Holy freakin' crap!*

Cateian, calm yourself.

"Oh, crap!" Cate drops to the floor and sits with her fingers on her temples. "Don't do that. You can't just talk to me."

I can and will. We are one, Cateian.

"Fine! What's with the fire? You could have killed me."

Cate can feel Rathleon's mirth. *I admit, I did not think the spell would work, Cateian.*

"You didn't think it would work and you still did it! What would you have done if you had killed me? Just, moved on?"

Unlikely.

"That's how the enchantment works. A human dies and the dragon just moves to the next human. Who cares if you risk my life?"

You are *risking your life. You fled from the Dragotian estate, ran through a forest of Watchers, accepted the help of the Kraeken, and drank poisoned water.*

"You set me on fire!"

Fire is my element and yours. You need not fear it.

"It's fire."

Dragons have different elements they connect with. For some, it is water and others air. All have an affinity for earth. A few connect with even rarer elements, like the Viator. Through their element, they open the veil that separates space and move between it.

"You're talking about Travelers? Like a hole ripped in the air that goes to another place."

Exactly.

Cate shivers hit by a sudden wave of heat and cold that ripples through her body. Bile rises in her throat, and she swallows it down. Pushing to her feet, she slowly descends the stairs, clinging to the rail the whole way.

Rimalon falls silent at the sight of her. Baen and Elar both turn. One moves to support her while the other goes to the kitchen returning with a glass of water. Baen helps her sit as she takes the water from Elar.

"You need rest."

Cate drinks half the water before responding. "You seem to think sleep fixes everything. It won't fix this."

The corners of Rimalon's lips twitch, near to a smile. "There is nothing to fix."

Cate finishes the water and sets the glass down. Elar sits beside her, his leg touching hers while Baen sits across from her. "How are you feeling?"

She laughs. The notes a bit too high and too forced. "Okay, I guess. Only my clothes burned."

"What about the lake?"

Cate takes a deep breath. "That. Yeah, I'm okay. Rimalon treated me and I feel much better."

"She nearly died." Elar says it like he's talking about the weather. "She needs to fully recover before she leaves."

"It was because of elves she was poisoned."

Elar's eyes narrow, the muscles in his jaw flex. Rimalon has never seen him this angry. Perhaps, it would be best if the girl left. Only, there's more to this girl and her dragon. His sire told him about Rathleon, the stories so vivid it is like they are his own memories.

"The Council sent emissaries to Aelvus for a full investigation." Elar shifts his attention to Cate. "You said if we found your friend that you would rest."

Cate glances between Elar and Baen. A wave of intense heat and cold ripples through her. She swallows against the nausea, her face pales. Elar doesn't ask permission. He pulls her on to his lap and stands, with Cate in his arms. "We can continue the conversation upstairs."

A few minutes later, Cate's lying on top of the bed with a light blanket over her. Elar sits beside her, while Baen leans against the wall and Rimalon sits in the chair. Cate covers her eyes with her arm.

It's Rimalon who breaks the silence. "I think humans call it possession when a spirit inhabits a living person. Is that correct?"

"It is." Baen answers.

"Over the centuries, elves have dealt with several types of possession. The kind humans are familiar with, as well as others. To shorten the tale, know that various artifacts and magics the elves protect draw the bodiless to us. Because of this, my sire developed a spell that forces the bodiless to reveal themselves when they are in possession of a living body."

"Why are you telling us this?" Baen sounds short-tempered. Cate keeps her arm in place and her eyes closed.

"I used the spell on Cate. It is what brought her dragon forward and why the fire spell was invoked."

"You what?" Elar shifts, Cate can feel the bed move and she imagines him turning his silver-eyed gaze on Rimalon.

"Cate is powerful." Rimalon lets the words hang in the air. "I needed to know who directs that power and their intention."

"You needed to know no such thing." Baen growls, sounding closer to a wolf.

"I protect the Valley and its inhabitants. It is my duty to know."

"What you know is that I am dragon-souled. You saw my scales." Cate sounds tired, her voice flat.

"I did and that is why I made your dragon reveal itself. Remarkably, your dragon knew my father. That connection did not keep her from warning me with the fire spell. Unless I am mistaken, that was your first-time using magic. The aftereffects will fade and the more you use magic, the less you will experience them."

"So, it was magic fire and that's why it didn't burn me?" Cate drops her arm, her eyes find Rimalon. "Why then did it burn the clothes?"

"The spell won't burn the caster; it will burn everything else."

Cate's gaze shifts to Elar. He had carried her to the shower. As if reading her mind, he turns back to her. "I am unhurt." He pushes up his sleeves to show his arms are unburnt. She glances at his chest, and he moves to take off the tunic.

"If you say you're not burnt, we believe you." Baen says, stopping him. "I don't know how much Cate has told you, but we're in a hurry. There are people looking for her."

"Yes, escaping an arranged marriage. Why are you helping her Kraeken?"

Baen crosses his arms over his chest. "I could ask you the same thing."

Rimalon's voice is like a balm, cooling the building tension. "The dragon Cate carries is the mage who, with a human and elf, cast the dragon-souled enchantment. Her waking is a sign."

"Of what?"

"A new era is in ascendence, and Cate is the catalyst."

Cate rubs her face with her hands and laughs. "You know how ridiculous that sounds? Me, a catalyst? All I want to do is find the stones."

"Once you have them, what will you do?"

"Free the dragons."

"Exactly. You are the rock around which the water ripples. Whatever decisions you make will have consequences on the world."

"It's not like I have any options. If I marry Viggo, he wants dragon souls to take over. The only way to stop him is to free the dragons."

"That would give reason for the Kraeken enchantment once more." Elar fixes his gaze on Baen.

"Our reason for the enchantment has never faltered."

"To kill dragons?"

"To protect our people. I will help Cate find the stones."

Elar slowly shifts his gaze to Cate. If she could disappear into the bed, she would. His voice is soft and low when he speaks. "Are you seeking the dragon stones to escape the marriage?"

"Yes, and no. Have you ever done something you thought right when you did it, but later you realized that though it was the right thing to do that maybe it wasn't the best thing to do?" Elar tips his head slightly and Cate takes that for acknowledgment. "When my dragon came up with the spell, she did it because she was hurting so much for her kind and for every race in the war. She wanted them to understand each other – especially the dragons and humans."

"It was meant to create empathy and understanding." Rimalon adds. "It was never meant to last this long. I cannot say the original intention was met. I can say that peace followed."

"Look, I don't even know if I can break the spell but at least I can find the stones in order to try."

Elar adjusts the blanket and stands. "With Baen here, are you willing to rest?"

"Yeah." Cate closes her eyes and is fast asleep.

✹ ✹ ✹ ✹ ✹

Viggo lies on the daybed, journals spread around him. Only the first had any in-depth reference to Xenothgorot's mate – Rathleon. It spoke of her shimmering blue-green scales. The magnificence of her wings, and that she was a queen of the sky.

He had respected her ability with magic, to the point of envy. That she was free with her knowledge irritated Xenothgorot. She had even taken several human apprentices, while at war with the humans. He could not understand her fascination with them.

Other journals talk about his search for her soul. At first, he feared she died during the war. Only after finding her body, did he know she didn't and her soul was in a human – somewhere. He built up wealth and acquired the land above the cave where her body slumbered and continued the search for her soul.

Over the centuries, he decided that her soul must still be slumbering and that's why he couldn't find her. So, he started looking for dragon-souled without gift manifestation. This led him to the Enderen clan. Through his notes, he started watching when a certain soul appeared. Scales would erupt and the host would gain basic dragon abilities – but never a gift.

That's when he crafted his plan for a new dragon race using the blood and bones of their human prisons. If he and Rathleon were born into the same generation, and if he could wake her, it would be more than possible.

The words "blood and bones of their human prisons" circulate through Viggo's mind. What will his body look like when Xenothgorot's plan comes to fruition? Will he even recognize himself?

A knock on the door startles him. "Come."

Hunter steps inside. He surveys the books. "I have an idea where Cate is, but it won't be easy collecting her."

CHAPTER 11

Cate felt fluish most of the night, either shivering or sweating under the covers. Rimalon carries in a tray with a bowl of oatmeal, an apple, and a glass of water. He sets the tray down and sits at the end of the bed. "You look much better. I apologize for not thinking about the reaction you may have to the reveal spell." Cate doesn't know what to say, so she remains silent as she eats the oatmeal. Rimalon continues. "Finding the dragon stones is no small feat, using them will be even harder. If you do find them, and if you will have me, I offer my services to be part of a mage triad."

"Thanks, but why would you do that?"

He smiles kindly. It warms his whole face, though looks a little out of place. "I thought long about what you and Rathleon said. Even though it may end peace and take lives, the dragons do not deserve an eternal prison."

Though not entirely hopeful, his words warm her. "I can't agree to you being part of a triad, when I don't even have the Stone. What I need help with is figuring out where to start. Rathleon remembers the stones were to be divided among the mages, but that's all."

Rimalon removes a ring from his pinky and hands it to her. "My father had this ring made after the enchantment was cast. He told me on his deathbed that the gem was a chip from the Dragon's Stone, which he found at the site after the stone was fragmented. Perhaps, it will help you find the pieces."

Cate studies the prismatic green gem. It almost looks like a peridot or emerald. Cate slips the ring on her thumb and there is a brief flash of light. She shakes her hand to rid it of the electric sting. "Thank you. Maybe Rathleon will know how to use it." Her body hums, like every nerve is alive, acutely aware of the ring's magic.

Rimalon absently pats her leg, like a grandfather comforts a child. "After the war, elfkind split into factions. The Valley of Mist is the epicenter of the southern elves. The northern elves cut themselves off from the world after taking heavy losses during the war. Since we do not have the dragon stone here, it is likely there."

"What about places like Aelvus?"

Rimalon considers the question, analyzing each remote elven village. "Not likely. Anything of magical import is kept under wards and guarded at the center of the Valley."

"Where are the northern elves?"

Rimalon sighs. "They use strong magic to keep themselves separate from the world – human and otherwise. All I know is that you need to head north." Rimalon gestures to the tray of half-eaten food. "Eat, you will need your strength."

❀ ❀ ❀ ❀ ❀

Elar sits at the council table, with ten other elves, all listening to an athletically built dark-haired dragon spin a tale of kidnapping and heartbreak.

Elar's blood boils. He can only be talking about Cate. Knowing that she ran away and was not kidnapped, does not lend Elar any patience. The man falls silent and Elar shifts his attention to the queen.

"If the Council agrees, we will send scouts to search for the girl. As only a Kraeken has entered the Valley."

"It was a Kraeken, of the Wolf clan, who kidnapped her."

Elar can see excitement in Viggo's eyes. He believes she's close. Unfortunately, she is but not in the Valley. The queen calls for a vote. Elar agrees to send out scouts – he must, not doing so would cast suspicion. Thankfully, it is a split vote.

The queen addresses Viggo. "Analise will escort you to a waiting room where you can refresh yourselves. Elar, join me in the Rose Suite."

Viggo stands, his chair noisily scraping across the wooden floor as the queen departs. Elar controls his emotions, schooling his expression to neutral as he follows the queen.

The Rose Suite is an enchanted room where roses bloom all year. The fragrance can be cloying. As soon as the door closes, the queen drops formalities. "What are you thinking? She's dragon-souled and the fiancée of a man who passes for no less than a king." Pacing, an uncharacteristic display of emotion, the queen waits for his response.

"She was dying. If I left her in Aelvus, he would have found a corpse. Besides, he is lying. She was not kidnapped."

"The Kraeken's tale was of rescue, as was yours. Either the girl is very cunning or very naïve. Has she recovered?"

Elar senses a trap in the question. "She had a setback last night."

The queen stops pacing to stand in front of him. Her stature and bearing convey authority. "Give her to the Kraeken and send them on their way."

"She carries Rathleon's soul."

The queen's mask of composure cracks with a sharp intake of breath. "Has Rimalon confirmed this?"

"It was his spell that revealed it. We know how powerful Rathleon is."

"She is locked inside the body of a human. Still, her appearance may have consequences." The queen approaches Elar and stands close enough that the hem of her tunic brushes against his legs. She tilts his head to stare into his eyes. "The council will delay Viggo for two days while we sort through any threats to elfkind."

Elar knows better than to argue. She gave him a gift. Two days to spend with Cate. Two days for her to heal. He waits until he is jogging through the Valley to allow himself another thought – two days to get away.

Passing through the mist, he moves to the trees. It's easy to track someone on the ground, less so from branches. Following a circuitous route, he reaches the cottage near sundown. Rimalon reads in the living room. In few words, Elar tells Rimalon about Viggo.

"She must leave if she is going to stay out of his reach. A pity."

Elar claps Rimalon on the shoulder before ascending the stairs, where he finds Baen watching Cate sleep. "Viggo is in the Valley. We leave now." That one sentence wakes Cate, as Baen leaps to his feet.

"We?" Baen is as tall as Elar, though thicker in build.

"I assumed you will continue traveling with Cate. Is that not true?"

"I assumed you will stay in your valley."

Cate is on the floor looking under the bed. "Where are my shoes?"

"The boots by the stairs are yours." Elar answers.

Cate stops and looks over her shoulder, one hand still holding the blankets. "But, what about my sandals?"

"Sandals are inappropriate in the forest. Let alone for climbing mountains. Take the boots." Elar carries them to her. She drops the blanket. The boots are supple and look a lot like moccasins. She slides her foot in, marveling at how well it fits. Like slipping on a pair of socks. She pulls on the other.

"They're beautiful."

"Rimalon cast anti-fire spells on the boots, a couple tunics and leggings." He retrieves a bag from his closet.

They join Rimalon downstairs. He addresses Cate first, "May your quest be successful." And then, he clasps forearms with Elar. "Until another day."

Hunter studies the cottage nestled high up in the trees. A staircase winds around the trunk and a trail leads into the mist.

He falls silent as people emerge, descending the stairs. Their footsteps light. Through the darkness, he can see three figures. Two men, and one slight enough to be a woman. Reaching the ground, one of them lifts his head as if sniffing the air. It must be the Kraeken.

Seconds pass before they move, skimming the border of the mist as they walk. Checking to ensure he remains downwind, he follows. Keeping his steps light, Hunter glides over twigs and leaves - anything that would make a sound.

They trot along the mist's edge until it thins and vanishes. Hunter slows aware he may be too close when the elf glances back. Hidden behind twin pines, he isn't worried about being seen only about being heard.

If they were dragon-souled, he'd have to be wary of Travelers. Seeing as Cate doesn't have that ability, he can give them a slight lead and follow their tracks. Waiting until ten minutes have passed, he cautiously advances.

Leaving the Valley of Mist, they climb an ever-steepening slope. The forest, no longer cultivated by elves, grows thick and wild. Hunter pauses to slow his breathing, the sound loud in his own ears. He studies the landscape. Without moonlight to guide him, he's lost their tracks and turning on a flashlight might give him away. Either he waits here and starts out in the morning, or he returns to the Valley.

He sits on a large tree root and leans against the trunk. It will be a long hunt; he might as well get some sleep.

Viggo reclines on a divan and sips tea sweetened with honey. It is the first time Viggo has dealt with elves, but not Xenothgorot.

A beautiful race. Well-mannered to the point of obnoxiousness. They seem reasonable though unwilling to interfere in human issues. Even an issue like finding Cate.

Xenothgorot's distrust seeds his thoughts. Could they have already found her? Are they keeping them apart because they know whose soul Cate carries? Viggo glances at the arched door. The vote to help him had been split. Will they agree?

What if the Kraeken ditched her somewhere? But, if he had, why come to the Valley? The only reason to come to the Valley is to ask the elves for help. But for what? Waking Cate's dragon? No, Viggo could help her with that.

Only, the girl is unwilling. It is the first time Xenothgorot has spoken to him since the engagement party.

"Not the girl, the dragon." He's used to Xenothgorot's long silences and does not expect a reply.

Use the elves. Find her and wake her. No other time have they allowed us in the Valley. Take this opportunity to learn what they know.

Viggo glances at Dane napping in a chair. Always on call, he doesn't begrudge him the sleep. Easing open the door, he steps into the hall. A fair-haired elf greets him. The muscles in Viggo's jaw clench, he'd hoped he was unguarded. "Do you have a library?"

"Of course, follow me."

As they leave the hall, another elf assumes the role of guard. Set in the enormous boughs of the Valley trees, the Elven city defies gravity and architectural rules. Bridges arch between buildings and platforms. It's difficult for even Xenothgorot not to be in awe.

His guide leads him over two bridges to a multi-story facade set directly in the trunk of a giant tree. Intricate scrollwork decorates the wood. Viggo runs his fingers along the sculpture as the guide opens the door. "No material leaves the library."

Viggo nods in understanding as he enters. Bookshelves at least four stories high line the walls. Ladders and staggered lofts provide access. It's a bibliophile's dream. "What filing system do you use?" When no one answers, he realizes his guide did not enter with him.

A willowy elf approaches, long white-blond hair bound in a loose braid, looking much like a professional student who prefers studying over working. "Welcome. You must be Viggo. How may I assist."

"How do you know who I am?"

"In a thousand years, we have never allowed a dragon into the Valley. Let alone two. Since you are in a place of revered knowledge, you are not the Traveler but the clan leader."

"Why not the Traveler?"

The elf turns her back to him, ignoring his question. He can either trail her like a lost puppy or stand his ground. He chooses not to move. At the base of the loft stairs, she pauses and glances back. "What interests you?"

"The end of the Dragon War."

"Up these stairs, North wall, tenth shelf, the series has blue covers." Without another word, she returns to her studies.

Viggo wastes no time. He starts with the earliest book. Reverently, he thumbs through the pages. The sketches are the only thing he can read, everything else is in elvish. He personally had never found the language interesting, perhaps Xenothgorot's bias influenced his taste. Grimacing, he returns the volume.

Looking around the massive room, he can find only one other besides the girl who greeted him. On the third level, near a rose panel window, a lean man sits at a table intent on the pages before him. Viggo's gaze flickers to the girl and then the man. Could either be trusted to tell him what the books say?

The library doors open, and a scholarly elf enters. It's difficult to tell with elves, but something about him makes Viggo think of an elder. Within minutes, he's at Viggo's side. "I am Rimalon. When the queen heard of your interest in the library, she thought I may be of assistance."

Viggo bites back a sarcastic retort. "I am curious about the elven version of what ended the dragon war."

Rimalon retrieves a book and sits at a long table. Casually, he skims page after page. Viggo sits across from him actively practicing patience. Toward the end of the tome, Rimalon stops turning pages and his finger moves along the lines of words.

"You are aware the elves took heavy losses during the war?" He asks and Viggo nods. "The remaining leaders met to discuss a novel approach by an unlikely source." Viggo doesn't move, his eyes locked on the foreign words. Rimalon clears his throat. "This may be unpleasant."

"Every fact is only one person's perspective that we universally accept to be true. Please continue."

"Near the battlefront, our mages were approached by a dragon who wanted to end the war. She was weary of watering the ground with blood. It took time to convince them of her sincerity, but at last she succeeded."

"Does it say how she convinced them?" Viggo rests his arms on the table and leans over the book as if the words might reveal themselves.

"Not in this account. The plan was simple. She wanted help in casting a spell to unite dragons with humans. Our leaders found the idea intriguing. It focused on the key antagonists and would let our kind recover."

"Opportunists."

"The dragons were dying. Who would be alive to raise hatchlings? Rathleon could see how it would end. She offered an opportunity for us all."

"How could she not know it would doom dragonkind? A triad to caste it, a triad must undo it and there are no more dragons."

Rimalon closes the book. "Is not fact only one man's perception accepted as truth?"

CHAPTER 12

Cate sits on a boulder watching the sunrise, her arms wrapped around her legs. Baen and Elar left a little before dawn to scout their trail.

Incendiere. The thought is Rathleon's. A small trickle of fire, little more than a lighter's worth, escapes from her lips. It's exhilarating to dip her fingers into the flames and feel them tickle her skin, without burning.

"That'll surprise Viggo."

She jumps, nearly turning the small flame into a torch. Closing her lips, the flames dance on her tongue. Hunter stands behind her, illuminated by the pink light of dawn. Her gaze searches the woods.

"If you are looking for my brother, he isn't here." Hunter squats beside her. "If you don't want to marry Viggo, why didn't you talk to your father?"

"My father gave me away!" Fire punctuates her words. Rathleon cuts it off. "No one was going to help me. So, I helped myself."

"You could have died."

"What do you care?"

"You are marrying my brother that makes you family."

Cate pushes to her feet. "I am not your family."

They both turn at the sound of a cough. Baen and Elar stand among the trees. "Elar thought a man skilled enough to track us wouldn't fall for such a simple trick as leaving Cate alone. Tell me, how do plan to steal her away?"

"I am no thief. I am here to bring her home when she is ready." Hunter steps in front of Cate, as if protecting her. "I assume you are the wolf that saved her from the Watchers and hid her in your cabin. Thank you for protecting her, but she is too naïve, too grounded in the world of science and technology. That's the only excuse for trusting a wolf. That one room cabin you stayed in was quite cozy." Baen moves before Hunter can react, his fists twist in Hunter's shirt, their faces inches apart.

"Careful." The word comes out more like a growl.

"Dragon-souled and Kraeken are like a match to tinder." Hunter leans close to Baen, uncaring of the threat he poses and whispers, "Viggo was at the cabin. He was particularly enraged by the scents on the bed."

Cate turns three shades of pink as she realizes what Hunter's insinuating. Stepping around Baen, she works to rein in her emotions only saying, "You make assumptions."

Elar studies the men, as Baen releases Hunter. His words are meant for Cate. "It is a risk to let him go."

"It's a risk to keep him with us." She holds out her hand to Hunter. "Give me your phone."

"If you want it, you'll have to go back to the Valley. I left it in my bag. Look, I am the best tracker Viggo has. As long as I am with you, you don't have to worry about being caught."

"Are you seriously suggesting we take you with us?" Cate's gaze flickers between Hunter and Baen. "Why?"

"If I am with you, I can assure my brother of your safety. And, when you're ready, I can take you home."

Cate rolls her eyes. It is clear he isn't listening, but not having to worry about being followed is a win. She turns to Elar. His cool silver eyes assess Hunter, the muscles in his jaw flex.

"How can we guarantee your compliance?"

"You can't."

"Honest answer. You stated you are here to take Cate home, when she is ready. Baen and I will hold you to that. Even if she is never ready."

Kith studies his latest drawing. A man, with scales covering most of his body, standing next to Cate. Behind them looms the shadow of a dragon, its wings spread as if preparing for flight. Everything about the piece is ominous.

His chest feels hollow, as if all these years of waiting have reduced him to a husk. Just a few more days and he'll talk with his daughter. Judging by Emily's reactions, he'll have a long road ahead to forge any relationship with her.

A swift knock is all the time he has to turn the drawing upside down, before Tatiana enters, her foot tapping, and her arms crossed over her chest. He quickly guides his niece from his room, shutting the door behind him.

Like his sister, she resembles a Viking maiden - tall, fair-haired, fair-skinned, and fearless. She was born dragon-souled. A Traveler.

"Uncle," before they enter the great room, she turns on him, "I have been helping the clan for four years as a Traveler. I am more than capable of taking you to the Dragotian estate or anywhere else for that matter. Why have you forbidden it?"

He gently places his hand on her shoulder. "My daughter is already committed to them. I don't need them grasping for you too." He knows his argument is wrong as soon as he makes it. He shouldn't have taken the "keep you safe" argument. Even if it is true.

"I can bring her home anytime you want; all I have to do is go there once."

"You don't think Viggo knows that? He only allows his Travelers to and from his estate. This isn't about your bravery or ability. It is about my daughter's safety and well-being. It's about the perpetuation of dragon-kind. I am not arguing about this."

Tatiana tosses her braid over her shoulder and stomps away. Kith watches as she leaves. He joins the others in the great room, sitting beside his wife. She tucks her small hand into his. It's always amused him how delicate she feels, when in reality, she is anything but.

Oksana sets a thick file of papers on the coffee table. His sister has always been good at arguing, making a career out of it as a lawyer suits her well. Beside her sits Kalon, her husband and his best friend.

Kalon sips from a mug, by the smell of it – chai. In the spring, he shaved off most of his beard, leaving only a goatee. He's the only man around that makes Kith feel small. He makes the couch look like a love seat.

"I am not backing out of the agreement." Emily starts to pull her hand from his and he grips it tightly.

"Everything about it favors the Dragotians. Why didn't you at least let a contract lawyer review it before you signed?"

"Who says I didn't?"

Oksana gives him a look and taps the file. "She is to move-in with them on her seventeenth birthday. Marry him on her eighteenth birthday and have at least two kids by her twenty-fifth birthday. Whatever made you think this was a good idea or even a good agreement?"

"It isn't about my daughter. It is about dragon-kind."

"Not about your daughter?" Emily yanks her hand from his.

"Em, my gift is being a Dreamer. I see things that will happen. My dragon has been Dreaming since its birth. We know things, things that I wish we didn't know. We don't always understand what we Dream, but we know it will come to pass. For dragon-kind, Cate needs to be in this agreement."

Unable to speak, her emotions too raw and ragged, Emily storms from the room slamming the door behind her. Kith turns to Oksana.

She and Kalon calmly sit on the couch, their eyes locked on his. "You know this hurts me, but I can't be selfish."

"I know this hurts a lot of people. I wish it weren't the ones you love." Oksana leaves the papers on the table and follows Emily out. Kalon sits forward, his arms on his knees.

"I promised you I wouldn't say anything to my wife or yours, but maybe you should."

Kith shakes his head. His heart hurts. "How can I explain what I am not even sure of myself?"

"If you don't try, you might lose Emily for good this time."

Bitterness wells in Kith. He tried explaining to Emily when she was pregnant and again after their beautiful daughter was born. He even tried the night before she ran away. None of it helped. How would it help now?

Kalon's dragon and his had both known Rathleon. They'd been as close to her as another could be without being a mate. She had trusted them and they her.

He'd tried to explain to Emily how important it is to wake Rathleon, how all the pieces are aligned. How Rathleon is the key to dragon-kind's future. But she couldn't understand. Especially without magic or a dragon's soul to consult. He glances at the closed door. "It would have been simpler if I'd married a dragon."

"If you'd married a dragon, Cate wouldn't exist and Rathleon's soul would still be tucked away in peaceful slumber."

Sourly, Kith acknowledges Kalon. "You are right. My Dream led me to the mountain that day. It didn't make me fall in love though, that was all Emily's doing."

"And together, you produced a girl that will change this world. It isn't easy being the parents of a savior."

Kith closes his eyes and leans back on the couch. That word – savior – had been used after Rathleon's sacrifice by the humans and elves, even others of magical descent. Now, it's being used again.

"Time will tell."

Tatiana sits on a bench under a large tree, opposite the entryway to her uncle's house. It's one of her favorite spots – whether reading a book or daydreaming – it's always made her feel secure and at ease. Not today.

She'd thought about following her aunt, but what do you say to a woman whose child is missing? A woman you don't really know and have no connection with. I'm sorry and it'll be okay – just sound like empty words.

It was a relief when mom appeared, following Emily down the road, and calling out to her. Tatiana lies on the bench, staring at the clouds through the leaves and branches. She'd tried putting herself in her cousin's place. Imagining being betrothed and not knowing it until people showed up out of thin air and kidnapped you.

It reads like a romance novel. Only, judging by her aunt's reactions and the fact that she ran away with Cate years ago, there's something up with this plot. Is it just that she's against arranged marriages?

Tatiana can't blame her. Who would want to marry a stranger?

Only, maybe there is something to it. Parents invest time to make a good match for their kids, the kids get to know each other… maybe if more people spent time up front there would be less divorce.

Not fair. That's like comparing apples and oranges. To really know if one is more successful than the other, she'd need to look at the divorce rates of arranged marriages and those of love marriages separately. But how would you determine a control group?

"Tatiana?"

She jumps up at the sound of her uncle's voice and sits properly on the bench. He joins her. "I would like you to come with me when I visit Cate."

Tatiana's heart pounds painfully with excitement. "Are you sure?"

He slowly nods. "Just keep your Gift hidden and get to know the place as much as you can while we're there."

❋ ❋ ❋ ❋ ❋

Viggo stands at the balcony railing enjoying the Valley view. He doesn't turn at the sound of footsteps nor at the scent of roses. He bows his head at the queen as she stands beside him. "Did you enjoy your visit to our library?"

His lips twitch into a smirk before he controls his expression. "If I read elvish, I would have enjoyed it more. I was arrogant to think you would have books in English or even one of the dragon languages."

"It is good to recognize one's own arrogance. It is something I have been working on among my people. Separating ourselves from the other races has led to a feeling of superiority. Whether valid or not, it means we think we have little to learn from others. That is untrue. One can learn even from the basest of creatures."

"Has the Council arrived at a decision?"

"It has only been a day. A task will take exactly as long as the time we give it."

"Then, to what do I owe the pleasure of your company?"

The queen smiles, enjoying the revelation of the dragon's feelings. It is clear he detests her and is merely tolerating her presence. "Rimalon shared that you are interested in the end of the dragon war. I know this history."

Viggo turns from the view and focuses on the queen. "Why did Rathleon do what she did? Nowhere in our histories does it recount her reason." The queen opens her mouth to speak, and he forestalls her. "I'm not interested in the history rewrite. That she did it to save us or that she was tired of watering the ground with blood. I want the real reason."

"Then, you will have to wait until your souls are born in the same era and ask her yourself."

"She has been reborn in the body of my betrothed. I will stop at nothing to find her."

"Was she kidnapped or did she runaway?"

Viggo takes a menacing step towards the queen. The elf does not flinch, her eyes remain on his. "I have already answered that."

"I remember that Rathleon was mated to a dragon… his name was… Xenothgorot." Viggo's eyes flash revealing the queen's guess to be accurate. "It is unfortunate they became rivals during the war. Unable to see the other's viewpoint. I wonder what he thinks now that he has lived among humans for so long."

Viggo's flat-eyed stare displays his lack of interest in the queen's game. He turns back to the view. "Xenothgorot merely wanted to preserve his kind and their right to hunt."

"The dragons right to hunt was never under challenge. It was what they hunted that we disagreed on."

Viggo laughs. If Rathleon had not done what she had, it is possible he wouldn't be standing before the queen to argue. It's a point he cannot disagree on even if Xenothgorot once did. "Is there any way I can convince you to help without waiting for the Council's vote?"

"If I am not mistaken, you are a mage. Rimalon is our eldest of mages. Perhaps, he has a solution."

Viggo grimaces. Something about Rimalon angers him. The queen falls silent at his side. The wind whistles around them, shaking leaves and tugging at their clothes.

The wind carries unfamiliar scents. No matter how frequently she visits, she can't get used to the Reaches. V'Lana shakes her loose mane of silky black hair, wishing she were in wolf form rather than human. Her eldest son reclines lazily on a chaise, enjoying a sunbath.

The balcony of their shared suite overlooks the courtyard, with much of the terraced city in view. Her stomach rumbles and she glances at the appetizers on the table. Since sending Baen off with that dragon, her acid reflux has been too strong to enjoy eating.

Did she do the right thing?

As a girl, v'Lana had been enamored with mages. She had read everything she could in hopes of one day discovering her own untapped abilities, only to discover the Kraeken enchantment prevents shapeshifters from wielding magic.

In her studies, she stumbled on the history of the Dragon War as told by the losers. It fascinated her to think about the trio who cast the Dragon spell. Let alone about the type of people lucky enough to carry dragon souls.

She shivers. Her mate had been dragon-souled. Her eyes shift to d'Gar. If she had picked a Kraeken, perhaps both sons would have been shifters. Instead, her eldest cannot change. As nonchalant as he tries to be, v'Lana knows the pain and jealousy he hides.

Feeling her gaze, his eyes meet hers. "What do you think about courting Ka'Lea?"

He sits, no longer at ease. The twins are day and night. Where Baen is broad and wild, d'Gar is lean and elegant. He runs his fingers over dark stubble, thinking about his options before answering. "Wolves have never bred with another clan."

"Perhaps that should change."

"Why? Are you feeling guilty about lying to the queen?"

V'Lana laughs. She leans on the balcony rail. "There is a fine line between truth and lie, I merely walked it."

They both turn at the sound of a door opening. A few seconds later, one of the wolf clan escorts Ka'Leel into the room with Viggo's sister on his arm. It's like looking at a living incarnation of ying and yang. Ka'Leel guides IlliaVaa to a chair. Her glossy black hair blends into her black silk tank and peasant skirt.

"I hope we are interrupting." IlliaVaa helps herself to tea, pouring a glass from a pitcher sweating on the table.

"Absolutely, what can we do for you?"

IlliaVaa smiles making her even lovelier. V'Lana returns the smile as she maintains her relaxed pose. "We've narrowed down where my sister is. It's a densely wooded area obscured by mist. That makes reconnaissance by the Eagles nearly impossible. Not so for wolves."

"You mean that poor girl in a loveless arranged marriage, right?"

IlliaVaa's eyes shift, the pupils elongating. V'Lana comfortably returns her stare, while d'Gar tries to hide his unease by refilling his glass. "Truth can be a bitter pill. It's one I have eaten daily for years. Are you eager to experience it?"

"Those who walk in light do not fear the shadow."

Ka'Leel chuckles drawing IlliaVaa's intense gaze. She stares at him until her eyes return to normal. With a frown etching lines into her brow, she shifts to V'Lana. "There's no need to discuss this further, though I enjoy our banter. You will send scouts; I have seen it. A courier will bring a map in a few hours."

Ka'Leel bows before escorting IlliaVaa from the terrace. The dragon's voice, though a whisper, carries. "We need to talk."

CHAPTER 13

Viggo's body aches, his head dully throbs even in sleep. Reclining on a red velvet sofa, his arm over his eyes, he can feel Xenothgorot beside him in the Dragon dream.

Elven magic is nothing like dragon magic nor the modified version practiced by dragon-souled. It is visceral, innate, part of their very nature. To his credit, Rimalon earnestly attempted to teach how to tap into the energy of the forest. In theory, it was a brilliant idea. Using the very life of the forest as his scout, but practice did not bear fruit.

Viggo groans. Xenothgorot huffs a plume of sulphureous smoke, a clear sign of his displeasure. "How did she endure them?"

"How do you endure me?"

The great dragon sets a talon larger than Viggo on the back of the couch. Its weight makes the wooden frame creak. "Necessity."

Viggo cradles his head in his hands. The dull throb is on the verge of a migraine. Ever since learning of the role he plays in bringing dragons back into the world, he's wondered what it would be like to be the hosted soul – living and not living, undying.... Without control.

Vertigo rocks Viggo and he rolls to his side, preparing to vomit. He opens his eyes, expecting to see Xenthgorot's scales, and not the rolling green lawn of his estate. He pushes to his feet. Not far from him, Cate sits in a meditative position her eyes closed.

Viggo staggers to her side, quietly sitting beside her. The air holds scents of pine and fresh lawn clippings. If his youth had been spent flying kites or playing ball, he might feel nostalgic. He takes another deep breath, hoping to catch a hint of her scent. But, in her Dream, there is nothing.

"If you miss it, why don't you return?"

Cate's eyes remain closed. Her voice is soft, nearly peaceful. "I can return anytime I want, no strings attached, when I close my eyes."

Ignoring the ache in his head and battling nausea, he studies her. This version of Cate seems confident, self-assured. His gaze drifts to her neck and the scales hidden beneath her hair. "Why did you run?" Maybe it's the headache, but his tone sounds vulnerable. He expects her to laugh or give a sarcastic quip.

"You're a stranger who kidnapped me."

His first inclination is to argue that he abided by the agreement, that he didn't kidnap her. Instead, he addresses the only thing he can change. "I won't be by our wedding."

"I want to date, go to college, and figure out what I want to be in life. Not get married."

"Date me. Go to college online. Figure out life at my side."

Cate opens her eyes and focuses her intense gaze on him. "You don't want me. You want my dragon so you can transform the dragon spell. No thanks, I like being in control of my own body."

"It took a triad to cast it, it will take a triad to break it. Together, we can explore possibilities."

She leans forward so that their noses are almost touching and softly says, "You have beautiful eyes."

The argument on his lips drops unsaid. He blinks unsure if he heard correctly.

Cate sighs, her gaze moves from his eyes to his mouth. "I've never been kissed, except in my dreams." She blushes, her voice taking on a husky quality, as she leans into him. Lightly, her lips brush against his. He shivers, his hands cup her head, his fingers entangle in her hair. Their lips meet again, warm, and moist.

This. He wants this. He wants her.

Gently, he pulls away, his hands holding her close. "Where are you?"

Cate's eyes sparkle with mischief. She leans close her mouth near his ear, her breath warm on his skin. "I don't know."

He nearly jumps when her tongue caresses his ear. His hands tighten in her hair. "Careful." He groans.

She giggles. "It's just a dream."

"We are in the Dragon Dream. Anything that happens here, really happens."

Cate pulls away and he lets her, his hands slip from her hair. Emotions flit across her face like colors in a kaleidoscope. "You mean, if I hit you here, you'll wake up with a bruise?"

"Yes."

Her hand moves to her mouth, while her eyes move to his. "We really kissed?"

"More than once." He smirks thinking about their previous encounter in the Dream. "I know you're with the Elves. Come to the Council. Return home with me."

"You know nothing."

It feels like a hot spike drives through his head and colors dance in his vision. He lies down, squeezing his eyes tightly closed and curls into a ball. It has been years since he has had this kind of reaction to magic. Years since he's had a migraine like this.

There's a light touch on his shoulder. "Are you okay?"

"No." He whispers. "Wake up. This is your Dream. I am trapped here until you wake."

Cate opens her eyes, and a canopy of pine needles comes into view. Baen sleeps beside her, while Elar keeps watch from the branches of an adjacent tree.

Out here, in the middle of nowhere without a power line or radio tower in sight, she can imagine she's entered a fairy tale or gone back in time. It feels like a separate world.

An alarm on Baen's watch chimes and, after a few seconds, he taps it into silence. He sniffs the air and stretches. Cate admires the way his shirt pulls against his body. He chuckles. "I can tell your thoughts by your scent."

Her cheeks heat. The feeling of Viggo's lips fresh in her mind.

"Wishful thinking on your part." Hunter tosses Cate a berry as he appears from behind the dense foliage.

Elar drops lightly to the ground. His silver eyed gaze locks on her. "A human approaches." The humming of an engine filters through the soft sounds of the morning.

"Maybe they have a phone." Hunter suggests, leaning against a tree.

A quad comes into view with a park ranger sitting astride it. He changes direction to intercept them. "You folks all right?" As he pulls up to them, the quad settles into an idling purr.

"Yeah thanks." Cate answers.

The ranger studies them. "You're near private land. Head northwest to get back on the trail. You'll come out at the lighthouse trailhead."

"Thanks." Hunter shifts the ranger's attention to him. With a nod, the man reverses and disappears amongst the trees with only the whine of the engine in the distance.

As they gather their bags, Baen says, "I take it we're not heading northwest.'

Elar's lips twitch into the faintest smile as Baen and Hunter lead the way leaving him to walk beside Cate. "How do you feel?"

"Great. Really." She kicks a pinecone, and it bounces off Hunter's heel. He glances back, his gaze flitting between them. "Can all Elves work magic?"

"All Elves are conduits for magic. Some learn how to control the flow while others never do. It is like breathing. Most never think about it, while others master it and use it to control pain or improve concentration."

A massive shadow glides over the open ground. "What was that?"

Interlacing branches makes it difficult to discern. Baen grabs Cate's hand pulling her deep into the trees. "Kraeken shapeshifters. They are eagles we call kraa."

"Why are we hiding?"

"They stay near the Reaches. They don't venture out unless ordered by the queen."

"You think Viggo convinced the Kraeken queen to find Cate." Hunter scans the little bit of sky he can see. "Not a bad plan." Staying close to the trees and beneath interlacing branches they run.

Ka'Lea leans against the stone wall, enjoying the way the wind whips her hair and tugs at her clothes. Ever since she learned most people fear heights, she's used the tower roof as a sanctuary.

The dragons backed her in a corner after they brought proof of the Wolf clan's involvement in the girl's disappearance. Ka'Lea's lips curl at the thought of v'Lana's smug arguments.

One might expect contrition or fear. Not from the Wolf matron. According to V'Lana the Dragotian's seek to alter the dragon spell, which is why they want the girl. And IlliaVaa did not deny it. She just smiled, her too big eyes soaking up Ka'Leel's beauty.

Ka'Lea's fingers clench the stone. Rage boils inside her at the thought of her dead husband entertaining an overly eager bimbo in their suite. Not the first.

Only death made him monogamous.

Ka'Lea laughs, a cold harsh sound stolen by the wind. Tears fall from her eyes and dry on her cheeks. What would a change in the dragon spell mean to the Kraeken?

Dragons and Kraeken have silently worked behind the curtain of world governments to ensure their prosperity, safety, and relative independence.

But Kraeken are dependent on dragons. It is why we exist. At first, it was to hunt and kill them. Then, the hunt changed. Even the definition of survival changed. Only an enchanted or dragon-souled is strong enough to live through giving birth to a shapeshifter.

If they change the spell, will we still want them and they us? Will they even be human enough to breed?

Too much inter-marrying is a bad thing, it causes genetic abnormalities. Without dragon-souled, will our enchantment fail, or will the new dragon form cause more enchanted to be born?

If he's only marrying her for the spell....

Is it better to marry a wolf that can't shapeshift or a dragon? D'Gar is handsome, from a wealthy and influential family.

It's a good match.

As for Viggo, he's handsome, fearless, powerful, wealthy. Everything about him makes her heart race. Their offspring would rule Kraeken and Dragotians. The only downside is that he's already engaged.

Does he have to marry her to use her for whatever spell?

Ka'Lea pulls an errant strand of white hair from her face, and it makes her think of Ka'Leel. He's always been steadfast and loyal. If she asked him to leave IlliaVaa alone, he would. Or, if she asked him to get close to her....

She pushes thoughts of marriage aside. The future of the Kraeken is at risk. Fewer enchanted are born every year, several of the lesser houses can no longer shift. Would changing the dragon spell be a blessing or a curse?

The girl's a wildcard. V'Lana thinks the girl will try to free the dragons. But it can't be done. Imagine the devastation, the deaths. How could anyone be so naive as to think freeing dragons a good idea?

Images flash in her mind – fighter planes, drones, bombs, and nuclear weapons. Humanity may very well destroy itself trying to defend against the magnificent maelstrom of power that is a dragon. Would helping Viggo find her prevent such a stupid mistake or only compound it?

Maybe the girl will have an accident and none of this will matter. Ka'Lea sighs, as one can only hope.

❋ ❋ ❋ ❋ ❋

Cate screams as the ground gives way, dirt, and debris cascade around her. She thumps against the ground and air explodes from her lungs. Gasping, she struggles to inhale. Tears leak from her eyes.

Elar lands beside her and wipes dirt from her hair, telling her to take slow breaths. Satisfied, she is unharmed; he glances at the wide earthen tunnel bolstered by support beams.

"You, okay?" Hunter calls, blocking the light as he tries to peer into the hole.

"Yes." Elar answers ducking low and wandering down the tunnel. "This is very sturdy, well-maintained. There should be an exit somewhere."

"We'll look for something to use as a rope or ladder." Shadows move and light enters the space. From above, Hunter complains about carrying bags while Baen mutters something about wolves. Cate pushes to her feet and sediment falls from her clothes.

Her eyes shift, her pupils elongate. Details of the tunnel emerge as light dances from small pieces of glinting rock into her dragon-enhanced vision. She steps close to the wooden supports. "It lacks the smell of rot and oddly holds the scent of cologne."

Elar smirks. "I do not smell cologne." Together, they start down the tunnel.

Cate feels her dragon stir. It's like a thing hidden deep in her subconscious uncoils. Her skin feels feverish and sensitive, even the touch of fabric from her clothes feels rough and raw. She coughs, trying to rid herself of a dry scratchy throat.

She'd felt this way before, the first time she discovered her scales. It was just over a year ago. The doctor thought she had a virus and kept her from school for a week. The whole time, her body felt on fire and every inch of skin felt itchy and painful.

She pulls at her clothes. Her fingers grab the hem of her tunic, and before she can think, she's pulling it over her head. Elar grabs her wrists and gently eases the tunic back in place. Silver eyes stare into her own, his fingers bruising tight. "What are you doing?"

She pulls at his grip. "I want it off."

With one hand still on Cate, he wrenches a bit of stone from the wall and gently presses it to her face. She leans into it, as if it were an ice pack and sighs. He moves the stone to the back of her neck and her legs wobble as she visibly calms. He draws her close, keeping the stone in place, and guides her along the tunnel.

"What are you doing?"

"A hunch, it won't hurt only help."

Emotions swirl in Cate like a tide pool. The smell of rock fills her with longing. She can feel the elements in the stone, and it makes her both sad and safe all at once. Elar's pulse thrums through his touch.

He draws to a stop, and she opens eyes she didn't realize she'd closed. She sucks in a quick breath. They stand in a massive cavern. "It's like staring at a thousand stars in a sea of night."

"I see only the dark."

Cate takes the stone from his hand. "You really can't see this?"

He laughs. It makes him sound human. "I am not a Drow. The dark places are not my home and they do not welcome me." He releases her wrist and his fingers run down to hers, entwining. "If you let go, I will be lost."

Cate squeezes his hand. "How did you know to do that with the stone?"

"A guess, based on my readings of dragon accounts. All dragons have an affinity for earth, which is why many make dens deep in mountains. Do you see a way out?"

Now that her skin no longer feels like it is trying to peel itself from her bones, she analyzes the cavern. There are four exits. The one on the left is the largest. "I think we go this way."

Leading Elar by the hand, they leave the sparkling cavern. The tunnel is wide enough to drive a car through. Gradually, familiar scents begin to fill the air. Gasoline, oil... it's like they are in a garage.

Cate stops and Elar bumps into her. At the same time, a light illuminates the space blinding them. Blinking back tears, she squints at a stocky man standing in a shadowy doorway. In the distance, vehicles rest as if in a storage hangar.

"How'd you get in here?" The man's voice is deep, tinged with a northern accent.

"We fell. The ground gave way and we found ourselves in a tunnel."

Cate's eyes shift from dragon to human, making the LED bulb tolerable. She starts to pull her hand from Elar's, but his grip tightens. The man crosses his arms over his broad chest. "You fell because you were trespassing."

"We were headed back to the trail. Sorry, we were lost track."

The man's steely gaze shifts to Elar. "I find it difficult to believe an Elf lost his way in the woods." It's a clear challenge, one Elar ignores. "An Elf and a dragon holding hands...."

"It gets stranger. There is a human and a werewolf looking for us." Cate tries to free her hand, but Elar does not let go. "If you could just show us out...."

The man pushes open the door and tells them to follow.

With a sideways glance at Elar, Cate passes through the door and enters a concrete walled hall, lights run along the top. After the natural beauty of the rock, it feels stark and cold. It isn't long before they pass through another doorway and enter an opulent circular room filled with custom bookshelves, artwork and plush overstuffed furniture.

"The exit is several floors above. This way." The man leads them to a door and a catwalk that crosses a cavernous grotto before climbing two flights of stairs. Cate's eyes are drawn to doors and walkways throughout the space.

"This is incredible."

"We've been expanding it for the last hundred years. It's first life was as a mine."

"Why didn't you just take us to the hangar exit?"

The man gives Cate a flat stare. "Maybe there are things I don't want you seeing."

"Like the military grade vehicles?"

The man stops near the top of the stairs and glares down at Cate. "You shouldn't get involved in things that aren't your business."

"Right? Back home, they have people who tell you how long your grass should be or when you can water." Cate's tone is light, and she flashes a smile.

The man laughs. It transforms his oversized features, making him cute if not handsome. "Where are you from?"

"Colorado."

"You're a long way from home. Why are you on my land with an elf?"

"We're just passing through."

"An elf, a dragon, a werewolf and a human - it sounds like a bad joke."

"Only if you add a dwarf in the mix." Elar moves to the step below the man and towers over him. "The door?"

The man grimaces. Pushing open a door, he waits for Cate and Elar to pass through before stepping inside. The room is a modern living room, with couches and a large flat screen TV. He gestures to the door. "There's the exit. If I catch you on my property again, let alone inside my house...."

Cate's head tilts to the side as if she's listening to something. She shushes their host and wanders toward the far wall. Elar steps in front the man blocking his access to Cate as she kneels before an intricately carved chest.

"What are you doing?" Anger and curiosity twine like vines in the dwarf's voice.

Cate's fingers run along the intricately carved wood. Leaning close, her breath bathes the latch. It pops open and she carefully lifts the lid. Inside, nestled in a bed of velvet is a giant oblong... thing.

"Do you hear it?" Cate asks, her eyes find their host as Elar steps aside.

The man's gaze shifts between the box and Cate. "That box has been sealed since the dragon war. How did you...?"

"You seriously don't hear it?" Cate cannot believe neither of them can hear the gentle melody coming from the thing in the box. It sounds like wind through heavily laden branches, like water babbling in a lazy brook, like... Spring and Fall dancing across the same field.

Elar kneels beside Cate. Lightly, he touches the box. His fingers hover over its contents. "It is a seed." He closes the lid and the latch clicks. "A treasure, if I am not mistaken, as it is the only remaining seed of the Somnolence Tree."

The dwarf shoulders them aside and attempts to open the box, neither the latch nor the lid gives. He grabs Cate's arm and Elar grabs him. The man ignores Elar. "Open it."

"Let go of me." Anger supersedes fear as Cate's pupils elongate.

Elar releases the man and steps back, aware of the flames that could leap from her. The dwarf pulls her to him, his breath hot on her face and smelling of salami and anchovies. "Open it."

A delicate flame dances on Cate's lips and the dwarf backs up but doesn't let go. With a sneer, she sends a stream of fire along her arm. His eyes widen and he curses as the flames reach his fingers.

Locking gazes, he stubbornly refuses to let go. Cate silences the flame. The fabric on her arm is darker than it was but unburnt. The enchanted fabric worked!

"Let me go unless you want me to set fire to this room."

Flexing charred fingers, the dwarf relinquishes his hold. "Please, try again to open the box. I need to know if it was just a fluke."

Cate glances at Elar but his expression is blank. "Sure, why not. Move."

The dwarf steps back as Cate kneels before the box. Not sure what she did the first time, she runs her fingers over the intricately carved wood and leans close to the box. Nothing happens. Frustrated, she heaves a heavy sigh bathing the latch with her breath - it pops open.

"Amazing. I have a few other chests we've never been able to open... would you be willing to try?"

"Do you have a phone?"

CHAPTER 14

Standing, in the middle of the Elven Council, arms upraised, veins bulging with the effort, Viggo sneers. Power pulses through him, raw and violent. "Three days wasted and for what? For you to tell me in a holier-than-thou tone that you won't help?"

Wind, drawn by the power he holds, whips through the chamber like a cyclone. His head throbs from yesterday's efforts but he ignores the pain. "I approached you as an equal. Why, when I know she is near, won't you help?" He drops his arms to his sides and the wind abates. Power encases him in a red tinged aura. "Have you not loved?"

The queen's features remain passive as she speaks, displaying no anger over his display nor empathy for his position. "Dragons can be capricious creatures, as can humans. Your display was impressive, and I acknowledge the power you wield. Understand, many here wield such. The decision was the Council's to make, and they voted to decline your request." The queen's gaze slowly shifts to each Council member in attendance. "Since we have many missing members, I will grant you this. Rimalon will consult with the forest and will tell you what it shares. That is the most we will do." Standing, she leaves the chamber followed by everyone except Rimalon.

The elder approaches him, garbed in gossamer green robes trimmed in ivory fabric. He doesn't speak. Reaching the center of the chamber, he closes his eyes and folds his hands. A soft magic hue lingers around him. With a lilting voice, he hums.

Viggo watches with excitement. Finally, something is happening. A vine emerges from the ground at the elder's feet. It dances like a snake being charmed, until it's as high as Rimalon's waist. Though it grows no taller, it flattens creating a table with a basin. "Bring me water."

Before Viggo can move, a lean acolyte pours water from a ceramic vase into the basin. Rimalon grips both sides of the vine table and leans forward, peering into it. Whispering in Elvish, he doesn't blink. Seconds tick into minutes. After an hour, Rimalon releases the vines. In a voice tinged with the sound of leaves rustling, he says, "North, on foot traveling with three others. Deep, where roots feed, they wander." The elder blinks and steps away from the basin.

"What does that mean?"

The vines recede and water splashes to the ground. Rimalon coughs. His eyes retain the mist of magic. "A girl, traveling with three men, is headed north. They are several days from here and somewhere underground. That is usually what 'where the roots feed' means."

"Three men? She was with a Kraeken. How do you know it was her?"

The power aura around Rimalon swells. "I asked if they had seen a girl, traveling with a spirit wolf, that's what they call shifters. It is possible there is another girl traveling near here."

"And the other two?"

"An elf and a human."

"An elf." Viggo's power swells, nearing the point when he can no longer control it. "Did you make me wait three days to give them a head start? Do you expect me to believe you?"

Someone clears their throat. Viggo turns to find Dane standing in the chamber doorway. "Sir, Hunter's missing. He went scouting and never came back."

Viggo glances at Rimalon, the power aura that surrounds him fluctuates like flames dancing over logs. "Thank the queen for her hospitality."

❀ ❀ ❀ ❀ ❀

Greed lights the dwarf's face. Licking his lips and rubbing his hands, he straightens and addresses Cate. "I've been a horrible host. Stay for dinner, and while it's being prepared, I could show you many of the treasures we've collected."

"No need." Elar answers, his hand twines with hers once more.

His skin is smooth, his touch warm. The contact grounds Cate. She glances at him and then back at the chest. The song still trills softly from inside. She knows the dwarf is using her. But does it matter?

"Only if I get to keep one of the treasures, a treasure of my choice." Her eyes lift from the chest to find the dwarf's gaze. His face contorts before smoothing out into a smile that doesn't touch his eyes. "After all, you would never know what is inside without me. Right?"

Tension fills the room as they stand staring at one another. Elar steps toward the door, pulling Cate with him and the dwarf barks out, "Deal."

Elar's fingers grip her hand a little tighter as he turns back to the dwarf. "Since you have chosen to be our host, what is your name?"

"Rayland."

"Well, Rayland, if you wish us to join you for dinner, then we will need you to locate our companions. The human and werewolf."

The dwarf nods. "Of course, my son knows this land well." Pulling a mobile phone from his pocket, Rayland presses a button enabling short wave communication. "Rueman, I have invited guests to dinner but two of them are lost on our land. Find them and let Sivin know to add four plates for dinner."

The phone beeps as a voice returns, "Copy."

Rayland leads them back to the catwalk. "This way."

Elar walks ahead of Cate, his hand gripping hers. Nothing about his posture displays his dissatisfaction with her choice, but still… it's there. Rather than watching their route or the wonders of the caverns and rooms they pass, she finds her eyes continuously drawn back to the elf.

Metal scrapes across metal as Rayland pushes open an aged gate blocking an old mine elevator. They duck inside and Rayland closes the gate before flipping a large switch. The stone wall slides by before them, their ears pop as they rapidly drop in elevation.

With another flip of the switch, the elevator glides to a stop. There's an almost indistinguishable tremor in Elar's fingers. Rayland opens the gate and beckons them forward. Elar ducks low, the height of the tunnel not enough to accommodate his stature. Cate squeezes his hand; she expects him to glance at her, but he doesn't.

"It was a prolific mine in its heyday. Made the neighboring town wealthy. Unfortunately, they started blasting too near one of our historic sites. We couldn't risk them finding an ancient dwarven city, so we caused a fault near their blasters and there was an accident that claimed a hundred or so lives."

"That's awful."

Rayland points to a boarded tunnel on their right as he keeps walking. "We kept the tunnel shut down in honor of those who died. The mine stopped producing soon after and my family bought it."

The rough lights overhead flicker ominously. Cate's eyes wander to the now distant tunnel where so many died. How many mining accidents are related to dwarves? How much blood do they have on their hands to keep their world secret?

She wants to look over her shoulder to see how far away the elevator is but resists. Rayland turns down a secondary tunnel with steps carved into the stone leading down. The passage is narrow enough that they have to travel one-by-one.

They emerge into a temperate, well-lit cavern decked in treasure. Gems, coins and bars of various metals, chests, and paintings. "Now you know why we are so careful with our security."

"Why don't you use a bank or at least a safe?" Cate pulls her hand from Elar's drawn to objects on the far side of the cavern.

Rayland watches her move, his eyes once more glinting with greed as he follows. Cate stops before a series of chests, each intricately carved and set with unique inlays representing wildlife and nature.

"You've never opened these?"

Rayland's silence is the answer. Cate dusts the top of one chest and leans close to it. There is no song or voice inside, just cold silence. Exhaling, her breath bathes the latch, and it pops open. Slowly, she eases aged hinges that squeal in protest. Rayland edges her aside, wanting to be the first to see the contents.

The box is empty.

He slams the lid shut and points to another. Cate brushes dust from her hands and obliges, studying the next chest she again leans close and breathes on the latch. This time, she doesn't wait for Rayland. She moves to the next while he examines the contents.

Out of the dozen chests only five contain anything: a red polished scale the size of a serving platter, a gem the size of an ostrich egg, a plain-looking short sword, a two-handed battle hammer ornately carved with runes, and a crown.

"I wonder whose head that sat on." Elar muses.

Covered in dust, Cate coughs and steps away from the chests. Each feel... sorrowful. The objects in them emanate despair and loss. "I think that's a ring, a dragon's ring that fit over a talon."

Rayland removes each object and sets them on top of their respective chests. "Just so. Legend has it they are funerary remembrances from the beginning of the Dragon War."

Cate shivers. "If we're done, I'd like to clean up."

Rayland scans the cavern. "We're done, in this chamber anyway. Dinner is waiting."

The trek back is even more of a blur than the trek there. Cate's mind keeps returning to the objects and the way they made her feel. Overwhelming sorrow. Grief – deep, biting into the core of her soul. Pain – not physical yet managing to set every nerve on edge.

The last thing she wants is to eat.

"What is this?" Rayland bellows as they enter the living room where the first chest rests.

The room is in chaos, furniture broken and shoved against the wall. Cate blinks, not believing her eyes as Viggo wrestles with a massive wolf. Both pause at the sound of Rayland's voice, their attention drawn to Cate.

She pulls her hand from Elar's suddenly self-conscious about the contact. Viggo tosses the wolf against the wall and stalks toward her. She barely registers that Dane and Hunter stand at ease with a red-faced dwarf near the door.

The wolf snarls, back on its feet, its hackles raised, and teeth bared. Elar moves to intercede but Cate steps forward to meet Viggo, fire erupting from her mouth to bathe her body. His eyes rove over her, raw hunger in his gaze. "The wolf wasn't enough? You had to find an elf too?" Ignoring the fire, he grabs her waist and pulls her against him. The flames cover his clothes. He winces but doesn't let go. "You are mine."

The bone-jarring grief from moments before transforms into righteous-rage. A dragon's rage watching death march through her family, her friends, her world. All because this man – no, this dragon – wouldn't see the war for what it was. His desire. His fight. His cause.

She leans into him, feeling the fire spread, smelling the char as it reaches his flesh. "I am mine." Her pupils elongate as power fills her.

Viggo senses the change, like watching water pour into a pitcher. He opens his own well releasing the magic within, surrounding his singed flesh in a simple protection spell. His mouth finds hers. She doesn't respond. It isn't Cate, and he's had no time to win Rathleon.

Cate shoves him and he stumbles backward. The wolf stalks around him to stand at Cate's side while Elar stands on her other. Viggo wipes blood from his lip, a gift from Cate's teeth. "I see your dragon has awakened."

Rayland steps between them, his arms outstretched pointing to the devastation in the room. "Whatever this is, whoever you are, take this outside!"

Viggo's lips curl in a snarl. "Watch yourself dwarf."

"Watch myself! This is my house. Get out."

"Dane." The name echoes throughout the chamber. The Traveler steps forward and a gaping portal opens in front of him. "Cate." The demand is clear.

She laughs.

"You are legally mine."

"Not until I turn 18."

"So, you admit you *are* mine." Fire dances high above Cate. Rayland dives across the room and out of the way. Words trail from Viggo's lips and Cate's feet leave the ground. His gaze meets hers. "Come to me."

"No." Her progress across the room stops, as if her feet are suddenly anchored to the stone. "Elar, the chest." He doesn't ask which chest. Grabbing the chest, he returns to Cate's side. "I have never said I will marry you. Leave me alone."

Words spill from her mouth in a silent fountain and the fire surrounding her leaps from her body, coalescing into a swirling ball. Within the ball, a world emerges similar to Dane's portal. "Elar, Baen, you are first."

They don't argue, don't hesitate. Their faith in her makes Cate's heart swell as they step into the fire and vanish. Her eyes find Hunter. "To think I trusted you." Before Viggo can react, the anchor holding her in place vanishes, and she disappears into the flames.

The ball winks out of existence the moment she vanishes.

CHAPTER 15

Rathleon adjusts her wings as the wind shifts. The mountain range below, yet untouched by war, is a balm to her grieving soul. Names and faces flicker across her vision, blurred by tears. Banking to the right, she seeks a valley to land.

Not long ago, she happily flew beside her mate, a dragon unmatched in beauty, intelligence, and strength. Not long ago, they imagined a world where their hatchlings would grow and soar.

The ground rises to meet her, and she tumbles across it, nearly catching her wing on a tree. She curls into a ball, tucking her head into the fold of her wings. Her heart feels like it's shattered, torn apart by the weight of grief.

An image of a laughing human, full of light and joy, vanishes under the sight of Xenothgorot's talons. She sobs. This. This is not him. A creature of unmatched rage, unmatched viciousness.

She could understand if the humans killed one of their clan, any of their clan, without reason. But, they had not. Griesh attacked first and they defended what was theirs.

Xenothgorot had brought the entire clan. Not just a few skylords, but all of them, even the smallest dragons that serve as nursemaids to the hatchlings.

Rathleon takes a shuddering breath and forces herself to unfurl. The wind has changed, blowing in rain. Studying the mountainside, she spies a large overhang where she can shelter.

❀ ❀ ❀ ❀ ❀

"Where did she go?!" Viggo's voice echoes in the dwarven room.

Dane shrugs. "I've never seen that type of portal. It isn't a Traveler's technique. I can't read it."

Viggo crouches, pushes his hair from his face and takes a good look at the room for the first time since entering. "Why was she here?"

Rayland glares as he tips a three-legged chair upright, its fourth leg hangs askew. "A little late to be asking, but they fell into one of my tunnels."

Viggo gestures to the room. "Text me the bill."

Dane tosses Rayland a business card before opening a hole in the air, which they step through leaving the dwarves with a mess.

Sitting on the patio, looking lovely in a teal summer dress, IlliaVaa waves to them over the heads of a lean white-haired man and the recognizably bulky frame of Kith, his father-in-law. The guests stand as Viggo joins them.

"A pleasure to host you." Viggo's lips twitch in the imitation of a smile.

"It looks like you were in a fight." Ka'Leel smirks, taking his seat and staring at IlliaVaa.

Viggo combs his fingers through his hair and straightens his shirt, ignoring the stinging pain near his eye where the wolf's claws caught him.

"IlliaVaa was just telling us of the intense training regimen you created for Cate. It's a shame I won't be able to visit her as I expected." Kith's fingers drum against the table.

"It is a blessing her gift manifested. Unfortunately, at her age, it requires more focus than I anticipated." Viggo returns, sitting at the table with them.

"I am encouraged to hear of her dragon waking. What technique did you use?"

"Peril." Viggo's dark gaze pins Kith.

Tension ripples through Kith's frame, the muscles in his jaw flex. He pushes to his feet. His eyes once again lock on Viggo's purpling skin and bloodied face. "I must be off." Dane joins him as a leggy blond emerges from the house, her icy beauty a contrast to IlliaVaa's dark velvet looks. "I hope you don't mind that I brought my niece. I wanted to introduce the girls."

"Of course not." Viggo acknowledges the girl with a nod before Dane escorts them from the estate through a portal.

Ka'Leel bows to IlliaVaa. "Call me." Then, he too joins Dane.

IlliaVaa grimaces, her eyes scanning Viggo from head to toe. "You look like hell."

"Feel like it. What's with the Eagle?"

"Nothing, yet. I take it you didn't find Cate."

"No, we found her. And, then we lost her." He pushes his hands through his hair and grabs the back of his neck, the feel of his scales a reminder of who he is. "Her power is intriguing. She can breathe fire and create something like a portal with it."

IlliaVaa leans forward resting her elbows on the table. "Cool! Did you get hurt?" He extends his arms and shows the tender burns he received before he enacted his protection spell.

He heaves a sigh. IlliaVaa's eyes shift from human to dragon. Her power rises to assuage her curiosity. Pain blurs with desire. He really wants Cate, but is it love? Her gift attempts to sort the images - dual layers, it isn't just him but his dragon too.

A passionate kiss. A hunger to be whole. Want of power. Want of an equal.

Her eyes shift back. Viggo sits with slumped shoulders. IlliaVaa heaves a heavy sigh and leans against the table. "Truth is raw. Most people prefer it sugar-coated, but not you. Stop searching for her. She needs this... time... to realize her potential and her dragon's.

Rathleon was ever passionate about what she believed. Do you think Cate any different?"

"How can I convince her to be with me, for Rathleon to be with Xenothgorot, if she is on her own?"

"In the Dream."

He laughs, surprising IlliaVaa. "She's already pulled me into the Dream."

"Hopefully, you made good use of the opportunity."

Viggo's eyes focus intently on his sister. "What of the men she travels with?"

"Don't mind them, by her birthday, it will come down to the two of you."

"Tell me of the reason for Ka'Leel's visit."

Schooling her features, something she learned at the hands of their father, she chooses to hide Ka'Leel's interest in her. "Kraeken is unstable. It's rumored Ka'Lea killed her husband and few of the enchanted families want to sacrifice a son to be the next king. The Wolves are the likeliest candidate."

"Makes sense. D'Gar is strong but not a shifter. It would also bring v'Lana to heel after her eldest son aided – continues to aid – Cate."

IlliaVaa drums her fingers on the table. "If you weren't betrothed, would you court Ka'Lea?"

He laughs, a genuine sound that lifts the corners of his mouth and dimples his cheeks. "She's not my type."

"Right, she's the wrong kind of dangerous."

✾ ✾ ✾ ✾ ✾

Huddled under an overhang, protected from icy rain and the biting wind, Cate sleeps. War, bloody and raw, fills her dreams.

Steel rings against steel. Dragon talons tear flesh. She covers her ears and closes her eyes, but the images and sounds won't go away.

Screaming, she startles awake.

Baen lifts his lupine head. He sniffs the air, glances at her, then settles back down. Cate wipes sweat from her forehead, unable to clear the vestiges of fear that cling to her like a fine mist. She pushes to her feet and moves to sit beside the cold fire.

Their shelter isn't large, just big enough for the three of them and the few bags they carry. Elar had built the fire as close to the edge as he could without the rain dousing it. Which means, he should be right here but there are no signs of the elf.

Maybe he needed a bio break.

She rubs her arms as a chill settles over her. Clouds obscure the night sky, and the wind driven rain obscures the landscape. She blows a thin stream of fire onto the wood, but it's slow to take. Thick smoke from wet wood fills their space.

Resigned to let the fire be, she moves further from the opening. Baen coughs. "Can't sleep?"

"I had horrible dreams. Even now, it's like I'm still living them. The sounds and images won't leave my mind."

"If you're cold, lean against me."

Cate glances at the fire and the layer of smoke under the rock ceiling, then moves to sit where her body touches Baen's fur-covered back. "Thanks."

It's not long before his warmth lulls her back to sleep.

She wakes when Baen moves, feeling a little awkward draped across his back and snuggled into his fur. Stretching, she asks, "Where's Elar?"

"He's been gone since last night. Unlike you, he can take care of himself. Stay here." Without another word, he leaps from the ledge down the mountain.

The ledge feels cold without him. Angrily, Cate mutters about fire and holes in the air as she searches their bags for food. Finding a granola bar, she sits with the Dwarven chest on her lap and opens it. It's like the seed is calling her. Just seeing it, running her fingers over it as she eats, settles her mind. "Who or what are you, little one?"

"A treasure."

Cate slams the chest closed and looks at a girl standing on the ledge in black jeans, hiking boots, and a black tank top. White hair, braided on each side like a Viking, leather bracelets, a leather choker, and ear cuffs in the shape of twisting vines - black eyeliner draws attention to light blue eyes.

"Who're you?"

The girl scoffs. "Why do you have a somnolent seed?"

Cate sets the chest down and stands, pushing it behind her with her foot. "I don't want trouble."

The girl's mouth curls into a smile. "I do. Give me the chest." She steps closer. "No use waiting for your friends. The wolf's chasing shadows, and I took care of the elf last night."

"What did you do to Elar?"

The girl extends her hands. "The chest."

Cate squares her shoulders and lifts her chin. "The elf."

The girl smiles coldly. "You think you can stop me from taking what I want?" A small ball of fire appears on the girl's open palm.

Cate's eyes widen. She'd been stupid to think she's the only one who can create fire. She extends her own hand, mimicking the girl. Flames dance along her fingertips and coalesce into a swirling ball of blue and purple.

"Interesting." The girl studies Cate, both still holding fire. "What's your name?"

"Where's the elf?"

The girl stops her fire first. "I'll take you to him. Bring the chest."

Reluctantly, Cate extinguishes her flames and lowers her hand. "Why should I trust you?"

The girl laughs. "You shouldn't. If you want to save the elf, bring the chest, and follow me." She leaps from the ledge, not waiting for a reply.

Gritting her teeth, Cate picks up the chest and follows the girl. As they walk a winding path around the mountain, Cate purposefully touches branches and scrapes her feet on the ground. Anything to help Baen find them.

In this light, the girl's skin is bluish in tint. Without thinking, Cate blurts, "You're a Drow."

The girl pushes aside a curtain of vines and steps into a cave. Cate follows, a feeling of déjà vu settles over her. The cavern is unlit, and Cate's eyes shift.

They walk along a sloping tunnel for what feels like hours when the girl pushes on a flower shaped outcropping. A door swings open. She gestures Cate inside and remains in the tunnel. "Give me the seed and you can walk out of here."

The room is small but cozy only the lack of light, the smell and rough walls mark it as being underground. The daybed, chair and side table look as if they were bought at a big box store. "Where's the elf?"

"About two rooms down." The girl leans against the rough doorframe. "Why care about a traitor? Worry about yourself. Unless you give me that seed, you're not getting out of here."

Cate sits on the bed, the box on her lap. "Even if I give you the box, you can't open it. Besides, I can leave anytime I want."

"Keep believing that." The girl steps back and the door swings shut.

Cate closes her eyes, since first calling fire in the Valley of Mist, it's felt like fire runs through her veins. Imagining the ball of flames she conjured to escape Viggo, she opens her eyes and looks up. Nothing. Not even a flicker on her skin.

She plops on the bed. *Rathleon.* She can feel the dragon awaken as if stretching her wings. In seconds, another pair of eyes see through her own. *This is not where we went to sleep.*

Cate fills her in.

Drow? She stares at the box in her hands then lies down. *This is exactly what I hoped for.*

You hoped to be isolated from Baen and Elar, and locked in a room?

Rathleon chuckles. *When I left Xenothgorot, I came to this mountain. I found a cave and nursed my injuries. Later, I discovered a clan of Drow shared the mountain.*

Cate taps the box. *You let my friends walk into a trap.*

You will need to demonstrate who you are and what we can do for the Drow to trust you. Rathleon folds her wings and sinks into Cate's   subconscious. *Wait! I am not done talking to you.* No reply. Just random drips of water from somewhere down the hall.

Ka'Lea sits in a wing back chair, her eyes pin v'Lana to the windows, but the Wolf matron doesn't notice, her attention on the far mountains. "What are your thoughts on Dragotia?"

"That I am wasting time and money searching for a girl that brings no benefits to Kraeken."

V'Lana faces the young queen. "Viggo plans to change the dragon-souled spell."

Ka'Lea levels her gaze on her mother's old friend, in politics there is no place for affection. "What effect do you think it will have on our enchantment?"

"If he succeeds, dragon souls will be primary. We don't know what that will do to the bodies that carry them. On the other hand, if the girl releases the dragons, there would be purpose for the clans once again."

Ka'Lea coolly studies V'Lana's features. The words echo her own thoughts. "Is that why Baen is with the girl?" A Kraa scout searching for the runaway reported seeing the shapeshifter in the mountains, near a dwarven settlement.

"It is time we take back our place in the world and if that means releasing dragons, then I will release them."

Ka'Lea stands, rising to her full height and tosses her white hair over her shoulder. "You dare to presume what is right for Kraeken."

V'Lana is done cowering before the child in front of her. "I *presume* to do what is right for our people. The enchantment fades. Fewer children in every generation are born with the ability to shift. After a few more generations, shifting will be a memory." V'Lana steps close enough to the Queen to smell the peppermint in her breath. "I know you are strong enough to do what is right, that is why I will agree to d'Gar's marriage with you."

"First, you presume to release dragons. Now, you presume I'll marry your son."

"We have never mixed our bloodline with another clan. Your marriage will be the first. It is time to ensure our survival. You know it and I know it."

Ka'Lea's lips curl over white teeth. "The Lion clan thought to gain power through marriage, even making me believe L'Syle loved me. I will not be fooled again."

"d'Gar is wayward. He needs a strong woman to curb his wandering. Do you not find my son handsome, intelligent, ambitious?"

Ka'Lea slowly blinks hooded eyes. "Blame me not for a short life, should he wander."

"The blame would be his."

"You are a hard woman, v'Lana. I will entertain marriage with d'Gar, should he approach me himself. As for the runaway, for now, we will let her go."

❀ ❀ ❀ ❀ ❀

Emily sketches in her book, new ideas for tattoos. It is nearly impossible not to worry about Cate, only Kith's drawings soothe her. They show her daughter safe. Kith's visit to Viggo had been unproductive, but happily vague, supporting the images in his Dreams.

But, as a mom, knowing her seventeen-year-old is wandering on her own is terrifying. She has no money, no clothes, nothing. The pencil snaps. Emily stares at the wooden fragments between her fingers.

The last time she felt this way was when she left her parents. She'd grown up isolated, living in a cottage deep in the forest and off the grid. Leaving them had been the hardest thing in her life, until now. But it was also the best decision she ever made.

Kith enters the room, sweat glistens on his skin, weight-lifting has been his escape like drawing has been hers. "Dinner?"

Emily tosses the pencil in the trash. "Sure. Whatever you want."

He pauses in the doorway to the bathroom. "She's okay. She's not with Viggo, but she's okay. She has an Elf and a Kraeken with her."

"I know, I know, but…."

"We can't stop her destiny."

"Fate is what we make of it, not what it makes of us."

Kith leans against the bathroom doorway and crosses his arms over his broad chest. "Time will never change how much I love you, but destiny separated us for fourteen years. It is what is, and though we live under the illusion of choice it is only that, an illusion." He gives her a grim smile before disappearing into the bathroom and turning on the shower.

Emily opens a desk drawer and digs in it for another pencil. She can't think like Kith, never could, that's why she ran with Cate. Free will is the purview of all humans. Predestination may be, but it is God's thing, not man's.

Taking a deep breath, she sets her pencil to paper and outlines a gryphon.

❀ ❀ ❀ ❀ ❀

Baen howls cursing himself for letting Cate search on her own for the elf. Sniffing around the ledge, he finds her scent, the elf's scent, and another.

He closes his eyes and focuses. It's difficult to separate Cate's. The wolf in him wants to grab on with its teeth and never let go. He snarls. There's no need to separate them, she's the one he needs to find.

He lowers his head and deeply inhales. Opening his eyes, it's as if her scented footprints light up. He can see exactly where she went. With lips curled over canines, he snarls and leaps.

He'd warned her she was too trusting.

She should have stayed where she was and let him find the elf, but no. She has to follow a stranger down the mountain. His instincts take over as he rants, anger building at her, at himself, and at the elf.

Fear mingles with anger – what if the stranger has ill intentions? What if it's another dragon bent on taking her back to Viggo?

He slows. Is that such a horrible thing? If she marries that god-forsaken dragon, then she'd be his problem. He shakes his head, fur lifting and settling. Of course, it's a problem. She's innocent and sweet. Viggo isn't.

According to v'Lana, he wants to use Cate to change the dragon-souled spell – and that's the only reason they are engaged. He takes a breath, remembering the feel of her lying across him as they slept. Since first meeting her in the ravine and saving her from the Watchers, he's tried to keep an emotional distance.

At a logical level, he knows the pheromones draw him to her; but, with her missing, again, he has to admit there's more to it.

His ears twitch. Voices.

Silently, he stalks toward them keeping the scent in his nose. It carries him into the mountain. Down a tunnel worn by time and the passing of feet, he stops as the voices get louder.

"He's here." It's a girl's voice.

"Come forward." A man.

Baen bares his teeth as he turns a blind corner and enters a large cavern, dimly lit, but well enough for him to see. A man reclines at a table, calmly eating, while a girl leans against the stone wall.

"Like you, I've just arrived. My companion was filling me in on the situation. Care to join me for a meal?" Small bells in his many braids tinkle as he leans forward to offer Baen a plate.

"No thanks." He growls. "Where's the girl, and the elf?"

The man grins and takes a bite of chicken. He gestures for the girl to take over the conversation. Instead, she gives him sass. "Why are you entertaining the wolf?"

When the man at the table does not answer, she heaves a weighted sigh. Rather than talking to the wolf, she continues the conversation she was having with the man before the wolf arrived. "As I was saying, she thought to intimidate me with a fireball."

"Yes, yes, where is she now?"

"In one of the quiet rooms. The elf's in another a few down. This one, I thought to distract. I did not think he'd stick around."

Setting the chicken bone on the plate and licking his fingers, the man's attention shifts to Baen. "What is your connection to them?"

"What does it matter? I want them back."

The man stands and wipes his hands on his pants. "That's a bit of a problem. See, the elf, even if he isn't personally a traitor, is kin to traitors. He'll be treated accordingly. The girl, if Channa's right, is too interesting to let go."

"Then, I rip your throat out and take them."

The man laughs, a full-throated hearty belly laugh. It is not the response Baen expected. "Kraeken were bred to destroy dragons. I'd heard that in the last thousand years they started bedding them instead but hadn't seen such passion myself. Interesting. Don't worry, wolf, we won't hurt her.

Our people made a pledge a thousand years ago to aid the dragons in bringing peace to this world. We keep that pledge today."

"Then, why is she locked up?"

The man smiles. "Not all dragons seek peace. Come, let me reassure you she is well."

A short walk later and the man knocks on stone, it hollowly reverberates. Without waiting for a response, he presses on an outcropping and a door swings open. Cate sits in darkness on a bed holding the dwarves' treasure box. She lifts her head; dragon eyes catch a glint of light and eerily shine.

The man steps inside. "Hello, I am Rook, and the girl is Channa. Are you comfortable?"

Cate softly replies, "What is this room?"

"It's a quiet room. The stone has a unique quality that represses certain magics. Do you want for anything?"

"Freedom and my friends."

Rook steps aside so that Baen can enter. "I believe he is a friend. As for the elf, he will be tried for treason."

"Who did he betray?"

"Not him specifically, but his people. It is a burden all fair folk carry from withdrawing during the war."

Cate stands and steps closer to Rook. "Ridiculous! That was a thousand years ago."

"Only a generation or two for us, now who is the dragon you carry?"

❀ ❀ ❀ ❀ ❀

Elar wakes. His mouth is dry and cottony. Rubbing his head, he touches a tender lump. He remembers watching the fire and keeping it lit despite the rain, and then a shadowy figure in the deluge.

He'd stepped away from the ledge to investigate and.... He looks around the complete darkness, unable to even see his hand before his face.

A door opens, flooding the room with light. Blinding him. Only with complete self-discipline does he prevent himself from shielding his eyes.

"See? Unharmed." It's a man's voice. "We leave in two hours."

"We'll stay with him." It's Cate. He blinks against the pain of the light, his eyes watering. Her outline slowly comes into focus.

"Your choice."

He hears her enter, feels her sit beside him and slip her hand on top of his, then the door closes and darkness returns.

CHAPTER 16

E lar squeezes Cate's hand, reassuring himself of her presence. All he can see is a faint outline around her - a small glimpse of the soul her body houses. In this hideous maze of tunnels, she is a star shining brightly on a moonless night.

Since his earliest memories, he's heard tales of the Drow. None of them pleasant. He shivers, the tremors reach his fingers. Cate draws closer. She does not speak.

He appreciates her silence. His shame hidden from all but her. He can hear Baen panting, the space tight even for the wolf. He reminds himself who he is and the heritage he represents, straightening his spine and squaring his shoulders he refuses to give the Drow the satisfaction of seeing his weakness.

A faint glow of light illuminates the tunnel ahead. Elar shades his eyes with his free hand, the light painful, as tears clear to reveal a fairytale forest with massive trees and buildings artfully cut from stone.

Rook bows to Cate. "Welcome to the Frozen City."

Her grip on Elar's hand loosens. "I can't believe no one knows this exists."

Chana pushes past them to a narrow walkway that leads down into the forest. Rook prevents Cate from following. "The Elf is a criminal. Once we reach the trees, he will be taken...."

Cate interrupts, her tone matter of fact, "He will stay with me."

Rook gazes at Elar's hand holding Cate's. "You have much to learn, dragon. We are not the villains."

"Neither is Elar."

Rook sighs as he watches them lightly descend the narrow path heading toward what he knows awaits them. "How do you stand it?" Rook walks close to the wolf's tail, neither concerned about the treacherous width of the trail. "She is radiant. Each hour with her, it's like looking at a new person. When did her magic awaken?"

"Recently."

"And already she wields fire. It's an innate magic but difficult to master."

More than a dozen Drow encircle Elar and Cate as they reach the forest floor. Baen snarls, leaping to land at Cate's side.

"I warned you the Elf would be taken prisoner." Rook joins them, his words ring with authority.

Flames spread from Cate's mouth to dance along her limbs. Reflexively, Elar let's go of her hand. Cate's eyes shift to dragon and her voice gains the depth and timbre of a much larger being. "What disgrace is this? Have you lost the grace and manners of your ancestors?"

The Drow encircling them do not move. Rook is the only one to approach her. Flames appear in each of his hands, leaping with different shades of blue. "Welcome, Lady. The war took its toll on us all. Had the Elves not withdrawn, perhaps it would have ended sooner. After your departure, the Council named their race Traitor and deemed any who enter our boundaries as criminals. This elf meets that criteria."

"I brought him. So, I will bear the punishment for his crime of trespassing, but he is no Traitor."

Flames dance up Rook's arms from the mesmerizing balls in his hands. "Take him." He orders the Drow behind him. Two males step forward.

"*Tuero.*" Cate/Rathleon whispers. A shimmering light encircles the three of them. The Drow tentatively touch it. It's as if they touch a thick glass wall. "I do not want to hurt you. Allow us to stay together and I will abide by your trial for trespassing."

"You will allow us to prosecute the elf?"

"I will take his place."

Elar lightly sets his hand on Cate's, ignoring the flames that singe him. Her eyes meet his and the flames vanish. "I will represent my people. Put down the barrier."

"They've already judged you guilty."

"I trust that with you at my side, the trial will be fair."

"Are you sure?"

He closes his eyes and nods. Cate/Rathleon whispers, *"Fin'e."* The shimmering barrier vanishes. The Drow take Elar into custody and shuttles him through the trees out of Cate's view. Cate/Rathleon turn their fierce gaze on Rook. "Mistreat him and I will destroy this haven."

He bows. "I understand, Lady. This way."

Baen glances in the mirror and adjusts the t-shirt. Though the Drow have modern clothes, they prefer a slim fit. He had to pick jeans too big for his waist to fit over his thighs, and the shirt conforms to the lines of his shoulders and chest a little too well. If he were the type to show off, the outfit wouldn't be bad.

His ears twitch. Someone opened a door. He steps into the hallway, nearly colliding with Cate. She smells like vanilla and lavender, her hair's still damp, and her cheeks are flushed from the heat of the shower. He steps aside so she can pass.

It's nearly impossible not to inhale her intoxicating scent. Since waking her dragon, her scent has changed and, with each new type of magic she learns, a new scent emerges. "Amazing." He exhales.

"What?" She turns back, a beam of sunlight in her hair.

Baen swallows reminding himself that she is engaged and not someone he can have. "Nothing." He follows her into the living space and sits on a sofa as far from her as he can. Cate closes her eyes and rests her head against the back of the chair.

"You look tired."

She rubs her face. "I am, but how can I sleep when Elar's in jail."

Baen smiles. "Perhaps seeing where he is being held will help you relax. Drow are elves after all. Though they are more visibly emotional than their counterparts, the Drow are still a lot like them. Their jail is nothing like a human jail. He will be safe and comfortable until he is found guilty, then he will be harshly dealt with."

"He's not guilty."

"Of trespassing, we three are guilty. Of some race thing, I agree with you – he's innocent."

"How do you do it?"

"What?"

"Be so calm."

He laughs and a dimple appears on his cheek when he smiles. "I'm not calm. Simply good at appearing so, especially when it comes to you." Cate blushes. "With everything you've been through, this is the first time I've smelled fear."

"I talk to a dragon in my head. If anything, I feel like I've gone crazy. But, when you have scales, what isn't crazy?

My classmates thought it was cool my mom owned a body modification and tattoo shop. They even thought it was cool when my scales appeared, thinking my mom had done it for me. It was a great excuse.

And when I couldn't take listening to them whisper about me, mom would let me stay home. She helped me accept myself. Working at her shop, I saw other people who were different – because they were born that way or paid to be."

"She sounds amazing."

"She is. I wish I could tell her I'm okay. I can't believe that in this day and age it is so hard to find a phone."

"Maybe they have internet here. At least you could send an email." He scoots forward and leans his elbows on his knees, his hands under his chin. "What was that thing you did in the forest?"

Cate yawns. "The barrier?" She shrugs. "It's something my dragon did."

"Could you do it again?"

"Probably."

Baen stands. "Let's visit Elar, come on. After you see him, you can rest."

Cate follows him outside. It's like she's on the set of a movie. Everything is beautiful. Heads turn and eyes follow as they pass. Whispers shroud them like mist. Cate's ears redden at some of the guesses of who Baen is and why he's with her.

He clears his throat and climbs stairs to a platform nestled about halfway up a massive trunk. A guard stands at either side of the door, both dressed entirely in black. "We've come to see the Elf."

The guard smirks, his eyes on Cate. "He's popular with the women but we must refuse."

"He's our companion and the Lady needs to ensure he is well cared for." The guards' eyes widen at the word "Lady." With a shared look, one opens the door while the other leads them into the hollow tree. A winding staircase takes them several levels underground.

Not far from the stairs, the guard unlocks a plain-looking door. Elar sits on a bed in a well-lit room, his legs stretched out before him, thumbing through a book. On a side table is a plate of fruit and chilled pitcher. Cate steps inside. She peeks behind a door in the wall at the foot of the bed and finds a closet-sized bathroom.

Facing Elar, she asks, "Are you okay?"

"I am good. Chana visited before you and brought the food and drink. She said I will stay here until the trial. Do not worry, they will not mistreat me before the verdict. Something about you tearing down their haven if they should."

Cate laughs her cheeks heating. "I'm glad you're okay. I'll get you out of this, I promise."

"Perhaps now you can sleep." Baen whispers.

Elar moves with grace to stand beside her. Lightly, he tilts her chin to study her face. "Take care of yourself." A small smirk lifts the corner of Elar's mouth, drawing her attention to the lines of his lips.

Baen clears his throat and Cate steps away from Elar's touch. "We have a lot of work to do to clear the charges and Cate needs to sleep before that happens."

"You sound like her brother. It is a good role for you."

"Then, as a brother, you won't mind if I share her quarters... or, her bed." With a grin meant to cause a fight, Baen steers Cate from the cell. A guard closes and locks the door behind them.

Cate glances over her shoulder at the cell as they climb the stairs. Something about the way Elar holds himself, the way he talks makes her feel like he remains in the cell by choice, that he could leave if he wanted.

Thoughts swirl in her head as they return to their quarters breaking free when the door to their suite closes. "What was that back there?"

Baen sits on the couch. Sunlight crowns his raven hair and lights his eyes. He's ruggedly beautiful. She lowers her gaze to the carpet, suddenly losing confidence.

"You don't have experience with elves."

"What does that have to do with anything? You have your own bed, why'd you say that?"

"He needed a reality check. For an elf, he is awfully expressive." Baen leans forward, his elbows on his knees. "Get some sleep. I'll wake you in a few hours and we'll work on proving Elar innocent. Maybe along the way we'll see what they know about the Stones."

Cate sits beside him. "Reality check? Really?" Despite his arrogance, something about his quiet demeanor and tacit understanding makes her comfortable. "Stop pushing his buttons when you all are together. It's annoying, and thanks, you know, for taking me there."

"Why don't you thank me by laying down and closing your eyes."

Cate extends her legs over Baen's and rests her head on the arm of the sofa. She closes her eyes and slows her breathing, trying to steady the rhythm of her pounding heart. At some point, sleep claims her.

She's sitting on a boulder overlooking the sea, a light wind lifts strands of hair off her shoulders and from her face.

"You're doing great, just a few more minutes."

She turns at the sound of his voice. Viggo sits on a lower rock, sketch pad in hand and pencil moving. "There." He starts to close the book but stops when Cate asks to see it.

She joins him sitting close enough that he can feel her warmth. Her eyes rove over the drawing. "Why did you have me model if you weren't going to draw me?"

He smiles and it softens the hard lines of his face. "It is you. You can hold it up to any mirror to compare." He turns the page to a previous drawing. It's Cate with a fire portal hovering above her.

"You're good."

"Thanks. I wanted to be an artist before my father died. Now, I run the family business."

"What kind of business?"

"It's a conglomerate. We own farms and wineries, even tech companies. Then, there's management of the clan." He sets the book down and looks into her eyes. "I confess, at first, you were just another business transaction left by my father."

"Flattering."

"It was easy to think that way until our engagement party when I saw you, for you."

Cate rolls her eyes. "I can't even get away from this in my dreams. I might as well wake up."

"Don't, I won't talk about it."

She laughs, taking pleasure in his vulnerability. "What do you think we're going to do, if we're not talking, kiss?"

"Why not?"

He reaches out and gently pulls her to him, then rests his forehead on hers. "Power. That was our parents' reason, and my obligation. I miss you." His voice breaks, softening her resolve.

"You don't know me."

"You didn't give me the chance." His fingers uncurl, releasing her. "Stay safe."

The dream dissolves. Cate opens her eyes to the sound of Baen dozing beside her. She blushes at the memory of Viggo in the dream, with the feel of Baen's legs beneath hers.

Why are her dreams filled with him? And, even if it is a dream, why does she always respond like that to him? She closes her eyes again. Maybe it's because he's good looking. Even if his personality sucks. Even if she doesn't want to marry him, she can at least dream of a scenario where he's a nice guy once in a while.

CHAPTER 17

Ka'Lea tugs at her jacket's hem, straightening any wrinkles that might have appeared since the last time she touched it. Suits have never been her go-to, much preferring flowing gossamer gowns over any corporate uniform. The elevator lurches to a halt, a digital voice announces the floor. The doors open and she steps onto shiny marble tile.

The dragons know how to impress. Every dozen feet another burly man, obviously security, stands against the wall like a Grecian statue. At the end of the hall, she enters a massive boardroom, gently tiered so that the person who sits at the center is higher than any other.

Familiar faces greet her. As a shareholder, she has a right to attend these meetings, even if she's not one of the dragon clan leaders. But, without a dragon soul, she is seated near the back of the room at one of the lowest tables. It grates on her.

As if on cue, the room quickly fills, and Viggo enters followed by his executive assistant, Dane. Both are well cut, in tailored suits. Either would make a fine boyfriend, though only Viggo would rate husband. Ka'Lea smiles, thinking of d'Gar waiting for her at the hotel.

Though he cannot transform, his family is a strong carrier of the enchantment. It is likely any heirs they produce will have the ability whether born wolf or eagle. She blinks, realizing her mind has wandered, and forces herself to focus.

Viggo's speaking, it takes a minute to realize he's talking about market shifts and what the Fed may do in the next year to curb inflation. She never enjoyed economics and it's hard to pay attention. When the conversation changes to technology and advances that his teams are working on, she sits on the edge of her chair.

The Kraeken have long used technology to disguise their hamlet, and to protect their people from would-be were-hunters. He turns the floor to Dane who talks about the financials, and then Dane introduces different industry presidents to discuss their company's strategic goals and overall plans for the next three years.

Shareholder meetings do not hold the same allure as they did the first time she attended three years ago. Someone taps her shoulder. She nearly snaps the messenger's fingers before politely smiling and leaning in to hear the youth whisper that Viggo would like to speak to her after the meeting.

She quietly rises and follows the lithe black-clad teen from the room to the elevator. The meeting was almost over anyway, no reason to stay. The messenger swipes a key card and presses the penthouse button. Neither speak as the elevator doors close.

Viggo thanks the shareholders for attending, promising to meet them in the banquet hall before dinner, then steps from the dais and exits the board room. Focusing is difficult. His mind keeps wandering to the Dream and Cate.

By the time he reaches the penthouse, Ka'Lea stands at the windows gazing over the ocean. Her long white hair is plaited, hanging heavily against her cream-colored jacket. "Thank you for coming." She turns at the sound of his voice. He removes his own jacket and hands it to Dane, then sits in a leather chair. He casually crosses one leg over the other and leans back. "Congratulations on your pending marriage."

"Thank you." A cold smile lifts the edges of her lips. "The Kraa scouts found nothing useful. We've aided per the treatise. What else do you want?"

"Where are the Drow?"

"They've mingled long with humans." She spread her arms and gestures to the city below. "So, everywhere. Why?"

"Send me the location of the hidden Drow capital and I'll transfer two percent of my stocks to you."

"Only two percent?"

"Make that one percent. Ask again and you will be working for free."

She shrugs, giving him the location of the Drow is nothing. Now, the slight to her pride and her status…. "If there's nothing else, I have a plane to catch."

"You're not staying for dinner?"

"We're visiting wedding venues." She turns and pulls open the door, before she can leave, he says, "More than five generations of our people have interbred, maybe it is time to consider the Kraeken one of the clans."

Tatiana thumbs through the clothes in the closet. Very few have been worn, most have a thin layer of dust on them. The bathroom is similar, makeup that's been used maybe once, but nothing else.

No personal items anywhere. Not in the closet, not in the bathroom, and not in the bedroom. It's almost as if her cousin didn't really live here. Maybe he has her living somewhere else for training.

Laughter carries to the room from outside. Staying behind the curtains, she peers below. IlliaVaa sits on the patio with a white-haired guy. It's clear she's into him, the way she smiles and laughs at his jokes. Tatiana grits her teeth. She wishes she had better news to give her aunt.

A portal appears on the lawn, Viggo and Dane walk through. That's her cue to exit. Dashing into the bathroom, she faces the full-length mirror and chants. Unlike Dane, she can't make a portal in thin air, but any reflective surface – like a mirror – is fair game.

Stepping from the Dragotian manor into her bedroom, she immediately grabs a blanket and covers her standing mirror. If she can use it to Travel, so can someone else. Pulling her phone from her pocket, she takes it off silent and checks her messages.

Mom wants to meet. She slips her phone back into her pocket and jogs down the stairs. It's a short walk to the café, Mom's favorite spot when she's working on a difficult case.

The bell over the door rings as she enters, and Mom looks up from a stack of papers. Hilde waves at her and starts filling a large, sweet tea, no ice, from behind the counter. Sliding into the booth across from Mom, Tatiana swipes a fry off her forgotten plate. Neither says anything until after Hilde drops off the tea with a smile and small talk.

Keeping their voices low, nearly inaudible to human ears, they discuss Tatiana's recent foray into the Dragotian estate. Oksana grimaces as she holds up a piece of paper covered in fine print with narrow margins. "Whoever drafted this is good. I've yet to find any clause I can exploit."

"You will. I have faith." Tatiana's phone dings and her fingers itch to check the text. "I'm going to dinner with Vek."

Oksana's eyes meet hers. She can feel a judgmental response forming on Mom's lips, but after a second, she shakes her head. "Be safe. I want you home by eleven."

"It's Friday night."

"Fine, midnight, no later or Dad'll come looking for you."

Tatiana grimaces. "I almost forgot, that Kraeken prince is still hanging around IlliaVaa." Stuffing another fry into her mouth, she kisses Mom's cheek and hurries from the café.

Cate wakes with a start. Wiping drool from her mouth, she blinks. She had been having a dream about the Dragon War. She was flying over a bloody battlefield filled with wounded and dying of all races.

She stretches, her back and neck hurt. She had only meant to rest her head on the desk, pillowed on her arms. Not sleep. The windows outside are dark. Table lights illuminate the library. Baen is nowhere in sight.

Rook stares at her from a chair in the corner. She closes the book and stretches. "Found anything?"

"I'm not sure you want me to."

He smirks and pushes to his feet. "I have nothing against the Elf. Want to get some air?"

"I'll wait for Baen."

"The wolf's hunting." He moves within a few feet of her. Dark braids frame his face, highlighting the deep blue of his eyes. She takes a step back. "Magic, like any other muscle, needs work to grow. Take a break and come with me."

He does not wait for her response. Reluctantly, Cate follows him from the library. The branches and land below are illuminated by bluish-white sparkling lights. It is as if thousands of stars descended to rest among the branches.

It is a sight she'll never get used to.

They walk until they reach the edge of the Frozen City, Rook stands in an open field, darkness eats the land beyond. He turns to her as fire erupts on his palm. Lifting his hand, he nods at her to do the same.

Flames dance along her tongue, unaided by magic words, she lifts her hand and blows on her fingers. Heat transfers to her hand as she closes her lips. The flame is still there should she open her mouth.

"Fascinating. Extinguish the flame and, this time, call it forth from your flesh only. Do not breathe it into existence." He closes his fist, and his own flame vanishes. The field is even darker without its light.

With her free hand, she smothers the flames. Keeping her hand open, palm towards the sky, she concentrates on fire emerging from her pores. Nothing happens.

It feels like forever before she exhales, a small burst of fire puffs out with the air. "I can't." Rook's finger brushes her palm. She jumps. She'd been so focused she hadn't realized he moved. With one hand he grabs her wrist and with the other he works her hand until the fingers unfurl.

"Relax your hand, it is but the vessel which will hold the flame. Fire is within you. It doesn't need created; it only needs released." Still holding her wrist, his tone is soft. "See the fire, expect the fire, know it will come when called."

Cate stares at her hand. The pressure of his fingers makes it feel like her hand is the only thing that exists in the dark. She imagines a blue-white fire, like the lights in the city, dancing over her palm. The pressure vanishes as flames appear – just as she imagined.

"Excellent. Now, to make them go away, simply see them vanish." The flame disappears. Rook pats her arm. "Very good."

"What else can you teach me?"

"More than you have time to learn. Practice calling fire."

"I didn't come here to learn magic."

"Then, what did you come here for." They both turn toward the dark woods at the sound of Channa's voice. She steps forward, her white hair nearly glowing in the absence of light.

"If you'd asked instead of kidnapping my friend...."

"He shouldn't have trespassed. His kind knows better."

"His *kind*...."

"Cate." Baen's wolf voice says entering the field. She'd forgotten how big his wolf form is. "Tell them why we're here."

Wishing she could punch Channa in the face instead of asking for anything, she blurts, "I need the Dragon Stones."

Channa enters the field with flames bouncing on her palms. "Too bad, I don't care." Rook steps away as Channa throws a fireball where Cate had been standing.

"What's wrong with you?!" Reflexively, Cate catches the fire and squashes it. Flames appear in her own hands. Channa squares off in front of her, fire covers each girl's fists.

"Knock it off." Rook commands. Channa sneers, looking every bit the petulant child, but doesn't drop her fists. "I said that's enough." Slowly, Channa obeys, and Cate follows. "The Dragon Stones...."

Cate lifts her hand signaling for silence. Baen's ears twitch. "Do you hear that singing?"

"Ignore it." Channa glares at Rook as she crosses in front of him on her way back to the city. "It's just a dryad."

The singing gets louder, its tune mournful. "Why is it so sad?"

Rook extends his arm toward the city. "We should return." As Cate walks behind Channa, Rook answers. "The dryads lost a precious seedling long ago. Every ten years, they sing." He tosses his braids over his shoulder; fine frown lines deepen between his brows. "I apologize for Channa."

"What's her problem?"

Rook smiles in earnest. "Me. She's been my protégé for the last twenty years and has developed an attachment."

"Control her before someone else does." Baen growls from behind them.

"It's good to get fighting experience. Drow are not as refined as our forest dwelling cousins, and misunderstandings can occur."

"Weak excuse."

Cate agrees with Baen. Channa had been ready to take her head off, but if Rook hadn't brought Cate out to practice would Channa have even attacked? The dryad's haunting melody fills the night, only when they cross the boundaries of the city does it fall to a nearly inaudible level.

It's midnight before Baen emerges from his room, in human form and hair still wet from a shower. He's wearing pajama pants, and no shirt. Cate blushes, her eyes drawn to his fit body and muscular abdomen. She buries her face in the book she was reading as he pours a glass of water.

They'd covered why she'd gone to the clearing with Rook. It hadn't been a bad idea, and the fresh air was good. Exercising magic was like exercising her body, but Baen made her agree not to do it again without him. It didn't matter that she argued he couldn't do anything if something went wrong. It only mattered that she finally agreed. That's when he'd fallen silent and went to shower.

Lowering the book her eyes fall on a strange sentence. "Baen, listen to this. The accused may choose to sit on the Obsidian Throne in lieu of a trial. If the throne releases the accused, they are deemed innocent."

"I wonder why Rook hasn't mentioned it."

"Let's ask tomorrow." Cate yawns. Setting a piece of paper in the book to mark the page, she puts it down and stands. "I think I can sleep now."

"I'll be here if you need me."

Nodding in thanks, she slips into her room and under the covers. She's asleep almost as soon as her head hits the pillow.

She wakes up the next morning after a night of miniature golf and dinner with Viggo. She might have thought the dream weird if she hadn't forgotten about it by the time she'd showered and eaten.

It takes more than half the day to find Rook and another few hours before he has time to talk. Handing Cate a soda, he sits beside her. "What would you like to know?"

"What is the Obsidian Throne?"

He chokes on his drink, coughing he says, "The Obsidian Throne?" She nods. Clearing his throat, he answers. "It is the rightful throne of the Drow ruler."

"Why would there be a clause in your trial system that says the accused can sit on the throne and if it releases them, they are innocent?"

"Because the throne kills anyone who sits on it. If you are a criminal who dares to sit on the throne, you are challenging for the right to lead the Drow. Only the rightful ruler can sit on it. It's a death sentence." He finishes his soda and tosses the bottle into a nearby trash bin. "There's no shortcut to the law."

Cate's shoulders droop. Elar's already been in jail for a week. "How am I supposed to find evidence of his innocence for something his people did a thousand years ago?"

Rook shrugs. "I am of the mind that he bears the responsibility and therefore the punishment." Standing, he lightly pats her shoulder before returning to his office.

Cate's request stops him at the door, "Tell me what happened,"

"At first, the Elves were part of the alliance fighting against dragon tyranny but then they withdrew. If Rathleon hadn't stopped us back then, we might have finished them off before her spell was cast."

"Why did they withdraw?"

"Ask the Elf."

As much as she hates to admit it, he's right. Rather than starting with books, she should have started with Elar. Finding the jail is easy and, with Rook's seal, getting in is even easier.

Cate enters the cell while a guard waits outside the closed door. Elar looks up from a scroll. Rolling it, he sets it on the table. "Are you well?"

"I should be asking you that." Cate sits on the bed beside him. He doesn't answer, waiting for a response to his question. "I am. Tell me about why the Elves withdrew from the alliance during the Dragon Wars. What happened?"

"Our population was on the brink of extinction. If we did not withdraw, we would have perished."

Cate rubs her eyes. The reason feels valid. "How did they go about it?"

"They returned to the Valley of Mist."

Thinking about her time with Elar, in his house, their travels through the woods, even now – he is very formal and matter of fact. Black and white. When he says they returned, does he mean they just left?

"When did they return, how did they leave?"

Elar turns to her, his silver eyes study her face. "They returned after the battle of shadows. From the history, they packed up and left."

"There was no planning with their allies, no discussion?"

"No. It was their decision, not the alliance's decision. Why would they need to consult them before returning home?" Elar moves a stray strand of hair from Cate's face and tucks it behind her ear. His touch is careful and gentle.

"I think that's the problem. When you are in an alliance, you are no longer individuals. You are part of the collective. By thinking as individuals and not considering the collective, the Elves wounded the whole." Though she has no idea what the battle of shadows is, she has a better idea of why the elves are considered traitors.

"You will not find evidence to prove my race innocent."

"The only thing you are guilty of is being with me."

He moves faster than she can see, his hand behind her head tilting her head up so that their lips meet. The kiss is soft, his lips and breath warm. His eyes remain open, staring into hers. Separating only enough to speak, he whispers, "Am I with you?"

Cate's heart feels like a hammer against her ribcage. Her stomach is a mess of fluttering. She leans in to feel the press of his lips on hers. He gives in to his desire, kissing her once more before releasing her. "Find the Stones. When you are ready to leave, no one can keep me here." He brushes his fingers through her hair. "You must remain innocent." Her soul shines brightly through her eyes. "Be wary of those around you and find the Stones."

The guard knocks and opens the door. It's time to leave.

Cate's lost in thought when she enters the apartment. Surprise and outrage flare as Baen grabs her shoulders and presses her against the door, his grip tight and possessive, his nose pressed against her hair. "What are you doing?"

"I'll kill that Elf." The words are a growl. He shudders, his fingers dig into her. His heart's beating so fast, she can hear its rhythm.

Her own heart beats quickly and it is becoming difficult to control her outrage. "Let go of me." With his nose pressed to her hair, she whispers the words.

His breath hitches. "I'm sorry." The words sound desperate, a plea. He can't explain why he hasn't moved any more than why he grabbed her in the first place.

He takes another long slow breath. This one is steadier, calmer. His fingers start to relax. He rubs the side of his head against hers and takes another breath. His heart rate is slowing. Consciously, he moves one finger than another until he no longer holds her. His body is heavy against hers. He inhales again and takes a step back. Her shoulders ache where he'd grabbed her.

"What the hell was that?"

He plops onto the couch, his head in his hands. "Go to your room."

Her voice rises, the control on her anger slipping. "What the hell was that?!"

He lifts his head; his gaze holds hers. "He… touched you." His eyes shift to her mouth.

It feels like a thousand butterflies are trying to tear through her middle. The way he looks, so vulnerable for such a big guy, and the way his voice sounds – both draw her in a way she's never felt before. "So?"

He laughs. It's a sound that rips at her heart. "So? You're right. I have no reason to be jealous. You're engaged to another man. Who am I to you?"

"My friend."

He pushes to his feet and strides down the hall to his room. At the door, he says over his shoulders, "Friends don't feel the way I feel. Maybe we've spent too much time together. I told you dragons attract my kind." The door slams behind him.

CHAPTER 18

The next few weeks are spent researching the battle of shadows, the Elves, and the Drow. None of it gives the information she needs to free Elar. With Baen sulking in wolf form, she feels like she gained a pet and lost a friend.

Though, in wolf form, she feels comfortable lying beside him, her head against his belly or her arm wrapped around his neck. Every now and again, she'll find herself idly stroking the fur on the top of his head or playing with his ears.

As they are leaving the library, Channa falls into step beside her. "I thought you should know that the box you brought with you was stolen."

Cate stops dead in her tracks. "What?"

"That dragon treasure box. It was stolen."

Rook approaches, his eyes murderous. He acknowledges Channa and asks Cate to follow him. They take the most direct route from the city to a stream. Perched on a fallen tree, bridging the banks, is a willowy woman with long greenish colored hair and skin the color of bark. In her lap is Cate's chest.

When the woman speaks, it's like the wind whistling among branches. "Help me." Tears glisten in her eyes as her hands search the box for a latch.

Rook scowls and looks from the woman to Cate. "That box does not belong to you. It belongs to her."

Cate takes a moment to decipher Rook's statement and then wades into the stream, icy water fills her shoes. She extends her hands. "I can open it, if you let me."

The dryad hands Cate the box. Taking a deep breath, Cate exhales over it and the latch springs open. The dryad slips her fingers inside and removes the singing seed. Tears flow like rivers down her cheeks.

Sliding from the tree, the dryad lands in the water beside Cate. "Thank you." Grabbing Cate's wrist, she magically moves them through interconnected roots to the home of the Mother, a somnolent tree whose seed Cate found.

From the trunk of the tree, an elegant woman emerges. Tall, strong, with hair the color of amber and skin the color of fertile earth. Diamond tears fall from wide eyes. "My seed has lain dormant for too long. It needs heat, as if from the sun, or it will never sprout."

"I think I can warm it."

The elegant dryad approaches and gestures for the maiden who brought Cate to hand over the seed. Still, it sings. Cate wraps her hands around it and brings it close to her mouth, then breathes a steady stream of fire over it until she worries it'll roast rather than incubate.

The seed glows red when Cate extends it to the Mother. Roots the size of her thigh emerge from the ground and dig a deep hole. "Place it inside." Cate whispers kind words to the seed before she releases it. As it settles, the roots fill the hole and gently pat the disturbed dirt until it's smooth.

"Thank you." The elegant dryad returns to its tree, as one of its roots gently caresses Cate's cheek. She feels herself fall, as if in slow motion, caught be the dryad who brought her.

"Sleep." Whispers the maiden.

❀ ❀ ❀ ❀ ❀

B'ian paces the forest outside the Den. The enchantment was cast to protect the Kraeken from dragons, now he bargains with one. It is almost too much. He stops in his tracks, catching a dragon's scent.

What appears is not a dragon, but a woman. Shorter than him by a head, with long blue-green hair. Her clothes are simple, leggings worn beneath a light gown. Her whole bearing is regal. Even as the alpha of the Wolf clan, he feels a powerful desire to bow to her on bended knee.

"What is your decision?" Her voice is low for a woman, strong and steady.

"The Wolves will protect the cave for a full day and night. No more, no less."

She bows to him and departs. No extra words. No platitudes.

He watches her leave and glances overhead, wondering where the dragon was that watched the interaction.

Cate zooms out of the scene, keenly aware that it is a dream but one in which she has no control. Her consciousness follows the woman.

In a cave, bedecked more like a house than a cavern in the woods, the woman moves among tables. On a cooper pedestal, sitting in the middle of the floor, is the pulsing green stone.

A young woman enters carrying firewood. She is lean, athletic, with dirty blonde hair tied back in a rough braid. "When will the others arrive?"

"The day after tomorrow." The woman turns to gaze at the girl storing the wood. "Promise me you will follow the plan."

"I promise. I know what this means."

"Veralyn, stay near Arraniean. He has sworn to protect you."

"I would even if he hadn't."

The woman nods once and returns to the tables, her hands moving among vials.

Cate struggles to wake up but cannot. The scenery shifts. The woman with the light blue-green hair argues with a young Elf maiden. Both are angry enough that they no longer hear each other. "Then, I do not need you. We will end this war on our own." The woman storms away from the Elf maiden, leaving her on her knees in tears.

Cate rolls over and rests her head on Baen's bare chest. His eyes open and the grip on her waist tightens. "Just a little more sleep." His eyes close. Coyly glancing at him, she lightly toys with the fine hair on his chest. "You're making this difficult." His other arm comes around her and he lifts her on top of him, their faces close together. His mouth finds hers. It's like her body ignites on fire, though thankfully, it doesn't. The kiss starts deep and passionate, then softens until he releases her. She blushes and quickly leaves the bed. "We didn't...?"

He smiles and it overtakes his face. "We didn't, though it was hard not to."

Cate jumps from the scene, floating above it, and realizes that it isn't her and Baen – it's the woman and B'ian.

She's standing over the stone. Beside her is a Drow and human. Each have their fingers resting on the pulsing rock. Words rain in torrents from their mouths, as the stone gets brighter and brighter.

At the far end of the cavern, the girl slips inside. Staying close to the wall, she squats down and watches. Her eyes make contact with Cate hovering by the tables.

❋ ❋ ❋ ❋ ❋

Viggo has slept more in the last two months than the last two years. Every time he closes his eyes, Cate waits for him in the Dream.

They golfed, swam, hiked, drew, ate, and even danced. Never has he gotten to know a girl so well, or like her so much.

Every moment with her is delightful torture as he holds himself back, teasing her with light touches and stolen kisses. All knowing that in six short months, she'll be his.

CHAPTER 19

Elar clenches his fists. He's waited long enough. Before the guard opens the door to drop off food and scrolls, he employs a cloaking spell. After that, it's simple to slip out and up the steps.

He first follows Rook, then Channa but neither leads him to Cate. It takes tracking Baen before he finds Cate's apartment. "Show yourself." Baen growls. Elar drops the spell and enters the chambers. "Took you long enough. I thought the threat of leaving us alone would be enough."

"Where is Cate?"

"Sleeping. This way." Baen leads him to the first door in the hall. "She's been sleeping for two months. Rook says it's the effect of a Somnolent tree."

"Where did she run into one?"

"You know that Dwarven treasure box with the seed? Yeah, well… it was a Somnolent seed and its Mother found us."

Elar opens the door and sits beside Cate on the bed. She resembles the tale of the maiden who slept after pricking her finger – vulnerable and beautiful. He gently rests his fingers against her wrist to feel her pulse, then lightly touches her forehead and cheek.

Magic pulses beneath her skin. If he can disrupt the magic, he should be able to wake her. Baen bares his teeth from the doorway. He's had Cate to himself for three months, letting anyone touch her is like cutting his own flesh. "I'll wait in the other room."

Elar removes a needle hidden in the hem of his sleeve and pricks his finger, then hers. Her blood is slow and thick. Pressing the cuts together, he patiently waits for each heartbeat to push a little of his blood into her and a little of hers into him.

After an hour, he seals both cuts, closes his eyes and calls to the magic in his blood. It is faint in her veins – extraordinarily little, but enough, he hopes.

Cate grimaces. Closing his eyes, he lets his soul call out to hers while using his magic to wake her. Slowly, her pulse quickens. What was sluggish now naturally flows. He opens his eyes and checks her pulse.

The magic is fading but not fast enough. Removing the needle, he pricks all ten of her fingers, watching as little swells of blood blossom. Using a cloth, he gently wipes them away and repeats the prick if they start to close.

Still not fast enough.

He bites his top and bottom lip, then bites hers. Pressing their lips together, he mixes her blood with his. This process is more effective, and he admits – more enjoyable. Her eyes flutter open, and he kisses her for real.

Ending the kiss, he wraps his arms around her. It has been so long. His eyes feel heavy. He can no longer keep them open.

Cate cries out and Baen rushes in as Elar collapses. She's too weak to help. Baen carries the Elf to his room and lays him on the bed. Returning to Cate, he spies the damage to her fingers and mouth.

"He must have exchanged blood with you."

"Why?" Her voice is hoarse with disuse.

"To wake you." He helps her sit, then brings a bowl of broth and a glass of ginger ale. "Channa has been taking care of you physically, while you slept, but it was hard to get you to eat anything. Take it slow."

Cate nods, accepting his help to hold the bowl while she sips. "How long did I sleep?"

"A little over two months."

"What? Why didn't anyone wake me sooner?"

"We tried." Baen's thumb gently rubs across her wounded lips, wiping away broth. "Maybe it takes Elven magic, not Drow. Whatever it was, it worked. I thought you'd sleep a hundred years."

"It feels like I slept a hundred years. Is Elar free, what happened?"

"I think he escaped. After you opened the box, the dryad vanished with you. Not long after, she returned with you sleeping in her arms. She said it was your reward." He sets the empty broth bowl down. "I'm glad you're awake. Want me to draw a bath for you? I think you'll be too weak to shower for a while yet."

"Please." Images from her dreams replay in her mind. Two months, it feels like two lifetimes. Was the gift these dreams? What was real and what wasn't? She blushes thinking of the time she spent with Viggo – was that only wishful thinking? And the times she was another woman in a wolf's arms.

Her fingertips and lips ache. What did Elar do to wake her? Whatever it was, she owes him.

Elar knows he is dreaming. It is not a dream from which he can willingly wake. Below him is the battle of shadows. Death reaps on all sides. The hardest hit are the Elves.

It's like watching stars disappear from the night sky. Brilliant, flashing – empty. His heart weeps for the loss. Seeing it, he understands the order to withdraw. Elves do not reproduce quickly, like humans. Yet, looking at holes left in the lines, he also understands the resentment of the other races. If the Elves had stayed, what would have been the result? Would the dragon spell have been cast?

A woman with bluish-green hair stands in challenge before the Elf court in a multicolored gown, a sword on her hip and a bow on her back. The weapons are not her power – fire dances over her open palms.

"It is neither cowardice nor deceit to withdraw." Speaks the Elk King.

The fire dances high and then vanishes. The woman's deep voice is strong and commanding. "Only when you have no fear of death are you free to bravely act. As of now, the Elves are no longer part of the alliance." The woman turns to leave and Elar can clearly see her face. Though beautiful, it's her emerald eyes that draw him.

"Wait." The woman stops but does not face the council. The Elf queen stands to her full imposing height. "Take this stone. Though we cannot participate in casting the spell, we can give you an amplifier to intensify the magic."

The woman accepts the large green stone. At her touch, it pulses as if with a heartbeat all its own. The color and intensity match her gaze. "Your gift is accepted with its intention. We will end the dragon threat."

"Delay it, perhaps. You cannot end it without destroying dragon-kind."

A single tear rolls down the imposing woman's cheek to fall on the Elves' gift.

Elar had known the Elves were not part of the spell that cast dragon souls into humans; but he had not known the Queen was responsible for gifting the Stone. Interesting gift the dryads gave, to experience the past through dream.

❀ ❀ ❀ ❀ ❀

Cate leans against the wall. The dryad's magic kept her body safe during sleep, and the Drow's magic kept her nourished. But, still, she lacks stamina. Gathering her energy, she completes the walk to the main room and sits on the couch.

Baen has a plate of mashed potatoes with mixed vegetables and a small side of lean beef waiting for her. He's already cut the meat and drizzled it with barbeque sauce. It tastes wonderful!

She slowly savors each bite. When she's done, he clears the plate and leaves a tall glass of ginger ale. The carbonation helps her stomach, and the sugar gives her much needed calories. "Thank you for taking care of me."

He smiles and her treacherous heart beats faster. "You're welcome. Have you come up with an idea to save the Elf? The trial's at the end of the week."

"How? I've been asleep! How was I supposed to prepare? Did you find any leads, anything I can use?" Panic swells in her chest, and a lump in her throat chokes her at the realization of how little time left she has to save Elar, find the dragon stones and rid herself of an unwanted marriage.

CHAPTER 20

When she'd made the request, Rook thought her insane. Channa laughed. But, this morning, each brought gifts – clothes and jewelry.

Feeling stronger, more vital than ever, she slips into a Drow made black dress and a pair of matching leggings, then slides her feet into boots with a low heel and puts on bold hoops with stars dangling from them and a star choker. She gathers her hair into a high ponytail, then paints her lips with a deep shade of red.

No matter what happens, she's going to look good doing it.

Elar sleeps on Baen's bed. Where he's been since he woke her. She lightly touches Elar's sweeping cheek bone, then the edge of his ear to end at its tip. "This time, I'll save you."

More resolved than moments before, she leaves the apartment. Baen doesn't say a thing. He falls in step behind her. At the forest floor, they're met by Rook and the entire Drow Council.

They too had thought her request a joke. Why would she risk her life to save an Elf? They'd tried to talk her out of it and failed. No amount of negotiation would stop her from her choice nor their enforcement of Elar's crime.

This is the only way.

The walk to the mountain entrance takes an hour. The simplicity of the entrance – just an open doorway, framed by a stone arch carved with vines – feels anticlimactic. They enter, one-by-one.

Gently, the narrow tunnel slopes upward. The walk feels like it takes a lifetime. They enter a vast cavern, the floor of which is a series of concentric rings, held together by a bridge at each cardinal direction, with an endless drop beneath.

The Council solemnly marches to stand on the second ring. Drow elders fill the third, and the last ring, which is at the wall of the cavern, fills with onlookers. Rook addresses Baen. "You may stay at her side, as her attendant. I warn you, do not touch the throne." To Cate, he whispers, "Are you ready?"

She nods.

Rook faces the gathered assembly. "The acting representative of Elar, accursed Elf accused of treason and trespassing, has requested to forego the trial, and prove his innocence by the Obsidian Throne. Do you concede to the throne's decision?"

When the echo of his voice fades, the Council answers in unison, "We abide by the throne."

Cate takes that as her cue. With Baen two steps behind, she confidently strides across the stone bridges, passing each circle until she reaches the center. At the heart, squats an imposing obsidian throne. It glistens in the fey light.

Taking a deep breath, she steps up to it, turns, takes a deep steadying breath, and sits.

It takes a second to realize that her spirit has been transported somewhere else. Snow swirls around her with icy gusts, her clothes batter her legs, and her ponytail whips her eyes. Lifting her arm for protection, she strides forward.

This must be part of the test. At any rate, she's still alive.

Leaning into the wind, she crosses an empty expanse for what feels like days. At length, she stands before an imposing tower. No other buildings, just the tower. Pushing open the door, she stumbles inside.

Her skin burns from the wind and cold. Blinking against darkness, she spies the vague outline of a winding staircase. Straightening her clothes and hair, she slowly ascends until she reaches the tower top. Throwing open a trap door, she climbs outside.

The sky is clear, and stars brightly sparkle. It's as if she's standing in the middle of space. The wind and snow are far beneath. On this platform, there's only silence and a giant mirror. Haltingly, she stands before it.

At first, she sees a reflection of herself, then the image changes to her mother. She reaches out and gently touches her mother's face. "Mom." She brokenly whispers.

The image shifts into a tall lean man with white-blonde hair and amber eyes. He has high cheekbones and ears that end in tips. Cate blinks, wondering who he could be. His skin has a slight blue hue and he's wearing black armor. He smiles at her; it isn't a comforting expression.

His image wavers, replaced by a woman with bluish-green hair and emerald-green eyes. Cate saw this woman in her dreams. Why is she in the mirror?

The tower shakes with a sound like thunder. She rushes to the wall, holding tightly to the stone as she peers below. A massive white dragon bellows from the ground. When she looks back, the mirror is gone.

Jumping through the trapdoor, Cate races down the stairs, holding on to the railing to keep from falling. The tower shakes again, debris rattles loose from stones. At any moment, the dragon could bring the tower down.

Racing through the open door into the howling wind, Cate stops at the dragon's claws. They are as tall as she is. The dragon lowers its head, peering at her with an eye the size of a car. "I am the Guardian. Who dares to enter my refuge?" Its voice rattles the bones in her body.

"I am Cate. I sit on the Obsidian Throne." Cate's eyes shift from human to dragon. Fire erupts from her mouth and dances over her body. "I am the bearer of Rathleon's soul."

The white dragon steps back. Its print left in the snow is deep enough Cate could break a leg if she fell in it. "Is it time, finally, to end this curse?"

"You are no more cursed than any other of our kind. Veralyn was to give you a piece of the Stone. Where is it?" The voice speaking is no longer Cate's.

The dragon extends its foot to Cate. There's a green pulsing stone embedded in its claw. "If you can remove it, it is yours. If you cannot, you die."

Stepping close to the stone, Cate examines how it is set in the nail. It looks like someone melted it there. There's no metal or anything holding it in place.

Deeply inhaling, she exhales white-hot fire. The nail reddens, the snow around it steams, but the Stone stays in place. Light-headed, Cate staggers. The dragon taps its claw in front of her, "I'll give you two more attempts."

Glancing about, there is nothing to use to pry it loose. "Dragon, please set your nail in front of me so that I can better see it."

The dragon complies, the stone is set at the height of Cate's head. Not afraid of residual heat, Cate reaches out and rubs her fingers along it. The stone doesn't only seem fused, it seems part of the nail. How can she remove it?

Quaerere, the thought forms in her mind as she imagines a tool like a knife or flathead screwdriver, something to use to dig at the edges of the stone. From out of the howling wind, a stone implement hurtles her way. She opens her hand in time to catch it; it looks like a mix between a knife and screwdriver.

Too focused to think about how the item came to her, she sets to working the edges of the stone attempting to loosen its setting in the talon. Around and around, she goes, chipping at the nail.

Nothing.

"Second attempt failed." The dragon's voice showers her from above.

Cate's hands hurt from the cold. There must be a way. Maybe she could freeze the talon and shatter it? But it's already so cold, if it hasn't frozen already, would it?

Incutio. Snow swirls around her until there is nothing more than white. Gathering it into a mass, she hurtles it at the nail blasting it repeatedly. Then, she picks up the screwdriver knife and hammers at it. It cracks but doesn't shatter. The stone pulses in the talon, undisturbed.

"Third attempt failed."

The dragon lifts its foot. Cate tries to run, but the dragon stomps her to the ground before she even takes a step. Pain shoots through her bones. Is this how she's going to die? The weight is too much, she can't breathe.

The foot lifts and Cate pushes to her knees, her chest heaves as she sucks in air. *Tuero*. A pulsing green shield surrounds her. The dragon's foot presses down. The shield sags like a bubble but doesn't burst. Cate struggles to her knees. "Please, I need the Stone." The words come out as pained gasps.

The dragon's talon taps the shield. Testing its strength. It pushes harder and Cate screams, the strength of her newly awoken magic waning. The bubble shrinks. There's no way out. Smaller. Smaller. It now only covers her body by an inch.

Is this really how I die?

Instinctually, she reaches up to grab the talon as the dragon bursts the shield. Cold, hard, it pushes her deep into the snow. No, this is not how I die. I do not end here! Releasing pent up fear and rage, she screams and with her arms wrapped around the talon puts her shoulder against it and pulls. Something pops, cracks – hot rain showers her.

The snow around her vanishes. The wind falls silent. A roar echoes in her ears as she opens her eyes. In her hands is a large pulsing stone, drops of deep red blood steam from it. Blinking, she realizes she sits on the Obsidian Throne. Voices echo throughout the cavern, chanting. The words are foreign, but their meaning is clear. "Long live the Queen."

❀ ❀ ❀ ❀ ❀

Kith wakes in a cold sweat. His heart thumps a wild rhythm. Grabbing a sketchbook and pencil, his hand moves across the page with frantic intensity.

Since the engagement party, he'd been unsure which path Cate would take. Even now, a parallel path lies close to her steps. Will she agree to the Dragotian plan or set the dragons free?

He sets down the pencil and looks at the page. Cate stands in front of a large throne surrounded by Drow. In her hand, she holds a stone half the size of a football.

Kith's shoulders sag. She's successfully acquired one of the three Dragon Stones. Setting the sketch down, he crosses the room and opens the biometric safe in his closet. Retrieving an envelope, he licks dry lips and leaves the bedroom.

He finds Emily in the living room distracting herself with a true crime show on TV. He sits beside her and hands her the envelope.

"What's this?"

"I drew it after you left. I thought it might be important in the future, and I think that time is now. Open it."

Turning off the TV, she opens the manilla envelope and slides a piece of sketch paper out. The picture is of her – and her parents – in front of the cottage she grew up in. Tears well in her eyes. She hasn't seen her parents since she made the decision to leave.

Her fingers lightly trace over their faces. Painfully accurate, every detail. "You knew?"

"Not at first. It took me a little while to understand." He tucks her hair behind her ears. "You have none of the traits."

She sobs. "Why now?"

"Because this is a key to where Cate is."

Emily grabs Kith's hand. "Where?"

"Do you know where the Drow keep a large black throne? It is in a cavern, the floor of which is concentric rings." He can tell Emily is thinking, accessing memories she tucked away long ago. Setting the sketch on a side table, she blows her nose and wipes her tears.

Taking a ragged breath, she nods. "I think so but there's no way there, not unless a Traveler can take us."

"Exactly what I was thinking, think of a location near this place that has a reflective surface, like a big pool of water."

※ ※ ※ ※ ※

Cate sinks into the tub, hot water covers everything up to her chin. Her hair floats about her. Even though she hadn't really been in snow, hadn't really been near frostbite, she felt it. She felt colder than she's ever been.

She shivers, nausea ripples through her in waves. The walk back had been unreal. In her hands, she carried one of the Dragon Stones – a pulsing magic relic. She'd sat on the Obsidian Throne and lived.

She'd survived. Somehow, she'd ripped the dragon's talon off and when she woke the stone remained.

Slipping beneath the water, she runs her hands through her hair removing blood and soap. Like the Stone, when she came to, hot dragon's blood dotted her body. Breaching the surface, she takes a breath.

Another ripple of nausea. Stepping from the water, she dries off and puts on a soft, thick robe wrapping her hair in a towel. She glances at the Stone on the bathroom counter. She'd cleaned it first. It hadn't felt right leaving it soiled.

Her body tingles as her fingers lightly rest on it. She closes her eyes. It's like she's an empty glass and touching the Stone fills her. Picking it up, she carries it into her room. Setting it on the bed, she lies beside it and closes her eyes.

Viggo pulls her into his arms, wrapping her in a tight embrace. He gently kisses the top of her head. "Where have you been?"

"I don't know."

He laughs, tipping her head to smother her mouth with his. The kiss is warm, filled with desire. His hands move over her back to rest in her hair, his fingers touch her ears. He opens his eyes; his gaze holds hers. "What have you done?"

He pushes back her hair. His eyes rove her features. "What is this?"

She wakes up with a start. Pulling the towel from her head, she crosses to the dresser and the mirror on top of it. Panic swells in her chest. What is going on? She turns her head to look at her left, then right ears. They're no longer rounded but upswept in a graceful curve. Leaning close to the mirror, she examines her complexion.

There's a slight bluish hue to it. She grabs her hair searching for the driest piece. It's paler than it used to be. Pulling her hair to the side, she drops her robe to examine her scales. Blue-green iridescent scales several inches wide line her spine. At least they haven't changed.

She picks up the robe as the bedroom door opens. Pressing it to her front, she screams, "Shut the door!"

Baen stammers something, his eyes locked on her bare back.

"Shut the door!"

It slams shut. Cate takes a deep breath and slides the robe on. Embarrassed and angry, she yanks the door open. Baen stands in the hall, pink tinges his cheeks and neck. "Sorry…."

"What do you want?"

"Rook is here with some of the Council Members. I'm sorry, Cate. I thought you were sleeping. I was going to…."

"Knock next time." She returns to her room, dresses, and combs her hair. Tired, nauseous, and irritated by having to meet with anyone, she enters the main room of the apartment.

Rook leans against the far wall while two Council members sit on the couch. One is a man who looks to be in his mid-thirties while the other is a woman who looks to be in her late twenties. Both are beautiful with the signature white-blonde hair of the Drow. They stand as she enters.

"Hi." She feels more than a little awkward, unsure how to address them.

Rook comes to her aid. "Cate, this is Smoke and Simall." Smoke bows, his silver eyes hold hers for a second longer than is comfortable. Simall bows next, her pale blue eyes make Cate feel like she is under a microscope. When Cate sits, they sit.

"What brings you?"

"Your security." Simall's voice is refined, her manner of speech soft.

"Though you have a wolf at your side, the Council suggests you accept an elite corps of bodyguards." Smoke's eyes lift to the hall behind Cate. She knows Baen stands there without even looking.

"I'm good, thanks."

Smoke smiles. His look gives her chills. "With due respect, *your majesty*, you now belong to the Drow. You are a treasure to be protected."

Cate laughs, the smile on her face far from welcoming. "Whatever. See yourselves out."

"What did you think would happen if you survived the Obsidian Throne?"

Cate cocks her head, her eyes narrow as she thinks of her response to Simall. "That Elar would be found innocent, and we would continue our search for the Dragon Stones."

"Why do you want the Stones?" Simall's tone is purely neutral.

"To free the dragons so I don't have to get married."

Simall laughs. The sound, though innocent, is hurtful. Cate pushes to her feet and Simall waves her back. "I apologize, your majesty. With your new position, no one can force you into anything. You have every Drow on this planet at your beck-and-call. Why do you need to fear an unwanted marriage? As for the Dragon Stones, they are power. Power is good in measured doses, too much becomes destructive."

"Are you telling me to give up on finding the Stones?"

"Yes."

"I won't. Freeing the dragons isn't just about getting out of an arranged marriage. It's the right thing to do."

"Is it?" Smoke's eyes linger on Baen's shadow. "Why do you think the Kraeken were created? Why do you think the wolf aids you?"

Cate glances back. Baen's eyes meet hers. "They protected people from dragons." Smoke nods, waiting for her to come to the same conclusion he has. "Are you saying that Baen's only helping me so that I can bring back the dragons and a reason for the Kraeken to exist?"

"Is that so far-fetched?" Smoke directs his next question to Baen. "Tell us, what is the state of the Kraeken clans? How many born can shapeshift?"

"That's none of your business." Baen's response is more of a growl, than a sentence. Smoke and Simall let it hang in the air.

Rook claps his hands, startling everyone. "Get some rest, your majesty. Tomorrow night there will be a banquet to celebrate your ascension. After that, we can discuss your security. In the meantime, Smoke and Simall will add trusted members of the three corps to oversee your physical security – outside the apartment."

It's a clear dismissal. Smoke and Simall bow to Cate, as they are ushered out the door by Rook. When it's quiet, Baen joins her.

"Is it true?"

He doesn't need to ask what. He knows what she's asking. "I am helping you because I want to and because v'Lana asked. As for my mother's reasons, I do not know." He sits on the table in front of her chair. "Since finding you in the ravine with the Watchers on your trail, I have wanted to help you. That is the truth."

"Why?"

He smirks and gives a little self-deprecating laugh. "You are different. Strong-willed, opinionated, beautiful, and brave. Even without being a dragon, I would find you attractive." His eyes trace the new lines of her cheekbones and ears, following the length of her hair with its new white-blonde highlights. "It's just… you're engaged, and not even eighteen. I have no right." Cate stands and he grabs her wrist. She looks at his hand. "Even though I have no right, I want to stay by your side."

"Why? I don't even know who or what I am anymore."

His smirk lifts into a smile. "You're part Drow. Siting on the Obsidian Throne brought it out and you're dragon-souled. I don't think there is another person like you in this world." Cate's heart tightens, remembering the way Viggo reacted to her ears in the dream. Was that only her subconscious or was that really how he felt? Why did his reaction hurt so much? It's not like they're really a couple.

"You are beautiful."

Cate gently removes his hand from her wrist. "Thanks." She takes a mind clearing breath. "For everything." Even if she doesn't believe it, hearing it helps.

CHAPTER 21

A push kick sends the standalone kick bag into the far wall. Viggo looks for something else to hit, but he's demolished the gym. He hadn't even stopped to wrap his hands; the throb of his knuckles is a welcome distraction.

What was she thinking? Pulling off his sweat-soaked shirt, he heads to the shower. He catches a glimpse of his scales in the reflection. An image of Cate's scales fills his mind. The feel of upswept ears lingers on his fingers.

Disgusted, he strips and steps into a steaming shower. Water traces the curves of his lean muscles, washing away the feeling and memory. The most real part about the last few months was the Dream and falling in love with Cate. Not because he had to, but because he wanted to.

Learning that she can't bowl, hates fish, loves instrumental music, is endearingly clumsy, stunning under the moonlight, and can't tell a joke. He yearns to spend every moment with her.

He turns off the shower and pushes wet hair from his face. There's no way she can be an Elf or Drow. The bearer of a dragon's soul must be human.

Why then had it felt like the Dream?

To hell with IlliaVaa's Truth. It's already been months, when will Cate return?

❋ ❋ ❋ ❋ ❋

IlliaVaa gathers the playing cards together after another losing round of solitaire. Since Viggo returned to the city, the estate's been a little too quiet. Only Ka'Leel's visits provide any distraction.

They'd first met in college, but lost track after she quit. Too many people, too many Truths. It made her head spin. She shuffles the cards. Most people shine with a myriad of color, their Truths undecided. Not Ka'Leel. He shines brightly, an enigmatic bluish-white. It draws people to him.

Ka'Lea, on the other hand, shines just as bright but with an orange-tinged light. It makes people wary of her, and they should be. Where Ka'Leel is warm and genuinely caring, Ka'Lea is cold and self-absorbed. For twins, they couldn't be more opposite in temperament and more alike in looks.

IlliaVaa sets the cards and glances at the cup of tea across from her. It had been hot two hours ago. Unlike a Dreamer, she can't see the future, but her Gift sometimes edges that boundary. The patio door opens. "Please, join me. I sent Hunter on an errand, so we won't be bothered." A leggy blonde with Nordic good looks sits across from her. "I'm IlliaVaa."

"Tatiana."

"Ah yes, Cate's cousin. You came with Kith a few months ago. How is he? And the clan?"

Tatiana glances at the cold tea and IlliaVaa's red tinged hands. She's been outside for a while. "Where's Cate?"

"Training."

"Both of us know that's a lie."

IlliaVaa smiles, the look on her face patronizing. "It is Truth. She is training, just not with any Dragotian. I am sure Kith has Dreamed as much or he wouldn't send you as regularly as he has to check on us." She glances at the low hanging clouds. Snow is coming. Hunter will be back soon. Her eyes shift to dragon as her gaze returns to Tatiana. "What an interesting role you have should Cate succeed. Seek the eggs and you will understand." Her eyes shift back to human, and she closes them for a second to reorient herself. "Go Cousin."

Tatiana stands. "Cousin? What do you mean if Cate succeeds?"

"Our time is up. If you see Cate before I do, tell her I miss her." IlliaVaa gathers the cards, no longer feeling like a game of Solitaire. As a portal forms on the lawn, the backdoor clicks behind Tatiana.

IlliaVaa tucks the cards in her pocket and dumps the cold tea on the lawn. Dane catches her eye and gives her a nod, stepping aside from the portal as Hunter emerges. The men don't say a word to each other. With a quick smile, aimed at her, Dane disappears through the portal, and it winks out.

"Got everything you wanted." Hunter shows her the bags in his hands. "It's too much food for the two of us."

IlliaVaa takes bags from his hand. "But you're such a good cook and I hate eating Thanksgiving at a restaurant. It makes me want to throw-up what I just ate, seeing all those Truths."

Hunter opens the door for her. The twins had been his salvation and condemnation. They'd shifted their father's attention, and when he'd reached puberty without any hint of scales, had freed him from their father's passion. They'd also become his wards, and he, their servant. He'd hated this house, hated its isolation. That was before their father died.

Now, it's his home. His place. Viggo despises it for the memories of their father. IlliaVaa sees it as her sanctuary, a place to freely breathe, a stop-over in life. While he, he sees it as his home. It's easy to take care of your home, and those who fill it.

Hunter sets the groceries on the counter. "Did that girl say Cate's okay?"

IlliaVaa hesitates, the refrigerator door open and a quart of eggnog in her hand. If Hunter saw her, did Dane? "No, they don't know where she is either."

"You sure she is safe?"

She shrugs and puts the quart on the shelf, then shuts the door. "The Truth is that she needs to be on her own right now. I don't know if she's safe or who she's with, except maybe that Wolf." IlliaVaa empties the contents of the bag on the island. "You know what Father wanted and what Viggo is trying to fulfill, right?"

Hunter sits at the island. "Yeah."

"Well, what if Cate doesn't agree with their plan?"

"I'd rather like that. I'm not good with my family becoming hosted souls."

IlliaVaa warmly smiles. "Me neither."

"So, you are playing both sides."

With a bitter laugh, IlliaVaa shakes her head, ebony curls bounce on her shoulders. "I am playing the only side I can. Truth must win out – it is my lot in life." Hunter comes around the island and wraps his sister in his arms. If he could, he'd protect her from the Truth, but it is the one thing he can never do.

Tatiana covers the mirror in her room, her hand on her chest feeling her heart race. It'd been close. What would have happened if she'd been caught? Anything? Nothing?

The first time she saw Dane, she'd felt a shudder of revulsion. There's something about that dark-haired perfectly attired man that makes her think of a serial killer.

IlliaVaa had called her cousin. It'd thrown her off until she realized that the marriage would make them in-laws. "What was that about eggs?"

Leaving her room, she grabs a soda from the fridge. As she pops the tab, there's a knock at the door. Chugging the drink, she unlocks it. It pushes open, knocking her backwards. She splutters, most of the soda covers her with what remains in the can spilling on the ground. Two long-haired, heavily bearded men in black barrel inside. "Take her."

She kicks her assailant in the groin. He grunts but pushes forward. He wraps his arms around her, pulling her back to his chest. Her teeth lodge in his arm. He doesn't even flinch. The first man returns. "No one else is home. Let's go."

Tatiana screams, hoping someone will hear her, as they drag her from the house and into a black SUV with dark tinted windows. Lodged between the two men on the back seat, she struggles to no avail. The engine revs and the car takes off. Her neighborhood passes by, then the town, then they are on the dark highway.

"Why are you doing this?"

"It would be better if she were quiet." The driver's voice is soft and deep.

The man next to her removes a cloth from his pocket. She tries to cover her mouth with her hands, but even with her dragon-strength he is able to pull them aside and place it over her mouth and nose.

In short order the world around her collapses and her eyes close.

Waking to a throbbing headache and cotton mouth, Tatiana squints against the light. Shading her eyes with her hand, she studies the small windowless room. A cot, no blankets, with a sink and a toilet.

It looks everything like a jail cell.

"Hey!" She screams and immediately regrets it. Her head feels like it's going to fall off her neck. "Hey."

The door to the room soundlessly opens. A woman stands outlined by light. Stocky, yet feminine, she steps inside and offers Tatiana a glass of water. "You'll feel better after drinking this."

Not caring if it's poisoned, she just wants her head to stop aching, Tatiana guzzles the water. "Who are you? Where am I? Why did you kidnap me?"

"I'm U'Sana. You are at my ancestral home. My father will answer the last question. I apologize for B'Rethle's ardor in applying the anesthetic. He's not the brightest of my brothers. You did take a chunk out of his arm though, so let's call it even."

"Call it even? You kidnapped me and we're supposed to call it even?"

U'Sana smiles and steps out of the room. "Come with me."

Staggering to her feet, Tatiana follows U'Sana down a long hallway to an elevator. Clutching the handrails, she feels like her knees are going to give when the box moves. She almost retches when it lurches to a stop. The doors open and she exits.

They stand in a massive atrium at the center of a mansion. The interior walls are far enough away that it appears as if they stand in a forest.

"Impressive, isn't it?"

"Yeah." Whatever was in the water is starting to make her headache go away. U'Sana leads her to a series of couches in the middle of the trees. A broad-chested man with hair curling around the collar of his shirt and at the base of his sleeves stands to greet her.

"Welcome. I apologize for the crude way in which you came. I am U'Sar, head of the Bear clan."

Light bulbs go off in Tatiana's head. No wonder she couldn't escape. "Why am I here?"

"Please, sit." U'Sar gestures to a couch as he sits and crosses one leg over the other. Tatiana chooses the couch opposite him. "U'Sana gets her another drink. Her eyes show the medication hasn't worn off yet." The girl dashes through the trees and out of sight. "May I say that even disheveled, you are beautiful."

"No."

U'Sar laughs, a hearty belly-shaking laugh. "Have you considered marrying outside your clan?"

"No."

"Will you give me more than one-word answers?"

"Depends on your question."

"Are you familiar with the marriage agreement of the Enderen and Dragotian clans?"

"Yes."

"Hmmm, do you know why the agreement was made?"

"Because two clan leaders wanted their kids to marry."

U'Sar growls, his lips curl into a frown. "You are smarter than that even with a throbbing headache. The real reason?"

"Something to do with the dragon spell originally cast a thousand years ago." U'Sana returns and Tatiana downs the proffered glass of water. Coughing, she glares at the were-bear. "Is that what you wanted?"

U'Sar roars with laughter and U'Sana joins him, her beady eyes darting between her father and Tatiana. "Sani, take our guest back to her room. She's a Traveler, don't let her near any reflective surfaces."

"Yes, Father."

"That's it! You just wanted to ask me if I knew about the marriage agreement and you're locking me up again?"

"I like her spirit." Tatiana turns at the sound of a melodically low female voice. A woman emerges from the trees, tall, muscular, with tawny red hair. "Perhaps you were right, U'Sar." She leans against the couch, arms crossed under an impressive bosom.

"Who're you?"

"Someone preparing for war and looking for allies. U'Sar, give her the information we've gathered and return her to her family. I don't want anyone on our side who was forced to join."

"As you wish." U'Sar pushes to his feet and leads Tatiana through the atrium. She glances back at the red-haired woman only to find she's already gone.

CHAPTER 22

Cate stands naked before the mirror. She doesn't look like herself, or at least the memory of herself. Months under the Dryad's spell removed the fat from her body. Lean, with bluish skin, her scales glittering along her spine, her hair with strands of white, and her ears upswept – she is no longer an awkward teen.

She grimaces at the dress draped over the edge of her bed. Knee-length, with a deep V-neck in the front and plunging back. Not something she would ever pick for herself. Choosing instead black pants and a black tank top, she braids her hair and pins it like a crown. Dressed, she slips her feet into black heels and opens the door.

Elar stands with his hand raised to knock. His mouth falls open at the sight of her, as hers falls open at the sight of him. "You're awake!"

He lowers his hand and steps forward; she steps back making space for him in her room. He quietly shuts the door. His silver eyes take in her appearance from head to toe. "Tell me everything."

She sits on the bed and he beside her, reciting the trial of the Obsidian Throne. "When I returned, I looked like this."

He gently touches an upswept ear, his lips curve into a rare smile. "You are brave and loyal. Thank you."

She blushes. "You're welcome and, don't forget, I found one of the Stones."

There's a knock at her door. She jumps to her feet. "I nearly forgot the coronation!"

Elar's smile widens. "The dress is far more suited to a coronation. Shall I help you?"

Every bit of Cate's exposed skin flushes hot. "No, I'm not wearing that." She pulls open the door and Baen glances at her, then Elar.

"You're awake." Though his tone is flat, his eyes flash fire. "Smoke is about to tear down the apartment. Let's go."

Baen is dressed as a Drow bodyguard, in light black armor. He follows a step behind her. Two Drow, a male, and a female, wait for Cate at the door. They grimace at her appearance but say nothing. Elar's smile is gone as he brings up the rear of Cate's entourage.

It's like a dream. Something happening to someone else. She steps onto a palanquin carried by four men. It barely rocks as they lift it. Baen walks on one side and Elar the other.

Throughout the ride, she reminds herself to breathe – long, slow breaths. More people than the Frozen City can hold line their path. Some cheer, others stoically watch. At the mountain, Cate leaves the palanquin.

Instead of walking up to the throne, they take a dark path leading deep below it. She shivers. Elar reaches out to comfort her and Simall's cool voice stops him, "She will face far worse than cold."

Marching in silence, they reach the ceiling-less cathedral. Smoke bows, touches his heart and forehead, then enters. "Only her chosen guard may enter with her." Simall counsels, making the same gestures before stepping through an ornately carved doorway.

Elar coolly studies Cate, his silver eyes linger on her newly shaped lobes. "I cannot change what you went through to clear my name and I am wise enough to know second-guessing my past decisions benefits no one. Drow, dragon-souled or human, I am always your ally." His gaze shifts to Baen. With a brief nod by both, Elar enters the cathedral.

Cate takes a steadying breath, straightens her shoulders, and strides through the doorway with her head held high. Baen is an intimidating force at her heel.

Icy white lights hang from the stone walls, not touching the inky blackness above. Drow sit in pews on either side of the aisle. Cate doesn't look at any of them, her eyes focused on the narrow stone bridge before the first row of pews that leads to a rock pedestal on which the high priest waits in dark purple robes.

Reaching the bridge, she glances down. Only shadows greet her. Refusing to show any fear, she crosses the bridge and turns to face the assembled. Baen guards the bridge entrance, sword drawn and held at the ready.

The high priest raises his arms, head thrown back. "O goddess of the night, weaver of life's thread, devourer of the wicked, we ask that you acknowledge the rightful ruler of the Drow and bestow upon her your blessings."

A hushed silence falls. Nothing is happening.

Cate squints, trying to read the crowd. They all look up. Ever so slowly, as not to draw notice, she tilts her head. A wave of cold fear washes over her. She wants to scream but can't. Descending on a massive web is a white spider the size of a car. Swallowing a lump in her throat, she looks back at the crowd.

Goosebumps pepper her arms. By sheer willpower, she remains still. One white leg, then another settles on her shoulders. Her breathing comes short and shallow. A weight settles on her head, a spider silk crown, the legs lift and a silver substance weaves from one shoulder to another, bestowing a cape.

Finished with its task, the massive arachnid ascends its web and vanishes into darkness. The priest's voice rings like a bell, "Long live the Queen."

"Long live the Queen." Echoes in the chamber, filling the mountain halls. The Drow lift their heads, eyes shining.

Cate steps onto the bridge as white spiders the size of mid-size dogs climb from the shadows beneath to line the stone before the pews.

It's like living her best daydream and worst nightmare all at once. Baen drops to one knee, his hand over his heart as she reaches the cavern floor, "Until my death." His words are drowned out by the chorus of Drow voices as he falls into step behind her. She strides down the aisle and from the chapel.

In the dark hall, Rook bows low. "This way, my Queen." He touches his hand to a stone sigil, a door swings open. Cate and Baen follow inside to a lavishly decorated well-lit room. The door slides closed. "We'll wait here until the cathedral is cleared."

Cate does her best not to squeal, as she does a very unqueenly totally squeamish dance. Her hands go to her head to the spider woven crown and the cape on her shoulders. "Are there any on me?"

"They are the size of dogs. If they were on you, you'd know." Baen laughs.

"The goddess has never woven a crown or cape, only coronets. Her webs are fireproof, shatterproof, and... you may find the crown hard to remove."

"What do you mean?"

"It's naturally sticky."

"Great." Cate shivers. "Anything else?"

"Her blessing gives dominion over her children."

Cate levels Rook with a deadpan stare. "Are you telling me I can control spiders?"

"That's exactly what I am saying." His calculating eyes sweep her outfit. "Why did you not wear the dress?"

"Not age appropriate."

"It was intended to display your beauty and scales."

"My *beauty* can be shown without a revealing outfit."

"I agree." Baen chimes.

Rook glares at him and steps close enough that he is nearly nose to nose. "You know our laws well, wolf. As the first to take a life oath, no one may question your loyalty or remove you from her side. It was supposed to be Smoke."

Baen smirks and says nothing.

Baen crossed the line. He pledged his life to Cate, an unbreakable pledge sealed by coronation magic. Elar grinds his teeth. He knows full well how innocent Cate is. She sat on the throne only to save him; now, here she is, a dragon-souled Drow Queen with a werewolf bodyguard.

Resting near the mountain entrance with thousands of Drow, who await her appearance, he wonders if this was her fate all along. When he met her, she had been searching for an Elf to find the Dragon Stones. But, maybe, it had never been the Elves who could help her.

Why would Rathleon have entrusted the Stone to a race who betrayed her? Why had Rimalon not thought of this or had he always known and sent them north to find the Drow?

Time seems to stand still as a hush falls over the crowd. Wearing a sparkling spider-silk crown and royal cape, Cate emerges from the shadowy mountain doorway. Trailing her are Baen and Rook.

Her eyes scan the crowd until they find him. She holds his gaze for a split second, long enough for him to see the glimmering soul within. The transformation has not changed her. She is still Cate. With a confident stride, she glides through the crowd to her palanquin.

He can no longer see her over the heads of the crowd as sound returns with a frenzy of cheers. Under his breath, he casts a cloaking spell and wends his way to Cate's apartment.

❀ ❀ ❀ ❀ ❀

It had been nearly impossible to rid herself of Rook. Only with a promise to attend the coronation feast at sunset, wearing the dress, was she finally able to shoo him out. Baen closes the door, but it pushes open again before he can latch it.

Baen grabs an unseen body as he shoves the door closed. "You're lucky I know your scent." Elar drops his cloaking spell and narrows his eyes to the werewolf.

Baen loosens his grip, then finally releases him. Elar doesn't touch his neck. He gives no sign of injury, though red fingerprints mar his skin.

"I know a little about Drow coronation magic. With your oath, you will know whenever Cate is in danger or pain. You may even experience her more intense emotions."

Cate pauses in removing the cape. "Coronation magic?"

Elar's eyebrows rise. "You did not tell her? I am surprised that Rook was not forthcoming. When you left the pedestal, do you remember Baen taking a knee?" Cate's eyes shift from Elar to Baen. She nods. "At that moment, he pledged his life to you."

"You what?" The cape falls loose. "Why would you do that?"

"If I hadn't, Rook or another Drow would have. I couldn't see you bound to them. I…."

She lifts her hand to silence him, trying to understand what Elar said and what Baen said as the events of the coronation replay in her mind. She had been so concerned with the spiders, with surviving, that she hadn't even given Baen's fealty a second thought. "What about coronation magic?"

Elar picks up the cape and drapes it over the back of the couch. "There was little to do in jail but read. Coronation magic is especially potent for Drow. You even more so, blessed as you are by the goddess. Your *dro-sargtlin* is a life warrior roughly translated. You are linked. No matter where you are, he will feel you. If you are hurt, he will share your pain. Some books claim that a *dro-sargtlin* can also share your pleasure. Or your hate."

Cate shakes her head and retrieves the cape. "I can't deal with this right now. I have to get ready for the feast." Not wanting to believe anything Elar said, but by the look in Baen's eyes knowing it to be true, she walks into her room and closes the door.

"What was that?" Baen challenges.

"You tell me. She is engaged to be married. You say she is not free, that she is too young, yet here you are tying yourself to her in the most intimate way. How will you handle it when she lies with her husband?" Baen snarls and lunges, but Elar's too fast. He merely steps aside. "A horrible trick and you did not give her a choice. In the end, it will not be Cate who suffers."

"I will make sure she never suffers." Baen growls, his lips curl over sharp canines.

"To live is to suffer. No life is free of pain. It matters not if it is one hour or a thousand years in length." Elar lightly touches Baen's shoulder. "Whoever Cate chooses as her partner in life, you will stand by her side. Can you handle this?"

"I will have to."

Elar smirks. "You are honest, at least. As for me, I care not whether she is engaged nor whether you two are bonded." He runs his fingers over his tunic. "I must prepare for the feast."

CHAPTER 23

E lar wears all white, his long mahogany hair loose except for braids above either ear, his silver eyes sparkle as he bows. "May I escort you?"

She slips her hand onto his. The corners of his lips hint at a smile. "I appreciate Rook switched gowns." Blood-red, with a plunging back, it has a modest collar and a simple A-line skirt. The spider crown rests regally on top of loose curls through which the tips of her ears peek.

She smiles, feeling more at ease and lets him lead her to the main room. Baen holds open the door. Dressed all in black, he looks both dashing and menacing.

Every baker, every cook has been hard at work since the moment she survived the Obsidian throne to feed the populace of the Frozen City. Hues of violet soften the sky, as the sun sets behind the mountains. Thousands of twinkling lights float in the trees. There couldn't be a more magical night.

The head table sits on a platform so that all who attend can view the Queen. Cate takes a calming breath, as she focuses on not tripping over her skirt. Baen pulls out a chair for her and she carefully sits while he stands behind it, a looming shadow. His intense gaze studies the crowd. Elar sits on her right as Rook launches the festivities.

Cate's stomach growls. She's had almost nothing to eat all day. She digs into buttery mashed potatoes with a hint of garlic and perfectly seasoned asparagus.

Light conversation drones about them like a sweet cloud. Deviled eggs, rolls, ham, pineapple, chocolate covered strawberries – she leans back and quickly washes it down with what she believes is water.

"That wine is light but has a kick." Rook cautions. He signals and music washes over the crowd.

Elar extends his hand. "May I have this dance?"

Cate nervously looks over the crowd. Once she stands, all eyes will be on her. She swallows and places her hand on his. He rises and leads her from the platform.

Anyone eating, stops. Anyone talking, hushes. Taking her free hand, he places it on his shoulder, then slides his hand down to her waist. Gracefully, they dance across the forest floor, their eyes locked.

One song fades into another. Nothing exists but them.

The music stops. It takes a few seconds for either of them to notice. Someone stalks toward them from the edge of the tables. Tall with black hair, wearing a tuxedo.

A tuxedo? Cate blanches.

"Viggo?!" She lets go of Elar's hand, embarrassed as if she was doing something she shouldn't.

Baen growls, leaping the table to land lightly on his feet. He moves to block Viggo's path. Rook forestalls the Drow guards, curious about what is happening.

Viggo's dark-eyed gaze shifts between Cate and Elar, then back to Baen. "Step aside. This isn't about you, unless you make it."

"I don't take orders from you." Growls Baen.

"Let me see him." Baen hesitates, then moves a little, so that he isn't blocking her view. "What do you want?"

"To bring you home." His eyes move to her crown, and carefully study her appearance. His fists clench and his jaw tightens. "You look beautiful."

Cate pushes her hair behind her ears. "Are you sure about that?" She spins in a slow circle, showing him the scales that run the length of her spine and the bluish tint of her skin.

Dane pushes through the crowd, Cate's Dragon Stone in his hands. Cate's eyes widen, anger washing over her in hot waves. "That's mine!"

Viggo's smile is cold. "It'll be waiting for you at home."

"I said. THAT. IS. MINE." Cate's eyes shift from human to dragon. Bluish-green flames sprout from her mouth with every breath and cover her skin.

Spiders race through the forest en masse – reacting to her uncontrolled emotion. The world tilts, wine coursing through her system.

Smirking, Viggo whispers under his breath. Something... like a magical bubble... encircles Cate, smothering the flames. She collapses to the ground clutching at her throat, gasping.

Baen punches Viggo, catching him in the solar plexus, forcing him to suck in air. The bubble vanishes and Cate wheezes. Tears roll down her cheeks. She pushes to her knees and collapses as a scream rips from her.

Elar scoops her into his arms as she arches her back, wailing. With his eyes on Viggo, Baen calls for Smoke and Simall. Viggo quietly watches Cate in Elar's arms, as Dane creates a portal. "When you want the Stone, you know where it is." They step through and the portal closes to the sound of her screams.

Rook leads them to the Council Hall; it is closer than Cate's apartment. Elar places her on a couch. Her hands clutch the fabric, her nails gouge the wood. "Oh, it hurts." She pants, tears squeeze from beneath her closed lids. Her limbs shake as she rolls to the floor, arching her back.

Baen kneels in front of her, grabs her shoulders and looks into her eyes. There is no way what he is feeling can be happening. "Cate, look at me. Look at me!" He shakes her and she lifts her head. Her eyes find his. Dragon eyes. No trace of human stares back at him. Scales, petite blue-green scales, edge the corners of her eyes. The fine bones of her face are breaking.

He can feel it.

This is a transformation. Like when he changes from man to wolf. How? "Remember who you are. Remember what you are. You are human, Cate. Human." Her breathing is ragged and sharp. Her body's dumping adrenaline, the pain is receding, euphoria replacing it, as she succumbs. If he doesn't do something....

"Cate!" He pulls her to him. His lips find hers. Hungry, terrified, protective. His passion shocks her. She pulls away and slowly the little scales disappear. Her bones begin to mend.

She blinks, confused. He helps her to the couch. She plops down, her head in her hands. "Why'd you do that?'

"Well, it was kiss you or slap you."

"Neither was a good option." Elar interrupts.

"You should sleep. Your head will feel better when you wake."

Cate curls on the couch. Rook finds a blanket in a closet and covers her. "Who was that man?"

"Cate's fiancée." Baen answers.

"Interesting." Rook glances at Cate then quietly exits, leaving the queen with her sworn bodyguard and the Elf.

Viggo broods over the Dragon Stone resting on his desk. Every time he touches it, it flares with light. When he'd walked through the Drow, he kept hoping his dream of Cate had been only his imagination, that she couldn't have changed in appearance. But, she had.

Then, to see her in the arms of that Elf, his rage flared hotter than the sun. He'd used all his business skills to hide his emotions.

It didn't matter. In the end, she'd be his. At least, until they undid the spell. Then, *they* wouldn't be together, Xenothgorot and Rathleon would be.

He heaves a sigh and rests his hand on the Stone. Its magic makes his body thrum. For centuries, his family has worked to change Rathleon's spell and reunite her with Xenothgorot. Now that it is close at hand, he wonders if it is the right choice.

Shouldn't *he* be with the woman he loves? Why should he give up his life, his ability to touch and hold her, so Xenothgorot can be with the woman/dragon he loves?

And, what happened to Cate? Why was she screaming in pain? His spell shouldn't have harmed her, only removed the oxygen. He never would have smothered her. A little coughing was expected, but not pain. Not, the screams he heard when he left. Even now, they echo in his soul.

He lifts his hand from the stone. "She didn't try to argue or fight until she saw you. Until then, we were civil… even with how angry I was seeing her in someone else's arms. It was you." He pats the Stone and moves to lie down on his leather couch. "I need to see her."

Cate sits in an empty auditorium staring at the stage. She'd missed the production. She'd tried to get here on time, but no matter what she did, she just couldn't make it. Traffic, getting lost, locked doors, forgetting her locker combination – they all contributed.

The door opens and someone enters. Cate grabs her things to leave, but someone grabs her wrist. "Please wait."

Her brows narrow as she turns to face him. He looks familiar, though why anyone that handsome would talk to her is beyond her understanding.

"Please." He pleads. She shrugs and they sit. "How are you feeling?"

"I'm fine."

He gently taps the underside of her wrist three times to bring her into the Dream. She blinks and her expression changes. "How are you feeling?"

"Why did you take my Stone?" Her tone is cold enough to freeze hot chocolate.

"For safe keeping."

Her eyes narrow. "How did you find me?"

"I got lucky. What happened?" Releasing her wrist, he gently touches the edge of an ear lobe.

"*I* got lucky. I risked my life for a friend and came back with the Stone and a crown."

"I'd like to hear the story." Cate gives him a brief version of the events. "You risked your life for the Elf?" The muscles in his jaw flex.

"I risked my life for my friend. He wouldn't have been there if I hadn't brought him when we escaped from you."

Those words sting. "You have no reason to escape me. Our marriage is set. I only want what is best for you, your happiness...."

"And, to change the dragons. Is that why you crashed my coronation feast and stole my Stone?"

"It's here when you want it. All you have to do is come home." He leans close enough that she can feel the heat of his breath on her mouth. "How are you feeling?"

"I hurt. My head feels like it's splitting open, and my bones feel like they've been broken and re-set. What did you do to me?"

"That wasn't me. I just put out the fire."

"All you did..."

"Cate, I would never hurt you." He leans in, his mouth presses against hers. Gentle, soft and tasting sweetly of him. Heavy-lidded eyes meet hers. "Come home."

Her dream shifts. The auditorium and Viggo are gone. She stands in front of a quaint cottage in a weird forest with bioluminescent trees and flowers. The door opens and a lean middle-aged woman, with long ash-blonde hair steps out. Her mouth falls open at the sight of Cate. "Who are you?"

"Who're you?"

"Veralyn. How did you find me?"

That name sounds familiar. Where had she heard it before? "I didn't."

Pain wakes her followed by an urgent need to wretch. Baen holds a trash can with one hand and her hair with the other. Her stomach seizes and she groans.

Elar places a cool wet cloth on her neck. Another heave and her stomach empties. She accepts a tissue and wipes her mouth, then lies back.

"If you're up to it, we should get back to your apartment."

"Yeah." Cate pushes to her feet and sways. She presses a hand to her head and Elar gently lifts her into his arms. Baen's jaw tightens, but he says nothing as he leads the way from the Council Hall.

Spiders are *everywhere*. Cate closes her eyes and shudders. Elar reminds her that they came for her, and she can just as easily dismiss them.

She sincerely tries, but nothing happens. Tears leak from her eyes – her head throbs, her body aches like she has the flu, and her arachnophobia has her frozen.

"They sense your emotions. You will need to clear your head and calm yourself."

Cate focuses on Elar. The feel of his arms, the sway of his walk, the heat of his body. She thinks about dancing with him, his eyes locked on hers. She avoids thoughts of Viggo. If her mind wanders, she recalls it to this moment.

"Whatever you are doing it is working." His voice is silky, softly deep. It makes the inside of her ears tingle and warms her core.

Cate opens her eyes. They are back in the apartment and there are no spiders. Elar carries her to her room and lightly sets her on her feet. She sways and falls, sitting on the bed. She forestalls him from reaching out. "I'm okay."

Baen leans against the doorframe with his arms crossed over his broad chest. "I need to talk with Cate, alone."

Elar glances between them. He bows his head to Cate. "Good night, Queen Cate." Walking to the door, his mouth set in a thin line, he waits for Baen to step into the room. Neither speaks, their gazes communicating.

As Elar exits, Baen closes the door. Cate's dream-filled eyes turn to him as he sits beside her. "What happened? I saw Viggo encase you in the bubble and I could feel you becoming light-headed but…."

"I don't know. Viggo says it wasn't him."

Baen's eyes narrow and his brows drop into a deep V. "Viggo says? When did you talk to him?"

She doesn't meet his eyes, her gaze shifts to the floor. "When I was sleeping." Silence stretches uncomfortably and Cate wrings her hands. "Can we talk about this later? I really don't feel good."

"I know. Our bond lets me feel your pain, remember. What you experienced was…." A knock on the door interrupts them.

Smoke enters and deeply bows. "We found a group of intruders in the forest near the Frozen City. They claim to be here for you, my Queen."

Baen helps Cate to her feet. She smooths her dress and leaves the apartment. With each step, she becomes stronger and steadier, as if her body is remembering how to move.

A crowd waits at the Council platform. Smoke leads Cate to a new chair set on a small platform to make it higher than the others. Its height is the only differentiating factor.

She leans against the chair but doesn't sit. Without Rook to guide her in protocol, she's not sure what to do. Elar arrives, his voice clear silencing the crowd. "Hail Queen Cate, blessed by the goddess, ruler of the Drow." Voices echo him, as they fade, he continues. "This audience is now in session. Present your pleas."

A guard in black armor with unique badges on his chest drops to his knee and bows. "We found these intruders near the city. They claim to be unrelated to the events of the feast. We have troops inspecting every entrance to ensure the safety of our borders."

Cate glances at Elar then Baen, unsure if she should speak. "Bring them forward." The circle of guards and a gaggle of Drow surrounding them opens and three figures step onto the platform: a tall, beautiful girl probably Cate's age or close, a bear of a man with blonde hair and beard, and…. Cate blinks in disbelief and exclaims, "Mom!"

CHAPTER 24

They'd returned to her apartment, Cate had changed into a comfortable tunic and leggings, and spent the better part of the night catching up with her mom. Baen, on the other hand, spent that time sharing his view of events with Cate's father.

Now, the four of them sit together in the great room. The awkwardness between Cate and her father is palpable. Unsure of what to talk about, Cate blurts, "I have to find the Dragon Stones."

"We know." Kith pulls a square of paper from his pocket and unfolds it. He hands it to her. "I am a Dreamer. I see future events."

The drawing is Cate standing in front of a cottage facing a woman framed in the doorway. Around them are giant mushrooms and odd trees. Cate's expression shifts. Pointing at the paper, she says, "I dreamt of this place."

"We think it is where you will find the next Stone." Kith's voice is shaky with emotion.

"When I saw what your father drew, I couldn't believe my eyes." Emily takes the drawing and stares at it.

"What do you mean?"

"Think about who visited my shop. Most of them were not human. Before I met your father, I left the Frozen City, but this isn't where I am from." She points to the paper in Cate's hand. "That is."

"Do you know how to get back?"

Emily locks eyes with Kith and he encourages her to go on. "I do. At least, I think I do. When I left, I was told there was no way back for me, but that doesn't mean there isn't a way for you."

Baen sets his hand on Cate's shoulder. "She's exhausted. It has been a long and emotional day. Before we continue this conversation and make any plans to find the next Stone, Cate needs sleep."

Elar knows Baen is speaking about what he feels through the bond, not just out of concern for her well-being. Still, seeing his hand on Cate makes him want to remove it with one clean slice of his hunting knife. He blinks. When had such emotion crept into his being?

"Rook prepared an apartment for you, not far from Cate's. Simall has a guide waiting." Baen leads them to the door. Emily's reluctance is plain as she lingers but, at length, the three leave.

Cate leans against the back of the chair and presses her fingers to throbbing temples. "I want so much to believe he loves me." The hurt in her voice is like a knife to the chest.

"It's clear he does." Baen scowls, Cate's pain his pain.

"Why is he helping me find the Stones? He arranged the marriage to Viggo. He clearly wants to help the Dragotian's change the spell, so why?"

"Maybe he does not want it changed in the way you think he does." Elar takes her by the shoulders and gently guides her down the hall to her room. "Some intentions are not as clear as they seem."

Cate studies his face. She wants to ask him something but instead says, "Thank you for staying with me. Both of you."

The corners of Elar's lips lift in a near approximation of a smile. "It is my pleasure."

"And mine. Now, get some sleep."

Cate hesitates. "I don't want to dream." When she'd slept at the Council Hall, she'd seen Viggo. In fact, every time she closes her eyes, he's there.

Since the coronation and whatever blessing she received, it's like the dreams she had during the Dryad's sleep have been separating. Some feel more like memories, others vague like dreams, and a large part of them like the Dragon Dream where everything is real. "Do you have a spell or something?"

"Something." Elar answers. "Let's sit on the bed. Let me teach you a technique akin to meditation. It will let your body rest and heal without opening yourself to dreams."

Tatiana stares out the window, her mind not on home, but on the words of the Bear and Lion clans.

When she's sure Kith and Emily have fallen asleep, she asks the Drow attendant to lead her back to the queen's residence. It's strange how beautiful the Frozen City is, how quiet. She'd always thought the Drow a scheming, raucous, ruleless race. The few Drow she'd met in the world had been beautiful, deadly, and without morals. How could such a place like this exist?

Outside the queen's apartment two guards, all in black, stand at attention. The attendant addresses them and explains who Tatiana is. The guards' eyes lock on her. She can feel their assessment. "The Queen rests. She takes no audience."

Tatiana sneers, her clear blue eyes narrow. Her dragon laughs. "I go where I choose. It is a courtesy that I ask entry."

A female appears behind her – so quiet in her movements that even with dragon-enhanced hearing she is surprised – it is the knife at Tatiana's throat that announces her. "You were asked politely." The knife's edge draws a thin bead of blood. "We've shown you respect, Traveler, by not setting a guard on you. Do not test our patience."

"She is my cousin."

"Who you just met, if I am not mistaken."

The door of the queen's apartment is open. The queen's outline can be seen behind her wolf guard, who leans against the door frame; his keen eyes move between each figure before him. The woman at

Tatiana's back releases the pressure of the blade so that it no longer touches Tatiana's skin but hovers within a hair of it. "What brings you to the Queen's apartment at this hour?"

"Information."

Baen rubs his thumb along his jawline. It's dark with black stubble. His eyes glow with an animalistic light. The queen's voice carries easily into the night. "It's okay, Baen, Simall, let her in." The wolf moves, the woman releases her and Tatiana steps between the guards to enter the queen's apartment.

Tatiana studies her cousin. After spending so many hours observing the Dragotians' in Cate's room, talking to others about her – she isn't what Tatiana thought she'd be.

The queen gestures for her to sit as she makes herself comfortable on a couch with her wolf beside her. He's big, good-looking in an untamed way. The apartment door closes, leaving the three alone.

"What information do you have?" She sounds like she isn't feeling well, her skin is pale, and she looks a little green.

Tatiana glances at the wolf. "Since you went missing from the Dragotian estate, your dad's had me trying to find you – or what information I could about you."

"If your information is about my father, I really don't care." Cate moves to stand, and Tatiana cuts her off.

"It isn't. Sorry, just trying to feel a little less like a traitor."

"A traitor?" It's the wolf who asks.

Tatiana reluctantly nods. "See, everyone wants Cate to marry Viggo. Then, they can do some magic and change the dragon spell. Only, I don't want my dragon to takeover. I like myself just how I am.

My dragon likes it too. She's never lived outside her shell. She has no idea how to *be* a dragon. We think there are likely others like us too."

Cate scoots to the edge of the cushion and leans toward Tatiana. "What if I said I don't want to change the spell either? Because I don't."

Tatiana's eyes narrow and her brows furrow. "What do you want to do?"

"I want to free the dragons."

The queen watches Tatiana, scrutinizing her every reaction. It's like having dinner with her mom. Tatiana considers how best to negotiate this turn of events. "Free them?"

"Your little dragon could learn how to *be* a dragon. You could even teach her."

An image of her dragon frolicking beside her warms Tatiana. Travelers are known to be small, maybe she'd be the size of a Great Dane at most. "I have no idea where her egg is."

The queen shrugs and sits back on the couch. "The more dragon eggs you find, the likelier it is that one of them is hers." Covering her eyes with her hand as if to protect them from the dim light, she wearily says. "Why are you here?"

"On my way back from Viggo's, I was kidnapped by the Bear clan." The wolf's eyes flash and his lips curl over his teeth. "The Lions are dissatisfied with the Kraeken Queen. They think if they capture you, and force you to... well, do exactly what you just said, that they can move on the Eagles."

"What is their reason for Cate releasing the dragons?"

Tatiana's eyes focus on Baen, her mouth purses. "To strengthen the enchantment."

He takes a deep breath and nods as if he is considering past conversations. He addresses the queen. "What she says is likely true. The Lions have no love of the Eagles with L'Syle's death. Even worse, with their suspicions of his murder at Ka'Lea's hands, usurping the throne is something L'Nora would do if she thought it putting L'Syle's people in their rightful place.

Your purpose, you, would be just a pawn to them. Either ruler would seek to strengthen the enchantment to demonstrate their rightful rule – repositioning the Kraeken as a world power."

The queen pushes to her feet and sways. "I'm going to free the dragons. It doesn't matter whether it helps the Kraeken or not, sorry Baen. As for the Eagles and the Bears or Lions... they can do whatever. I'm going to bed before I throw up."

Tatiana watches the queen walk on unsteady feet to her room. The wolf clears his throat. "L'Nora's cunning. If she kidnapped you, she let you go just for this moment."

"I know. She's not what I expected. The queen, I mean."

Baen chuckles his gaze following the path Cate trod moments ago. "She isn't what anyone expects. How are you related?"

"My mom's her dad's sister." Tatiana pushes to her feet and crosses to the door. "Does she really mean to free the dragons?" Baen nods, "Do you think she can? I mean it's not possible."

"She's done many impossible things."

Cate closes the door and leans against it. The room feels like it is spinning whether her eyes are open or not. Her stomach churns and bile rises in her throat. Sweat runs down her spine as she shivers beneath her clothes.

Elar had meant well, teaching her wakeful sleep. A sleep akin to meditation that keeps the body alert and the mind calm, outside of dreams, but she couldn't maintain it.

A whimper escapes as she climbs into bed, fully clothed, and pulls the covers up to her chin. She's never felt this bad, not even when her scales first appeared. The door opens and a large body climbs into bed beside her on top of the covers and holds her close. *Baen.* Since the coronation, she's started to feel his presence, to know where he is even without seeing him. With his warmth, her body stops shivering. A part of her says she should be embarrassed or push him away, but that part is a tiny voice amid a maelstrom of pain. In his arms, sleep overtakes her.

She lies beside Rathleon as the dragon suns herself on a massive boulder. It feels like they have been peacefully enjoying the stillness for some time. A playful breeze kisses her cheek, cooling it, and moves on to dance along the tops of evergreens as it passes to the valley below.

Rathleon turns her massive head to stare at the girl. The dragon taps a claw on the rock. "I wondered why you are so powerful. I thought perhaps it due to my own abilities that you inherited my gifts as a mage. I was vain."

"Of course, my magic is your magic."

Rathleon chuckles. "Your Drow transformation bespeaks otherwise. I was there when the Drow priests created the Obsidian throne. I know how its magic works. Only a Drow with royal blood can sit on it. Anyone else will die an immediate and painful death. You were foolish to sit it for your friend. And, by all rights little one, you should be dead. Instead, you are very much alive. That is why you are queen. It is your birthright.

You are human through your father; thus, you carry my soul. You are Drow through your mother; thus, you sit the throne. What else are you?"

Cate scratches at the scales on the back of her neck, then studies her hands. Something had happened in the fight with Viggo.

It had felt like her bones were starting to break and reposition themselves, that her skin was no longer supple around her eyes, that…. "I don't know."

"I once knew a Kraeken who explained shifting. It reminds me of our experience. Could you be a Kraeken or possess their enchantment? They are, after all, mostly human. Perhaps, over the last thousand years, one of your ancestors was Kraeken and the incident brought out the beast?"

Could she be Kraeken? Cate stands with her arms wide and shrugs. "I don't know. Would it mean I can't undo the spell?"

Rathleon's head whips to the side, a snarl that makes the ground tremble rips from her throat. A massive red dragon approaches. "It's Xenothgorot. Go little one." Cate glances from one dragon to the other. Rathleon's wings spread wide. "Go."

The Dream shifts. Disoriented, Cate wonders if she is still in the Dream or back in one of the Dryad's spell-invoked memories. It feels so real, but… it's as if she's looking through someone else's eyes. A woman stands beside her at a workbench, grinding seeds with a mortar and pestle. "Careful, do not over grind them. The powder should be course." The words are from Cate. She blinks and turns back to the workbench.

Her hands move among vials and containers adding a little of this and a little of that to a small stone bowl resting on top of a miniature fire. With a couple drops of liquid, the contents begin to bubble. The woman beside her adds a pinch of the powder she'd been grinding. Cate steps from the bowl and the woman glances into it. "When the liquid becomes a solid, it will be done. Is that correct, Mother?"

Elar leans against the doorframe watching Cate sleep in Baen's arms. Only the oath-sworn bond prevents him from ripping the werewolf apart. The bond would bring Cate pain if the wolf dies. So, he'll have to keep him alive and make him regret having made his choice.

It is time to bring the Elves together. It is time for the millennia old feud to end. With a last glance at Cate, he leaves the apartment. Invoking the cloaking spell, he moves undetected through the Drow.

It is like moving through the Valley of Mist, only with more emotion. Drow mingle on platforms in the trees, fill restaurants and argue in the streets. They are alive. The Valley of Mist is like a library filled with scholars who rarely interact, banal and predictable. There is nothing predictable about the Drow. Elar smirks, the Elves are about to change.

He finds Rook sipping an amber liquid from a crystal glass studying a chess board on the patio of an apartment high in the trees. Rook gestures to the empty chair opposite him. "Join me."

Elar drops the spell and sits. Unsurprised that this powerful Drow sensed him. Rook pours Elar a glass of amber liquid. "Welcome." Together, they drink. Brandy, not Elar's favorite. "How is the queen?"

"Resting."

Rook nods and moves a piece on the board, then sits back in his chair and gives Elar his attention. "What brings you?"

Elar studies the chess board thinking about how to phrase what he wants and how much to reveal. "Why were you on the mountain?"

"Even the council takes turns guarding our entrances. Besides, Channa is my apprentice. The outer caves provide opportunities to train and guide our youth. Is that truly what brought you?"

"How will you train and guide the queen? She is young, Rook. What is your plan?"

Rook takes a sip and smiles. "Who dares train the queen? Young or not, she is blessed by the goddess. She sat on the Obsidian throne. She is who she is."

"And the Council will continue to rule while she sits on the Obsidian throne. A figurehead." Elar swirls the amber liquid, his eyes seemingly on the drink though they never leave Rook. The Drow does not respond, keeping his volatile emotions in check. "What of her quest to find the Dragon Stones?"

Rook's face darkens. He downs the remainder of the brandy and sets the glass next to the chess board. "Her quest ended when she saved you and became our queen."

Elar smirks. The Drow is trying to bait him. "I doubt she sees it that way. Let her complete her quest. It will change nothing, even if she were to die. Though, I will protect her with my life, as will the wolf."

"You came to plead for her?" Rook's eyes narrow as he tries to figure out Elar's next move.

"The queen of the Drow saved the Crown Prince of the Elves, Elarian son of Valrius. Through her actions, she redeemed the traitorous Elves." Elar schools his face, keeping it perfectly impassive.

Rook's eyes darken and his cheeks heat. "*You* are Elarian? The aloof wandering prince of the Elves. The prince who prefers the woods to his valley?" Elar bows his head in acknowledgement. Rook lunges over the table, narrowly missing Elar's throat, as Elar dodges. Rook's lips curl over his teeth in a sneer. "Leave. This. Place."

"When I was some random Elf, you tolerated my presence because of the queen. Now, you want to expel me. Do you think she will allow it? When I go, she goes."

"Traitors' spawn." Rook's on his feet. "The Council will never allow Valrian's heir to marry *our* queen. To have traitor's blood sit *our* throne."

Elar stands. Calmly, he looks down at Rook, being of a taller height. "I propose joining our people – no more Elves and Drow – only the *People*. Is that not worth considering?

I know you lead the Council. They will defer to your judgement. Consider it, Rook. Consider what it would mean to our *people*."

Elar allows a smirk. The Drow are very emotional. "Cate is her own person. She does not know your ways nor mine. Whether the Council agrees or not, she will complete her quest. She will rid herself of the human that thinks he can bond her. And, when she does, we will become one."

❋ ❋ ❋ ❋ ❋

Viggo wakes and runs his hands through his hair. He had hoped to find Cate in the Dream but instead Xenothgorot led him to Rathleon. They had sparred, with their teeth and talons, and with their words.

After a thousand years, Rathleon's anger is still very real, her outrage still bright. But you cannot have hate without love. Once, she had to have deeply loved Xenothgorot to feel such intense hatred.

Viggo checks the time on his watch before lying back on the pillow. He needs sleep, real restful sleep, not time in the Dream. Dane informed him that something was happening with the Kraeken, that while Ka'Lea plans her wedding someone is planning a coup. Normally, he wouldn't have cared but Ka'Lea is a stockholder.

He'd told her not long ago that perhaps she should consider herself part of the clan; how can he turn his back on anyone in the clan?

He covers his eyes with his forearm. If he keeps thinking, he'll never get back to sleep. He tries to set aside Dane's news and clear his mind, but images of Cate fill its emptiness. Cate's eyes brimming with hurt at their first meeting; Cate turning to him as he stepped into the room on the day of their engagement party; Cate's lips pressed against his; Cate challenging him on the night of her coronation.

He sighs. At this rate, he isn't going to sleep. Might as well get up. Pulling back the covers, he slips into jeans and a black t-shirt. At least he knows she's okay. But can he wait for her return?

He needs his sister. He needs to know the Truth.

IlliaVaa presses her hand to her throbbing head. The pain has her off balance and she stumbles to her bedroom door. Straightening, she takes a deep breath and pulls it open. Viggo's fist is raised to bang on the offending wood. His mouth hangs open like a fish gulping air. She growls. "Do you know what time it is?"

"You look like crap."

She shuts the door in his face and staggers back to bed. He pushes it open and follows. Grabbing her arm, he leads her to a set of chairs near the window and helps her sit. "You, okay?"

IlliaVaa's eyes flutter open. "If I could sleep away this headache I might be. What do you want?"

He pushes his hand through his hair. IlliaVaa closes one eye and focuses the other on him. He looks haggard, his eyes bloodshot and dark. With a heavy sigh, she gives in to her dragon. Her eyes shift, and surprisingly her head hurts less. Images float around him.

One makes her heart skip a beat. She knows he'll pick up on the change in her breathing, but she can't help it. No wonder he isn't well. It goes against everything their father taught them, everything he pounded into Viggo. It's never taken this long to see the Truth and he's becoming suspicious. She gasps as her eyes return to normal.

Collapsing into the chair, she closes both eyes and presses her hands to her head. For the moment, happy to have the excuse of the migraine.

He clears his throat. She opens her eyes to answer as a wave of nausea strikes. With the speed of someone who doesn't want to vomit everywhere, she makes it to the bathroom just in time to heave into the toilet. Viggo follows, pulling her hair back and holding it out of the way.

When her stomach's empty, dry heaves pump through her. Viggo gently braids her hair and gets a cool damp washcloth, placing it on the back of her neck. Spent, she leans against the edge of the tub.

"Where's your medicine?"

She clears her throat. "It didn't work. Don't worry, I just need to sleep now. I always feel better after throwing up." She lifts her eyes to his. "A seed is blooming in your heart. For the first time, you see yourself as more than a dragon's vessel. For the first time, you question your purpose."

Viggo's skin flushes and his eyes narrow. It's a Truth he hadn't even admitted to himself. How could he? Anything he knows, Xenothgorot knows.

"Rathleon did not leave because she ceased to love Xenothgorot. She left because she saw that all life as valuable. That is the nature of her curse. She wanted the dragons to understand that the humans also had mates and children, families to protect."

Viggo sets his large hand on the crown of her head, gently stroking her hair. Something he hasn't done since their father's abuse. "Will she really return to me?"

IlliaVaa closes her eyes. "Yes." It's what Viggo needs to hear. He lifts her from the bathroom floor and puts her into bed before leaving. Tears gently fall from her eyes, not from the pain in her head, but from the pain in her heart.

CHAPTER 25

Baen's cheek rests against the top of Cate's head. Her scent fills him, warms him. From the moment she approached his wolf in the canyon, she has filled his thoughts.

He'd tried to push her away. She was engaged to Viggo, not even eighteen. But v'Lana insisted. As his mother, as the matron of the pack, he couldn't refuse her.

The cabin had been torture. He wanted nothing more than to hold her, like now. He'd managed to resist, only by shifting into his wolf. Then, at the lake, she'd vanished. He'd hunted until he found her… with Elar.

It's like the elf laid claim to her. Always near, often touching, seemingly patient. Never respecting she's spoken for. Never giving credence to her age. He'd tried to tell himself it didn't matter. She wasn't his. She was Viggo's. Only, it did matter.

When Elar was locked up and it was only the two of them, Baen realized he couldn't ignore her any longer. He couldn't be without her. So, when the idea came to him to become her oath-sworn, he didn't pause.

Even if she married Viggo, even if Elar tried to claim her, she would always be connected to him; he would always be near her. No one could separate them. Ever.

It was his choice to stand by her side and protect her. To always protect her. It is hers to decide who she someday gives her heart to. He holds her a little tighter. Even if it isn't him; he would survive the pain and intimacy the oath-sworn bond gives when she is with another. Because, no matter what, a piece of her will always be his and he is fully hers.

A knock at the door rouses her. "Yes?"

"Milady, your mother requests an audience."

Cate sighs and pulls from his arms. "I'll be there in a minute." She shivers, feeling the lack of his warmth. Rubbing her arms, she glances at her clothes. She hadn't cared to change last night before crawling into bed.

"Do you want me to come with you?"

She shakes her head, picking a new tunic and a pair of jeans from the dresser. She pauses before opening the door and heading to the bathroom. "Thank you, for last night."

"You're welcome. We should probably talk about what it means for me to be your oath-sworn."

She nods before disappearing into the hallway. He can feel her jumbled emotions in his head, thankfully, she no longer feels the physical pain that Baen can only associate with shifting.

❀ ❀ ❀ ❀ ❀

After a quick shower and clean clothes, Cate feels better. She joins her mom in the main room where fresh coffee, fruit, cheeses and sweet rolls wait. Emily pours her a cup of coffee and hands her a small plate with a roll and pile of grapes. "How are you feeling?"

"Better."

"I'm so sorry. I tried to get you away from them, but I couldn't find you. That's when I went to your father. Your aunt is a great lawyer, but she couldn't find a loophole in the marriage agreement."

Cate sips the coffee and picks at the roll, finding it difficult to meet her mother's eyes. "I understand. I don't blame you. I know you were looking for me. After I got away, I wanted to let you know I was safe, but I couldn't find anyone with a phone."

"I'm not blaming you either. I'm blaming myself. I am so sorry I let them find you." Silent tears trail down Emily's cheeks.

Cate bites her lower lip and reaches out to touch her mom's leg. It's a light touch, filled with forgiveness. Emily's gaze finds hers. "It's okay. I got away. I'm alive and safe." She softly laughs. "If this hadn't happened, I wouldn't be the Drow Queen."

"I just wanted you to have a normal life. When your dad told me about the agreement and his Dream, I just… I just… I couldn't stay. I thought you needed a chance to be you, not whoever everyone else thought you should be."

Taking Emily's hand in hers, she considers how to word her thoughts. "Being normal is all I wanted. Even when Viggo poured his heart out to me, all I could think was that I wanted to go to college and that I haven't even had a boyfriend." She hugs Emily. When they separate, she holds her mom at arms' length. "I'm not normal, Mom, and that's okay."

"Of course, it's okay."

"No, I don't mean it that way." Cate sits back, her eyes searching Emily's hoping to help her understand. "My life isn't normal because *I* am not normal. I am not human. I am dragon-souled, only I am not just dragon-souled if anyone can say just dragon-souled. I am Drow. I am a dragon-souled Drow, Mom. No one else is like that. Just me. I am the only one. I am the only one who can define normal, for me."

Emily tucks a piece of Cate's hair behind her ear. "You're right. Like you, my mother is one-of-a-kind. I think you two should meet. I can't return to where I grew up, but maybe you can."

Cate's smile lights her eyes. "The cottage? I thought your parents were dead."

"To this world, they are. I wasn't born in this world. It's a long trip to where I entered, and it is deep below the temple in the mountain. Do you feel up to it?"

"You mean, like going right now?"

Emily's throat tightens and she swallows hard. "Yeah, right now. I don't know if the Drow Council will let us go and it is something I feel very strongly you need to do."

"What about Baen and Elar?"

Emily's eyes lift to Baen's silent form, leaning against the wall and within earshot. "I don't think I could separate you if I tried."

Two hours pass before they enter the mountain. Baen carries a pack full of water and another full of food. Elar has a pack with LED flashlights. Cate glances over her shoulder at the silhouettes of her father and cousin, framed by the light outside. Emily was adamant they could not come.

"This isn't a casual hike," she'd told them. Kith had wrapped his arms around Emily and whispered into her ear before pulling Cate in for a fierce, and awkward, hug.

Straightening, Emily gestures to the path leading to the temple. "We start there."

Elar clicks on a light and tosses it to Emily, then clicks on another for himself. Baen's eyes shift, as do Cate's. Colors in the cavern, her human eyes can't see, spark to life. They walk in silence down the tunnel to the temple.

Only a few days ago, she'd walked this path wondering if she would live. Oddly, it feels much the same. Reaching the ornately carved doorway, Emily takes a breath and scans the walls. "Are you looking for the waiting room?"

Emily shakes her head. "No, there's a door that opens to another tunnel."

Cate shivers, thinking about the spider that dwells above the temple. Closing her eyes, she imagines its children showing her the way. She fights a scream as tiny white spiders emerge from the wall outlining a rectangle. "Um, Mom." Cate points to it and Emily glances from the spiders to her daughter.

"Can you make them leave? I don't want to touch anything that might offend them."

Cate imagines them moving from the door and they spread out. Emily steps forward, running her fingers along the door's edge until they find a trigger. Pressing it, the door slides open. Emily quickly enters, leading them deep into the mountain.

Cate's legs burn. They've been walking down steps and sloping ledges for hours. She doesn't even want to think about walking back. The lights from the flashlights barely illuminate the path. "How did you find your way out?"

Emily shrugs. "By feel mostly. At the end, I climbed the wall up into the temple. Imagine their expressions when a girl emerged over the edge instead of a giant white spider! My hands, arms, legs, and feet were all scraped and bloody. Dirt covered me from head-to-toe. I was a mess."

"The ground is leveling out." Elar's clear voice calls from ahead. Sheer walls surround them. They are at the bottom of the mountain. Opening his pack, Elar removes all but two flashlights. Lighting them, he lodges them in rocks and fills the space with light.

The black walls look like glass, the ground beneath their feet fine glittering black sand. "Mom?" Cate turns to Emily who presses her hand against the mirror-like rock.

"It's here."

There's nothing, not even her reflection. "What's here?"

"The Dream." Emily sighs and moves to sit in the center of Elar's light ring. The others join her. "I am not a dragon, and I cannot enter the Dream. Not even in my sleep. But here, after the Dragon Wars ended, a powerful mage opened a door to the Dream. She did it to save the man she loved – still loves."

Emily asks Baen for water. He passes a bottle to everyone. She drinks half of hers before continuing. "What she did has never been done, before or since. You see, the Dream is out of time and space. I cannot even really describe it, only that it is exactly what the person Dreaming needs."

"Mom, I didn't need to spend the day descending into a mountain to reach the Dream. I could've just gone to sleep."

Emily blinks, then laughs. "You're going in wide awake and in-the-flesh."

"How do I do that?"

"I don't know."

Cate rolls her eyes.

"If you can enter the Dream through sleep, can any dragon?" Elar's eyes focus on Cate.

"Of course." She answers dismissively.

"When you were in the dryad's sleep were you in the Dream?" Elar's voice is soft, not echoing at all in the chamber.

Cate shifts her stare from her mom to him. His intensity makes her fidget. "Sometimes. I think I was. It was all so real, all of it. It's hard to tell when I was seeing a vision of the past, in the Dream, or just dreaming."

"Wolves have something like this Dream. We too move through it, communicate with one another in it. Perhaps, I can help you." Baen can feel Cate's unease through their bond, and he doesn't like what Elar is suggesting.

"Has *he* been with you all along?" Elar's question softly leaves his lips, though his eyes hold an edge to them.

Cate blinks. Unsure of what he is asking or why. "Who are you talking about?"

"That lech of a dragon who calls himself your fiancée." Elar's lip curls in a sneer. His hard stare pins Cate where she sits.

"Such display of emotion is out of character for your kind." Emily notes.

Elar's eyes narrow and he gives Emily a cold stare before focusing on Cate. "I will have your answer."

"You mean Viggo? Yeah, he was in my dreams. So were you and Baen and mom and dad and so many people I don't know, I was asleep!"

"In this Dream where everything is real. Where he can get to you, and we cannot."

Baen understands now. It is a place where Cate is unprotected, a place where Elar cannot go. "As I said, Wolves have something similar. Perhaps, I can enter with her. Guard her, as I do here."

Elar's eyes flicker between Cate and Baen. "What has been done cannot be undone, but perhaps we can prevent his interference with Cate in the future."

Emily finishes her water and squeezes the plastic until it crumples. "As I was saying, I don't know how to open it." She tosses the crumbled plastic to Baen and walks to the sheer mirror-like wall. Resting her hands on it, she slides them along the cool surface. "But however you get there, this is the door to the Dream."

Sighing, Cate joins Emily. *Rathleon, any ideas?* Her dragon stirs, waking to stare from her eyes. The silence is long. After a time, Emily rejoins Baen and Elar. No one speaks.

It reminds me of how Travelers use reflective surfaces.

Cate nods. She'd had a similar thought. Rathleon urges her to step forward and place both hands on the stone. She rests her forehead against the cool surface. First one finger then another taps the rock. Words flow from her mouth, foreign and from another time.

Each tap sounds like a massive doorknocker banging against a giant gate. It reverberates through the chamber and up the mountain.

"What are you doing?" Emily looks skyward, fearful of falling rocks and spiders alike.

Cate doesn't respond. Her entire focus on the rock. A blue-green aura surrounds her, brighter even than the flashlights. The wall begins to shimmer. Baen leaps to his feet. On instinct, he grabs hold of Cate's waist as two arms emerge from the stone, wrap around her wrists and pull them into the mountain.

❀ ❀ ❀ ❀ ❀

Baen holds her close as the arms release her. They stand in a tranquil forest. Birds chirp overhead and the air is comfortably warm. Before them stands a familiar woman. She's been beside Cate in her dreams, grinding herbs, concocting potions, learning spells. But it is not Cate who speaks, it is Rathleon through Cate's voice. "Veralyn."

The woman crosses her arms and studies Cate. "She is quite safe here, wolf-man." Baen releases Cate and the woman tilts her head studying them. "How much time has passed?"

"I don't know." Cate answers, unsure of what Veralyn speaks.

Rathleon responds, "A thousand years."

Veralyn shakes her head and turns from them. They follow as she purposefully walks a well-worn path through the cheerful wood to a quaint cottage tucked into a glen with a bubbling spring that feeds a small stream.

She pulls open the cottage door and beckons them inside. "I have a stew over the fire. It won't be ready for a few hours. Water?"

"No thanks." Cate responds as they sit in beautifully carved chairs.

"You look like her." A small smile lifts the corner of Veralyn's mouth. "Actually, you look a little like both of them. I guess that's fitting since you carry Rathleon's soul."

"Are you, my grandmother?"

Veralyn's face lights up and her smile brightens the room. "I am Cate's grandmother and Rathleon's daughter."

Cate sits back. The only sound in the room the bubbling of the stew. How can that be? How can Veralyn be Rathleon's daughter? An image of a dragon crashing into a mountain, fleeing its crazed mate, comes to mind. Rathleon had fled when she realized she was pregnant.

"But, if that's true, why isn't your soul in the body of a human?"

Veralyn tucks her feet beneath her and takes a deep breath. "I was born human."

Cate feels like she's on a merry-go-round. Nothing makes sense and her head is spinning. "Rathleon's a dragon, how were you born human?"

"This is the Dream mother. You need not be enslaved." Veralyn's clear gaze holds Cate's. In seconds, Cate feels her body tingle. Beside her stands an enchanting woman with bluish-green hair and emerald eyes.

"Hello Cate." Rathleon's voice is resonate even as a human. Her eyes sparkle. She leans down and wraps Cate in an embrace. Then, she moves to draw Veralyn into her arms.

"Why didn't you tell me?" Tears travel Cate's cheeks in tracks like Veralyn's own. Mother and daughter separate, still holding hands they sit side-by-side.

"It is my greatest secret."

"Your secret! It's my life, Rathleon. You're… you're…."

"How could I tell you that you carry your grandmother's soul? I was not sure at first. Then, your Gifts began to appear, I started to wonder. It wasn't until this very moment, I was sure."

"I've lived your memories through the dryad's sleep, and you weren't sure?!"

"Cateian, those memories could have been given to you through the enchantment. I needed to really know. I had to be certain."

"Why? Tell my why you had to be certain?"

Veralyn answers. "Rathleon is a dragon. I am human. How can that be? Think about it, really think about it for a minute."

Cate's eyes dance between the women. A torrent of emotion swirls inside her making it difficult to clearly think. "You couldn't have conceived with a human…."

"No." Rathleon shudders.

"Then… how…?" Cate shakes her head.

Rathleon glances at Baen before choosing to speak. "I learned how to shift. I discovered that a dragon could shift into a human. I birthed Veralyn as a human and she has lived her days as a human. She has never shifted to her dragon form."

"So, the enchantment didn't send her soul into a human, because it was already in a human?"

"Exactly."

Cate blinks and wipes the tears from her cheeks. She sits straighter and glances at Baen. He isn't looking at Rathleon and Veralyn. He's looking at her. She licks dry lips and asks, "Does that mean my mom's a dragon?"

Veralyn shrugs. "I've never been a dragon but that doesn't mean I *couldn't* be a dragon. Dragon magic runs through me. It's how I created this place. It's how I saved your grandfather." Her head tilts again as her eyes take in Cate from head-to-toe. "Has your skin always had a bluish tint? Your mother's skin never did."

Cate shakes her head. This is all so much to take in. "No, it only became that way after I sat on the Obsidian throne."

They hadn't heard the door open. It isn't until he speaks that they turn to him. "You did what?" Everyone stands. His presence commands attention. He closes the distance between them, and Cate finds herself face-to-face with a tall lean man with white-blonde hair and amber eyes. His skin has a slight blue hue. The man from her vision during the trial.

He reaches out to touch her and Baen forestalls him. Their eyes lock. Baen defers and steps back. The man tilts her chin, his amber eyes take in every facet of her features. "You are?"

"This is Cateian, King Arraniean, your granddaughter." He releases her at the sound of Rathleon's voice. He had momentarily forgotten her. "Cateian, this is Arraniean, King of the Drow, the only man worthy to marry my daughter and be called Son."

"How are you here?" he asks, as Veralyn takes his hand and guides him to a chair.

"It is time." Veralyn answers. He heaves a sigh, his eyes drift between Cate and Rathleon. "It has been a thousand years already, my love."

"Much has changed." Rathleon muses.

Veralyn nods. "We had to wait for Cate. No matter how long it took."

Cate feels the weight of Arraniean's gaze. He runs his hands through his hair and sits on the edge of his chair. "How is Emilean?"

"If you mean my mom, she's good. Goes by Emily. She owns her own business and is a really great mom." Cate assures him. Her heart races. She had no idea what finding them would feel like. She'd always wanted to know them, but she'd been so focused on breaking free from the marriage agreement and finding the Stones, she hadn't really thought what it would mean to find her grandparents.

He nods and studies her features. "You sat on the throne?"

"Yeah, I'm the queen now."

Arraniean laughs, surprising everyone. Cate stifles a jump and cautiously smiles. "Of course, you are. You are my granddaughter. Only you and your offspring may sit on the throne. It was made of our blood, for our blood. I never told Emilean, but I thought she understood."

"Mom lives as a human. She didn't stay with the Drow."

"What led you to sit the throne?"

"She did it to save our companion." Baen answers. "The changes you see were almost instantaneous." Arraniean's hard gaze fully turns to him. It's as if he is deconstructing Baen, seeing into his very soul.

"We have not been introduced."

"I am Baen, first son of v'Lana, twin of d'Gar, alpha of the Wolf clan, oath-sworn of Queen Cateian." Arraniean's eyes flicker to Cate and back to Baen. "I will protect her with my life."

Rathleon frowns at Baen's declaration. "Now that introductions are complete. We are here for a purpose. Cateian is betrothed to a boy who carries Xenothgorot's soul."

"What?" Veralyn's pulled from the familial moment.

"Xenothgorot plots to corrupt my enchantment, for the dragons' souls to take control of the humans' who provide for them."

"I won't let him do it. I'll free the dragons first." Cate declares.

Veralyn nods slowly at first, then faster with a broad smile overtaking her features. "Yes, yes, it is time. It is easy to be distracted here, to lose focus, to forget."

"Except when we scout him. He has been terribly busy lately, gathering dragons, holding meetings. It's been the same, year after year, only now there is an urgency to him. A need." Arraniean's eyes stay on Cate. "Now, I know why. Xenothgorot feels the end is near. One way or another, he'll be in control again."

Veralyn frees her hand from Rathleon's and approaches Cate. "Come with me." Rathleon makes a shooing motion. When Cate stands and follows Veralyn, Arraniean stops Baen from going with them.

They leave the sitting room and pass through a small kitchen with the amazing smelling stew. Veralyn opens a plain looking door and guides Cate into a mage's workroom. Beakers, vials, workbenches filled with oddities line the walls. Veralyn goes directly to a trunk underneath the farthest bench.

She unbuckles its straps and flips it open. Cate stands in the middle of the room, fearful of touching anything. Her gaze is pulled to a series of sketches half-drawn near the window. Veralyn clears her throat. She stands in front of Cate with something wrapped in a cloth held out in her hands.

Cate takes it and immediately feels a flood of power fill her. Her head leans back, her mouth falls slack, as power escapes her eyes, ears, and mouth. "You must control it. Guide it back to the Stone." Veralyn's voice calls to her.

Cate closes her eyes, envisioning the power retreating from her cells to return back to the cool facets beneath the cloth. She takes a breath as the final wisp leaves her.

When Cate's eyes open and focus on Veralyn it looks as if the weight of the world is on Veralyn's shoulders. "I am sorry. We are not much different, you and I." She leans against a bench and thinks about how to phrase what she wants to say. "I am Rathleon's only child. Xenothgorot is my father. I am fully dragon, but I have never *been* a dragon. Arraniean knew. Your mother never did. Emily believes she is human and Drow. If you tell her...."

"I won't."

Veralyn takes a trembling breath. "That means you, my lovely granddaughter, are dragon and Drow from your mother's side and human from your father's. You are the triad. Dragon, Drow and human. Only you can break Rathleon's enchantment."

Cate's reaction isn't what Veralyn expected. At first, she just blinks. Then, she starts to laugh. She laughs so hard that tears stream down her cheeks. It takes a while for her to calm down and catch her breath. "I knew it. I just knew it."

"Why?"

"Because that's all I want to do. I just knew there had to be a way and it was me all the time. It was me!" She laughs again.

"Rathleon will help you with the spell. You only need to find the Stones."

"Exactly! That's what I've been doing. I already have two pieces. I even have a small shard that was made into a ring."

"You've been collecting the Stones?"

"I found the first piece in the trial for the throne. Now, I have the second."

Veralyn absently nods. "I left a piece with the Drow. They must have thought the trial would protect it. And, of course, I took a piece with me into the Dream. The third piece was given to the humans. It could be anywhere."

"I'll find it. Don't worry."

"When will you marry the boy with Xenothgorot's soul?"

Cate glowers at the question. "The wedding will be on my eighteenth birthday."

"That will be the day Xenothgorot moves."

"I'm not marrying him. I'll stop Xenothgorot by freeing the dragons and when I do the marriage agreement is void."

Veralyn rests her hand on Cate's shoulder. "We've been watching the boy and Xenothgorot. When they are here, they are not often together. It seems the boy no longer wants what Xenothgorot wants."

"What do you mean?"

Veralyn drops her hand and pulls Cate into a hug, the stone between them. "I mean he doesn't want to change the enchantment. I think he doesn't want Xenothgorot to take over his body and suppress his soul."

Cate pulls away and shrugs. "Who would?"

Veralyn knows Cate isn't catching her meaning, but she doesn't push it. "Come, now that you have the Stone, let's catch up for a while. It has been forever since I've seen my mother and I want to know more about you and my daughter."

Stepping back into the mountain, Cate hands the Stone to Baen and hugs her mom. Emily warmly returns it, the women silently enjoying each other. "I love you, Mom."

"I love you."

Emily sighs and releases Cate. "We have a long climb out. Ready?" Holding Emily's hand, Cate nods. Elar collects the flashlights, and they begin their trek. "How are they?"

"Good. They miss you."

Emily's mouth lifts into a small smile. "Living in the Dream was serene and peaceful, but I had no one to play with or fall in love with. It was very lonely." Cate squeezes Emily's hand. "But then I met your father and had you. I will never be alone again."

✾ ✾ ✾ ✾ ✾

Elar fights the need to release the tension in his shoulders. Waiting for Cate felt like a lifetime, an Elven lifetime. His lips curl in a slight sneer as his eyes land on the werewolf. After the wolf's vow, the light of Cate's soul has started to surround Baen. It agitates Elar.

As they climb the stairs towards Cate's apartment, a new color dances among the shimmering hues that envelop Cate. It's as if each Stone she collects is awakening something she is unaware of. Goosebumps pepper Elar's flesh. He takes a deep calming breath.

No one, except Veralyn, has ever physically traveled into the Dream – before Cate. Magic-wielders will want to know how she did it. They will want to dissect her talent and her power. Good luck with that. Elar allows a soft chuckle and misses Baen's sidelong glance.

Cate is in a league of her own in terms of power. Emily holds Cate close, whispering in her ear, before she kisses her cheek and follows another branching path to her own guest apartment.

They enter Cate's apartment, and she flops on the couch. Baen takes the Stone from her while Elar sits beside her. "Would you like anything?"

She leans her head back, closing her eyes. "A bath and bed. I knew climbing up would be far worse than down." Cate yawns. "My legs ache, my feet hurt, I smell and I'm sure I'm covered in dust and dirt."

Elar leans close, scoops her into his arms and carries her into her room. Though her eyes open wide in surprise, she does not protest.

Baen softly growls, his gaze meeting Elar's. Awkwardly, they face each other until Baen retreats closing the door behind the Elf.

"Um, I'm good now. I can handle the shower part on my own."

Elar's eyes shift to stare into Cate's, his irises dilating. "Baen sleeps in your bed. Do you know how that makes me feel?"

Cate swallows hard as she holds his intense gaze. "We just sleep. The vow he made... he knows when something is upsetting me and it's soothing to have him close."

"Is it just the vow?"

Cate breaks eye contact. "Truthfully, I don't know. And it doesn't matter, I'm engaged. You both know that."

"To someone you do not want to marry."

Cate exhales a long heavy breath. "Does it matter?"

The bedroom door bursts open. Baen's chest heaves and his eyes are no longer human. "Cate, the Kraeken are at war."

CHAPTER 26

Ka'Leel scowls at the screens: some show troops movements, others deployments of weapons and machines, others stores and bunkers. He runs his hand through his hair. Never had he thought it would come to their own kind fighting one another.

He had planned against the humans finding them. Run scenarios about being detected and how to deflect an engagement. He had not planned on his own kind turning on them. He should have known it was a possibility, especially the way Ka'lea treated the king.

With her wedding a few days away, L'Nora could not take the slight to L'Syles's memory. The king had not been chaste, nor good to Ka'Lea but he had been a remarkably strong and charismatic leader. Two things Ka'lea is not.

Ka'Leel turns his thoughts back to the screens. So far, intel reports that the Bear, Mountain lion, Serpent and Badger clans have joined the Lions. With Ka'Lea marrying d'Gar, the Wolves are allied with the Eagles. Old alliances with the Fox and Wolverine clans still stand. If only the Horse, Hawk, Falcon and Deer would join.

He takes a swig of water wishing it were something stronger. A gangly youth races up the causeway and barges into the command room. With a quick salute, he reports that there's been a breach of the main hall.

Ka'Leel blinks, glances at his water wondering if it indeed wasn't something stronger, when the youth explains that the five "just appeared" and one of them is Lord Baen.

Ka'Leel leaves the command room and jogs to the main hall. When he arrives Ka'Lea and d'Gar greet Baen, an Elf and a... girl? Or is she a Drow?

Lord d'Gar's eyes wander over Cate in her all-black Drow armor, her hair pulled back in a tight ponytail. She's flanked by two Drow guards. "Brother!" He says while clasping Baen in an unreturned hug. "I'm glad you could make it for the wedding."

"I'm not here for your nuptials, brother."

Ka'Lea clears her throat. No one in the room bends a knee. The Kraeken Queen's eyebrows rise in displeasure. "Why do you not recognize your Queen?"

Baen only bows his head. "My apologies, Queen Ka'Lea. My loyalty and life are pledged to Queen Cateian."

Ka'Lea blinks. Her gauzy gown flows around her with a gentle breeze created by the air conditioning. Her eagle-like eyes shift to the Drow guards and then to Elar. She appraises him as d'Gar did Cate. "A Drow Queen and an Elven Prince, interesting company you keep Lord Baen." The word Lord comes out as a verbal sneer. "Why are you in my keep, uninvited?"

"We are here to help you defeat the Lions." Cate answers, feeling Baen's irritation through their bond.

Lord d'Gar steps close to Ka'Lea and gently sets his hand on her waist. His touch causes her to look up into his eyes. Her posture relaxes and she faces Baen. "Why would you think we would want or accept your help?"

Ka'Leel doesn't give Baen or anyone in his party a chance to respond. "Because I told him about the war. Baen is good at what he does and any help he is willing to give will buy us time as we hopefully work toward a treatise."

"There will be no treatise! That lying, conniving, *Lion* does not deserve leniency. L'Syle was not an upright man. He was not the role model of a husband a king should be. Perhaps it was one of his lovers' husbands who killed him, but I did not. This war is ludicrous! It deserves no acknowledgement."

"Whether we acknowledge it or not, it will come. People will be hurt and die if we do not do something." Ka'Leel steps between Ka'Lea and Baen. His long white hair captures the light from the window, creating a halo effect. "Focus on your wedding and let me do my job, my queen."

She stares long at her brother before turning on her heel and haughtily gliding from the room. D'Gar glances at Cate, then at Baen, Elar and her guards before following. Ka'Leel extends his hand to Baen. "Thank you for coming."

Baen clasps Ka'Leel's arm. "I am still Kraeken."

"Come, let's retire to the strategy room." Releasing Baen, Ka'Leel grimaces. "Perhaps I can offer you all a room to relax while Baen and I meet."

Elar's jaw muscles flex as he grinds his teeth before answering. "We are a unit. Where Baen goes Cate goes, and where Cate goes, I go. As for her guards, they are her shadow which never fades."

"I see." Ka'Leel scowls as Baen shrugs. "Follow me then."

He leads them from the main hall, along walkways and through wide halls, through small courtyards and bustling areas filled with soldiers. He keys a code on a touchpad and a door swings open. Stepping into the room, the walls are lined with monitors displaying satellite images, video feeds, predictive modeling, and security footage. Before them is a glass table. Ka'Leel passes his hand over it, and it lights up as he swipes through menu options in an unknown language.

A 3-D rendering of the Eagles' Reaches pops into view. "I think she's likely to come from the northern valley."

Baen shakes his head and points to areas on the mountain. "They may make it, but their allies won't. No, I think it more likely they'll stay in their human skins and enter through the town. Once through, they'll detonate points along the wall. It'll be easiest to scale the mountain here and here. After that, it'll be a full-on blitz."

"Why are you assuming only a ground assault?"

They both turn to look at Cate. "Because none of the clans can fly."

Cate laughs out loud and quickly covers her mouth, shocked and embarrassed at her reaction. "Sorry, but just because the clan has an animal shape, they can take doesn't mean they won't make use of the technology at hand. You have. Why won't they use drones to drop bombs? Or, to carry in a smaller shifter to infiltrate you?"

"Or other creatures like insects to spy?" Xon adds. His deep voice is a surprise to all as they shift to stare at the Drow. His blue-black hair hangs loose down his back and his amber eyes feel out of place on his lightly tinged skin.

"Why would they use insects? Do you mean like bugs?"

"What other definition of insect is there?"

Ka'Leel shakes his head. "No, I mean devices that allow a person to hear what another person is saying even when they are not in the same room."

Xon tips his head in thought. "That too I suppose. But, no, I meant bugs. Our queen controls arachnids, I thought perhaps your species could do something similar." His smile is vicious. "I should not have assumed."

Ka'Leel fights a desire to shiver. "Spider Queen, huh?"

Cate makes a face and focuses on the rendering. She knows nothing of warfare. Never studied it. Never imagined herself fighting in one.

Ka'Lea checks her image in the mirror and brushes her hair off her shoulders. War. Like L'Nora has the nerve to actually lay siege to the Reaches.

Spider Queen, hah! How dare Baen serve another? He's Kraeken. A wolf. He's her subject.

Lord d'Gar wraps his arms around her waist and leans his head against hers, his nose tilted to inhale her scent. "You are beautiful."

"Your mouth says beautiful words yet your eyes wander."

His arms tighten. "I will look. It is in my nature to admire beautiful things. I will not wander. I am yours and yours alone."

"As I am yours." She responds, turning into his arms to press her lips against his. "With L'Nora threatening a military coup, perhaps we should move up the wedding. Everything is ready."

He leans back to read her expression. "Are you sure? I don't want you pressed into anything."

"I am sure."

"Then, when do we wed?"

"At midnight."

He leans in and kisses her deeply. "I should go then. The groom isn't supposed to see the bride on the day of the wedding until she walks down the aisle."

Ka'Lea blushes as d'Gar pulls away and reluctantly leaves the room. Picking up a phone, she relays to the steward her change of plans. With an evil grin, she sashays to her personal suite where she'll call Dane.

"She what?!" Ka'Leel slams his palm on the table before wiping it down his face in frustration.

Baen shakes his head and glances at Cate. Xon and Smoke flank her while Elar explains the topographical challenges of assailing the Reaches.

Flopping into the nearest chair, the Eagle prince runs his hands through his hair. "The wedding is now tonight, midnight."

"How does that force L'Nora's hand?"

His eyes meet Baen's. "Every head of every clan is to be there."

"It opens the door to the rebels and gives us an opportunity to capture them."

"And it gives them the chance to kill Ka'Lea, and you, and end the Eagle line."

"She changed the date and time. Maybe it'll throw them off their game."

"You willing to bet your life on maybe?"

Ka'Leel shakes his head. "At least now we know what to plan for. Why don't you take your Queen to a guest suite? I can spare you for an hour and though attractive in her battle suit, she will need a dress for tonight."

Baen turns his head to stare at Cate. With Xon and Smoke, and Elar, the risk to her is minimal. "You're right. But not a guest suite. I'll take her to the Wolf Suite."

Having studied the 3-D rendering, Cate knew the Reaches was large but walking through it made it hit home. Centuries of art collections line the walls, rooms with different eras of furniture. She glances at Baen in the mirrored wall of the elevator as its animated voice announces the floor and its doors slide open.

"My grandfather had the lift installed. The Eagles prefer the outside stairs that zigzag up the wall. Grandfather did not."

Cate laughs at the thought of having to climb hundreds of stairs to reach the suite, thankful for the investment.

The only door in the narrow hall opens, revealing V'Lana, the Wolf matron. Clothed in a designer gown, a black so deep, her long raven locks blend into it, she beckons them inside the suite. Her keen gaze assesses each as they enter, first the Drow, then Elar and Cate. Baen growls, a low resonate sound, when v'Lana reaches out to stop the young queen. Her lips press into a thin line as she slowly lowers her hand. "What is your relationship that you threaten me?"

Closing the door of the suite, Baen faces his mother. "Oathsworn."

Her brows lift and her eyes narrow. "What oath did you swear?"

"My life."

The air feels heavy, the silence thick. V'Lana closes her eyes and takes a long slow deep breath. Baen guides them into the great room.

Xon stands where he can see every entrance while Smoke studies the windows. When v'Lana joins them, she is calm. "What brings you to our suite?"

"At the Reaches, the only person I trust with Cate, is you."

V'Lana glances at Smoke and Xon. "I have little doubt she is well protected, but I will do what I can."

Leaning close to Cate, he whispers, "I will meet you at the ceremony."

Cate watches him leave and then directs her attention to V'Lana. "I'm sorry for intruding. We'll just hang here; you don't need to worry about entertaining us."

V'Lana folds her hands together. "There is nothing for me to do with the wedding, except show up. If spending time with you frees Baen's mind to focus on the defense of the Reaches, then it is worth my effort. Come, let us find you an outfit befitting your station." She points at the Drow and Elar to punctuate her next statement. "Stay here. You are in the Wolf Clan suite; nothing will happen to her."

CHAPTER 27

Viggo adjusts his silk tie, checks his watch, and waits as Dane makes a portal. Earlier in the day, he'd sent a hundred special forces trained bodyguards to the Reaches, in support of one of his shareholders.

Now, he must look the part of the richest most dangerous man in the world, because he is. He smirks. His black hair is perfect. His Italian handmade suit, perfect. His brown leather shoes, perfect. IlliaVaa slips her hand onto his forearm, joining him as he steps from his home to the Eagles' lair.

Cool mountain air caresses his skin. Here in the mountains, the sun has already set, the sky a soft purple. "If you've come to see Ka'Leel, he is busy."

"I came as your plus one. Besides, you wouldn't want Cate to get the wrong idea should she see some pheromone-induced Kraeken besieging you."

Viggo's jaw tightens. With that Wolf attached to Cate, he suspects she'll attend the wedding and may even participate in the defense of the capital, which is why he chose to use Ka'Lea's shareholder status as an excuse for sending his elite guard.

A tall lean man with angular features, wearing a long-flowing white robe greets them. "My lord and lady, please follow me." Viggo scowls at his back, as he follows the man, IlliaVaa still firmly attached to his arm and Dane trailing.

White drapery, white flowers, and platinum decorations line the hall, the railings, and descend into the family chapel. The attendant leads them to one of four balconies above the sanctuary. "The ceremony will soon begin." Bowing, he leaves them.

Viggo escorts IlliaVaa to a chair, then stands at the balcony and studies the room. Directly across from them, Cate leans against the balcony railing with an Elf at her side and two Drow behind her. Viggo's breath catches and his heart flutters. Her hair is curled into a messy pile on top of her head, with ringlets kissing bare shoulders. An emerald choker encircles her fair neck, and a strapless emerald gown hugs her flawless figure. Silk gloves hide her delicate hands, the fabric ending just above her elbows.

"Who is that beside Cate?"

He blinks, remembering himself. "What do you see when you look at him?"

IlliaVaa sighs. Viggo gives her time to really *see* the Elf. "An ancient tree, straight and healthy. Half of its branches are covered in white flowers, the other half with deep purple. It's almost like staring at the sun, beautiful and blinding."

The sanctuary doors open. Guards, wearing ceremonial white armor, march along the aisle positioning themselves one to each pew. Their armored boots produce an echoing clack against the stone floor. Next, a snow-white eagle, the size of a man, ducks through the doors and walks to the altar. Its head twitches as it seeks to see each part of the sanctuary. Fluffing its feathers, it settles at rest beside the dais. A massive black wolf proudly pads down the aisle. It bows its head to the eagle and takes its position on the opposite side of the altar. Seated, it's taller than most men.

Next, the groom enters. Clad in a black tuxedo with white satin trim, white vest and shirt. He looks like he just stepped from a fashion magazine. His even steps take him to stand beside the wolf.

A gentle tune lures the Kraeken gentry inside, the orchestra hidden on a balcony high above the sanctuary. Each sit, by rank, on a specific pew. Lady v'Lana is in the first, her seat near d'Gar and the wolf, while the opposite pew by the eagle is empty.

Once all clans, except the lion, are present and seated, the orchestra silences and an ethereal sound fills the hallowed space.

Wearing a diamond tiara, her long white hair hanging loosely down her back, clad in a simple lace dress and wearing a cloak of feathers, Queen Ka'Lea enters. Framed by the doorway, backlit by a rose-hued stained-glass window, she looks every bit like the formidable queen.

Viggo's eyes shift from the spectacle below to the woman across from him. Cate's beauty, no less than Ka'Lea's, is pure and warm, whereas, Ka'Lea's is cool and hard. The music changes, and everyone stands. IlliaVaa taps his shoulder to get his attention. Reluctantly, he returns his focus to the ceremony and stands for the prayer.

The words wash over him, like a stream of sound. He mumbles something under his breath and sits, his attention back on Cate. She looks up from the sanctuary floor, her gaze finding his own. He tips his head. She doesn't respond, her gaze moves back to the sanctuary and the dais.

Boom! Viggo surges to his feet as the sanctuary doors burst open, the massive wood nearly shattering against the stone walls. A lean woman with a crown of strawberry blonde hair marches purposefully down the aisle to a cacophony of gasps and exclamations of outrage. Queen Ka'Lea turns, poised and composed, to face the intruder.

"All clans must be present at a royal wedding." Seethes the newcomer, her voice deep yet still very feminine.

"Then, you are just in time L'Nora. Be seated, and we shall proceed." Interjects v'Lana, slowly standing and facing the leader of the Lion Clan.

"Lady v'Lana, I thought you wiser than to unite with the Eagles. They claim to mate for life, only such claims hold no value, when they can just kill their spouse."

"King L'Syle's death was most unfortunate. The clans and nation grieve for him still."

"Yet, the queen reweds." Snarks L'Nora.

"It is her due," responds v'Lana with no hint of emotion.

The guards along the last two pews step in between L'Nora and the dais. She faces them as one would annoying, yet harmless, pests. Behind her streams an army of soldiers, around the sanctuary and down the aisle. L'Nora's white teeth can be seen from the balcony as she flashes a smile. "I object to this wedding." She steps closer to the guards. "Actually, I object to this rule."

The eagle and wolf on either side of the dais screech and growl as they face the soldiers nearing them. V'Lana approaches the wolf and rests her hand lightly on his head. Leaning close she whispers in his ear. Reluctantly, it settles. Its hackles lying flat though its teeth still show like daggers. Facing L'Nora and edging closer to the couple, V'Lana asks, "How did you enter the Reaches?"

L'Nora shrugs, a smug smile lifting her lips. "You think you're the only one who can use dragons?"

Viggo surges to his feet, angered by her tone if not her words. "Careful, brother." Warns IlliaVaa.

"Use is a harsh word. The dragons are our brethren, not our tools." V'Lana stands at d'Gar's side.

"Brethren? Just because they are nice to look at, and *use*, in human form does not make them our equal. Of course, they are tools. Isn't that why you encouraged your own son to…." She screams as the massive wolf launches, his teeth barely missing her throat as she springs backwards, tearing into the armor of her shoulder.

Animals snarl and scream, squawk, and squeal as the Kraeken elite transform. Metal clashes on metal and odd sonic bursts pop as they fire specialized weapons. "What are you waiting for? Get her out of here!" Shouts Viggo to the men with Cate.

Through all that unfolded below, she remained calm. Rising to her feet, he watches as her eyes begin to glow and light encircles her. "She's joining in the battle." IlliaVaa's voice echoes his own thoughts.

"Why won't she leave?" His heart beats against his ribs like a moth against a lamp. IlliaVaa points to the wolf still engaged with L'Nora, only the latter is now a lioness. Viggo's lips curl. The wolf.

The wolf who is always near her, in her dreams, and…. In. The. Way.

Xenothgorot roars. A fierce predatory claim of dominion. The cacophony in the sanctuary stills, all eyes lift to find who made such a sound. Shadows dance around him like flames licking his skin. He raises his hand, where a ball of fire forms between his fingers. "This ends here." Like a division one pitcher, he hurtles the fire.

Light blooms around the wolf as the fire hits, spraying the lioness and anyone near with its vicious sparks. Screams of terror and pain stab the ears. Viggo readies another fireball, only to see that the wolf is untouched. He stands staring up at the balcony, his teeth bared, and his snout curled. Fire hurtles towards him again and he doesn't move, the flames slide along a glowing barrier of light.

Soldiers flee, while a steward runs to engage the sprinkler system. L'Nora writhes in agony. Someone throws a tapestry over her and tamps out the fire. Water sputters and rains down, dousing dancing sparks. The globe of fire in Viggo's hand hisses with each drop of water that hits it but does not go out.

"It is done." Ka'Lea announces coldly from the dais. "This uprising, it is over. The Eagle and Wolf clans are united; the wedding ceremony is complete."

Xenothgorot/Viggo had forgotten the ceremony. Various animals drag the injured from the sanctuary while others bow in homage to their Queen and her new King Consort. The wolf does not. He continues to glare at Xenothgorot/Viggo, his lips curled. "This is not how you win her to you." IlliaVaa cautions. The Dragon Lord chuckles darkly, placing one foot on the banister and balancing his weight.

"I do not have to win the child to have the dragon." With lighting speed, he launches soaring over the sanctuary to the opposite balcony. Drow swords greet him. A barrier of steel, like a cage of dragon teeth, to his human flesh. Cate stands behind them, her eyes cold and blazing. Beautiful. Dragon-eyes. He catches his footing on the railing, balancing on its edge, just inches from the steel.

"Who do you fight for, Viggo?" Cate's words rake his spine, like talons on ice.

"Myself." Xenothgorot/Viggo answers with a casual grin.

Cate's breath hitches and she takes a step back, making room for the Elf to shield her from Xenothgorot's/Viggo's gaze. "You are not Viggo. Why did you attack Baen?"

"Rathleon is mine and you are Viggo's. No one shall come between us."

"This isn't our fight." Cate growls, her voice changing in depth and timbre.

"Ah, my gem, for once I agree. This is not our fight. It is time to end all this. Time for you to return to me."

Rathleon/Cate laughs breathily, curls bounce on her pale shoulders as she shakes her head. "I will never return to you. A thousand years has not changed you. You have not grown in compassion or understanding, only in hate and jealousy."

Viggo slips over the railing, the Drow swords rest on his chest as he stands to his full and imposing height. He ignores the Drow, his eyes on the Elf. "It is rare for Elven royalty to be so far from the Valley of Mist."

"Not so rare these days." Elar drawls with a bored tone.

I do not have scales to shield my flesh. If you move any closer, you'll have to wait another twenty years to find her. Viggo warns as Xenothgorot reaches for the irritating Elf.

Xenothgorot growls. "Rathleon, come to the Dragotian estate and receive what is your due."

"Cate is the Drow Queen and not subject to a human agreement made between dragon clans." Coolly challenges Smoke, his sword-arm aching to press his blade into flesh.

"She is dragon-souled!" Viggo roars. "And, as such, is subject to our laws."

Someone clears their throat and everyone on the balcony shifts their attention to a winged woman hovering over the sanctuary.

"You are all honored guests at *my* wedding and under treatise." Ka'Lea's white gown floats like a gossamer cloud about her as her wings beat to keep her aloft "The reception is about to begin in the banquet hall. I expect your attendance."

Cate grimaces. She dislikes the feel of Rathleon taking possession of her body. Queen Ka'Lea looks every bit like an avenging angel in her white gown, white wings, and shimmering white hair. Cate clears her throat and Rathleon recedes, nestling back inside Cate's body. Without a word or acknowledgement for Xenothgorot/Viggo, Cate turns on her heels and leads her party from the balcony.

Within minutes, they are met by Baen in his massive wolf form. He shoves his snout into Cate's hand to reassure himself she is okay. "I'm fine." She gently places her hand on his broad head. Pain stabs through their bond. "Viggo won't do anything here and I'm well-guarded. Tend to your wounds and join us in the reception hall."

Baen growls. With a bow of his head, he jogs out of sight. Cate continues to the hall. Bodies, lifeless and bloody, litter the ground. People pass by them as if they don't exist. A tremor runs through Cate as she steps over a growing pool of blood. Servants work to clean battle debris, as music wafts from a pair of double doors. "Kraeken are crueler than I imagined." Xon whispers.

"Life carries on." Replies an unaffected Smoke.

Elar offers his hand to help Cate step past the large body of a fallen Eagle while keeping an eye on Viggo who trails their party with his own.

The reception hall is intimate compared to the sanctuary. There's a table set above all others for the Queen and King Consort, and tables below for the guests. Cate finds her name card, and those with her, at v'Lana's table. The wolf matron looks untouched by the events of the wedding, her dress and hair impeccable. She bows her head to Cate as the young woman sits. "Thank you, for assisting Baen during the attack."

"He would not have needed it, if Viggo had stayed out of the fight." Comments Elar while pouring a glass of water for Cate. "I regret not having kept better tabs on dragon-souled politics the last several hundred years."

V'Lana absently toys with a champagne flute, twisting it back and forth by its stem. "It has not changed, really. You know of the dragon clans, yes?" Elar asserts that he does. "The clans remained when the dragons' souls were cast into humans. Eventually, they found each other and built societies. Xenothgorot is a high king, of sorts. He is the most powerful of the dragons, aside from his mate."

"Rathleon." Cate says softly.

"Yes, and their pairing was turbulent. It is said Rathleon left Xenothgorot midway through the Dragon War and joined the humans. His cruelty only increased with her absence." V'Lana waves at the room around her. "This stronghold was built to defend against him, now he sits within it. Such a strange world we live in."

The music silences and a herald announces the newlyweds. All in attendance stand. The royal entrance is somber. Ka'Lea's wings drape behind her like a feathered cape, their ends tinged red. Standing at the table, Ka'Lea addresses the assembly.

"Today, our brethren took up arms against us and paid with their lives. We do not honor traitors. Their clans are henceforth exiled, anyone caught within the Reaches or Kraeken lands will be killed on sight. Their ancestral assets are forfeit. Their enchantment, a curse. Let them live as the beasts they've become." A heavy spear pounds the floor three times.

"Long live the Queen." Prompts the herald.

"Long live the Queen." Choruses the clans.

Cate swallows, her lips clamp shut. As the attendees quiet, Queen Ka'Lea gestures to Viggo's table. "The crown extends a warm thank you to Viggo, clan leader of Dragotia. His elite team defended the sanctuary and prevented a greater disaster." Viggo bows.

"And, to Lord Baen, brother of our own King Consort, a special thank you from the Crown for defending the dais with Ka'Leel and allowing our ceremony to conclude unimpeded." Cate turns as the doors open and Baen enters. Dressed head to toe in black, with a mission-style collar, he makes Cate's heart pound so hard she feels faint.

She loses track of time, the blood rushing through her veins sounds like a raging river to her ears. Turning back to the table, she breathes deeply to calm herself as he sits beside Lady v'Lana. Elar glances between Cate and Baen, his eyes linger on her flushed cheeks and dilated pupils. He holds her chair as she sits.

Servants waste no time in serving food and drinks. A plate of steaming chicken with asparagus spears and rice is thrust in front of her, followed by another person pouring red or white wine. She politely declines the wine. She has little appetite, her mind still on the battle and the bodies in the hall.

"What progress have you made in your quest?" v'Lana asks, her tone polite, as if she is making idle conversation.

"Cate has all but the final Stone." Baen answers, as he cuts into his chicken.

Lady v'Lana sips from her glass, its red contents draw in the light. "Amazing, and in so short a time. You are truly motivated not to wed."

Cate sets her fork on her plate and rests her hands on her lap. She knows how sensitive dragon hearing is and imagines Viggo paying close attention to every word she says. "I only want a normal life. I want to date, go to college, and then someday marry. Is that an unreasonable request?"

Lady v'Lana studies the wine. "It is. For you, anyway. You are not normal. Any life you lead can is normal for you, as there is no one in this world like you nor will there be."

"She is right." Interjects Xon.

"You are the Drow Queen. You are dragon-souled. You are heir to the Enderen clan. And you are legally betrothed to the head of the

Dragotian clan. You have Drow bodyguards and my Oathsworn son protecting you. Do not expect to return to your human life. That is over."

Cate pushes back her chair as she stands. "Good night, Lady v'Lana." Without waiting for anyone, she strides toward the head table. The King Consort's eyes follow her the entire way. Ka'Lea's cool tone showers over her. "Queen Cate."

Cate bows her head to the couple. "I regret, I must leave. Congratulations on your wedding. And, on your... um, on... putting down the rebels."

"Thank you. When will Lord Baen be returning to the Wolf Clan?"

"That is his choice. Good night." Meeting first the queen's gaze and then the king consort's, Cate turns on her heel and strides confidently through the hall. Her guards, Elar and Baen fall in behind her.

Viggo starts to rise, but IlliaVaa grabs his arm. "Let them go. It is not time nor place."

"It better be the time and place soon." He growls.

"Soon, very soon." IlliaVaa soothes. "After all, things changed when she was crowned."

Viggo nods in agreement. Legal or not, with or without bloodshed, crown or no crown. She will be his. "Plan a meeting with Kith."

"Of course." IlliaVaa reflexively stares at Viggo with the Eye of Truth. The images she sees terrify her.

CHAPTER 28

"It is not that heavy. Move!" Tatiana growls, urging Tawn along as he waddles in front of her cradling a green flecked dragon egg the size of an award-winning watermelon. They deposit their precious cargo on the other side of the portal, then return passing Vek with an egg cradled in each arm like oversized footballs.

The sounds of battle rage above them, though buffered by layers of stone. Warm water, heated by natural hot springs, splashes up their legs as they search the cavern. "The pool at the far end, that's all that's left." Vek shouts over his shoulder.

With dragon-vision, it's easy for Tatiana to see the bulbous shapes nestled in the dark recesses. She points out two for Tawn and picks up the last. "This is it, let's go."

As she picks up the egg, the world falls silent. Tawn straightens, the eggs held tightly against his chest. Vek stands with one leg on either side of the portal. He beckons them to him, and they sprint across the cavern.

"Who do you think won?" Tawn whispers.

"Doesn't matter." Tatiana replies as he slips through the portal. She hands the egg in her arms to Vek and steps through, words of power already leaving her mouth as she touches the mirror to close the portal.

That had been the agreement with U'Sar, she'd create a portal for their armies to enter the Sanctuary if he found a way to get her access to the dragon eggs held captive by the Kraeken. All it took was to set her pocket mirror on a ledge. She didn't need to know where the cavern was if she recognized the resonance of the reflective surface.

Sweat dampens her skin and humidity makes her clothes stick to her as she surveys the egg nursey. "Let's get the eggs situated, then I'll make a portal home. I'm too tired to walk down the mountain."

"I second that." Tawn huffs as he retrieves the watermelon sized egg and gently submerges it in a warm pool.

"This cavern is perfect, Vek." Tatiana beams moving two eggs so that another can rest beside them in the warm water.

"At least my hours of hiking and spelunking paid off." Vek grins. Tatiana wipes sweat from her forehead with the back of her hand. Vek and Tawn couldn't be more different, as twins. Tall and leanly built, Tawn is built like a volleyball player. While Vek, short and thick, is built like a lineman. They've been friends most of her life, and only recently has Vek become more.

Opening a portal home, Tatiana graces both boys with a heartfelt smile. "Thanks for helping me."

"You're welcome." Vek's cheeks redden with more than exertion. Tawn makes a sarcastic comment about not having a day where he risks his life on some foolhardy errand. The boys step into her room, and she follows. As the portal closes, she tosses a cover over the mirror.

Vek and Tatiana plop on her bed and Tawn flops on to a beanbag. "So, not that I don't love a good rescue mission, but want to tell us what we volunteered for?" Tawn opens a mini fridge in arms' reach and pulls out three bottles of water, tossing a few at the bed.

Tatiana opens a bottle and chugs half before answering. "Okay, you all remember my cousin, the one that's been missing for years?"

"The one with the arranged marriage to the head of Dragotia?"

Tatiana rolls her eyes at Tawn. "Do I have more than one cousin that's been missing for years? Yes, that one. Well, she somehow hooked up with Lord Baen."

"The brother of Lord d'Gar?" Vek asks, finishing his water and crumpling the plastic bottle.

"The same. My aunt and uncle recently went to visit the Drow."

"Not a great vacation spot." Tawn interrupts. "Wait, what do the Drow have to do with the Kraeken?"

"If you'd stop interrupting, I'd get there." Tawn glares at her and closes his mouth. "Well, my cousin turns out to be the Queen of the Drow. And she took Lord Baen and this Elf, that's following her around, and probably some Drow guards... I don't know because even though she isn't a Traveler she can Travel... to the Kraeken."

"Bitter much?"

"You would be too if someone suddenly showed up to save the world while you're left holding the door, only to learn you're not even needed for that."

"Ignore him. How did you end up getting involved with the Kraeken?" Vek asks taking her empty water bottle and squishing it.

"A very convincing Bear." Answers Tatiana standing and leading the way from her room. "Mom's home, and I need a shower. No, that's not an invitation." She gives Tawn a sour look. "Thanks again for helping me. We'll figure out what's next after dinner." At the front door, she leans in hoping for a light kiss but Vek only smirks and waves as he trots away.

"I do not know what it is you see in them."

Tatiana shrugs. "Hi Mom, I'll take a quick shower. I won't be long, I promise."

"Fifteen minutes, and then I start eating without you." Oksana laughs as Tatiana takes two stairs at a time and vanishes into the bathroom.

Cate plops onto the couch as Baen disappears down the hall and Elar opens the cabinet retrieving a glass and filling it with cool water.

Elar sits beside her and hands her the glass. "Quite the day." She takes the water and guzzles it. "Turn around and I will work the knots." She complies, sweeping her hair to one side. His large hands settle on her shoulders and set to work.

Small whimpers of pain escape her lips. He pulls away but she urges him to continue. A menacing, chest-deep growl fills the room. Elar pauses. Cate looks behind her to see Baen in wolf form, lips curled over his teeth, snarling. "He isn't hurting me. Well, it does hurt but he's releasing the tension in the muscles." She pulls from Elar's grip and faces Baen. "Why are you in wolf form?"

"I'm exhausted and this is…safer." He pads into the room and settles at her feet.

"I'm going to get out of this dress." She steps over him and vanishes into her room.

Silence fills the space. Heavy, oppressive. Neither man willing to end it. They both involuntarily jump as someone bangs heavily on the door. A few seconds later, it opens, and a red-faced Emily and a grim-faced Kith enter.

"Where is she?" Emily's voice is raspy, as if she's been crying. Her eyes fall on the crown sitting on the table. Elar points to the hallway. Kith sits and Elar calmly faces him while Baen wanders to the closed bedroom door.

"What were you thinking?" Emily shrieks.

The bedroom door opens, revealing Cate clad in a pair of shorts and an oversized print t-shirt. "Mom, I've had a really long and really hard day. I don't want to do this right now."

"You don't… you don't want to do this?! I don't care what you want, we *ARE* doing this. You aren't even eighteen. You've already been kidnapped once, and now you voluntarily go to fight someone else's war?"

Cate's head lowers, her hair falls like a curtain across her face. "I wasn't in harm's way. Baen simply went to help shore up their defenses."

Emily crosses her arms over her chest. "Is that true?" Her head swivels to pin Baen. He nods, though slowly and it takes a second before he responds. His delay is enough for Emily. "What is true?

Did you go to shore up their defenses?" Again, Baen nods. "But she *was* in danger, wasn't she?" Baen doesn't look at Cate as he nods again. Emily rounds on her daughter. "You're grounded."

Cate laughs and her eyes meet her mother's heated gaze. "Grounded? Mom, that ship sailed. Long ago." She skewers Baen with a glare before focusing again on Emily. "I am engaged, a high school graduate, a queen! I don't care if I haven't turned eighteen. You have no control over my life, not anymore."

"You went to *WAR*. It's not like you stayed out late. People died, Cate."

"That's what happens when you defend what's right. People die."

"Was it right? How do you know you were on the right side?"

"Because I was on Baen's side. I don't care about the Kraeken, but I care about him. If his family is in need, then he gets my help. Just like I know he would help me. Besides, I had the Drow and Elar with me. Do you think anyone was getting passed them?"

"Do not belittle your own power, Cate. In truth, you can protect yourself very well." Elar interjects sidling next to Cate and wrapping his arm around her shoulder. Emily's eyes shift from him to his arm, to Cate and back.

Emily straightens her shoulders, her eyes flashing and her jaw tight as she grits her teeth. "As queen, you should never risk yourself unnecessarily. You have more to consider than your own welfare or that of your friends."

"You left the Drow. What right do you have to play the responsibility card?"

"That is enough!" Kith bellows. The deep timbre of his voice echoes off the walls, drawing the guards from outside to open the doors and check that all is clear. "You will not speak to your mother that way."

"What right do you have in this conversation?" Cate challenges, eyebrows raised and hands on hips.

Kith takes a menacing step forward and grabs Emily's wrist. "My right is as your father, whether or not I raised you. Your mother came here out of fear and concern. Fear that you may be injured, and concern over the choices you are making. You haven't heard a single word she's said. Come, Emily." Lightly pulling her by the wrist, he leads her to the door.

He pauses and turns back to Cate. "Never underestimate our love for you, nor believe it lacking. And, whether or not we love you, does not mean we respect you."

"Respect! You sold me in an arranged marriage." Cate growls, her eyes glowing and spurts of flames licking her lips.

Kith drops Emily's wrist and squares his shoulders. The mass of him makes the room feel small. "I did what was best for all dragon-souled."

"Whatever, *Father*." Cate shrugs out of Elar's grasp and storms into her room, slamming the door.

Silent tears wash over Emily's cheeks as she leaves followed by Kith.

Elar watches them go, the apartment silent once again. He crosses to Cate's bedroom, followed by Baen, and lightly knocks. The sounds of sobs filter through the wood. He knocks again. When there is no response, he opens the door and Baen pushes through, his massive wolf form driving the door into the wall. Cate lifts her head. "I don't want to talk."

Elar's eyes flicker to Baen lying at Cate's feet, the werewolf acting like a mere dog. "I am unfamiliar with the amount of emotion humans display, but not with what you feel." Elar sits beside Cate and hands her a box of tissues. "Your mother was wrong."

Cate sniffles and lifts her head to meet his gaze. "Really?" She sniffles again and Elar gently takes her hand and slips it into his, their fingers entwining.

"You are a queen. Queens need allies. Whether or not you assisted the entrenched Kraeken leadership because you were against their war, whether or not you support Ka'Lea and d'Gar, whether you just did it for a friend – your reasons do not matter. What matters is the result of the actions you took. Baen is oathsworn. He is an extension of you. By allowing him to provide strategic expertise to the Kraeken Crown, even if he is Kraeken born, you allied yourself with the Kraeken Monarchy."

"He's right." Baen growls.

"Whatever action or inaction you take no longer reflects on you, but all Drow. It is one of the strings attached to rulership." With his free hand, Elar tucks Cate's hair behind her ear. "As a crowned ruler, you can no longer think only as Cate and about what you want. You must think of yourself as the nation. What the nation wants and what is best for it." He gently squeezes her hand. "What Cate wants as a person and as a woman are now one with what Cate wants for the Drow."

A sob shakes her shoulders. "I only took the crown to set you free."

"And, in so doing, unwittingly stepped into a prison of your own. Gilded as it is."

Baen tilts his head to look up at Cate from the floor. He can feel the depth of her pain through their bond. He whines, and with her free hand, she reaches down and strokes the top of his head between his ears.

"My father doesn't even know me and yet he judges me." She pulls her hand from Elar's, wipes the tears from her face, and her mood shifts from hurt to anger. "This is his fault. All of it. And, he has the nerve, the nerve, to tell me off! He has no right to speak into my life, not after agreeing to marry me off to Viggo."

At the sound of that name, a spike of jealousy flares deep in Elar's heart. He lightly sets his hand on her lower back, needing to feel her warmth, to have contact with her. "Why did he attack us during the battle?"

Cate blinks and shakes her head, as if to clear unwanted thoughts. "Viggo didn't. That was Xenothgorot, Rathleon's ex. Only, he didn't get the memo they broke up."

Seconds tick by as silence spreads between then, broken by the harsh sound of Baen chuckling. Elar lifts one eyebrow, his cold eyes pinning the wolf. "What is funny?"

"The dragon war, and the resulting dragon-souled; and now, the Kraeken war are because of bad marriages."

"I do not find that funny." Elar continues to touch Cate's lower back, lightly drawing small circles with his fingertip.

"I'm tired." Cate pulls away from Elar and lies down, covering her face with her forearm.

"Would you like me to stay?" Elar offers.

"I'm okay. Baen's here."

The bed shifts as he stands. "Goodnight." After a few seconds, the door opens and closes. Cate lifts her arm to find herself alone with the wolf version of Baen lying next to the bed.

CHAPTER 29

Viggo stumbles from bed, nauseous and with a throbbing head. The Dream had been especially vivid. Xenothgorot gathering his generals, planning, drinking. He staggers into the bathroom and turns on the cold water in the shower. Not bothering to remove his clothes, he steps inside and lets the sting of the water wash away the lethargy and pain.

At length, he turns off the water and wraps a towel around himself. His gaze meets his eyes in the mirror and then travels the length of his skin. His scales are spreading. They wrap around the base of his neck and dip into a deep-V below his diaphragm. Glittering red drapes over his shoulders and edges toward his biceps. Unmistakable evidence that Xenothgorot is getting stronger.

There's a rap on his bedroom door, soon followed by another on the bathroom door. "Lord Viggo?"

"What is it, Dane?

"You've missed your morning meetings. I've rescheduled them, but need to know if I should cancel the remaining for this afternoon."

"Reschedule anything I have for the remainder of the week. Then, set up a time for me to meet with Kith Ender."

"You are not scheduled to meet with your father-in-law until the end of the month."

"Question me again and they will find your body floating in the bay."

"Yes, Lord Viggo. A request was delivered, by one of our Travelers, to meet with U'Sar, leader of the Bear clan. Considering your connections with the Kraeken royal family, I was uncertain if you would like to receive it."

Viggo opens the bathroom door, standing before Dane in only the towel. Dane's eyes glitter with malicious delight as his gaze travels to Viggo's new scales. "I will meet him. An investor is an investor, after all."

"I will schedule with both Ender and U'Sar." Dane bows his head and quietly departs.

Within an hour, Viggo is smartly dressed in black slacks, a black button-down silk shirt, and platinum jewelry. His hair is slicked back, his jawline accentuated by an early morning shadow. Sitting at the balcony table, he sips warm honey-water while sketching an image of Cate at the wedding.

IlliaVaa saunters into the room, pours a mug of coffee and joins him. He glances up at her entrance and returns to sketching. "You look like... a handsome piece of crap." He chuckles at her bold statement. "Did you get any sleep last night?"

"Xenothgorot was in the Dream. So, no."

When IlliaVaa remains silent, he sets down his pencil and looks at her. Her raven locks are in a loose ponytail. Her makeup and clothing are perfect. "What brings you here?"

"The wedding." She sips her coffee waiting for him to ask what about the wedding, but he never does. He sips from his mug in silence, then returns to sketching. "Are you going to move it up?"

"Yes."

"To when?"

"As soon as I can get Cate here. I don't care who is in attendance. I don't care what the decorations look like. I only care that there is an officiant."

"That is not how it is done. Not among people of our stature. It is demanded that we have pomp and circumstance. We have to put on a show."

"That can come after the ceremony. Have someone on standby. I expect it will happen soon."

"She's not even 18."

"She's a Drow Queen, dragon-souled! Who cares about her age." Viggo holds her gaze for a few tense seconds before returning to sketching.

IlliaVaa sips her coffee, her eyes flicker into dragon-sight. Truth never lies. She'd glimpsed it at the Kraeken wedding, and now seeing a psychopath like Dane act like a tame secretary, she'd assumed it. But the Truth is clear. Viggo is losing control. Soon, it won't be her brother looking through his eyes or moving his limbs. She finishes her coffee. "So, I know where to stash the officiant, where will you host the ceremony?"

"It doesn't matter." His hands never stop moving and he doesn't re-engage with her.

"The manor then. I can make sure it's pretty and ready to go, and have an officiant stay there as long as necessary." IlliaVaa pushes back her chair and stands. "I've got work to do. Call me if you need me." She doesn't wait to be dismissed, leaving as quickly and as arrogantly as she entered.

Viggo barely notices. His full attention is on his sketch. It's the only way he can quiet Xenothgorot and focus on his own thoughts.

Truth is unyielding. It is without sugar and often difficult to face. And, individually, it is subjective; understood based on one's own experience and biases. IlliaVaa closes one eye and narrow's the other enough to see where she is going without walking into a wall.

Unlike others, she must face Truth. It is her gift and her curse. The Truth is that Viggo will not be able to withstand Xenothgorot much longer. Generation after generation of Dragotians have prepared for this day, the day that Xenothgorot leads the dragons in taking over their human hosts. The day that dragons become free again.

But that truth is tainted. What is freedom when you steal another's body? Are you truly free? She unconsciously shakes her head, her body acknowledging the Truth even if her conditioned mind cannot.

How can she talk with Cate without Viggo knowing? How can she even contact her? There's always the Dream, but even the Dream has its risks. And there isn't a single Traveler she can trust that won't report right away to Viggo. Dane is definitely a no-go. She shudders at the thought of willingly asking him for a favor. Phone calls can be recorded, and texts can be traced and pulled from servers.

She takes a deep calming breath, holds it for the count of three, and then exhales. There has to be a way. Who can get close to her? Who…. That cousin of hers. The one that's been sneaking into and out of the manor. The Traveler. Can she be trusted?

Truth will tell.

Tawn and Vek are finishing off their second pizza. It's their payment for risking their necks to help her steal the dragon eggs. She swirls the ice in her cup, watching the dark soda bubble. "Did you all see the news?"

Tawn talks around bites. "You mean about what went down?"

"No, she's talking about hockey, smooth brain." Vek growls.

"Yeah, we saw it. They're calling it a terrorist attack. The Kraeken couldn't keep it under wraps from the humans, so they had to disguise it as something."

"I heard any clans involved in the rebellion were cast out, their properties confiscated."

"Sucks to be them."

"It's good you had the foresight to get the eggs out in advance. Who knows what would have happened to them had they stayed in those crèches."

"What if they connect us with the Bear clan or the rebellion? I mean, I *was* involved."

"So, we never talk about that again." Vek announces. "Didn't happen. We found those eggs where they are now, that's it. Nothing else."

"Right, nothing else." Tatiana's phone rings and she jumps. She forgot she had taken it off silent last night. She taps to answer it. "Yeah, Mom?"

Tawn and Vek continue eating. Tatiana makes a few noncommittal grunts and then responds with a reluctant, "yeah, okay, fine." She hangs up and sets the phone down.

"Everything okay?"

"She says she got a call from a client, dragon-souled, who wants her there today at 2 p.m. and she needs me to take her."

Vek glances at his watch. "So, you need to go. It's already 1:30 p.m. and your mom hates being late. Want me to drive you?"

She shakes her head and smiles. "Finish eating. I'll take care of the tab and see you guys later tonight." Taking a quick gulp of soda, she wanders to the counter and pays, then heads to the Women's bathroom.

Inside, she takes a few minutes to wash her hands, fix her hair and ensure the bathroom is empty before creating a portal with the mirror and stepping through to Oksana's office.

Stepping from a full-length mirror in the corner, she gets a friendly greeting from her mother. "You must have been with the boys. They're the only ones that can make you arrive on time."

Tatiana rolls her eyes and flounces into a white chair near the desk. As usual, Oksana's office is organized and tidy. Not even a scrap of paper on her desk. "Who are we meeting?"

"That's for me to know, they are *my* client after all. What you need to know is where we are going." Oksana hands Tatiana an address and a picture. Her daughter's gaze shifts between each. "Google it." Oksana replies. "You have fifteen minutes until we leave to familiarize yourself with it."

"Great." Pulling out her phone, Tatiana searches the internet for the address and all related pictures of the location. She then reviews the image her mother provided. The fifteen minutes pass too quickly for her comfort.

Turning to the mirror, she closes her eyes and envisions the location to travel. When she opens them again, the mirror reflects the image in her mind's eye. Oksana doesn't hesitate, she confidently steps from one location to the other followed by Tatiana.

They are in northern Washington State. Close to Seattle at a cozy bed and breakfast. A one-bedroom cottage with all the makings of a romance movie. Oksana checks her phone. "Wait here." She steps outside, and Tatiana searches for a television remote, then plops unceremoniously onto the couch.

The door opens as she's flipping channels looking for something to pass the time. Only, it isn't Oksana who enters. It's the most beautiful raven-haired beauty she's ever seen, the one and only IlliaVaa Dragotian. Tatiana hits the mute button and turns her attention to IlliaVaa as she sits across from her.

She focuses on not fidgeting under IlliaVaa's dragon-gaze. Rumors are that she is a Truth-seer. The only gifted with such sight. And she'd been in attendance at the Kraeken royal wedding. IlliaVaa blinks, her eyes returning to normal and sits back in the chair. A warm smile graces her timeless face.

"I am not one for small talk. I contacted Oksana because I need your help."

Tatiana blinks, her brows furrow. "My help? I thought you were my mom's client."

"I am. Let me ask you, where does your loyalty lie? Are you loyal to your clan? To dragon-kind? To humans?"

All sorts of alarms go off in Tatiana's mind. What is this woman fishing for? What does she want to know? "I'm loyal to my clan, of course, and dragon-kind. Why?"

"I am loyal to dragon-kind too." A soft smile spreads IlliaVaa's lips. "As part of the Ender clan, you likely do not know the full history of Dragotia. We have dedicated generations to restoring the dragons and returning the pre-eminent dragon to power."

"Xenothgorot." Whispers Tatiana.

"The same. Your cousin marrying my brother accomplishes this millennia old goal. It's quite astonishing really and dramatic to consider. The problem is that it puts him in power through a human, my brother."

"But that's what you want right?"

"No. I want the dragons to be released from the confines of human carriers. I do not want them suppressing human souls as they have been suppressed. Nothing about that is right." IlliaVaa absently toys with the arm of the chair. "I know I don't want to be an onlooker in my own body for the rest of my life."

"I'm confused."

"Understandably. Look, the reason I contracted with Oksana and am talking to you, is that I need you to warn Cate. I can't do it. I cannot get close enough to her without alerting Xenothgorot."

"Warn her?"

"My brother is losing control. He isn't the one leading, acting or controlling his own body most of the time anymore. It's Xenothgorot. He's figured out how to give dragons dominance. If he can master it, how much longer before he shares this information with his generals, his followers? And, when he does, what will it do to the bodies they inhabit? My brother's scales are rapidly covering his body." Tatiana meets IlliaVaa's stern gaze. "Think what that means."

"And what am I to tell Cate to do with this information?"

"Viggo or Xenothgorot, I'm not really sure which right now, is trying to move up the wedding. He wants to marry Cate as quickly as he can get his hands on her." IlliaVaa raises her hands to forestall any argument. "You will have to convince her this is a good thing. My family has a set of jewelry, passed down to each person who carries Xenothgorot's soul, meant for his bride. I believe the set makes up the last pieces of the Dragon Stone Cate needs in order to do whatever she can to set the dragons free. And, the only way she will get it, is to marry my brother."

Tatiana laughs out loud. She cannot help herself. "You want me to convince my cousin, who I really don't know by the way, to marry your brother after she ran from him? And has continued to run from him?"

"If your loyalty is truly to dragon-kind, you will do this. It is about saving two races, dragons and humans. If Cate doesn't act soon, there won't be any human dragon-souled left to save." IlliaVaa stands and sweeps her hair over her shoulders. She doesn't wait for a response from the girl and doesn't bid her farewell.

Tatiana sits in silence as the door bangs shut. A few minutes later, Oksana enters. She sits on the same chair IlliaVaa occupied. "As a lawyer, I do not want to know. As your mother, spill it."

Looking like a fish trying to breathe out of water, Tatiana gasps. "She wants Cate to marry Viggo as soon as possible."

Oksana's face is impassive. Her tone even when she speaks. "She paid me a hefty sum to put me on retainer only to get you to do what is already contracted to be done, and what I have fought against. Why?"

"Do you think it is really possible to free the dragons' souls and return them to their bodies?"

Oksana thoughtfully considers her answer. "Possible yes. Plausible, not really. Is that what this is about?"

"She says Viggo is losing to Xenothgorot, that soon her brother will no longer control his own body."

"And somehow marrying Cate will fix this?" Oksana sounds dubious.

"It sounds more like she wants to get her there so that Cate can get some jewelry that the Dragotians have been safeguarding."

"What do you think?"

"I think, it is really hard not to believe someone who is known for Truth."

"Just because she can see it, doesn't mean she lives it." Oksana gestures to the mirror. "I have another appointment in an hour. Let's head home."

Tatiana creates a portal back to Oksana's office. Her mind circles around IlliaVaa's words. If Viggo really is losing to Xenothgorot, what does that mean for every other dragon? Will she too be a prisoner in her own body, subject to another is will? A small voice deep in her subconscious connects that thought with her own Truth. Her body is already a prison.

CHAPTER 30

Cate nurses her coffee while scrolling through videos on a tablet in the great room. Smoke knocks and enters. She glances at him and goes back to scrolling. "Yes?"

He dutifully bows though she pays him no mind. "The High Council requests your presence."

"Why?"

Smoke smirks, his intense gaze meets and holds hers. "I'm not privy to that information."

"When?"

"Now."

She sighs, finishes her coffee, and stands. As she starts towards the door, Smoke stops her. "With all respect, my queen, you should dress with the dignity of your station."

"And what does that look like? Obviously, not the jeans I'm wearing in your opinion." Cate crosses her arms and taps her foot. Smoke gestures to the hall that leads to her room. Walking past him, she throws open her bedroom door, and startles a sleeping Baen, who is still in wolf form. He snarls. She acts like he's not there, throwing open her closet doors. "Tell me." She challenges Smoke, "What befits my station?"

Baen's lips pull back over impressive canines as Smoke thumbs through Cate's closet. Smoke glances at Baen, then dutifully ignores him. He pulls out a sleek red suit with black satin trim and weblike details embroidered along the arms. "Pair it with stilettos and you will carry yourself like a queen." Cate accepts the suit. Smoke nods to Baen and exits the room.

The wolf growls to himself, stands and shakes. Flipping his tail in agitation, he follows Smoke out of the room. Cate shuts the door and changes into the suit. The pencil skirt falls just below her knees, and the fitted jacket perfectly hugs her curves. She tucks the tails of the black tank into the skirt and buttons the jacket. She slips her feet into a pair of jet-black knee-high stiletto boots, zips them and strides confidently into the great room.

Human Baen, in a fitted black suit, stands beside Smoke. Both men's gazes move from her toes to her head. "All that is missing is your crown."

Cate runs her fingers through her hair and then positions the spider crown on her brow. Its fibers wrap in her tresses, making it impossible for anyone to remove but Cate. "Now, am I presentable?" Smoke bows in answer and opens the door to the apartment.

The walk to the council hall is brief. Smoke pushes open the double doors as someone in the background announces Cate. Holding her head high and her shoulders back, she strides into the room. Baen a step behind her.

Rook smiles and bows. The rest of the council follows his lead, as Cate ascends to a chair positioned slightly higher than the others. Baen stands behind her, his gaze studying each person in the room.

It's a modest hall. Windowless. The carpet lush and the furniture of the highest grade but lacking embellishment. It could be any boardroom at any company.

"Thank you, my queen, for joining today's council session." Placates Rook. "Our original agenda has been set aside to discuss what your rule, and your marriage, will look like."

Chana pushes back her chair and stands. Her voice resonates throughout the room when she speaks. "We are in unprecedented times. The queen is not a full-blooded Drow. We do not know what her lifespan will be, or how carrying a dragon's soul will affect her."

Cate fights the urge to leave. "My marriage is my business. As for my rule, what motions are on the floor?"

Channa bows. "Motion one is to infiltrate human society. Motion two is to take over the Kraeken. Motion three is to subjugate the dragons. Motion four...."

"Subjugate?" Cate's voice resonates with a timbre not her own. Dragon eyes stare down at the Council. To their credit, only a few squirm beneath her gaze.

"You, and the Drow, are at risk if the dragons do not accept the Drow as their sovereigns." A lean hawk-nosed Drow, with a voice fit for a larger man, argues.

Fire travels from Cate's mouth to dance along her skin. Her clothes begin to smoke. Baen leans close to her ear, ignoring the heat, and reminds her the clothing she wears is not fireproof. He then wraps his cloak around her to douse the fire.

"Dragons are subject to no one." She stands and meets the gaze of each council member. "I am the blood of Arranien, I choose my path. Your motions are no more than ink on paper. My rule. My marriage. They are mine to choose. Talk again about subjugation and I will personally see your end." Cate stalks from the hall with Baen in her wake.

The doors slam behind her. Bathed in an amber halo of sunlight, she closes her eyes. To anyone looking, it seems she is in an argument with herself. Seconds tick by as she straightens, her steps taking her not to her apartment but to the barracks of the Black Guard.

Xon glances up as the doors swing open. He moves to his feet as they close, the light glare fading and the image before him resolving into the queen. "My Lady."

"Who do they think they are?" She spins on Smoke. "I will not be *summoned* again, is that understood?" He bows low. She spins to Xon. "Am I the ruler of the Drow or is the Council?"

"The truth, my lady?" Xon asks. She curtly nods. "The Council rules the Drow. We've not had a royal leader in nearly a thousand years. That's a long time. Your appearance is surprising, and what you mean to the Drow must be defined. Will you rule? Will the Council? Are you a figurehead or are you more?"

Fire dances along Cate's tongue. It licks at her throat and teases her lips. Pain spikes her joints and flares along her ligaments. Rage blinds her. She screams, fire erupting from her mouth.

"Cate, you need control, or you will burn down the place." Baen cautions. Stepping close, he pulls her into his arms. He focuses on a feeling of calm, knowing the emotion will carry along his oath-sworn bond.

She fights his strong embrace; her anger battles his calm. Xon and Smoke both drop to their knees in deference. Baen holds her tight. "Fight it." He whispers. "Take the lead. See a clear smooth lake, not a ripple on the water's surface. Imagine the coolness of the water, fed by winter snow." Cate stills. "Your soul is at peace. Your mind at ease."

Tears leak from her eyes. He loosens his grip and studies her face. The fire is gone. Slowly, he releases her. She crumples to the ground. "I am nothing. Just a high school graduate, facing an unwanted marriage, playing queen. I just want this to end. I want to set the dragons free, and… and…." Tears brim in her eyes as she meets Baen's gaze. "I don't even know what I want anymore. I thought I wanted to go to college, date a few guys, fall in love and get married… to be normal. But now," she gestures to the world around her. "Now, I don't know."

"Normal is what you make it." Xon softly says. "You are queen. No one can deny that. You sat on the obsidian throne and lived. Your will *is* the will of the Drow and that is what has the Council on edge. Should you choose to claim it, the power is yours."

"Our world knows this, that is why your appearance at the Kraeken wedding matters." Smoke adds from the other side.

A knock on the door has Cate pushing to her feet and wiping her cheeks to regain a measure of dignity. Once she is composed, Smoke opens the door. Tatiana waits outside. "May I come in? When I went to Cate's house, they said she was here."

Xon grimaces. "By all means, follow me." He leads them to a windowless room with black leather furniture and a blue light for illumination. Cate sits and then offers a chair to her cousin, none of the men make a move to leave.

"Can we talk in private?"

Cate glances from Tatiana to Baen, Smoke and Xon. Reminding herself of her outbreak only moments before, she shakes her head. "No."

Tatiana sighs and settles into the chair. "You're rockin' that suit and I love your heels, in case anyone hasn't said how good you look. Don't take me wrong, I think women need to tell each other when they look good."

"Thanks."

"I know we're not friends, and we barely know each other. I know there's no reason for you to trust me. But I've got to try."

"Try what?"

"Do you know IlliaVaa?"

Cate tenses and nods once.

"Then, you know her gift of Truth. She arranged a meeting with me today. She wants me to convince you to return to Viggo, soon." Tatiana quickly raises her hands, to stop Cate from interrupting. "She told me that their family has an heirloom jewelry set for Xenothgorot's bride that contains pieces of the Dragon Stone. She thinks the wedding is how you can get them, and with them free the dragons."

"IlliaVaa wants to free the dragons?"

Tatiana absently toys with the hem of her shirt. "She said that Xenothgorot is taking over Viggo's body. His scales aren't confined to his spine anymore, and she isn't sure when she's speaking to her brother or the dragon." Tatiana scoots to the edge of the chair and leans towards Cate, fighting an urge to grip her hands. "She thinks that soon, Xenothgorot will train his generals how to take control of the human bodies that harbor them, forcing human souls to be imprisoned. Please, Cate, I don't want to live like that."

An image of Kith's drawings surface into Cate's memory, a drawing of humans bowing to two-legged dragons.

No, she cannot let it happen. She cannot let Rathleon's mistake perpetuate. Cate straightens her spine and meets Baen's eyes with a steel-hard gaze. A muscle in his jaw ticks, otherwise, he is statue-still.

Rising from the chair like the queen she is, Cate sets a hand on Tatiana's shoulder and gives it a gentle squeeze before leaving the Black Guard's barracks.

Two days later, Cate sits on the Obsidian Throne with Baen at her side. Her personal guards line the circle nearest the throne. The Drow Council, the Enderen elders, and members of the Wolf and Eagle Clans fill the remaining rings.

IlliaVaa enters the cavern as her name is announced. Her golden hair shines, even in the dim candlelight, her fitted white pantsuit a glaring contrast to the black garments of the Drow. In her hands, she carries the Dragon Stone that Dane stole the night of Cate's coronation. Voices hush as she passes. When she reaches the causeway to the throne, she bows from her waist.

"The throne acknowledges, IlliaVaa Dragotian, sister of Viggo. Do you accept the terms of marriage and ceremony?" Rook asks from the front row.

IlliaVaa takes a deep breath and enigmatically smiles. "The Dragotians have long prepared to celebrate the marriage of Xenothgorot and Rathleon, through the human bearers of their souls. If the Drow tolerates the presence of our priests, we will gladly hold the ceremony before the Obsidian throne and fulfill the contract of the Dragotians and Enderen. I bring the Dragon Stone as a token of our sincerity."

Rook looks to Cate and when she nods, he replies, "Your terms are acceptable to the throne. The marriage will take place in one week. The groom, his priests, and ten of his clan may enter our city anytime within the week to prepare."

IlliaVaa bows her head. "The wedding of Xenothgorot and Rathleon is as important to the dragons as finding an heir of Arraniean is to the Drow. Can we have, at least, one representative from each dragon clan in attendance?"

"The Dragotians may bring no more than ten attendees. We care not who comprise them."

IlliaVaa laughs, her voice carrying throughout the cavern. She gently sets the Stone on the ground, and she spins on her heels. "So be it." Without further ceremony, she strides from the ancient hall.

A feeling of dread settles deep in Cate's stomach.

That evening, Cate lies in bed, with Baen in wolf form on the floor beside her. "I don't know if I'm doing the right thing, but I can't do nothing." She sighs and rolls on her side so that her fingers can stroke the fur on Baen's back. "Has anyone heard from Elar?"

"No." Baen growls. "Try to sleep. I will guard your dreams, as I guard your room."

※ ※ ※ ※ ※

Xenothgorot gently rocks the crystal glass in his hands, watching the amber liquid it holds swirl. Everything is falling into place. In a week, he will once again be wed to the love of his life.

Surprisingly, the form she inhabits is not displeasing. He grins. Once he teaches her how to ascend and take control, forcing the human soul into submission, her human form will become even more stunning wrapped in brilliant blue-green scales.

Dane enters the dark study, sure-footed as ever. "My lord, our sources tell us that Kith Ender is not with his clan. It seems he has been with the Drow for some time."

The alcohol burns as he takes a sip. "Then, there is no reason to meet with him prior to the wedding. He will know of the Drow

Queen's decision." Setting the glass on the table, he grimaces. A white-hot pain shoots through his head, centered just above his eyes. Resting his elbow on the desk, he leans against his hand. "Ensure everything is ready for our departure first thing in the morning."

Hunter watches as Dane leaves the estate. His gaze travels among the well-known walls, the bookshelves, and titles that line them, to the windows and forest beyond. The house feels empty without Cate; no, his life does. She was the first to treat him as somebody. And he betrayed her.

Sadness tugs at him, he feels worn out and faded. Within the week, she'll be his sister-in-law. Another dragon in the house to serve. It's as if a fist squeezes his heart, soon they will all be dragons, not humans carrying the souls of dragons but dragons carrying the souls of humans. What little compassion they've shown him as their brother will be no more.

He locks the doors and turns off the lights. The future is not his to shape.

❀ ❀ ❀ ❀ ❀

Elar stands beside the Lady of the Valley, the Queen, his mother, overlooking a still mountain lake reflecting a pale moon. "What say you, Mother?"

She faces him, her eyes cool and demeanor composed. "As your mother, I am pleased. As your queen, I do not accept that a half-breed Drow is your match."

"My marriage with Cate unites the Elves."

"More than a thousand years of separation. There are reasons we are not one, my son. No, I do not agree."

"Whether you agree or disagree, whether the Council votes for or against it, none of these matter. I am informing you what will happen. You can accept it or not." Elar bows to the queen, turns on his heels and joins Rimalon. The elder does not speak. Together, they mount white stags. The beasts leap forward, racing north at break-neck speed.

✿ ✿ ✿ ✿ ✿

Cate leans against the wall, homework spread out on the comforter before her. She scratches the back of her neck, the pads of her fingers rubbing hard scale-like skin. She's going to have to say she's on her period to get out of swim class tomorrow. She leans back and rests her head against the wall. Which test is in the morning? Is it AP English or Biology?

There's a swift knock on the door. Before she can tell mom to come in, the door swings open revealing a tall muscular guy in blue jeans and a graphic t-shirt. "Sorry, but I think you should hear him out." He steps out of the doorway and an equally tall, but somehow more *human* looking guy with jet black hair steps inside. He looks haggard, like he hasn't slept well in weeks or like he's fighting a lingering sickness. Two large bruises are forming on his jaw and eye.

Her hand flies to her forehead as a searing white hot flash races from the top of her head through her eye. As it passes, she refocuses on the men. Her consciousness is now fully aware that she's in the Dream and before her stand Viggo and Baen.

"Is this how you guard me?"

Baen flushes. "Hear him out. I'm not going anywhere and he's too weak to try anything."

"Please." Viggo pleads.

Sweeping all the papers into a pile, she gestures for him to sit at the foot of the bed. He hesitates, but then sinks to the mattress. "Do not say anything, to me, that you do not want Xenothgorot to know. I am here to warn you. I am no longer in control of my body. He's succeeded in freeing himself, and in taking control."

"How are you here?"

"He's meeting with his generals in the Dream. I was able to follow him. Though he is the primary soul now, I am still me. It's just that I cannot always keep hidden from him what I want to hide. He's very good at figuring out what I'm up to."

"Should I assume he knows, or will find out, that you met me?"

Viggo chuckles and rubs his bruised cheek. "He'll know."

"Right, because what happens in the Dream is real. Thank you for the warning."

Viggo leans toward Cate and Baen steps into the room, menacing and coiled to strike. Instead of pushing himself on her, as he's done in the past, he stands. "For what it is worth, I am glad the marriage agreement happened. I would not have met you otherwise, and you are worth knowing." Viggo faces Baen. "Keep her safe for me and keep yourself in line." Without another word, he leaves the room.

Baen shuts the door and leans against it. Cate sighs and gestures to her homework. "And I thought this was hard! I hate Biology. Why am I dreaming about Biology?" She rolls off the bed and stands, wandering about her room picking up various things and setting them back down. "My life was easy when I was here. It was simple. Now? It is so messed up."

"You will sort it out."

"Thanks for the vote of confidence." She gestures to the door. "Did that defeated man look like Viggo to you? Was he anything like the guy I've been running from or fighting with?"

"He is just a man. Has been all along."

Cate rounds on him. "You are not helping!"

He shrugs. "That's why I let him in. He lost. The dragon won. Now, you know who you are facing." He can feel her unease and turmoil through their bond. Rather than using banal words, he grabs her wrist and pulls her against him into his arms. She settles her head against his chest, and he can feel her silent sobs. Soon, it will be over. Soon.

CHAPTER 31

Viggo and his entourage arrive the next day. They are greeted with little fanfare. Their lodgings are modest but beautifully decorated. Guards guide and shadow them, always present. Viggo/Xenothgorot admires the austerity and architecture of the Drow, with their dark aesthetics.

After settling in and being given a brief tour, they are led to the mountain and deep inside to the great hall. Drow stand on concentric stone rings. As they are led down one of the connecting aisles, heads turn and calculating eyes appraise them.

On the center ring sits the Obsidian Throne. The darkness between stone and the four aisles that unite them is fathomless. Voices fall silent.

The room darkens. He turns to watch as, down another cardinal aisle, a man and a woman in simple black robes lead a procession. Behind them marches the Drow Council. One by one, they line the edge of the circle facing the Throne. As the silence drags on, the queen enters. On her head sits a sparkling crown, on her shoulders a spider silk cloak. A gown of the deepest red hugs her curves like a second skin, falling all the way to her feet obscuring even her shoes. He holds his breath until she steps on to the walkway.

Her footfalls are silent. It's as if she glides on air. When she reaches the throne, she turns and faces the assembly. Her personal guard stands ready behind the throne. Gracefully, she sits. Her gaze shifts from one side of the room to the other, not even lingering on him for a second.

A councilman, with many beaded braids, walks ceremoniously to him and bows his head. "We welcome Lord Viggo, leader of the Dragotian Clan, bearer of Xenothgorot, to the Frozen City. In six days, we will gather in the temple to wed Lord Viggo and Queen Cateian. Until that time, Lord Viggo will be accompanied by Lady Channa."

Channa stands beside Rook, facing Viggo. Wearing black slacks, a black silk shirt, and black leather jacket with her long blonde hair bound into a tight bun at the nape of her neck, she looks every bit like a corporate executive and nothing like a Drow. She flashes a toothy grin at Viggo. "It will be my pleasure." He only glances at her, his eyes seek Cate once more.

"You will neither speak with nor see the queen until the day of your wedding." Rook continues. "She will be spending the time in seclusion, a part of our custom, to prepare."

Xenothgorot's had enough of the pompous posturing. Whispering words of power under his breath, he flicks his finger and moves the Drow out of his way. With long strides, he clears the bridge and finds himself standing inches from the throne. Cate stares up at him. Her mouth slightly parted, her eyes wide. Goosebumps pepper bits of her neck visible under the cloak. "You have made me wait long enough." His tone is soft, meant for dragon-hearing.

"You have not learned manners in a thousand years."

He shivers. The tone is Rathleon's. Her voice is like an aphrodisiac. He leans forward, placing a palm on each arm of the obsidian throne, intending to trap Cate. Instead, he screams. The sound foreign, the searing pain not his own. He yanks his hands back; blisters form on his palms.

"No one may sit the throne, nor touch it, unless they hold the blood of Arraniean." The Kraeken gloats from behind Cate.

"You overstep. This is *my* throne." Cate's voice carries throughout the room and echoes below them. "Leave. Do not approach me until the day we say our vows."

Viggo/Xenothgorot smirks. "There you are." Despite his wounds, he grips her face and fiercely kisses her. Baen grips him by the shoulders and pulls him back. Forcefully, he shoves him onto the bridge. Viggo straightens and arrogantly strides from the hall, his entourage following in his wake.

Cate/Rathleon watches him go. Looking every bit a Queen, they address the Drow. "The web is intricate and beautiful, the spider's prey unaware of the weave."

Once in the safety of her apartment, she releases the rage she felt at Viggo's violating kiss with an ear-splitting shriek. Every muscle in her body goes taut with the release. When her lungs hold no more air, she pants and straightens.

Someone clears their throat from across the room. Her gaze shifts to Elar and Rimalon sitting in the great room. They both stand and Rimalon respectfully bows. "It is wonderful to see you again, milady."

Embarrassment heats Cate's cheeks. "When did you… what are you doing here?'

"Lord Elar thought I could be of assistance to you. He has caught me up on your adventures and your success."

Cate removes the spider silk cape and crown, setting them in their appointed places, and joins them. Baen leaves them to catch up, silently slipping out of the apartment.

"Thank you for coming. I have all but the last Stone, and I should have it by the end of the week. I need to understand the Spell in the next five days."

Rimalon scratches his chin. "You have all but the last piece? Truly splendid. No wonder your power has grown. And, with the release of your Drow blood and characteristics, you are not the same dragon-souled young girl I met just a few short months ago." The old Elf's gaze shifts to Elar. "I understand, now."

Elar displays the smallest smirk. "If you can see her soul, you understand. Otherwise, you only think you do."

Realizing how far they traveled, Cate stands. "Do you want some water or something to eat? Has anyone showed you to your lodgings so you can rest and freshen up?"

Rimalon stands. "I would be honored to rest an hour and to bathe before we begin." Cate leads him to the door and gives orders. Within seconds, he is whisked away. Elar shuts the door, so that it is only he and Cate in the narrow hall.

"You are not marrying Viggo."

He's so close she can feel the heat of him, smell the scent of the woods on him. Loose strands of hair, freed from his mahogany braid, frame his features, and draw attention to his silver eyes.

The feeling of Viggo's blistered hands on her face, his lips on hers, fills her mind. Pushing to her toes, she tilts her head and presses her lips to Elar's. It takes a second for him to respond. Gently, he pulls her to him and deepens the kiss. For a few blissful moments, she lets herself disappear in it, then pulls away.

His arms wrap protectively around her. "I am never letting you go."

She doesn't respond, just rests in the warmth of his embrace.

For the next several days, Cate and Rimalon work deep in the bowels of the mountain to forge the Stones in her possession. Every spell, every attempt, fails.

One day before the wedding, Cate rests in defeat on a bench wrapped in the cool darkness of the underground. Rimalon left an hour prior to dig through historical writings in the Drow library, hopeful to find a hint.

She closes her eyes and rests her head against the stone behind her. Every part of her body is weary. Taking long, slow, even breaths she focuses on the hum of the stone. *Rathleon, do we even need to unite them? Why won't they work as they are?*

I never said they would not, Cateian.

Cate's eyes fly open, but the dark is so complete it doesn't matter if they are open or closed. *What do you mean?*

The Dragon Stone was merely a conduit, a focus. It will increase and redouble your ability. Its shape, material and facets were used as an amplifier. There is no reason why each piece could not be used in such a way as they are.

Cate takes the two Stones and sets them on the ground in front of her. Using the ring on her finger, she imagines funneling the magic from her arm through the ring to the first Stone, and then the first Stone amplifying it, and sending it to the second Stone for it to be amplified again.

Green light eerily fills the space. It arcs from the ring to the Stone to the other Stone. It is doing exactly as she imagined! Taking a deep breath, she reaches her other hand out to the second stone and the power arcs from it to her, closing the circle. Raw power surges inside her.

Every hair on her body stands on end. Her skin prickles. Her blood races. Power fights to break loose. Her mouth opens and her voice rips forth, each note encased in fire. Pain lances every joint. It feels like her limbs are trying to break and re-set. With sheer will, she cuts off the power. The room falls dark.

Panting, she collapses to the bed. She pushes sweat dampened hair from her forehead and starts to laugh, giddy, manic laughter.

It worked! It really worked.

Rathleon chuckles. *It did indeed. It will be difficult for you to control the power from all three Stones by yourself. Even I shared it with two other mages.*

"There is no one for me to share it with."

Rimalon will aid you.

Cate covers her eyes with her forearm. *This is my task, not his.*

Rathleon falls silent. Cate can feel her brooding, thoughtful, but she offers no advice, no wisdom, no words of caution.

Cate's body feels numb without the power. She pushes to her feet and staggers to the door. Drawing it open, she nearly runs into Emon's chest. With dragon-sight, his cropped blonde hair is like a beacon in the dark. "Collect the Stones. I'll return to my apartment."

He lets her pass and follows her instructions. Vykar walks softly at her heels, an expert in stealth and silence. If she hadn't seen him with Emon, she wouldn't even know he was there. Her legs threaten to give way halfway up the circuitous route, and she leans against the wall. This small delay gives Emon time to catch up.

With the proximity of the Stones, the ring on Cate's finger lights with power illuminating the path before them. She takes a steadying breath as power gathers in her veins. "Emon, please stay at least ten feet behind me. Any closer and we all might suffer."

He bows as she pushes forward. Another hour finds them leaving the caverns and entering a gray afternoon. Clouds hang low, shrouding the mountain caps. It feels like her blood is sizzling. "Take the Stones to the royal apartment. Vykar, take me somewhere to release this power. And, trust me, wherever it is, it should be fireproof."

"Then, we should return to the caves." He answers without blinking. "Or, if you want to punch something, we could go to the training grounds."

"Yes," Cate releases a controlled breath. "The training grounds." She watches as Emon carries the covered Stones away, then matches pace with Vykar as he leads her from the mountain and into the forest.

At first, they walk, then jog, then run. The exertion starts to burn away some of the Power. Her lungs ache as they pull to a stop. Not far away is a long building. Outside of it are several training courses, with different obstacles and challenges. Soldiers run in pairs through them, while another group jogs around the field, and another spars.

"Where do you want to go, my Queen?"

"Is that Baen?" She points to a figure sparring a team of five.

Vykar nods. "Yes, and over there is Lord Elar." He points in the distance to several shooting ranges.

"I don't know what I will do if I think Baen is in danger. I'd better not watch. Let's go to the shooting range."

Vykar smirks and leads Cate in a jog around the field to the distant ranges. Elar has a bow pulled taut and let's fly an arrow. Bullseye. He lowers the bow and focuses on Cate. As if able to feel her need, he steps aside.

Taking a steadying breath, she releases the pent-up Power. It burns through her, exiting as a ball of fire over her palm. With a primal scream, she hurtles it at the target. It hits and incinerates.

She does it again to the next target.

Everyone on the training grounds has stopped. All eyes are on Cate.

Feeling in control once more and no longer like there are ants crawling all over her, she takes a cleansing breath and smiles.

"Better?" Elar asks, the edges of his mouth curl in a near smile.

"Yes, thank you."

"Seeing as you are no longer sequestered in the cave, and your emotional release, should I assume that you were not successful?"

She shrugs. Elar hands his bow to Vykar and takes Cate's hand, without another word, he leads her through the crowds. Baen catches up to them and gestures to a golf cart. "Let's take the cart back." He jumps behind the driver's seat as Cate and Elar slip in behind him.

Cate wrinkles her nose. "Is that me?"

"Yes." Baen swiftly answers and Cate blushes. "It's natural after days in the caverns."

"Or, a few hours on the field in your case." Elar tosses back.

Baen barks a laugh. "Was that an attempt at a joke?" Elar doesn't answer. Instead, he shifts his gaze to their route.

"What has Viggo been doing?" Cate asks.

"Meeting with his people. The ten attendees they were allowed brought a lot of trunks with them over the last few days." Baen slows the cart as they approach the apartment. "Also, there's been a lot of unusual activity outside the mountain range."

"What do you mean?"

"Kraeken are gathering. So far, none of them have discovered the hidden entrances that lead to the valley. But that's not all. There are also signs of Elves."

Elar does not flinch. His gaze does not waver from the landscape. Cate looks from him back at Baen. The cart stops.

As they enter the apartment, Cate acknowledges the guards on duty, then rounds on Elar. "What aren't you telling me?"

"We will talk after your shower."

Her gaze shifts suspiciously between the two men before she retreats to her room.

Baen makes a beeline for the refrigerator, pulling out a cold bottle of water. He leans back against the counter and addresses Elar. The two of them have been avoiding each other since Cate went underground.

"I told you it would be difficult for you when she chooses another man."

Baen finishes the contents of the bottle, compresses it into a tiny ball and tosses it in the trash. "I will abide by whatever choices Cate makes. The key is, they need to be *her* choices. Not made by Viggo, her father, or you."

"You conveniently left yourself off that list."

"I support her. I don't tell her what to do."

"And what is it that you think I am deciding for her?"

"Don't play stupid. We both know that you are anything but."

Elar sits on the couch and leans back, his arms spread over the top. His silver gaze hardens. "When she does choose a husband, what then?"

"I am what I have sworn to be." Baen stalks passed him into the room he shares with Elar and slams the door.

An hour later, one of the guards announces the arrival of IlliaVaa. Neither Baen nor Cate are in the great room when she enters. Elar glances up from a book he is reading but does not stand. It is rare to meet someone unintimidated by her Gift. "Where's Cate?"

Elar slides a bookmark in place and rests it on his lap. "In her room."

"Which is hers?"

Elar does not answer, and instead opens the book he was reading. Without knocking, IlliaVaa pushes open a door and sweeps inside. Cate lies on top of the bed, sound asleep. IlliaVaa takes her time studying Cate and the myriad of images that swirl around her.

So. Many. Truths. IlliaVaa blinks and crosses her arms over her chest in an attempt to clear the visions. She calls Cate's name twice with no response, before shouting next to her ear.

Cate's eyes fly open as she yells back, "What?!"

"We have a lot of catching up to do. And, as your maid of honor, I would be remiss if we don't have a bachelorette party."

Cate rubs her eyes. "No."

"It's the night before your wedding. You are going to have some fun before you marry… well, you're going to have some fun."

"Who let you in?"

"I am IlliaVaa Dragotian. I let myself in."

"Of course, you did. I am exhausted and tomorrow is my big day. I don't have time to *have some fun.*"

IlliaVaa sits on the bed next to Cate. "I need an excuse to be with you. There're things you need to know, and the only excuse I have is a bachelorette party. Don't worry, it'll just be me, you, and your cousin."

Cate sits next to IlliaVaa. "What is this about? You're getting what you wanted. Tomorrow, I am marrying your brother."

IlliaVaa's shoulders slump, her head lowers and her gaze shifts to the floor. "Viggo is what our father shaped him to be. He carries the most powerful dragon's soul, Xenothgorot. He's my twin, Cate. Before our dragons manifested, I knew everything about him. Then, our father started our training.

When Xenothgorot showed himself, I was spared father's attention. Viggo had it all. I know he's arrogant, self-centered, egotistical. He's also incredibly responsible and caring. He has always looked after our Clan, with a long-term strategy of looking after all dragonkind.

The agreement our fathers made for you two to marry was to unite Xenothgorot and Rathleon. The only other dragon that can possibly match Xenothgorot's power is yours. Until you, she has never woken. Not in a thousand years.

All that time, dragonkind has lived trapped behind the eyes and flesh of others. Xenothgorot's found a way to trap the human soul and for the dragon's soul to become owner of the body."

"I knew it wasn't Viggo when he stormed my throne."

"Exactly." IlliaVaa wipes tears from her cheeks. "I love my brother. I don't want to lose him. I can't sit back and do nothing while he sacrifices himself. I've discussed it with my dragon and she's in agreement."

"How can I trust anything you say?"

IlliaVaa turns to face Cate, meeting her gaze. "I see Truth. It is ugly and beautiful, frightening and freeing. You need not trust me. Don't tell me what you are going to do, or how you're going to do it. Just help me save my brother."

Cate takes a deep breath. "Why my cousin?"

"You should have a talk with her." IlliaVaa flashes brilliant white teeth as she grins.

"What do you want to do?"

"Drink, talk, do our nails?" IlliaVaa laughs. "Nothing raunchy. We don't have time for that, and it wouldn't be any fun with your guards following us around."

"Fine."

IlliaVaa impulsively hugs Cate. "We'll be back in an hour. And you might want to ask the Elf and Wolf to take a hike."

Cate's eyes narrow. "See you in an hour."

Neither Elar nor Baen want to leave. They both voice their disagreement as they leave the apartment. They only quiet when Scyth and Simall enter.

A little more than an hour later, IlliaVaa and Tatiana sit on the couch and the former opens a bottle of wine. "Who are they?" She gestures with a glass to the Drow.

"Scyth is the Captain of the Black Guard." The female with shoulder-length black hair and intense silver eyes nods her head in greeting. "Simall is a cleric under her command." The slender female with white hair and light blue eyes gives a dip of her head at the introduction.

IlliaVaa shrugs. "Nice to meet you. I only brought three glasses. Sorry, do you have any extra?"

Scyth's eyes narrow, her words soft and her tone smooth. "We won't be drinking."

Pouring the wine, IlliaVaa hands a glass to Cate and Tatiana and then fills her own. "Suit yourself. I thought we'd start the night by playing a game. It's "How well does the bride know the groom"."

"I don't know him, at all."

"Exactly, so, first question: What is Viggo's favorite hobby?"

Cate sets the wine glass on the table, without taking a sip, and thinks about all the times she has seen Viggo. As she starts to open her mouth, IlliaVaa wags her pointer finger. "No, think not only about what you know about him in your wakeful life, but in your Dream life."

Tatiana nearly spits out the wine she had sipped and starts coughing. "You've been in the Dream with him?"

Cate looks from Tatiana to IlliaVaa. "I guess."

"Oh my gosh, what did you do? Everything. I mean *everything* you do in the Dream is real. It actually happens to a dragon-souled."

Cate blushes. She can feel her whole-body heat. "His favorite hobby is drawing."

"Correct!" IlliaVaa takes a sip of her wine.

"Wait, how is this game played? I don't know anything about the groom?" Tatiana asks.

"You and I ask questions. If she gets them right, we take a drink. If she gets them wrong, she takes a drink."

"What color are his scales?" Tatiana asks.

"That's too easy." IlliaVaa complains.

"Red."

Tatiana looks to IlliaVaa to confirm if Cate is right or not, then takes a sip of wine when she nods.

"Does he want to marry you?" IlliaVaa asks. Tatiana gasps at the question. IlliaVaa waves her off.

Cate remembers seeing his face the first day they met. He definitely did not want to marry her. But, if she thinks about all the times she has dreamt about him, and all of their conversations in the Dream and his actions and attitude since.... "At first, no. He was marrying me out of obligation. But now, he actually wants to marry me. But I don't know if it is him or Xenothgorot."

"We both drink on that one. Because you are right. He was marrying you out of obligation. So, I drink." She takes a long sip of wine. "But now, he's marrying you because he has fallen in love with you. Yes, Xenothgorot wants to be with Rathleon, but that isn't why Viggo the man is marrying Cate. So, you take a sip."

Cate silently considers IlliaVaa's answer as she picks up the glass and takes a small sip of the sweet white wine.

"I don't envy you." Tatiana's voice is small. "Like, the dragon's soul you carry is enviable, but I don't envy *you*. I would hate to be in an arranged marriage." She looks up from the table and at the expression on Cate's face quickly adds. "I'm sorry. I know you don't want this. Uh, next question, what's his favorite food?"

Cate shrugs and takes a sip of wine.

"Okay, enough of that game. How about two truths and a lie and we have to figure out which is the lie?" IlliaVaa asks with a friendly smile.

Tatiana shakes her head. "Nice try, but your Gift is seeing Truth. You'd win every time. Let's just go with the old tried and true Truth or Dare."

"Fine by me." IlliaVaa answers.

"Sure, why not." Cate responds.

"Okay, IlliaVaa, Truth or Dare?"

"Truth."

Before Tatiana can ask a question, Cate asks, "Why are you here?"

IlliaVaa smirks. "To free the dragons. If you free the dragons, you save Viggo from Xenothgorot."

Cate nearly drops the wine glass. She sets it on the table and wipes her palms on her pant legs. "Truly?"

"This *is* Truth or Dare." IlliaVaa answers.

Her voice a little hoarse, Cate turns to Tatiana. "Truth or Dare?"

"Truth."

"Why are you here?"

"To see if you can free the dragons. I rescued a helluva lot of dragon eggs from the Kraeken, and if you free them, I'm going to have one heck of a nursery to deal with."

Cate takes a slow breath, measuring both of the women before her. Are they telling the truth? Could they really want what she wants? And, if they are, how do they fit into the plan?

Is there a plan? Cate sits back on the couch, her heart racing. "I am getting married at 3:33 p.m. tomorrow. Before I say, "I do," I need to receive the Dragotian wedding set. How?"

"I was thinking about that. We haven't had a wedding rehearsal, so I don't know what to expect at a Drow/Dragon wedding. Is it like a traditional human wedding?" IlliaVaa asks.

Cate's brows furrow. She stands and starts searching the apartment. After a few minutes, she returns with a notebook. Opening it, she thumbs through the pages. When she stops, she reads aloud. "Viggo and I are to arrive in our separate staging rooms at noon. His is in a chamber on the second level, while mine is adjacent to the temple. Then, we go through whatever ceremonies and preparation work we each have. At three, Viggo enters the Temple. Ten minutes later, I make my grand entrance. Rook will welcome the guests, and conduct a ceremony honoring the Drow gods, then Rook begins the marriage ceremony. At 3:33, we say our vows and commit to one another."

"That's a very specific time to be saying your vows. What if something runs late?" Tatiana asks, finishing the wine in her glass.

Cate gestures to the schedule. "I'm just telling you what it says here. Viggo should have a copy."

"He likely does. I just haven't seen it. What if we make a small revision? In human ceremonies, they often have the lighting of a unity candle, or tying of a knot between the bride's and groom's joined hands. What if we add a unity ceremony where the groom adorns the bride with gifted heirloom jewelry?"

"So, he puts it on me in front of everyone before we say our vows?"

"That's what I am saying?"

"Would he do that?"

"Xenothgorot is so close to regaining Rathleon, I think he would do anything you ask. That's how I convinced him to let me bring the second Stone as part of his agreement to marry." IlliaVaa answers.

She glances at her watch. "We don't have much time. You only gave a few hours for your bachelorette party."

"I'll have Rook make the necessary changes. Just make sure that the jewelry he gives me is made from the Dragon Stone."

CHAPTER 32

The chamber, off the temple, is decorated with rich red silks. Cate watches in the mirror as a Drow stylist twists, curls, and pins her hair. Diamonds, blood rubies, and blue topaz are interwoven into the strands of blonde and white.

Only Cate and the stylist are in the room. Baen stands guard outside. When it is time for the ceremony, Elar and Rimalon will be seated in the first row with Cate's parents.

Her stomach twists. She wasn't able to eat this morning, her nerves too on edge. *You only have to connect the Stones.* Rathleon soothes. *I will guide the spell.*

If it doesn't work, I will be married.

We will be married. Rathleon corrects. *And, being sworn to Xenothgorot once is more than enough.*

"My queen," the stylist gently gets her attention. "It is time for you to slip into your dress."

Cate nods and stands. Her dress. It's not a dress she would ever have chosen for herself. She shouldn't have left it to the Council or the dragons. Thankfully, it isn't white. That helps it feel like she isn't cheating herself of one day marrying the man she truly loves.

Like the gems in her hair, it is a mixture of white, red, and topaz. The first part of the dress is a white silk sheath. The stylist bows her head as Cate removes her robe and steps into it. Its thin straps smoothly slide over her shoulders. "Ready."

Lifting her head, the stylist retrieves the next piece. A red lace overcoat. It hugs her curves and has a cathedral length train. Next, the stylist helps Cate into a silk topaz overcoat that has no sleeves and buttons beneath her bodice. Its train is half the length of the lace.

Adjusting the trains, the stylist unbuttons the back of each piece, layering them into hooks on the side, exposing Cate's scales. Other than the gems in her hair and the dragon stone ring on her right hand, she wears no jewels.

"Shoes?" Cate asks.

"You will be barefoot." The stylist checks the clock. "We should move to the hall. It will be time for you to enter in a few minutes."

Cate retrieves her crown from the pillow she'd set it on when she arrived and settles it on top of her head. The spider silk threads itself into her curls.

The stylist bows, then opens the door. Baen loudly exhales at the site of her. "You are stunning. If only it weren't for him." He offers her his arm and guides her to the temple doors. The stylist arrays her train behind her.

Cate takes a deep breath and leans on Baen. "Did Emon do what I asked?"

"Yes, everything is as you requested."

Cate nods and sighs. "It's really happening."

The temple doors open. In the distance, at the end of the aisle, waits Xenothgorot/Viggo. A haunting melody beckons them to enter. Tightly gripping Baen's arm, they take step after halting step. Drow fill the pews. She can feel their eyes on her. As they near the edge of the chasm, she catches sight of the dragon-souled, arrayed in suits and looking every bit like executives attending a cocktail party. At the end of the aisle are Emily and Kith. Sadness and hurt fill her father's eyes. Emily attempts an encouraging smile.

Rook bows at the waist and the music stops. "We are gathered here today to witness the union of Viggo Dragotian, leader of clan Dragotian, and Cateian Arraniean, Queen of the Drow."

Rook turns and addresses the chasm. "Welcome, goddess of webs, weaver of destiny. We invite you to witness this union, and to bless it as you have blessed our Queen."

An expectant hush falls over the Drow. Seconds tick into minutes, and the dragon-souled begin to murmur. Rook returns his focus to the bride and groom.

"Cateian Arraniean, if you enter into this union of your own will, step forward and join the groom."

Cate slowly removes her hand from Baen's arm and gathering her skirts joins Xenothgorot/Viggo in front of the bridge. As she does, Baen steps behind IlliaVaa at the chasm's edge.

"A marriage joins two people. In this case, it joins not only a man and a woman, a queen, and a clan leader, but two dragon rulers in their own right. To commemorate the event, and to recognize the unity this marriage brings, the groom will now present the bride with an heirloom wedding set."

Dane hands a velvet box to Viggo. He opens it and removes a necklace and pair of earrings, then hands the box back. First, he unclasps the necklace and sets it on her throat, reaching behind her to set the clasp.

He pauses to admire it resting on her chest. Unscrewing the earring backs, he places the posts in her ears and gently secures them. His touch is like fire on her skin. She shivers and he flashes a brilliant smile. "You are beautiful." He whispers.

"You are too." She whispers, licking her lips to wet them.

He quietly returns to his spot. Rook begins the ceremony to the Drow gods. Cate doesn't hear him. Her focus is on the stones set in the jewelry.

The magic in the stones is faint. Though her gaze rests on Viggo, she can no longer see him. Focusing on the Stone in her ring, she works to connect its power to the jewelry, then reaches her consciousness out to feel the Stones Emon placed.

They pulse beneath the front pews. Knowing the magic will arc to the Stones once she starts to connect them, she prompts Rathleon. *Anytime now.*

"What are you doing?" Xenothgorot/Viggo growls.

Cate opens her eyes. The Stones on her body glow brightly. She extends her reach to the other Stones and the magic arcs from one to the another, completing the circuit within her. Raw power fills her, pulsates in her, amplifies and continues through the cycle increasing with each rotation.

Rathleon' s voice echoes throughout the chamber and into the chasm. *"Reditamos colainn ziel. Reditamos colainn ziel. Reditamos colainn ziel."* Power rages through Cate. She lifts her head and screams, Rathleon's words continue to issue from her mouth as green light spews forth from her skin. The Stones beneath the pews light the cavern as if it were day.

"Stop it!" Xenothgorot/Viggo grabs Cate's arms and just as quickly releases her, as if burned.

A frightful scream rips through Cate and Baen shoves IlliaVaa to the side, shielding Cate from everyone's sight except Xenogorot/Viggo and Rook. The crowd is silent. No one moves.

Words continue to spew from Cate's mouth, interrupted only by screams. Green light fills the space. Xenothgorot/Viggo shoves Baen attempting to get to Cate. But the Kraeken does not move. Not even an inch, in spite of Viggo's dragon strength.

"Whatever you are trying to do will kill you. Stop it, now!" Xenothgorot commands.

The sound of cloth rending follows another horrific scream. The Stones glow brightly enough to make everyone clear the front pews and shield their eyes.

"Cate!" Emily wails. Kith grabs her by the waist and keeps her from moving, burying her face in his shoulder.

"Don't watch."

The crowd gasps as a massive blue-green wing expands over Baen. Without hesitating, he shifts his weight and barrels into Cate carrying her over the chasm edge.

Xenothgorot roars, reaching for her, but can only watch as she disappears into darkness. The Stones glow so bright that the light exposes the top of the chasm ceiling, revealing the white body of the Spider deity.

Air whooshes upward knocking anyone near the chasm edge toward the pews. Fire jets toward the massive spider causing it to move with uncanny speed to the other end of the ceiling. The mountain shakes and everyone covers their ears as a great beast vents its ire. Xenothgorot pushes to his feet. "It can't be. The dragons, we're all...." He looks behind him for the dragon-souled that accompanied him. A claw grips the edge of the chasm, covered in blue-green scales. Then another. A dragon's head emerges and soon the dragon's body, held unsteadily aloft by the beat of massive wings. The tips of which nearly brush each side of the cavern. A moment later, the beast carefully sets Baen on his feet away from the ledge.

"*Reditamos colainn ziel!*" The words aren't a chant. They are a command. The Dragon Stones flash and fall dark. Silence covers the cavern like ash. At length, someone in the back coughs. Someone else ignites the torches set in the walls, and the temple comes to life.

Viggo sits on a pew with his head in his hands. He blinks, unsure how he got where he is. Standing, he rushes Baen. "It is not possible. Where's Cate?"

Kith, who had been protecting Emily in the second pew, stands. He glances at his hands, then at Emily. "She did it." He scoops his wife into his arms and kisses her. "It wasn't for nothing. She really did it."

Emily turns this way and that trying to find Cate. "Where is she?"

Rook collects himself and returns to his place standing at the edge of the chasm. "Guards, clear the temple." Many of the Drow had left as the cavern filled with light. Those who remained file out, while the Dragotians are carried out weeping and whimpering in grief. Baen joins Kith and Emily. "She is well, but no longer in the temple. I will send for you when she is ready."

"But...." Emily protests.

Kith shakes his head, takes her hand, and leads her from the temple.

Viggo falls to his knees. Tears streak his cheeks. "How did she do it? Xenothgorot was so sure, so full of himself. He knew he was right. The dragon spell could not be broken, because all the souls of dragon-kind were sent into humans. There were no dragons left."

IlliaVaa kneels beside her brother. "That was Xenothgorot's truth. It was not Rathleon's."

"You knew?" The look of betrayal on his face nearly breaks her.

"I suspected. Between Rathleon and Cate, there are many Truths. It was difficult to tell where one ended and the other began."

"The dragon?" He asks.

She leans close and whispers in his ear, "Was Cate."

CHAPTER 33

Cold, naked, and oddly hungry, Cate climbs from the bottom of the chasm one handhold at a time. Stumbling onto a wide opening that leads to a tunnel, she crawls through and edges along the wall.

After a time, she can hear the voices of Drow. Wishing for something to cover herself with, she presses ahead. It isn't long before she spots a tall figure walking towards her. She frantically looks for someplace to hide her nakedness, but there is nowhere. With her dragon sight, she realizes that it is Elar and he cannot see in the dark.

"Here," she says, and he stops cold.

He holds out a cloak. She accepts it gratefully, wrapping it around her shoulders and clutching it tightly. "How did you find me?"

"Just like the first time we met, I heard your soul crying out and followed it."

"Thank you." She slips a hand from under the cloth to hold his. "This way." Together, they leave the bowels of the mountain and emerge into the purple of twilight. Just like the day she sat on the Obsidian Throne, Drow line the path into the city. Whispers precede them. Heads bow as they pass. Baen catches sight of them and ushers them into a golf cart.

Cate sits in back with Elar, her head rests on his shoulder. "You'll need to eat and to sleep. We'll have a lot to talk about when you wake." Baen counsels.

"Yes, of course." She mumbles, as her eyes close and she falls into a deep slumber.

When she wakes, she's tucked into bed. She lifts the covers and discovers she's been bathed, clothed, and laid on fresh sheets. The door opens, revealing Emily. "Mom?"

"Oh, thank goodness." She breathes, sitting on the bed and hugging her. "Baen said it was normal and you'd be okay, but it's been almost two days. What happened?"

"You tell me."

"Don't worry. I'm the one that cleaned and changed you, though Elar did put you in the bed. Where did that dragon come from? Baen wouldn't tell us anything, except that you were fine."

"Me mom. The dragon is me. And you, though you never knew it. Your mom is the last dragon. She was Rathleon's apprentice, human apprentice, and daughter."

"I don't understand."

"Rathleon learned how to shape shift from dragon to human. In human form, she gave birth to your mother. Your mother never learned to take dragon form so when the spell was cast, her soul wasn't moved. She was human and lived all her life that way. Just like you."

Emily shakes her head trying to clear her thoughts and urges Cate to continue.

"When Rathleon originally cast the spell that put dragon souls into humans, she did it with a Drow and a Human. Everyone always thought it would take three again to break it. Which it did, just all of them were in me."

There's a light knocking on the door. It's Baen carrying a tray laden with different plates of steaming hot food. Cate sits in the bed and leans her back against the headboard. He rests the tray on her lap. "After your first shift, you need to eat heartily to regain all the energy lost when you transformed."

"Thank you. For everything."

He smiles. "The first shift is hard, and you just had to do it publicly."

Emily shivers, "When Kith told me you pulled Cate over the edge with you.... Even now, I feel sick at the thought."

"She needed to be able to shift without everyone staring at her. It's a very gruesome and painful process."

"But you both could have died." Emily rests her hand on Cate's leg, needing to reassure herself.

"In the moment, that didn't matter. Only protecting her did."

Cate can feel her skin heating with embarrassment. She takes a hearty bite of oatmeal.

"How's Viggo?" Emily asks. "I never wished him ill, only that the blasted contract hadn't existed."

Baen answers. "Sick. He's being treated by his sister. Most of the dragon-souled are not faring well. Many are acting fluish, while others are grieving."

"What about, Kith?" Cate asks, unable to meet her mother's gaze.

"Your father is good. Surprisingly. But, then again, he saw it with his Gift long before it happened and came to terms with it." Emily shrugs. "We've decided to work on our marriage. I won't be moving back to Colorado."

"I'm happy for you, Mom. Really."

"Thanks." Emily wraps Cate into a tight hug, careful not to spill her food. "Now that you're awake, I'm going to get some sleep." She kisses Cate's forehead and leaves.

Baen takes her place, sitting on the edge of the bed, as Cate eats. "She hasn't left your side since we got to the apartment. We had to convince her to eat and nap once in a while."

"She's a good mom." Cate finishes the oatmeal and reaches for a plate of scrambled eggs.

"I'm glad you remember what happened. You're a shifter, like me. Only, you shift into a dragon and I a wolf. I thought it might be the case. The night of your coronation, you almost shifted. Did you know?"

Cate pauses with the fork over the plate. Her gaze finds his. "Remember when we went into the Dream and met my grandparents?" He nods but stays silent. "Veralyn all but told me. It took me a little while to understand, and I wasn't even sure if shifting was possible. There's never been a case of a dragon carrying another dragon's soul, so… I could only guess what might happen.

Rathleon even hinted at it many times. She never came out and told me, but that's why my magic is so strong. It wasn't just her Gift to me; it was my own ability, plus her Gift." She takes another bite of eggs.

"That's why you could do what it took three magic-wielders to do a thousand years ago."

"Yep." She finishes the eggs and sips the coffee, then chugs a glass of apple juice. "Not only am I a magic-wielding dragon, I'm also the Drow Queen, blood of Arraniean, and carried an enormously powerful dragon's soul. How's Rimalon?"

"I have never seen an Elf so excited. He's not affected at all by the bit of magic he added to the Stones. He, with Emon, collected them once everyone left the temple."

Cate picks at a blueberry muffin. "What about the jewelry and my crown? What happened to them when I shifted?"

"Your crown is anybody's guess. The Spider deity has created a new one. Its weave reflects who you are. It's impressive She still accepts you given that you nearly torched her." Cate almost spews coffee trying not to laugh. "I think she understands you couldn't control the fire at that time. As for the jewelry, you might want to look at yourself in the mirror." He moves the nearly empty food tray so that she can get out of bed.

Standing in front of the mirror, Cate pulls the pajama collar to see where the necklace had been. The gold setting is gone. The stones glitter from her skin, set into a distinct ring of scales where the gold had been. She leans closer and studies her earlobes, gemstones are embedded where her earring holes had been. "I guess Viggo isn't getting these back."

Baen laughs, a short burst, and then as if he can't hold it in a torrent that turns his face red. He doubles over, still laughing, trying not to overturn the tray.

"It's not that funny."

"It is." He wipes his eyes and stands. "Get dressed and come out. There's still more to talk about."

A few minutes later, Cate's sitting on the couch in jeans and a black t-shirt with her hair in a ponytail. "Where's Elar?"

Baen sits beside her on the couch and takes her hands in his. "You did the impossible. I want you to let that sink in."

"Okay." Her brows furrow and she studies their hands.

"Before the ceremony, the Kraeken and Elves had gathered on the other side of the mountain. But it wasn't only them. Xenothgorot had secretly gathered his forces. With what you did, they were rendered defenseless."

"I don't understand."

"They're sick, grieving, confused. They are also some of the richest people in the world."

Understanding begins to dawn and her mouth falls open. "You mean?"

"Fighting broke out. Elar, along with many Drow Generals, went to find out what happened. We haven't had any word yet."

"When did they go?"

"Yesterday."

Cate tries to stand, and he keeps her in place with gentle pressure on her hands. "You need to know what you're walking into before you make a move."

She squeezes his hands and pulls hers loose. "Take me to Viggo."

IlliaVaa wraps Cate in a crushing hug whispering thank you in her ear. "You really did it. You really saved us all."

"How are you feeling?"

IlliaVaa releases her and steps back, with a shrug she smirks. "I'm okay. I know my dragon is well, somewhere. She'll find me. Surprisingly, once I got over the feeling of missing a part of myself, I realized that my Gift remains."

"You mean, you can still see Truth?"

She nods. "Come." She leads Cate into the bedroom and throws open the drapes. Viggo groans and covers his eyes with his forearm. "Look who is here?"

He slowly drops his arm and blinks against the light. "Cate?" His voice is hoarse, as if he's been crying for a long time. Feeling awkward and unsure, Cate gives a small wave. "Come closer." Reluctantly, she moves to the side of the bed.

He pushes into a sitting position and leans against the pillows, then pats the bed next to him. She sits. "Thank you." His gaze holds hers as he says it. She can tell he really means it. "The last few months have been hard. He'd figured out how to takeover and was changing my body to one he wanted, and he'd locked my soul away." His eyes shift and he glances at IlliaVaa and Baen, then back to Cate. "I understand why you did it. It was long past time they were free."

Silent tears well in Cate's eyes and fall untended down her cheeks. "Thank you."

"It won't be easy. He is one of many who are incredibly angry; yet now that he's back in his body, maybe he'll forgive you."

"I have nothing to do with his obsession. That's for him and Rathleon to work out. I was just the intercessor." Viggo laughs, causing him to go into a bout of coughing. "Maybe when he figures out that he is my great-grandfather, he'll have a change of heart."

Viggo's eyes bulge and he chokes on his own spit. "Your what?"

"My great-grandfather. I don't know what you remember from the wedding, but I am a dragon. I was never just dragon-souled."

He blinks several times, his eyes narrowing as he glares at IlliaVaa. "Did you know?"

She checks her nails, not meeting his gaze, as she answers. "There were always so many images around Cate that they were hard to figure out."

"You knew." He whispers, nodding his head as he works out his own answer. "You're a dragon, a Drow, and a human. You are all three, that's why it worked." He slaps his own forehead. "I can't believe I didn't realize it sooner. No wonder you could enter the Dream so fully, even call me to you."

"What?"

Viggo clears his throat and gently smiles at Cate. "I guess we won't meet like that again. In the beginning, the first few times, it was you who pulled me into your Dream. It was not me."

Cate blushes and quickly stands. Viggo's face hardens as he addresses Baen. "I never liked you. The fact that you have been so close with her...." Viggo focuses on the ceiling as he gathers his thoughts. "None of that matters now. The contract is void. We're no longer engaged. Take care of her. I know you will, as her Oath-sworn."

"I never liked you either." Baen smirks. "Take care of yourself, Dragotian. You've a long road ahead of you."

It is past dusk by the time the Council gathers. For the meeting, Cate added a black leather blazer to her outfit, but nothing else. She strides into a cacophony of voices, all of which fall silent at the sight of her.

Channa rises. "Tuval, step forward and report."

A Drow with eyes the color of ivy approaches and in a rich baritone recounts the events of the last forty-eight hours. "The Kraeken civil war erupted on our border. At first, it was only them. Then, the Dragotians were attacked. They were weak with the release of their dragons. The Elves and Drow, led by Lord Elar, surrounded the Dragotians and fought back the Kraeken."

"You are dismissed." Channa commands. The Drow does not move. He kneels before Cate, with one fist pressed to the ground and his head lowered.

Cate leans forward, addressing only him. "I am listening. Tell me."

He lifts his head. "Your majesty, dragons have been sighted. The humans cannot believe what they are seeing. Videos are popping up all over social media. Some are not pretty."

Cate kneels in front of Tuval, and gripping his shoulders, helps him to stand. "Thank you. It is not wholly unexpected. Though, sooner than I had hoped."

He takes the fist that had been on the floor and covers his heart. "I, Tuval, son of Tuvair, pledge my undying loyalty and life in service to Cateian Arraniean, Drow Queen, and dragon."

"Thank you, Tuval." Cate gently smiles at him. He steps back, behind the Council members.

Cate's gaze moves from Drow to Drow until she has taken the measure of each. "You did not ask for a queen who is both a Drow and a dragon, but you have one. You did not ask me to free the dragons, but I did. You did not ask me to thrust us into war, but I have.

You asked me to get married and secure Arraniean's line. You asked me to be nothing but a girl with a crown on her head.

Understand. I. Am. Queen. I rule, not you. If you don't like it, leave. Our world has changed. We are no longer living in peaceful times.

Each dragon was ripped from their bodies, from their eggs, and placed generation after generation into the bodies of humans. Rathleon's intent had been no more than a few generations, but it lasted a thousand years.

Some will be sane and have developed an affinity for humans, and human-like species. Some will be insane, committed to violence. Some will fall somewhere in the middle.

Know this, I will defend our people. I will defend humans. I will defend dragons. With Scales and Stones. Together, *we* will build what the next era will be, and who will survive."

EPILOGUE

Tatiana pushes sweaty hair from her face and resumes scrubbing the scales of a small black dragon. It extends its neck for her to work down to its breastbone. "Vek, are you done with Shyugar?"

"Yeah, she's with Kith and Emily. If Blue would hold still...." He grumbles. Tatiana looks over her shoulder to see a blue dragon the size of a pony trying to catch a butterfly with its nose. She laughs and returns her focus to her task.

It is hard to believe it has been almost three months since dragon souls returned to their bodies. Finishing with Jett, she releases the dragon and stretches her back. The media paints dragons as mindless, voracious beasts. The military is at high alert and all but the air force stopped flying. People do not understand. Tatiana gently caresses the black snout thrust under her hand.

"Vek, we need to put the truth out there. The world needs to know there are good and bad dragons, just like there are good and bad humans. We must protect them."

"I agree." He says, finishing with Shyugar. He points to the trees around them. "I put up trail cameras when we brought the eggs back from Eagles Reaches. I wanted to make sure they were safe." She rushes into his arms and hugs him tightly. "I have hours and hours of video. It might help to interview Cate and any other dragon willing to tell their story."

"That would make her a target." Tatiana pulls back and looks into his eyes. "She already risked everything to free them."

He kisses Tatiana's forehead. "She has Elar and Baen at her side and is herself a fire-breathing dragon. Let anyone try to hurt her."

ABOUT THE AUTHOR

Depending on the day, **AD Krasikov** may be outgoing or reserved, flamboyant or traditional, a chatterbox or quiet. She is an observer, a storyteller, a strategist. It is her purpose in life to make a difference.

Raised by an engineer and a serial entrepreneur, she learned from an early age to use facts when making a request, and that failure is only a setback towards success.

She is ever curious and built a lengthy career in financial services. AD graduated from the University of Colorado at Colorado Springs with a Bachelor of Arts degree in Cultural Anthropology.

AD is a speaker, author, and mentor. She is passionate about humans – each individual person – and strives to make a difference, as best she can, in the lives she touches.

An avid reader, she enjoys a wide array of genres and admits to an addiction to original voiceover, subtitled, foreign dramas.